Joanne Harris is the author of *Chocolat* (made into an Oscar-nominated film with Juliette Binoche and Johhny Depp), and twelve more bestselling novels. Her work is published in over fifty countries and she was appointed MBE in the 2013 Queen's Birthday Honours list. Born in Barnsley, of an English father and a French mother, she studied Modern and Medieval Languages at Cambridge and spent fifteen years as a teacher before (somewhat reluctantly) becoming a full-time writer.

She lives in Yorkshire with her family, plays bass in a band first formed when she was sixteen, works in a shed in her garden, likes musical theatre and old sci-fi, drinks rather too much caffeine, spends far too much time online and occasionally dreams of faking her own death and going to live in Hawaii.

The novels of Joanne Harris – have you read them all?

CHOCOLAT

When the exotic Vianne Rocher arrives in the French village of Lansquenet and opens a sinful chocolate boutique directly opposite the church at the start of Lent, the villagers are split into opposing camps.

'Mouthwatering . . . A feelgood book of the first order'
Observer

BLACKBERRY WINE

A bottle of home-brewed wine left to him by a past friend provides the key to an old mystery and a terrible secret for Jay Mackintosh.

'Touching, funny and clever'
Daily Telegraph

FIVE QUARTERS OF THE ORANGE

A tragic childhood in Occupied France comes back to haunt a secretive widow.

'Vastly enjoyable, utterly gripping'
The Times

COASTLINERS

On a tiny Breton island, Mado returns after a ten-year absence to fight the tides and attempt to bring a dying community back to life.

'A writer of tremendous charm, who creates a winning blend of fairy-tale morality and gritty realism'
Independent

HOLY FOOLS

In seventeenth-century France, Juliette takes the veil, only to find that a man from her past returns to haunt her behind the convent walls.

'With this bold, inventive book, Harris confirms her position as one of Britain's most popular novelists'
Daily Mail

SLEEP, PALE SISTER

A blackly gothic evocation of Victorian artistic life: Joanne Harris's second novel, first published before she won worldwide recognition.

'A hauntingly evocative laudanum-dream of a novel'
Time Out

GENTLEMEN & PLAYERS

At St Oswald's, a Northern boys' grammar school, a dark undercurrent stirs, of obsession and revenge.

'A gripping psychological thriller...
with pace, wit and acute observation'
Daily Express

THE LOLLIPOP SHOES

Vianne Rocher seeks refuge in Paris with her two
daughters, but encounters a dangerous adversary.

'*Chocolat* was a hard act to follow but Harris has
managed it in style'
Daily Express

THE EVIL SEED

Joanne Harris's haunting debut novel, a gothic vampire story.

'A dark, gothic romance filled with mystery,
jealousy, and violence . . . a thrilling read'
Style

blueeyedboy

A dark tale of a poisonously dysfunctional family, a
psychological thriller that makes creative use of all the
disguise and mind games that are offered by life
on the internet.

'Delivers an almighty twist in the tale . . .
brilliantly atmospheric and at times heartbreaking'
The Times

PEACHES FOR MONSIEUR LE CURE

When Vianne Rocher receives a letter from beyond the
grave, she has no choice but to follow the wind that blows
her back to Lansquenet, the village in south-west France
where, eight years ago, she opened up a chocolate shop.

'Immerses the reader in a bath of seductive imagery
in a brave and grippingly confected story'
Sunday Times

Other books by Joanne Harris

JIGS & REELS

Joanne Harris's first collection of short stories:
sly, funny, sometimes provocative.

'Tantalising and suggestive, and leaves us wanting more'
Sunday Times

THE FRENCH KITCHEN (with Fran Warde)

A beautifully illustrated cookery book
of Joanne Harris's French family recipes.

'Simple yet stylish recipes from the heart of a French family'
Sunday Telegraph

THE FRENCH MARKET (with Fran Warde)

A mouth-watering collection of recipes inspired
by fresh, seasonal French market produce.

'Crammed with authentic local recipes... A glossy,
uplifting book'
Sunday Tribune

RUNEMARKS

Joanne Harris's first book written for a younger audience,
an epic tale set in the world of the Norse gods.

'If you liked Philip Pullman's *Northern Lights*, try this'
Heat

RUNELIGHT

Two girls. With new runes. And the end of the
world is coming. Again.

'One of my favourites...The author's wonderful
imagination is showcased to great effect'
The Sun

RUNEMARKS

JOANNE HARRIS

BLACK SWAN

TRANSWORLD PUBLISHERS
61–63 Uxbridge Road, London W5 5SA
A Random House Group Company
www.transworldbooks.co.uk

RUNEMARKS
A BLACK SWAN BOOK: 9780552778985

First published in Great Britain
in 2007 by Doubleday
an imprint of Random House Children's Publishers
Corgi edition published 2008
This edition published in 2012 by Black Swan
an imprint of Transworld Publishers

Addresses for Random House Group Ltd companies outside the UK
can be found at: www.randomhouse.co.uk
The Random House Group Ltd Reg. No. 954009

Typeset in Palatino

2 4 6 8 10 9 7 5 3

The Random House Group Limited supports The Forest Stewardship
Council® (FSC®), the leading international forest-certification organisation.
Our books carrying the FSC label are printed on FSC®-certified paper.
FSC is the only forest-certification scheme supported by the leading
environmental organisations, including Greenpeace. Our
paper procurement policy can be found at
www.randomhouse.co.uk/environment

MIX
Paper from
responsible sources
FSC® C016897

Printed and bound in Great Britain by Clays Ltd, St Ives plc

To Anouchka

Acknowledgements

My heartfelt thanks go to the faithful warriors who stood by my side throughout all the adventures and misadventures that have befallen this book. To Jennifer and Penny Luithlen; to Peter Robinson; to Christian, who read it first; to Philippa Dickinson; to my fantastic editors Sue Cook and Nancy Siscoe; to David Wyatt for his illustrations and to Rachel Armstrong for publicity. To my P.A. Anne, who runs my life; to Mark, who runs the website and to Kevin, who runs everything else. Most of all, I am grateful to my daughter, Anouchka, who pestered me constantly for four years until I finished this story to her complete satisfaction...

Map of the Nine Worlds

ORDER
THE FIrMAMENT

asgard
(THE SKY CITADEL)

THE RAINBOW BRIDGE

yggdrasil
(THE world tree)

world above   the middle worlds

the one sea

outlands

inland

world below
THE fundament

hel
(THE underworld)

dream

netherworld
(THE black fortress)

WORLD BEYOND
chaos

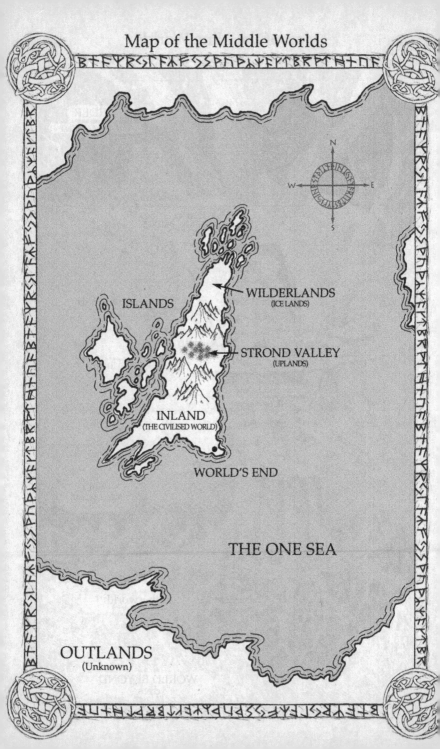

Map of the Middle Worlds

WILDERLANDS
(ICE LANDS)

ISLANDS

STROND VALLEY
(UPLANDS)

INLAND
(THE CIVILISED WORLD)

WORLD'S END

THE ONE SEA

OUTLANDS
(Unknown)

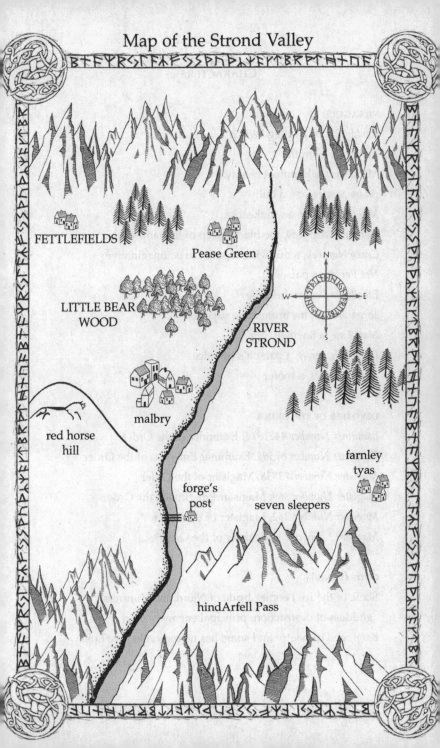

Map of the Strond Valley

FETTLEFIELDS

Pease Green

LITTLE BEAR
WOOD

RIVER
STROND

malbry

red horse
hill

farnley
tyas

forge's
post

seven sleepers

hindArfell Pass

CHARACTERS

VILLAGERS

Maddy Smith, a village witch

Jed Smith, a smith

Mae Smith, a brainless beauty

Adam Scattergood, a bully

Mrs Scattergood, an innkeeper

Dorian Scattergood, the black sheep of the family

Crazy Nan Fey, a midwife, reputed to be imaginative

Nat Parson, a parson

Ethelberta Parson, his wife

Torval Bishop, his immediate superior

Matt Law, a lawman

Daniel Hetherset, a parson's prentice

Audun Briggs, a roofer

DEVOTEES OF THE ORDER

Examiner Number 4421974, Examiner of the Order

Examiner Number 67363, Examiner Emeritus of the Order

Magister Number 73838, Magister of the Order

Magister Number 369, Magister Emeritus of the Order

Magister Number 262, Magister of the Order

Magister Number 23, Magister of the Order

GODS (VANIR)

Skadi, of the Ice People, bride of Njörd, the Huntress, goddess of destruction; principal enemy of Loki

Bragi, god of poetry and song; has no reason to love Loki

Idun, Bragi's wife, goddess of youth and plenty; was once abducted by Loki and handed over to the Ice People

Freyja, goddess of desire; once mortally insulted by Loki

Frey, the Reaper, Freyja's brother; no friend to Loki

Heimdall, gold-toothed sentinel of the gods; hates Loki

Njörd, sea god; once married to Skadi but now separated due to irreconcilable differences; agrees with her on a single subject – dislike of Loki

GODS (ÆSIR – SEER-FOLK)

Odin, chief of the Æsir, blood-brother of – and ultimately betrayed by – Loki

Frigg, his wife; lost her son because of Loki

Thor, the Thunderer, son of Odin; has more than one bone to pick with Loki

Sif, his wife; once went bald because of Loki

Tyr, god of war; lost his hand because of Loki

Balder, son of Frigg; died because of Loki

Loki

OTHERS

Sugar-and-Sack, a goblin

Hel, Mistress of the Underworld

Lord Surt, Ruler of World Beyond, Guardian of the Black Fortress

Jormungand, the World Serpent

Ellie, also known as Old Age

Fat Lizzy, a pot-bellied sow

The Nameless

RUNES OF THE ELDER SCRIPT

$\digamma$ *Fé*: wealth, cattle, property, success

$\cap$ *Úr*: strength, the Mighty Ox

$\flat$ *Thuris*: Thor's rune, the Thorny One

$\digamma$ *Ós*: the Seer-folk, the Æsir

R *Raedo*: the Journeyman, the Outlands

Γ *Kaen*: Wildfire, Chaos

H *Hagall*: Hail, the Destroyer, Netherworld

Υ *Naudr*: the Binder, distress, need, death

$|$ *Isa*: Ice

$\Lsh$ *Ár*: plenty, fruitfulness

Λ *Yr*: the Protector, the Fundament

$\mathcal{5}$ *Sól*: summer, the sun

$\Uparrow$ *Tyr*: the Warrior

B *Bjarkán*: vision, revelation, dream

Υ *Madr*: mankind, the Folk,

Γ *Logr*: water, the One Sea, the Middle Worlds

RUNEMARKS

BOOK ONE
World Above

There was a Seer who foretold the end of all things . . .
Never trust an Oracle.

Lokabrenna, 9:1

1

Seven o'clock on a Monday morning, five hundred years after the End of the World, and goblins had been at the cellar again. Mrs Scattergood – the landlady at the Seven Sleepers Inn – swore it was rats, but Maddy Smith knew better. Only goblins could have burrowed into the brick-lined floor; and besides, as far as she knew, rats didn't drink ale.

But she also knew that in the village of Malbry – as in the whole of the Strond valley – certain things were never discussed, and that included anything curious, uncanny or *unnatural* in any way. To be *imaginative* was considered almost as bad as *giving oneself airs*, and even dreams were hated and feared, for it was through dreams (or so the Good Book said) that the Seer-folk had crossed over from Chaos; and it was in Dream that the power of the Faërie remained, awaiting its chance to re-enter the world.

And so the folk of Malbry made every effort never to dream. They slept on boards instead of mattresses; avoided heavy evening meals; and as for telling bedtime tales – well. The children of Malbry were far more likely to hear about the martyrdom of St Sepulchre or the latest Cleansings from World's End than tales of magic or of World Below. Which is not to say that magic didn't happen. In fact over the past fourteen years the village of Malbry had witnessed more magic in one way or another than any place in the Middle Worlds.

That was Maddy's fault, of course. Maddy Smith was a dreamer, a teller of tales, and worse; and as such, she was used to being blamed for anything irregular that happened in the village. If a bottle of beer fell off a shelf; if the cat got into

3

the creamery; if Adam Scattergood threw a stone at a stray dog and hit a window instead – ten to one Maddy would get the blame.

And if she protested, folk would say that she'd always had a troublesome nature; that their ill-luck had begun the day she was born; and that no good would ever come of a child with a ruinmark – that rusty sign on the Smith girl's hand –

– that some oldsters called the Witch's Ruin, and that no amount of scrubbing would remove.

It was either that, or blame the goblins – otherwise known as Good Folk or Faërie – who this summer had upped their antics from raiding cellars and stealing sheep (or occasionally painting them blue), to playing the dirtiest kind of practical jokes, like leaving horse dung on the church steps, or putting soda in the communion wine to make it fizz, or turning the vinegar to piss in all the jars of pickled onions in Joe Grocer's store.

And since hardly anyone dared to mention *them*, or even acknowledge that they existed at all, Maddy was left to deal with the vermin from under the Hill alone and in her own way.

No one asked her how she did it. No one watched the Smith girl at work. And no one ever called her *witch* – except for Adam Scattergood, her employer's son, a fine boy in many ways, but prone to foul language when the mood took him.

Besides, they said, why speak the words? That ruinmark surely spoke for itself.

Now Maddy considered the rust-coloured mark. It looked like a letter or sigil of some kind, and sometimes it shone faintly in the dark, or burned as if something hot had pressed there. It was burning now, she saw. It often did when the Good Folk were near; as if something inside her were restless, and itched to be set free.

That summer it had itched more often than ever, as the goblins swarmed in unheard-of numbers, and banishing them was one way of putting that itch to rest. Her other skills remained untried and, for the most part, unused; and though sometimes that was hard to bear – like having to pretend you're not hungry when your favourite meal is on the table – Maddy understood why it had to be so.

Cantrips and runecharms were bad enough. But glamours, true glamours, were perilous business, and if rumour of these were to reach World's End, where the servants of the Order worked day and night in study of the Word . . .

For Maddy's deepest secret – known only to her closest friend, the man folk knew as One-Eye – was that she *enjoyed* working magic, however shameful that might be. More than that, she thought she might be good at it too and, like anyone with a talent, longed to make use of it and to show it off to other people.

But that was impossible. At best it counted as *giving herself airs*.

And at worst? Folk had been Cleansed for less.

Maddy turned her attention to the cellar floor, and the wide-mouthed burrow that disfigured it. It was a goblin burrow, all right, bigger and rather messier than a foxhole and still bearing the marks of clawed, thick-soled feet where the spilled earth had been kicked over. Rubble and bricks had been piled in a corner, roughly concealed beneath a stack of empty kegs. Maddy thought, with some amusement, that it must have been a lively – and somewhat drunken – party.

Filling in the burrow would be easy, she thought. The tricky thing, as always, was to ensure it stayed that way. *Yr*, the Protector, had been enough to secure the church doors, but goblins had been known to be very persistent where ale was concerned, and she knew that in this case a single charm would not keep them out for long.

All right, then. Something more.

With a sharp-ended stick she drew two runes on the hard-pack floor.

Naudr, the Binder, might do it, she thought –

– and with it *Úr*, the Mighty Ox, set at an angle to the mouth of the burrow.

Now all it needed was a spark.

That spark. *That* was the only true magic involved. Anyone familiar with the runes – which were only letters, after all, taken from an ancient language – could learn to write them. The trick, Maddy knew, was to set them to work.

It had been difficult at first. Now, working the runes was easy as striking a match. She spoke a little cantrip – *Cuth on fyre* . . .

The letters flared for a few seconds, and then dwindled to a warning gleam. The goblins could see them – and so could Maddy – but to Mrs Scattergood, who despised reading (because she could not do it) and who thought magic was the devil's work, the runes would only ever look like scratches in the dirt, and they could all continue to pretend that the goblins were only rats.

Suddenly there came a scrabbling sound from the far, dark corner of the cellar. Maddy turned and saw a movement in the shadows and a shape, rather larger than a common rat, bob away between two of the barrels.

Quickly she stood up, lifting her candle so that its flame lit up the whitewashed wall. No sound could be heard;

nothing moved but the shadows that jerked and juddered.

Maddy stepped forward and shone the candle right into the corner. Still nothing moved. But every creature leaves a trail that only a few know how to see. There was *something* there; Maddy could feel it. She could even smell it now: a sour-sweet, wintry scent like roots and spices kept long underground.

A drunken party, she thought again. So drunken, perhaps, that one of the revellers, stupefied beyond all thought of caution by Mrs Scattergood's excellent ale, had curled up in some dark corner to sleep off the after-effects of a bellyful. And now it was trapped, whatever it was. Trapped behind a drift of stacked ale kegs, its burrow sealed, the cellar shut.

Maddy's heart began to beat a little faster. In all these years she had never had such a chance: to see one of the Faërie at such close quarters; to speak to it, and have it answer.

She tried to recall what little she knew of the Good Folk from under Red Horse Hill. They were curious creatures, more playful than bad; fond of strong drink and well-dressed meats. And wasn't there something else as well, something that lingered tantalizingly on the edges of memory? A tale of One-Eye's, perhaps? Or maybe some more practical trick, some cantrip to help her deal with the thing?

She left the candle on top of a barrel and came to peer into the corner. 'I know you're there,' she whispered softly.

The goblin – if it *was* a goblin and not just a rat – said nothing.

'Come out,' said Maddy. 'I won't hurt you.'

Nothing moved; just layers of shadow disturbed by the candle-flame. She gave a sigh, as if of disappointment, and turned to face the other way.

In the shadows, something lurked; she could see it from the corner of her eye.

She did not move, but stood, apparently lost in thought. In the shadows, something began to crawl, very quietly, between the barrels.

Still Maddy did not stir. Only her left hand moved, fingers curling into the familiar shape that was *Bjarkán*, the rune of revelation.

If it was a rat, *Bjarkán* would show it.

It was not a rat. A wisp – just a wisp – of Faërie gold gleamed in the circle of her finger and thumb.

Maddy pounced. Her strike was well timed. At once the creature began to struggle, and although Maddy couldn't see it, she could certainly *feel* it between her hands, kicking and twisting and trying to bite her. Then, as she continued to hold it fast, the creature finally went limp; the shadow dropped away from it, and she saw it clearly.

It – *he* – was not much bigger than a dog fox, with small, clever hands and wicked little teeth. Most of his body was covered in armour – pieces of plate, leather straps, half a mail-shirt cut clumsily down to fit – and out of his brown, long-whiskered face, his eyes shone a bright, inhuman gold.

He blinked at her twice. Then, without any warning, he shot away between her legs.

He might even have escaped – he was quick as a weasel – but Maddy had expected it, and with her fingers she cast *Isa*, the Icy One, and froze him to the spot.

The goblin struggled and squirmed, but his feet were stuck to the ground.

The goblin spat a gobbet of fool's fire from between his pointed teeth, but still Maddy would not let him go.

The goblin swore in many tongues, some animal, some Faërie, and finished off by saying some very nasty things about Maddy's family, which she had to admit were mostly true.

Finally he stopped struggling and sat down crossly on the floor.

8

'So what do you want?' he said.

'What about – three wishes?' suggested Maddy hopefully.

'Leave it out,' said the goblin with scorn. 'What kind of stories have you been listening to?'

Maddy was disappointed. Many of the tales she had collected over the past few years had involved someone receiving three wishes from the Faërie, and she felt rather aggrieved that in this case it had turned out to be nothing more than a tale. Still, there were other stories that she thought might contain more practical truths, and her eyes lit up as she finally remembered the thing that had been lurking at the back of her mind since she had first heard the suspicious sounds from behind the barrel.

'In yer own time,' said the goblin, picking his teeth.

'Shh,' said Maddy. 'I'm thinking.'

The goblin yawned. He was beginning to look quite cocky now, and his bright gold eyes shone with mischief. 'Doesn't know what to do with me, kennet?' he said. 'Knows it'll bring revenge if I don't get home safe.'

'Revenge? Who from?'

'The Captain, accourse,' said the goblin. 'Gods, was you brung up in a box? Now you let me go, there's a good girl, and there'll be no hard feelings, and no call to get the Captain involved.'

Maddy smiled, but said nothing.

'Ah, come on,' said the goblin, looking uncomfortable now. 'There's no good in keeping me here, and nowt I can give yer.'

'Oh but there is,' said Maddy, sitting down cross-legged on the floor. 'You can give me your name.'

The goblin stared at her, wide-eyed.

'*A named thing is a tamed thing*. Isn't that how the saying goes?'

It was an old story, told by One-Eye years ago, and Maddy had almost forgotten it in the excitement of the moment. At the beginning of the First Age, it was given to every creature, tree, rock and plant a secret name that would bind that creature to the will of anyone who knew it.

Mother Frigg knew the true names, and used them to make all of Creation weep for the return of her dead son. But Loki, who had many names, would not be bound to such a promise, and so Balder the Fair, god of springtime, was forced to remain in Underworld, Hel's kingdom, until the end of all things.

'Me name?' the goblin said at last.

Maddy nodded.

'What's a name? Call me Hair-of-the-Dog, or Whisky-in-the-Jar, or Three-Sheets-to-the-Wind. It's nowt to me.'

'Your *true* name,' said Maddy, and once more she drew the rune *Naudr*, the Binder, and *Isa*, to fix it in ice.

The goblin wriggled, but was held fast. 'What's it to you, anyroad?' he demanded. 'And how come you know so bloody much about it?'

'Just tell me,' said Maddy.

'You'd never be able to say it,' he said.

'Tell me anyway.'

'I won't! Lemme go!'

'I will,' said Maddy, 'as soon as you tell me. Otherwise I'll open up the cellar doors and let the sun do its worst.'

The goblin blenched at that, for sunlight is lethal to the Good Folk. 'You wouldn't do that, lady, would yer?' he whined.

'Watch me,' said Maddy, and, standing up, she began to make her way to the trapdoor – now closed – through which the ale kegs were delivered.

'You wouldn't!' squeaked the goblin.

'Your name,' she said, with one hand on the latch.

The goblin struggled more fiercely than ever, but Maddy's runes still held him fast. 'He'll get yer!' he squeaked. 'The Captain'll get yer, and then you'll be sorry!'

'Last chance,' said Maddy, drawing the bolt. A tiny wand of sunlight fell onto the cellar floor only inches from the goblin's foot.

'Shut it, shut it!' shrieked the goblin.

Maddy just waited patiently.

'All right then! All right! It's . . .' The goblin rattled off something in his own language, fast as pebbles in a gourd. 'Now shut it, shut it now!' he cried, and wriggled as far as he could away from the spike of sunlight.

Maddy shut the trapdoor, and the goblin gave a sigh of relief. 'That was just *narsty*,' he said. 'Nice young girl like you shouldn't be messin' with nastiness like that.' He looked at Maddy in reproach. 'What d'you want me name for, anyroad?'

But Maddy was trying to remember the word the goblin had spoken.

Snotrag? No, that wasn't it.

Sna-raggy? No, that wasn't it, either.

Sma-ricky? She frowned, searching for just the right inflection, knowing that the goblin would try to distract her; knowing that unless she got it completely right, the cantrip wouldn't work.

'*Smá—*'

'*Call me Smutkin, call me Smudgett.*' The goblin was babbling now, trying to break Maddy's cantrip with one of his own. '*Call me Spider, Slyme and Sluggitt. Call me Sleekitt, call me Slow—*'

'Quiet!' said Maddy. The word was on the tip of her tongue.

'Say it, then.'

'I will.' If only the creature would stop *talking* . . .

'Forgot it, hast yer!' There was a note of triumph in the goblin's voice. 'Forgot it, forgot it, forgot it!'

Maddy could feel her concentration slipping. It was all too much to do at once; she could not hope to keep the goblin subdued *and* make the effort to remember the cantrip that would bind him to her will. Already *Naudr* and *Isa* were close to failing. The goblin had one foot almost free, and his eyes snapped with malice as he worked to release the other.

It was now or never. Dropping the runes, Maddy turned all her will towards speaking the creature's true name.

'*Smá-rakki—*' It *felt* right – fast and percussive – but even as she opened her mouth, the goblin shot out of the corner like a cork from a bottle, and before she had even finished speaking he was halfway into the cellar wall, burrowing as if his life depended on it.

If Maddy had paused to think at this point, she would simply have ordered the goblin to stop. If she had spoken the name correctly, then he would have been forced to obey her, and she could have questioned him at leisure. But Maddy didn't pause to think. She saw the goblin's feet vanishing into the ground and shouted something – not even a cantrip – while at the same time casting *Thuris*, Thor's rune, as hard as she could at the mouth of the burrow.

It felt like throwing a firework. It snapped against the brick-lined floor, throwing up a shower of sparks and a small but pungent cloud of smoke.

For a second or two nothing happened. Then there came a low rumble from under Maddy's feet, and from the burrow came a swearing and a kicking and a scuffle of earth, as if something inside had come up against a sudden obstacle.

Maddy knelt down and reached inside the hole. She could hear the goblin cursing, too far away for her to reach, and now there was another sound, a kind of sliding, squealing, *pattering* noise that Maddy almost recognized . . .

The goblin's voice was muffled, but urgent. '*Now* look what you've gone and done. Gog and Magog, let me *out*!' There came another desperate scuffling of earth, and the creature reversed out of the hole at speed, falling over its feet and coming to a halt against a stack of empty barrels, which fell over with a clatter loud enough (Maddy thought) to wake the Seven Sleepers from their beds.

'What happened?' she said.

But before the goblin could make his reply, something shot out of the hole in the wall. Several somethings, in fact; no, dozens – no, hundreds – of fat, brown, fast-moving some-things, swarming from the burrow like—

'Rats!' exclaimed Maddy, gathering her skirt around her ankles.

The goblin looked at her with scorn. 'Well, what did you *think* would happen?' he said. 'Cast that kind of glam at World Below, and before you know it you're knee-deep in bilge and vermin.'

Maddy stared at the hole in dismay. She had intended to summon only the goblin; but the cry – and that fast-flung rune – had apparently summoned *everything* within her range. Now, not only rats but beetles, spiders, woodlice, centipedes, whirligigs, earwigs and maggots squirted horribly out of the hole, along with a generous outpouring of foul water (possibly from a broken drain), to form a kind of verminous brew that poured and wriggled at alarming speed out of the burrow and across the floor.

And then, just when she was sure that nothing worse could possibly happen, there came the sound of a door opening above-stairs, and a high and slightly nasal voice came to Maddy from the kitchen.

'Hey, madam! You going to stay down there all morning, or what?'

'Oh, gods.' It was Mrs Scattergood.

The goblin shot Maddy a cheery wink.

'Did you hear me?' said Mrs Scattergood. 'There's pots to wash up here, or am I supposed to do *them* an' all?'

'In a minute!' called Maddy in haste, taking refuge on the cellar steps. 'Just . . . sorting out a few things down here!'

'Well, now you can come and finish things off up *here*,' said Mrs Scattergood. 'Come up right now and see to them pots. And if that one-eyed scally good-for-nowt comes round again, you can tell him from me to shove off!'

Maddy's heart leaped into her mouth. *That one-eyed scally good-for-nowt* – that must mean her old friend was back, after more than twelve months of wandering, and no amount of rats and cockroaches – or even goblins – was going to keep her from seeing him. 'He was here?' she said, taking the cellar steps at a run. 'One-Eye was here?' She emerged breathless into the kitchen.

'Aye.' Mrs Scattergood handed her a tea-towel. 'Though I dunno what there is in *that* to look so pleased about. I'd have thought that *you*, of all people—'

She stopped and cocked her head to listen. 'What's that noise?' she said sharply.

Maddy closed the cellar door. 'It's nothing, Mrs Scattergood.'

The landlady gave her a suspicious look. 'What about them rats?' she said. 'Did you fix it right this time?'

'I need to see him,' Maddy said.

'Who? The one-eyed scallyman?'

'Please,' she said. 'I won't be long.'

Mrs Scattergood pursed her lips. 'Not on my penny, you won't,' she said. 'I'm not paying you good money to go gallivanting around with thieves and beggars—'

'One-Eye isn't a thief,' said Maddy.

'Don't you start giving yourself airs, madam,' said Mrs Scattergood. 'Laws knows you can't help the way you're made, but you might at least make an effort. For your father's sake, you might, and for the memory of your sainted mother.' She paused for breath for less than a second. '*And* you can take that look off your face. Anyone would think you were proud to be a—'

And then she stopped, open-mouthed, as a sound came from behind the cellar door. It was, thought Mrs Scattergood, a peculiar kind of *scuttling* noise, punctuated by the occasional thud. It made her feel quite uncomfortable – as if there might be something more down that cellar than barrels of ale. And what was that distant sloshing sound, like washday at the river?

'Oh my Laws, what have you done?' Mrs Scattergood made for the cellar door.

Maddy put herself in front of it, and with one hand she traced the shape of *Naudr* against the latch. 'Don't go down there, please,' she said.

Mrs Scattergood tried the latch; but the runesign held it fast. She turned to glare at Maddy, her fierce little teeth bared like a ferret's. 'You open this door right now,' she said.

'You really, *really* don't want me to.'

'You open this door, Maddy Smith, if you know what's good for you.'

Maddy tried once more to protest, but Mrs Scattergood was unstoppable. 'I'll wager you've got that scally down there, helping himself to my best ale. Well, you just open this door, girl, or I'll have Matt Law down here to take you both to the roundhouse!'

Maddy sighed. It wasn't that she *liked* working at the inn; but a job was a job, and a shilling a shilling, and neither was likely to be forthcoming as soon as Mrs Scattergood looked into the cellar. In an hour or so the spell would wear off, and the creatures would crawl back into their hole. Then she could seal it up again, sweep up the mess, mop up the water . . .

'Let me explain,' she tried again.

But Mrs Scattergood was beyond explanations. Her face had flushed a dangerous red, and her voice was almost as shrill as a rat's. '*Adam!*' she shrieked. 'Get in here right *now!*'

Adam was Mrs Scattergood's son. He and Maddy had always hated each other, and it was the thought of his sneering, gleeful face – and that of her long-absent friend, known in some circles as *the one-eyed scallyman* – that finally made up her mind.

'You're sure it was One-Eye?' she said at last.

'Of course it was! Now open this—'

'All right,' said Maddy, and reversed the rune. 'But if I were you, I'd give it an hour.'

And at that she turned and fled, and was already on the road to Red Horse Hill by the time the shrill, distant screaming began, emerging like smoke from the Seven Sleepers kitchen and rising above slumbering Malbry village to vanish into the morning air.

2

Malbry was a village of some eight hundred souls. A quiet place, or so it seemed, set between mountain ridges in the valley of the river Strond, which divided the Uplands from the Wilderlands to the north before finally making its way south towards World's End and into the One Sea.

The mountains – called the Seven Sleepers, though no one remembered exactly why – were bitter and snow-cloaked all year round, and there was only one pass, the Hindarfell, which was blocked by snow three months in the year. This remoteness affected the valley folk; they kept to themselves, were suspicious of strangers, and (but for Nat Parson, who had once made a pilgrimage as far as World's End, and who considered himself quite the traveller) had little to do with the world outside.

There were a dozen little settlements in the valley, from Farnley Tyas at the foot of the mountains to Pease Green at the far side of Little Bear Wood. But Malbry was the biggest and the most important. It housed the valley's only parson, the largest church, the best inns and the wealthiest farmers. Its houses were built of stone, not wood; there was a smithy, a glassworks, a covered market. Its inhabitants thought themselves better than most, and looked down on the folk of Pog Hill or Fettlefields and laughed in secret at their country ways. The only thorn in Malbry's side stood roughly two miles from the village. The locals called it Red Horse Hill, and most folk avoided it because of the tales that collected there, and for the goblins that lived beneath its flanks.

Once, it was said, there had been a castle on the Hill. Malbry itself had been part of its fiefdom, growing crops for the lord of that land – but all that had been a long time ago, before Tribulation and the End of the World. Nowadays there was nothing to see: only a few standing stones, too large to have been looted from the ruins; and, of course, the Red Horse cut into the clay.

It had long been known as a goblin stronghold. Such places drew them, the villagers said, lured them with promises of treasure and tales of the Elder Age. But it was only in recent years that the Good Folk had ventured as far as the village.

Fourteen years, to be precise; which was exactly when Jed Smith's pretty wife Julia had died giving birth to their second daughter. Few doubted that the two were linked; or that the rust-coloured mark on the palm of the child's hand was the sign of some dreadful misfortune to come.

And so it was. From that day forth, that Harvestmonth, the goblins had been drawn to the blacksmith's child. The midwife had seen them, so she said, perched on the baby's pinewood crib, or grinning from inside the warming pan, or tumbling the blankets. At first the rumours were scarcely voiced. Nan Fey was mad, just like her old granddam, and it was best to take anything she said with a dose of salt. But as time passed, and goblin sightings were reported by such respectable sources as the parson, his wife Ethelberta and even Torval Bishop from over the pass, the rumours grew and soon everyone was wondering how the Smiths, of all people – the Smiths, who never dreamed, went to church every day and would no more have flung themselves into the river Strond than truckle with the Good Folk – could have given birth to two so very different daughters.

Mae Smith, with her cowslip curls, was widely held to be the prettiest and least imaginative girl in the valley. Jed Smith said she was the image of her poor mother, and it almost broke his heart to see her so, though he smiled when he said it, and his eyes were like stars.

But Maddy was dark, just like an Outlander, and there was no light in Jed's eyes when he looked at *her*, only an odd kind of measuring look, as if he were weighing Maddy against her dead mother, and finding that he had been sold short.

Jed Smith was not the only one to think so. As she grew older, Maddy discovered that she had disappointed almost everyone. An awkward girl with a sullen mouth, a curtain of hair and a tendency to slouch, she had neither Mae's sweet nature nor her sweet face. Her eyes were rather beautiful, halfway between grey and gold, but few people ever noticed this, and it was widely believed that Maddy Smith was ugly; a troublemaker; too clever for her own good; too stubborn – or too slack – to change.

Of course folk agreed that it was not *her* fault she was so brown, or her sister so pretty; but *a smile costs nothing*, as the saying goes, and if only the girl had made an effort once in a while, or even showed a little gratitude for all the help and free advice she had been given, then maybe she would have settled down.

But she did not. From the beginning Maddy was wild: never laughed; never cried; never brushed her hair; fought with Adam Scattergood and broke his nose; and if that wasn't already bad enough, showed signs of being clever – disastrous in a girl – with a tongue on her that could be downright rude.

No one mentioned the ruinmark, of course. In fact for the first seven years of her life no one had even explained to Maddy what it meant, though Mae pulled faces and called it *your blemish* and was surprised when Maddy refused to wear the mittens sent to her father by the village's charitable – and ever-hopeful – widows.

Someone needed to *put things straight with the girl*, and at last Nat Parson accepted the unpleasant duty of telling her the facts. Maddy didn't understand much of it, littered as it was with quotes from the Good Book, but she understood his contempt – and behind it, his fear. It was all written down in the Book of Tribulation: how after the battle the old gods – the Seer-folk of that time – had been cast into Netherworld; but how in dreams they still endured, fragmented but still dangerous, entering the minds of the wicked and the susceptible, trying desperately to be reborn . . .

'And so their demon blood lives on,' had said the parson, 'passed from man to woman, beast to beast. And here you are, by no fault of your own, and as long as you say your prayers and remember your place, there's no reason why you should not lead as worthwhile a life as any of the rest of us, and earn forgiveness at the hand of the Nameless.'

Now Maddy had never liked Nat Parson. She watched him in silence as he spoke, occasionally lifting her left hand and peering at him insolently through the circle of her thumb and forefinger. Nat itched to slap her, but Laws knew what powers her demon blood had given her, and he wanted as little to do with the girl as possible. The Order would have known what to do with the child. But this was Malbry, not World's End, and even such a stickler as Nat knew better than to try to enforce World's End law so far from the Universal City.

'Do – you – understand?' He spoke loudly and slowly. Perhaps she was simple, like Crazy Nan Fey. In any case she did not reply, but watched him again through her crooked fingers until at last he sighed and went away.

After that, or so it seemed, Jed Smith's youngest daughter had grown wilder than ever. She stopped going to church, lived out in Little Bear Wood for days on end, and spent hours at a time talking to herself (or, more likely, to the goblins). And when the other children played jump-stone around the pond, or went to Nat Parson's Sunday school, Maddy ran off to Red Horse Hill, or pestered Crazy Nan for tales, or, worse still, *made up* tales about terrible, impossible things that she told the younger ones to give them nightmares.

She was an embarrassment to Mae, who was merry as a bluejay (and as brainless), and who would have made a brilliant marriage but for her unruly sister. As compensation, Mae was spoiled and indulged far more than was good for her, while Maddy grew up sullen, unregarded and angry.

And sullen and angry she might have remained, but for what happened on Red Horse Hill in the summer of her seventh year.

No one knew much about Red Horse Hill. Some said it had been shaped during the Elder Age, when the heathens still made sacrifices to the old gods. Others said it was the burial mound of some great chieftain, seeded throughout with deadly traps, though Maddy favoured the theory that the place was a giant treasure mound, piled to the eaves with goblin gold.

Whatever it was, the Horse was ancient – everyone agreed on that – and although there was no doubt that men had carved it into the flank of the Hill, there was something uncanny about the figure. For a start, the Red Horse never grassed over in spring, nor did the winter snow ever hide its shape. As a result, the Hill was riddled with whispers and tales – tales of the Faërie and of the old gods – and so most people wisely left it alone.

Maddy liked the Hill, of course. But then, Maddy knew it better than most. All her life she had stayed alert to rumours culled from travellers; to pieces of lore; to sayings, kennings, stories, tales. From these tales she had formed a picture – still maddeningly unclear – of a time *before* the End of the World, when Red Horse Hill was an enchanted place, and when the old gods – the Seer-folk – walked the land in human guise, sowing stories wherever they went.

No one in Malbry spoke of them. Even Crazy Nan would not have dared; the Good Book forbade all tales of the Seer-folk not written in the Book of Tribulation. And the people of Malbry prided themselves on their devotion to the Good Book. They no longer decked wells in the name of Mother Frigg, or danced on the May, or left crumbs by their doorsteps for Jack-in-the-Green. The shrines and temples of the Seer-folk had all been torn down years ago. Even their names had been largely forgotten, and no one mentioned them any more.

Almost no one, anyway. The exception was Maddy's closest friend – known to Mrs Scattergood as *that one-eyed scally good-for-nowt*, and to others as the Outlander, or just plain One-Eye.

3

They met in the summer of Maddy's seventh year. It was Midsummer's Fair Day, with games and dancing on the green. There were stalls selling ribbons and fruit and cakes; there were ices for the children; Mae had been crowned Strawberry Queen for the third year running and Maddy was watching it all from her place at the edge of Little Bear Wood, feeling jealous, feeling angry, but nevertheless determined not to join in.

Her place was a giant copper beech, with a thick, smooth bole and plenty of branches. Thirty feet up, there was a fork into which Maddy liked to sprawl, skirts hiked up, legs on either side of the trunk, watching the village through the crook of her left thumb and forefinger.

Some years before, Maddy had discovered that when she made this fingering and concentrated very hard, she could see things that could not normally be seen. A bird's nest underneath the turf; blackberries in the bramble hedge; Adam Scattergood and his cronies hiding behind a garden wall with stones in their pockets and mischief on their minds.

And it sometimes showed her different things – lights and colours that shone around people and showed their moods – and often these colours left a trail, like a signature for any to read who could.

Her trick was called *sjón-henni*, or *truesight*, and it was one of the fingerings of the rune *Bjarkán* – though Maddy, who had never learned her letters, had never heard of *Bjarkán*, nor had it ever occurred to her that her trick was magic.

All her life it had been impressed upon her that magic –

23

be it a glamour, a fingering or even a cantrip – was not only unnatural, but *wrong*. It was the legacy of the Faërie, the source of Maddy's bad blood, the ruin of everything good and lawful.

It was the reason she was here in the first place, when she could have been playing with the other children, or eating pies on the Fair Day green. It was the reason her father avoided her gaze, as if every glance reminded him of the wife he had lost. It was also the reason that Maddy alone of all the villagers noticed the strange man in the wide-brimmed hat walking along the Malbry road – walking not towards the village, as you might have supposed, but in the direction of Red Horse Hill.

Strangers were not often seen in Malbry, even at a Midsummer's Fair. Most traders were regulars from one place or another – bringing with them glass and metalware from the Ridings; persimmons from the Southlands; fish from the Islands; spices from the Outlands; skins and furs from the frozen North.

But if he was a trader, Maddy thought, then this man was travelling light. He had no horse, no mule, no wagon. And he was going the wrong way. He could be an Outlander, she thought, with his matted hair and ragged clothes. She had heard they sometimes travelled the Roads, where all kinds of people met and traded, but she had never actually seen one; those savages from the dead lands beyond World's End, so ignorant that they couldn't even speak a civilized language. Or he might be a Wilderlander, all painted in blue woad; a madman, a leper, or even a bandit.

She slipped out of her tree as the stranger passed and began to follow him at a safe distance, keeping to the bushes by the side of the road and watching him through the rune *Bjarkán*.

Perhaps he was a soldier, a veteran of some Outland war;

he had pulled his hat down over his forehead, but even so, Maddy could see that he wore an eyepatch, which hid the left side of his face. Like an Outlander, he was tall and dark, and Maddy saw with interest that although his long hair was going grey, he did not move like an old man.

Nor were his colours that of an old man. Maddy had found that old folk left a weak trail; and idiots left hardly any trail at all. But this man had a stronger signature than any she had ever seen. It was a rich and vibrant kingfisher-blue; and Maddy found it hard to reconcile this inner brilliance with the drab, road-weary individual before her on the way to the Hill.

She continued to follow him, silently and keeping well hidden, and when she reached the brow of the Hill, she hid behind a hummock of grass and watched him as he lay in the shadow of a fallen stone, his one eye fixed on the Red Horse and a small, leather-bound notebook in his hand.

Minutes passed. He looked half asleep, his face concealed by the brim of his hat. But Maddy knew he was awake; and from time to time he wrote something in his notebook, or turned the page, and then went back to watching the Horse.

After a while, the Outlander spoke. Not loudly, but so that Maddy could hear, and his voice was low and pleasant, not really what she'd expected of an Outlander at all.

'Well?' he said. 'Have you seen enough?'

Maddy was startled. She had made no sound; and as far as she could tell, he had not once looked in her direction. She stood up, feeling rather foolish, and stared at him defiantly. 'I'm not afraid of you,' she said.

'No?' said the Outlander. 'Perhaps you should be.'

Maddy decided she could outrun him if need be. She sat down again, just out of reach on the springy grass.

His book, she now saw, was a collection of scraps, bound together with strips of leather, the pages hedged with thorny script. Maddy, of course, could not read – few villagers could, except for the parson and his prentices, who read the Good Book, and nothing else.

'Are you a priest?' she said at last.

The stranger laughed, not pleasantly.

'A soldier, then?'

The man said nothing.

'A pirate? A mercenary?'

Again, nothing. The Outlander continued to make marks in his little book, pausing occasionally to study the Horse.

But Maddy's curiosity had been fired. 'What happened to your face?' she said. 'How were you wounded? Was it a war?'

Now the stranger looked at her with a trace of impatience. '*This* happened,' he said, and took off his patch.

For a moment Maddy stared at him. But it was not the scarred ruin of his eye that held her thus. It was the bluish mark that began just above his brow and extended right down onto his left cheekbone.

It was not the same shape as her own ruinmark, but it was recognizably of the same *substance*; and it was certainly the first time that Maddy had ever seen such a thing on someone other than herself.

'Satisfied?' said the Outlander.

But a great excitement had seized hold of Maddy. 'What's that?' she said. 'How did you get it? Is it woad? Is it a tattoo? Were you born with it? Do all Outlanders have them?'

He gave her a small and chilly smile. 'Didn't your mamma ever tell you that curiosity killed the kitty-cat?'

'My mamma died when I was born.'

'I see. What's your name?'

'Maddy. What's yours?'

'You can call me One-Eye,' he said.

And then Maddy uncurled her fist, still grubby from her climb up the big beech tree, and showed him the ruinmark on her hand.

For a moment the Outlander's good eye widened beneath the brim of his hat. On Maddy's palm, the ruinmark stood out sharper than usual, still rust-coloured but now flaring bright orange at the edges, and Maddy could feel the burn of it – a tingling sensation, not unpleasant, but definitely there, as if she had grasped something hot a few minutes before.

He looked at it for a long time. 'D'you know what you've got there, girl?'

'Witch's Ruin,' said Maddy promptly. 'My sister thinks I should wear mittens.'

One-Eye spat. '*Witch* rhymes with *bitch*. A dirty word for dirty-minded folk. Besides, it was never a Witch's *Ruin*,' he said, 'but a Witch's *Rune*: the runemark of the Fiery.'

'Don't you mean the Faërie?' said Maddy, intrigued.

'Faërie, Fiery, it's all the same. This rune' – he looked at it closely – 'this mark of yours . . . do you know what it is?'

'Nat Parson says it's the devil's mark.'

'Nat Parson's a gobshite,' One-Eye said.

Maddy was torn between a natural feeling of sacrilege and a deep admiration of anyone who dared call a parson *gobshite*.

'Listen to me, girlie,' he said. 'Your man Nat Parson has every reason to fear that mark. Aye, and envy it too.'

Once more he studied the design on Maddy's palm, with interest and – Maddy thought – some wistfulness. 'A curious thing,' he said at last. 'I never thought to see it here.'

'But what is it?' said Maddy. 'If the Book isn't true—'

'Oh, there's truth in the book,' said One-Eye, and shrugged. 'But it's buried deep under legends and lies. That war, for instance . . .'

'Tribulation,' said Maddy helpfully.

'Aye, if you like, or Ragnarók. Remember, it's the winners write the history books, and the losers get the leavings. If the Æsir had won—'

'The Æsir?'

'Seer-folk, I dare say you'd call 'em here. Well, if they'd won that war – and it was *close*, mind you – then the Elder Age would not have ended, and your Good Book would have turned out very different, or maybe never been written at all.'

Maddy's ears pricked up at once. 'The Elder Age? You mean *before* Tribulation?'

One-Eye laughed. 'Aye. If you like. Before that, Order reigned. The Æsir kept it, believe it or not, though there were no Seers among them in those days, and it was the Vanir, from the borders of Chaos – the Faërie, your folk'd call 'em – that were the keepers of the Fire.'

'The Fire?' said Maddy, thinking of her father's smithy.

'Glam. *Glám-sýni*, they called it. Rune-caster's glam. Shape-changer's magic. The Vanir had it, and the children of Chaos. The Æsir only got it later.'

'How?' said Maddy.

'Trickery – and theft, of course. They stole it, and remade the Worlds. And such was the power of the runes that even after the Winter War, the fire lay sleeping underground, as fire may sleep for weeks, months – years. And sometimes even now it rekindles itself – in a living creature, even a child—'

'Me?' said Maddy.

'Much joy may it bring you.' He turned away and, frowning, seemed once more absorbed in his book.

But Maddy had been listening with too much interest to allow One-Eye to stop now. Until then she had heard only fragments of tales – and the scrambled versions from the Book of Tribulation, in which the Seer-folk were mentioned only in warnings against their demonic powers or in an attempt to ridicule those long-dead impostors who called themselves gods.

'So – how do you know these stories?' she said.

The Outlander smiled. 'You might say I'm a collector.'

Maddy's heart beat faster at the thought of a man who might *collect* tales in the way another might collect penknives, or butterflies, or stones. 'Tell me more,' she said eagerly. 'Tell me about the Æsir.'

'I said a *collector*, not a storyteller.'

But Maddy was not to be put off. 'What happened to them?' she said. 'Did they all die? Did the Nameless hurl them into the Black Fortress, with the snakes and demons?'

'Is *that* what they say?'

'Nat Parson does.'

He made a sharp sound of contempt. 'Some died; some vanished; some fell; some were lost. New gods emerged to suit a new age, and the old ones were forgotten. Maybe that proves they weren't gods at all.'

'Then what were they?'

'They were the Æsir. What else do you need?'

Once again he turned away, but this time Maddy caught at him. 'Tell me more about the Æsir.'

'There is no more,' One-Eye said. 'There's me. There's you. And there's our cousins under the Hill. The dregs, girlie, that's what we are. The wine's long gone.'

'Cousins,' said Maddy wistfully. 'Then you and I must be cousins too.' It was a strangely attractive thought. That Maddy and One-Eye might both belong to the same secret tribe of travelling folk, both of them marked with Faërie fire . . .

'Oh, teach me how to use it,' she begged, holding out her palm. 'I know I can do it. I want to learn—'

But One-Eye had lost patience at last. He snapped his book shut and stood up, shaking the grass stems from his cloak. 'I'm no teacher, little girl. Go play with your friends and leave me alone.'

'I have no friends, Outlander,' she said. 'Teach me.'

Now One-Eye had no love for children. He looked down with no affection at all at the grubby little girl with the runemark on her hand, and wondered how he could have let her draw him in. He was getting old – wasn't that the truth? – old and sentimental, and it was likely to be the death of him – aye, as if the runes hadn't already told him as much. His most recent casting of the runestones had given him *Madr*, the Folk, crossed with *Thuris*, the Thorny One, and finally *Hagall*, the Destroyer, and if that wasn't a warning to keep moving on—

'Teach me,' said the little girl.

'Leave me alone.' He began to walk, long-legged, down the side of the Hill, with Maddy running after him.

'Teach me.'

'I won't.'

'Teach me.'

'Get lost!'

'Teach me.'

'Ye *gods*!'

One-Eye made an exasperated sound and forked a rune-sign with his left hand. Maddy thought she saw something between his fingers – a fleck of blue fire, no more than a spark, as if a ring or gemstone he was wearing had caught the light. But One-Eye wore no rings or gems . . .

Without thinking, she raised her hand against the spark and *pushed* it back towards the Outlander with a sound like a firecracker going off.

One-Eye flinched. 'Who taught you *that*?'

'No one did,' said Maddy in surprise. Her runemark felt

unusually warm; once more changing colour from rusty brown to tiger's-eye gold.

For a minute or two One-Eye said nothing. He looked at his hand and flexed the fingers, now throbbing as if they had been burned. He looked at Maddy with renewed curiosity.

'Teach me,' she said.

There was a long pause. Then he said, 'You'd better be good. I haven't taken a pupil – let alone a girl – in more years than I care to remember.'

Maddy hid her grin beneath her tangled hair.

For the first time in her life, she had a teacher.

Over the next fortnight Maddy listened to One-Eye's teachings with a single-mindedness she had never shown before.
Nat Parson had always made it clear that to be a bad-blood
was a shameful thing, like being a cripple or a bastard. But
here was this man telling her the exact opposite. She had
skills, the Outlander told her, skills that were unique and
valuable. She was an apt pupil, and One-Eye, who had come
to the valley as a trader of medicines and salves and who
rarely stayed anywhere for longer than a few days, this time
extended his visit to almost a month as Maddy absorbed
tales, maps, letters, cantrips, runes – every scrap of information her new friend gave her. It was the beginning of a long
apprenticeship, and one that would change her world picture
for ever.

Now Maddy's folk believed in a universe of Nine Worlds.
The first was the Firmament, the Sky City of Perfect Order.

Beneath their world was the Fundament, or World Below,
which led to the three lands of Death, Dream and Damnation
– and from which led the way to World Beyond, the Pan-daemonium; the home of all Chaos and all things profane.

And between them, so Maddy was taught, lay the Middle
Worlds: Inland, Outland and the One Sea, with Malbry and
the valley of the Strond right at the centre, like a bull's-eye on
a shooting target. From which you might have concluded that
the folk of Malbry had no small opinion of themselves.

But now Maddy learned of a world beyond the map's
edge; a world of many parts and contradictions; a world in

which Nat Parson or Adam Scattergood – for instance – might be driven to madness by as small a thing as a glimpse of ocean, or an unfamiliar star.

In such a world, Maddy understood, one man's religion might be another's heresy, magic and science might overlap, houses might be built on rivers or underground or high in the air; even the Laws of the Order at World's End, which she had always assumed were universal, might warp and bend to suit the customs of this new, expanded world.

Of course only a child or an idiot believed that World's End actually *was* the End of the World. There *were* other lands, everyone knew that. Once there had even been trade with these lands – trade, and sometimes even war. But it was widely held that these Outlands had suffered so badly from Tribulation that their folk had long since fallen into savagery, and no one – no one *civilized* – went there any more.

But, of course, One-Eye had. Beyond the One Sea, or so he said, there were men and women as brown as peat, with hair curled tight as bramble-crisp; and these people had never known Tribulation or read the Good Book, but instead worshipped gods of their own – wild brown gods with animal heads – and performed their own kind of magic, and all this was to them every bit as respectable and as everyday as Nat Parson's Sunday sermons on the far side of the Middle World.

'Nat Parson says magic's the devil's work,' said Maddy.

'But I dare say he'd turn a blind eye if it suited him?'

Maddy nodded, hardly daring to smile.

'Understand, Maddy, that Good and Evil are not as firmly rooted as your churchman would have you believe. The Good Book preaches Order above all things; therefore Order is Good. Glam works from Chaos, therefore magic is the devil's work. But a tool is only as good or bad as the one working it. And what is good today may be evil again tomorrow.'

Maddy frowned. 'I don't understand.'

'Listen,' said the Outlander. 'Since the world began – and it has begun many times, and many times ended, and been remade – the laws of Order and Chaos have opposed each other, advancing and retreating in turn across the Nine Worlds, to contain or disrupt according to their nature. Good and Evil have nothing to do with it. Everything lives – and dies – according to the laws of Order and Chaos, the twin forces that even gods cannot hope to withstand.'

He looked at Maddy, who was still frowning. She was very young for this lesson, he thought; and yet it was essential that she should learn it now. Even next year might be too late – the Order was already spreading its wings, sending more and more Examiners out of World's End . . .

He swallowed his impatience and started again. 'Here's a tale of the Æsir that will show you my drift. Their General was called Odin Allfather. You may have heard his name, I dare say.'

She nodded. 'He of the spear and the eight-legged horse.'

'Aye. Well, he was among those who remade the world in the early days, at the dawn of the Elder Age. And he brought together all his warriors – Thor and Tyr and the rest – to build a great stronghold to push back the Chaos that would have overwhelmed the new world before it was even completed. Its name was Asgard, the Sky Citadel, and it became the First World of those elder days.'

Maddy nodded. She knew the tale; though the Good Book claimed it was the Nameless that had built the Sky Citadel, and that the Seer-Folk had won it by trickery.

One-Eye went on. 'But the enemy was strong, and many had skills that the Æsir did not possess. And so Odin took a risk. He sought out a son of Chaos and befriended him for the sake of his skills, and took him into Asgard as his brother. You'll know of him, I guess. They called him the Trickster.'

Again Maddy nodded.

'Loki was his name; wildfire his nature. There are many tales about him. Some show him in an evil light. Some said that Odin was wrong to take him in. But – for a time, at least – Loki served the Æsir well. He was crooked, but he was useful; charm comes easily to the children of Chaos, and it was his charm and his cunning that kept him close at Odin's side. And though in the end his nature grew too strong and he had to be subdued, it was partly because of Loki that they survived for as long as they did. Perhaps it was their fault for not keeping a closer watch on him. In any case, fire burns; that's its nature, and you can't expect to change that. You can use it to cook your meat, or to burn down your neighbour's house. And is the fire you use for cooking any different to the one you use for burning? And does that mean you should eat your supper raw?'

Maddy shook her head, still puzzled. 'So what you're saying is – I shouldn't play with fire,' she said at last.

'Of course you should,' said One-Eye gently. 'But don't be surprised if the fire plays back.'

At last came the day of One-Eye's departure. He spent most of it trying to convince Maddy that she could not go with him.

'You're barely seven years old, for gods' sakes. What would I do with you on the Roads?'

'I'd work,' said Maddy. 'You know I can. I'm not afraid. I know lots of things.'

'Oh, aye? Three cantrips and a couple of runes? That'll get you a long way in World's—' He broke off suddenly and began to tug at one of the straps that bound his pack.

But Maddy was no simpleton. 'World's End?' she said, her eyes widening. 'You're going to World's *End*?'

One-Eye said nothing.

'Oh, please let me come,' Maddy begged. 'I'd help you, I'd carry your stuff, I'd not cause you any trouble—'

'No?' He laughed. 'Last time I heard, kidnapping was still a crime.'

'Oh.' She hadn't thought of that. If she disappeared, there would be posses after them from Fettlefields to the Hindarfell, and One-Eye put in the roundhouse, or hanged . . .

'But you'll forget me,' Maddy said. 'I'll never, ever see you again.'

One-Eye smiled. 'I'll be back next year.'

But Maddy would not look at him, and stared at the ground and would not speak. One-Eye waited, wryly amused. Still Maddy did not look up, but there came a single small, fierce sniff from beneath the mat of hair.

'Maddy, listen,' he told her gently. 'If you really want to help me, there's a way you can. I need a pair of eyes and ears; I need that much more than I need company on the Roads.'

Maddy looked up. 'Eyes and ears?'

One-Eye pointed at the Hill, where the dim outline of the Red Horse glowed like banked embers from its rounded flanks. 'You go there a lot, don't you?' he said.

She nodded.

'Do you know what it is?'

'A treasure mound?' suggested Maddy, thinking of the tales of gold under the Hill.

'Something far more important than that. It's a crossroads into World Below, with roads leading down as far as Hel's kingdom. Perhaps even as far as the river Dream, pouring its waters into the Strond—'

'So there's no treasure?' said Maddy, disappointed.

'Treasure?' He laughed. 'Aye, if you like. A treasure lost since the Elder Age. That's why the goblins are here in such number. That's why it carries such a charge. You can feel it,

Maddy, can't you?' he said. 'It's like living under a vulcano.'

'What's a vulcano?'

'Never mind. Just watch it, Maddy. Just look out for anything strange. That Horse is only half asleep, and if it wakes up—'

'I wish I could wake it,' said Maddy. 'Don't you?'

One-Eye smiled and shook his head. It was a strange smile, at the same time cynical, and rather sad. He pulled his cloak tighter around his shoulders. 'No,' he said. 'I don't think I do. That's not a road I'd care to tread, not for all of Otter's Ransom. Though there may come a time when I have no choice.'

'But the treasure?' she said. 'You could be rich—'

'Maddy,' he sighed. 'I could be dead.'

'But surely—'

'There are far worse things than goblins down there, and treasures rarely sleep alone.'

'So?' she said. 'I'm not afraid.'

'I dare say you're not,' said One-Eye in a dry voice. 'But listen, Maddy. You're seven years old. The Hill – and whatever lies underneath it – has been waiting for a long time. I'm sure it can wait a little longer.'

'How much longer?'

One-Eye laughed.

'Next year?'

'We'll see. Learn your lessons, watch the Hill, and look out for me by Harvestmonth.'

'Swear you'll be back?'

'On Odin's name.'

'And on yours?'

He nodded. 'Aye, girl. That too.'

After that, the Outlander had returned to Malbry once a year – never before Beltane or later than Maddy's birthday at the end of Harvestmonth – trading fabrics, salt, skins, sugar, salves and news. His arrival was the high point of Maddy's year; his departure, the beginning of a long darkness.

Every time he asked her the same question.

'What's new in Malbry?'

And every time she gave him the same accounts of the goblins and their mischief-making; of larders raided, cellars emptied, sheep stolen, milk soured. And every time he said: 'Nothing more?' and when Maddy assured him that was all, he seemed to relax, as if some great burden had been lifted temporarily from his shoulders.

And, of course, at each visit he taught her new skills.

First she learned to read and write. She learned poems and songs and foreign tongues; medicines and plant lore and kennings and stories. She learned histories and folk tales and sayings and legends; she studied maps and rivers, mountains and valleys, stones and clouds and charts of the sky.

Most importantly, she learned the runes. Their names, their values, their fingerings.

How to carve them into fortune stones, to be scattered and read for a glimpse of the future, or bind them like stalks into a corn dolly; how to fashion them into an ash stick; how to whisper their verses into a cantrip, to skim them like jumpstones, throw them like firecrackers or cast their shadows with her fingers.

She learned to use *Ár*, to ensure a good harvest –

– and *Tyr*, to make a hunting spear find its mark –

– and *Logr*, to find water underground.

By the time she was ten years old, she knew all sixteen runes of the Elder Script, various bastard runes from foreign parts and several hundred assorted kennings and cantrips. She knew that One-Eye travelled under the sign of *Raedo*, the Journeyman – though his rune was reversed and therefore unlucky, which meant that he had undergone many trials and misfortunes along the way.

Maddy's own runemark was neither broken nor reversed. But according to One-Eye, it was a bastard rune, not a rune of the Elder Script, which made it unpredictable. Bastard runes were tricky, he said. Some worked, but not well. Some worked not at all. And some tended to slip out of alignment, to tipple themselves in small, sly ways, to *warp*, like arrows that have been left in the rain and will rarely, if ever, hit straight.

Still, he said, to have any runemark at all was a gift. A rune of the Elder Script, unreversed and unbroken, would be too much for anyone to hope for. The gods had wielded such powers, once. Now, folk did what they could with what was left, that was all.

But bastard or not, Maddy's was strong. She quickly surpassed her old friend, for his glam was weak and soon exhausted. Her aim was as good as his, if not better. And she was a fast learner. She learned *hug-rúnar*, mindrunes, and *rísta-rúnar*, carven runes, and *sig-rúnar*, runes of victory. She learned runes that One-Eye himself could not work; new runes and bastard runes with no names and no verses, and still, he found, she wanted more.

So he told her tales from under the Hill, and of the serpent that lives at Yggdrasil's Root, eating away at the foundations of the world. He told her tales of standing stones, and of lost skerries, and of enchanted circles, of Underworld and Netherworld and the lands of Dream and Chaos beyond. He told her tales of Half-Born Hel, and of Jormungand, the World Serpent, and of Surt, the Destroyer, the lord of Chaos, and of the Ice People and of the Tunnel Folk and of the Vanir and of Mimir the Wise.

But her favourite tales were those of the Æsir and the Vanir. She never tired of hearing these, and in the long, lonely months between One-Eye's visits, the heroes of those stories became Maddy's friends. Thor the Thunderer with his magic hammer; Idun the Healer and her apples of youth; Odin, the Allfather; Balder the Fair; Tyr, the Warrior; falcon-cloaked Freyja; Heimdall Hawk-Eye; Skadi, the Huntress; Njörd, the Man of the Sea; and Loki, the Trickster, who on different occasions had brought about both the deliverance and the dissolution of the old gods. She applauded their victories, wept for their defeat and, unnatural though that might be, felt more kinship with those long-vanished Seer-folk than she had ever had for Jed Smith or Mae. And as the years passed, she longed ever more for the company of her own kind.

'There must be more of us *somewhere*,' she said. 'People like us – Fieries' – *family*, she thought – 'if only we could find them, then maybe, perhaps . . .'

In that, however, she was disappointed. In seven years, she had never so much as glimpsed another of their kind. There were goblins, of course, and the occasional cat or rabbit born with a ruinmark and quickly dispatched.

But as for people like themselves . . . . They were rare, he told her, when she asked, and most of them had no real powers to speak of anyway. A glimmer, if they were lucky. Enough to earn them a dangerous living.

And if they were unlucky? In World's End, where Order had reigned for a hundred years, a runemark, even a broken one, usually led to an arrest – and after that an Examination, and then, more often than not, a hanging (or Cleansing, as they preferred to call them in those parts).

Best not to think of it, One-Eye said, and reluctantly Maddy took his advice, learning her lessons, re-telling her tales, waiting patiently for his yearly visits and trying hard not to dream of what could never be.

This year, for the first time, he was late. Maddy's fourteenth birthday was two weeks gone, the Harvest Moon had worn to a sliver and she was beginning to feel anxious that perhaps this time her old friend would not make it back.

The previous year had seen changes in One-Eye: a new restlessness; a new impatience. He had grown leaner over the past twelvemonth, drank more than was good for him, and for the first time she saw that his dark-grey hair was touched with white. His yearly journeys to World's End were taking their toll; and after seven such reckless pilgrimages, who knew when the net might fall?

The runes had given her little by way of reassurance.

Maddy had her own set of fortune stones, made from river pebbles from the Strond, each painted with a different rune. Casting them upon the ground, she discovered, and studying the patterns into which they fell, was sometimes a means of divining the future – though One-Eye had warned her that runes are not always simple to read, or futures always set in stone.

Even so, a combination of *Raedo*, the Journeyman –

– with *Thuris*, Thor's rune, and *Naudr*, the Binder, filled her with misgivings.

One-Eye's runemark. A thorny path? And the third rune –
the Binder – the rune of constraint. Was he a prisoner somewhere? Or could that final rune be Death?

And so when Mrs Scattergood had said he was there –
there at last, nearly two weeks late – a great relief and a
greater joy had swept her up, and now she ran towards Red
Horse Hill, where she knew he would be waiting for her as he
always waited for her every year – as she hoped he would
every year, for ever.

5

But Maddy had reckoned without Adam Scattergood. The landlady's son rarely troubled her when she was working – it was dark in the cellar, and the thought of what she might be doing there unsettled him – but he sometimes lurked around the tap, awaiting an opportunity to comment or to jeer. He had pricked up his ears at the commotion in the kitchen – wisely keeping his distance from any danger of work to be done – but when he saw Maddy leaving through the kitchen door, his eyes gleamed and he determined to investigate.

Adam was two years older than Maddy, somewhat taller, with limp brown hair and a discontented mouth. Bored, sulky and doted upon by his mother, already a parson's prentice and a favourite of the bishop, he was half feared and half envied by the other children, and he was always causing mischief. Maddy thought he was worse than the goblins, because at least the goblins were funny as well as being annoying, whereas Adam's tricks were only ugly and stupid.

He tied firecrackers to dogs' tails; swung on new saplings to make them break; taunted beggars; stole washing from clotheslines and trampled it in the mud, although he was careful to ensure that someone else always got the blame. In short, Adam was a sneak and a spoiler, and seeing Maddy heading for the Hill, he wondered what business she might have there, and made up his mind to spoil that too.

Keeping hidden, he followed her, staying low to the bushes that lined the path, until they reached the lower slopes of the Hill, where he crept quietly up on the blind side and was in a moment lost to sight.

Maddy did not see or hear him. She ran up the hill, almost

43

stumbling in her impatience, until she caught sight of the familiar tall figure sitting among the fallen stones beneath the flank of the Red Horse.

'One-Eye!' she called.

He was just as she had seen him last, with his back to the stone, his pipe in his mouth, his pack on the grass beside him. As always, he greeted Maddy with a casual nod, as if he had been away for an afternoon, and not a twelvemonth.

'So. What's new in Malbry?' he said.

Maddy looked at him in some indignation. 'Is that all you have to say? You're two weeks late, I've been worried sick, and all you can say is *What's new in Malbry?* as if anything important was *ever* going to happen here . . .'

One-Eye shrugged. 'I was delayed.'

'Delayed? How?'

'It doesn't matter.'

Maddy gave a reluctant grin. 'You and your news. I suppose it never occurs to you that I might worry. I mean, it's only World's End you're coming from – and you never bring me news from there. Doesn't anything ever happen in World's End?'

One-Eye nodded. 'World's End is an eventful place.'

'And yet here you are again.'

'Aye.'

Maddy sighed and sat down next to him on the sweet grass. 'Well, the big news here is . . . I'm out of a job.' And smiling as she remembered Mrs Scattergood's face, she told the tale of that morning's work, of the sleeping goblin trapped in the cellar, and how in her clumsy haste she had summoned half of World Below in trying to capture him.

One-Eye listened to the tale in silence.

'And Laws, you should have *heard* the noise she made! I could hear it all the way from Little Bear Wood – honestly, I thought she was going to burst—'

Laughing, she turned to One-Eye and found him watching her with no amusement at all, but with a rather grim expression. 'What *exactly* did you do?' he said. 'This is important, Maddy. Tell me everything you remember.'

Maddy stopped laughing and set herself the task of recalling precisely what had happened in the cellar. She repeated her conversation with the goblin (at mention of the goblins' Captain she thought One-Eye stiffened, but could not be sure); went over every rune she had used, then tried to explain what had happened next.

'Well, first of all I cast *Thuris*,' she said. 'And then I just . . . pointed at the hole and sort of . . . shouted at it—'

'*What* did you say?' said One-Eye quickly.

But Maddy was feeling anxious by now. 'What's wrong?' she said. 'Did I do something wrong?'

'Just tell me, Maddy. What did you say?'

'Well, nothing, that was it. Just noise. Not even a cantrip. It happened so fast – I couldn't remember—' She broke off, alarmed. 'What's wrong?' she repeated. 'What did I do?'

'Nothing,' he said in a heavy voice. 'I knew it was only a matter of time.'

'What was?' she said.

But now the Outlander was silent, looking out at the Horse with its mane of long grass illuminated in the morning sun. Finally he began to speak. 'Maddy,' he said, 'you're growing up.'

'I suppose so.' Maddy frowned. She hoped this wasn't going to turn out to be a lecture, like the ones she sometimes got from well-meaning ladies of the village about *growing into womanhood*.

One-Eye went on. 'Most especially, your powers have grown. You were strong to begin with, but now your skills are coming to life. Of course, you're not in control of them yet, but that's to be expected. You'll learn.'

It *was* a lecture, Maddy thought. Perhaps not quite as embarrassing as the womanhood talk, but—

One-Eye continued. 'Glam, as you know, may lie sleeping for years. Just as this Hill has lain sleeping for years. I've always suspected that when one awoke, the other would not be far behind.'

He stopped to fill his pipe, and his fingers shook a little as he pressed the smoke-weed into the bowl. A string of geese passed overhead, V-shaped, towards the Hindarfell. Maddy watched them and felt a sudden chill against her skin. Summer was gone, and falltime would soon give way to winter. For some reason the thought almost brought tears to her eyes.

'That Hill of yours,' said One-Eye at last. 'For a long time it lay so quiet that I thought perhaps I'd misread the signs, and that it was – as I'd first suspected – just another nicely made barrow from the Elder Days. There have been so many other hills, you see – and springs, and stone circles, and menhirs and caves and wells – that showed the same signs, and came to nothing in the end. But when I found you – and with that runemark—' He broke off abruptly, and signalled her to listen. 'Did you hear that?'

Maddy shook her head.

'I thought I heard—' Something like bees, One-Eye thought. A hive of bees trapped underground. Something bursting to escape . . .

Briefly Maddy considered asking him what he meant by *with that runemark*. But it was the first time she had ever seen her old friend so nervous and so ill at ease, and she knew it was best to give him time.

He looked out again over Red Horse Hill, and the rampant Horse in the morning sun. Such a beautiful thing, the Outlander thought. Such a beautiful thing to be so deadly.

'Beats me how any of you can live here,' he said, 'with what's hidden under there.'

'D'you mean – the treasure?' breathed Maddy, who had never quite given up on the tales of buried gold under the Hill.

One-Eye gave his wistful smile.

'So it's really there?'

'It's there,' he said. 'It's been buried there for five hundred years, awaiting its chance to escape. Without you I might have turned my back on it and never thought of it again. But with you, I thought I might have a chance. And you were so young, so very young. With time, who knew what skills you might develop? Who knew, with that rune, what you might one day become?'

Maddy listened, eyes wide.

'And so,' he said, 'I tutored you. I taught you everything I knew, and kept a careful watch on you, knowing that the stronger you became, the more likely it was that you might accidentally disturb what lay sleeping under the Hill.'

'Do you mean the goblins?' said Maddy.

Slowly One-Eye shook his head. 'The goblins – and their Captain – have known about you since the day you were born. But until now they had no reason to fear your skills. Count on this morning's escapade to change all that.'

'What do you mean?' said Maddy anxiously.

'I mean that Captain of theirs is no fool, and if *he* suspects we're after the – treasure—'

'You mean the goblins might find the gold?'

One-Eye made an impatient noise. 'Gold?' he said. 'That old wives' tale?'

'But you said there was treasure under the Hill.'

'Aye,' he said, 'and so there is. A treasure of the Elder Age. But no gold, Maddy; not an ingot, not a nugget, not even a nickel penny.'

'Then what sort of treasure is it?' she said.

He paused. 'They call it *the Whisperer*.'

'And what is it?' Maddy said.

'I can't tell you that. Later, perhaps, when we have it safe.'

'But you know what it is, don't you?'

One-Eye kept his calm with some difficulty. 'Maddy,' he said, 'this isn't the time. This – treasure – may turn out to be as dangerous as it is valuable. Even speaking of it has its risks. And in many ways it might be safer for it to have stayed sleeping and forgotten.' He lit his pipe, using the fire-rune *Kaen*, and a clever little flick of the fingers. 'But now it's awake, for good or ill, and the greater danger would be if someone else were to find it – to find it and to put it to use.'

'What kind of someone?' Maddy said.

He looked at her. 'Our kind, of course.'

Now Maddy's heart was beating faster than one of her father's hammers. '*Our* kind?' she said. 'There are others like me? You know them?'

He nodded.

'How many?' she said.

'Does it matter?'

'It does to me,' said Maddy fiercely. There were others, and One-Eye had never mentioned them. Who were they? *Where* were they? And if he'd known of their existence all this time, then—

'Maddy,' he said, 'I know it's hard. But you have to trust me. You have to believe me when I tell you that whatever I may have hidden from you, however I may have misled you at times—'

'You lied to me,' Maddy said.

'I lied to you to keep you safe,' One-Eye told her patiently. 'Wolves of different packs do not hunt together. And sometimes they even hunt each other.'

She turned to him, her eyes burning. 'Why?' she demanded. 'What is the Whisperer? Why is it so important to you? And how do you know so much about it, anyway?'

'Patience,' said One-Eye. 'The Whisperer first. Afterwards I promise I'll answer all your questions. But now – please – we have work to do. The Hill has not been opened for hundreds of years. There will be defences to keep us out. Runes to find. Workings to break. Here . . . you'll need this.' He pulled a familiar object out of his pack and handed it to Maddy.

'What's this?' said Maddy.

'It's a shovel,' he said. 'Because magic, like leadership, is one-tenth genius and nine-tenths spadework. You'll need to clear the outline of the Horse to a depth of maybe four or five inches. It may take some time.'

Maddy gave him a suspicious look. 'I notice there's only one shovel,' she said.

'Genius doesn't need a shovel,' said One-Eye in a dry voice, and sat down on the grass to finish his pipe.

It was a long, laborious task. The Horse measured two hundred feet from nose to tail, and centuries of weather, abuse and neglect had taken their toll on some of the finer work. But the clay of the hill was dense and hard; and the shape of the Horse had been made to last, with wards and runemarks embedded at intervals to ensure that the outline would not be lost.

There would be nine of them, One-Eye guessed, one for each of the Nine Worlds, and they would need to find all of them before they were able to gain entry.

It was One-Eye who discovered the first, scratched on a river-stone and buried beneath the Horse's tail.

'*Madr*, the Middle World. The Folk. A good start,' he said, touching the rune to make it shine. He whispered a cantrip – *Madr er moldar auki* – and at once, a place at the Horse's head lit up with a corresponding gleam, and almost at once under the turf Maddy found the rune *Yr*.

'*Yr*. World Below. The Fundament. Things will move faster now.'

They did: *Yr* lit the way to *Raedo*, the Outlands, tucked underneath the Horse's belly, then *Logr* – the Sea – in the Horse's mouth –

– then, for each of its legs, *Bjarkán*, for the world of Dream, *Naudr* – for the Underworld –

– *Hagall*, for the Netherworld, and *Kaen*, for Chaos or World Beyond –

– and finally, right in the middle of the Eye itself, the rune of the Sky Citadel –

– *Ós*, the Æsir, brightest of all, like the central star in the constellation of Thiazi, the Hunter, that hangs over the Seven Sleepers on clear winter nights.

Ós. The Æsir. The Firmament. Maddy looked at the rune in silence. This was the moment of which she had dreamed, and yet now that she was so close, she felt a curious reluctance to proceed. It angered her a little; and yet she was conscious of a tiny part of her that wanted above all to step away from the threshold and to walk back to Malbry and the safety of its familiar cleft.

One-Eye must have sensed it; he gave a little smile and put his hand on Maddy's shoulder. 'Not afraid, are you, girl?'

'No. Are you?'

'A little,' he said. 'It's been so long . . .' He took out his pipe, re-lit it, and drew in a mouthful of sweet smoke. 'Foul habit,' he said. 'Picked it up from the Tunnel People on one of my trips. Master smiths, you know, but terrible hygiene. I think the smoke helps them disguise the smell.'

Maddy touched the final rune. It flared opal colours like the winter sun. She spoke the cantrip:

Ós byth ordfruma . . .

The Hill opened with a sliding crash; and where the Eye had been there was now a narrow, raw-sided tunnel sliding downwards into the earth.

6

Five hundred years ago, around the dawn of the New Age, there had been few strongholds more secure than the castle on Red Horse Hill. Built on a steep mound overlooking the valley, it commanded the entire plain, and its cannon were forever pointed at the Hindarfell pass, which was the only possible place along the Seven Sleepers ridge from which an enemy could attack.

In fact it was a mystery to the people of Malbry how the castle had fallen at all, unless it were by plague or treachery, because from the broken stone circle you could see all the way to Farnley Tyas to the north and, to the south, to Forge's Post, at the foot of the mountains.

The road was wide open, barely shielded by gorse and sparse scrubland, and the sides of the Hill itself were too steep for men in armour to climb.

But Adam Scattergood wore no armour, the cannon had long since been melted down, and it had been fully five hundred years since a lookout had stood on Red Horse Hill. As a result, he managed to climb the Hill unseen, and, crawling through the rabbit-tail grass to the lee of the Horse, he hid behind a fallen stone to listen to what the Witch Girl and the one-eyed scallyman were saying.

Adam had never trusted Maddy. Imaginative people made him nervous, and the world they inhabited – a strange, dark world where Adam Scattergood was neither noticed nor wanted – made him feel very uneasy indeed. But what he wouldn't admit to himself was that Maddy frightened him. That would have been too ridiculous. She was a bad-blood, wasn't she? No one would ever want her, not with that ruinmark on her hand. She would never amount to anything.

Adam Scattergood (Laws be praised) was a handsome boy with a brilliant future. He was already a parson's prentice; with luck (and with his mother's savings) he might even be sent to World's End to study in the Universal City. In short, he was one of Malbry's finest – and yet here he was, spying on the girl and her Outlander friend, like a sneak without any friends of his own. It annoyed him to think this, and he crept a little closer to the base of the stone, straining his ears for something secret, something important, something with which he could taunt her later.

When he heard the part about the treasure under the Hill, he grinned. There was a rich vein of mockery in that. *Goblin Girl*, he'd say. *Found any gold yet? Buy yourself a new dress, Goblin Girl? Get yourself a Faërie ring?*

The thought was so appealing that he almost left his hiding place there and then; but he was alone, and suddenly the girl and the Outlander didn't seem as funny as when Adam was with his friends. In fact they looked almost dangerous, and Adam felt glad he was safely out of sight behind the big stone.

When he heard about the Whisperer, he was doubly glad he'd hidden away. Adam wanted nothing to do with any relic of the Elder Age, however valuable – in any case it was probably cursed, or possessed by a demon. And when it came to opening the Hill, Adam could have hugged himself with glee, for although he had a lively terror of anything uncanny, it was clear that this time, Maddy and her one-eyed friend had overstepped the mark.

Opening the Hill to World Below! Nat Parson would have strong words to say about *that*. Even Matt Law, who had no love for the parson, would have to admit that this time Maddy had gone too far. There could be no ignoring such a blatant violation of laws laid down in the Good Book.

This could mean the end of the Witch Girl, once and for all. The people of Malbry had long tolerated her peculiarities for her father's sake, but such conjuring was a serious crime, and the moment Nat Parson found out (as Adam fully intended that he should), Maddy might be Examined, or even Cleansed.

Adam had never seen an actual Cleansing. Such things didn't happen much outside World's End – but civilization was marching on, as the parson was often wont to say, and it could only be a matter of time before the Order established an outpost within reach of Malbry. It couldn't happen too early for Adam. An end to magic; the Hill dug out, its demons burned, and Order restored to the valley of the Strond . . .

But as time passed, and nothing happened, Adam grew sleepy behind his rock. He began to doze, and when at last Maddy drew open the Horse's Eye, he was jolted awake with a gasp of astonishment. One-Eye looked up, his fingers crooked, and Adam was suddenly sure the Outlander could *see* right through the ancient granite of the fallen stone to where he was hiding.

A great terror gripped him, and he flattened himself even more closely to the ground, half expecting to hear heavy footsteps coming towards him across the Hill.

Nothing happened.

Adam relaxed a little, and as the seconds passed, his natural arrogance began to return. Of course he hadn't been seen. It was just this place, he told himself – this Hill, with its ghosts and noises – that had unnerved him. He wasn't afraid of a one-eyed scally. And he *certainly* wasn't afraid of a little girl.

What was she doing, anyway? Maddy seemed to be lifting her hand; from his position, Adam could just see her shadow on the grass. He couldn't have guessed she was using *Bjarkán* – but now she too could see the boy hunched against the fallen stone, his face a blur of fear and malice.

Maddy needed no workings to know what her enemy was doing there. In that second she understood everything. She saw in his colours how he had followed her; how he had spied on her and One-Eye; and how he meant to run back to the village with his stolen knowledge and spoil everything, as he always spoiled everything.

And now her rage at last found an outlet. Quite without thinking, and with her bastard runemark glowing hot on her palm, she hurled her anger and her voice, like the stones Adam had so often thrown at her, towards the crouching boy.

It was instinctive. Her cry rang out across the Hill, and at precisely the same time there was a flash of light and a deafening *crack* as the standing stone split into two pieces and granite shavings spackled across the brow of the hill.

Adam Scattergood was left crouching between the two halves of the broken rock, his face the colour of fresh cheese and a wet stain spreading over the crotch of his fine serge trousers.

Helplessly, Maddy started to laugh. She couldn't help it. The attack had left her almost as terrified as Adam himself, but still the laughter came and would not stop, and the boy stared at her, first in fear, then in awe, and finally (as soon as he realized that he was unhurt) in black and bitter hatred.

'You'll be sorry, Witch,' he stammered, climbing shakily to his feet. 'I'll tell them what you're planning. I'll tell them you tried to murder me.'

But Maddy was still laughing, out of control. Tears ran from her eyes; her stomach hurt; and even so, the laughter felt so good that she couldn't stop, could hardly breathe. She laughed until she almost choked, and Adam's face grew darker still as, breaking away from the circle of stones, he fled back down Red Horse Hill towards the Malbry road. Neither Maddy nor One-Eye tried to stop him.

Now Maddy went up to the broken stone. The laughter had fled as fast as it had erupted, and she was left feeling drained and a little sick. The granite had stood three feet high and almost as broad; nevertheless it had been split clean in two. She touched the break: it was rough and raw-edged, and inside it, here and there, nuggets of mica shone.

'So, you can throw mindbolts,' said One-Eye, who had followed her. 'Well done, Maddy. With practice, that may be a useful skill.'

'I didn't throw anything,' said Maddy numbly. 'I just threw . . . my voice. But it wasn't a *rune*; it was just nonsense, just random shouting, like today in the cellar.'

One-Eye smiled. 'Sense,' he said, 'is a concept of Order. The language of Chaos is nonsense by definition.'

'The language of Chaos?' said Maddy. 'But I don't *know* it. I've never *heard* of it—'

'Yes you do,' said One-Eye. 'It's in your blood.'

Maddy looked out across the Hill, where the distant figure of Adam Scattergood was getting smaller and smaller along the Malbry road, occasionally giving vent to a shrill scream of rage as he ran.

'I could have killed him,' she said, beginning to shake.

'Another time, perhaps.'

'Don't you understand? I could have *killed* him!'

One-Eye seemed unmoved. 'Well, isn't that what you wanted to do?'

'No!'

He smiled, but said nothing.

'I mean it, One-Eye. It just happened.'

One-Eye shrugged and relit his pipe. 'My dear girl, things like that don't *just happen*.'

'I don't understand.'

'Oh yes, you do.'

And she did, Maddy realized – she was not the daughter of a smith for nothing. The thing she had thrown at Adam – the mindbolt – had not sprung out of thin air; it had been *forged*. It had been heavy, like a crossbow quarrel, and she had cast it at Adam with the strength – and intent – of years of pent-up anger.

Once again she felt a moment of dread as she imagined what might have happened if the stone had not taken the impact. And with that fear came the even more terrible knowledge that she could (and would) do it again.

One-Eye must have read her thoughts. 'Remember what I taught you?' he said gently. 'Fire burns, that's its nature. Use it or not, but remember this: a mindbolt isn't a blunderbuss. It won't go off on its own.' He smiled. 'As for the boy – no harm was done. It's a pity he heard us, of course. It gives us less time. But it changes nothing.'

'Wait a minute,' said Maddy, looking into the open tunnel. 'You don't think we should go in right now, do you? After what happened?'

'After what happened,' said One-Eye, 'what choice do we have?'

Maddy thought about that for a time. By now Adam would have made his report – unless he'd stopped to change his trousers – no doubt embellishing it with as many tales of demons as his limited imagination could invent.

Jed Smith would have to be told, and Matt Law, and the bishop, not forgetting Nat Parson, who had been waiting for such a crisis since his legendary pilgrimage to World's End and who would be delighted to have such an important violation to deal with. And whatever else happened, the incident would go down in the Malbry ledger alongside the most important events of the village's history, and Adam Scattergood would be remembered until long after his bones were dust.

The sun was high in the sky now, and the valley was green and gold in its pale light. A little smoke rose over the rooftops, and the scent of burning stubble reached Maddy from afar, filling her eyes with sudden tears. She thought of the smithy, and of the tiny house abutting it; of the smell of hot metal and smoke; of the ring of marigolds around the front door.

This was her world, she thought; and until this moment, when she was close to leaving it, she had never realized how much it meant to her. If she fled now, she tacitly admitted her guilt, and things could never go back to what they had been before.

'Is it worth it, One-Eye?' she said. 'This Whisperer, whatever it is?'

One-Eye nodded. 'It's worth it,' he said.

'More than gold?' said Maddy.

'Much more than gold.'

Once more Maddy looked out across the valley. She could stay and argue her case, of course. She would at least get a fair hearing. There hadn't been a hanging in the valley since Black Nell – a saddleback sow with a ruinmark on her back – had eaten her piglets ten years ago. But One-Eye was an Outlander – one of a tribe of beggars and bandits – and his trial was likely to be short and harsh. She had no choice – and besides, with the Hill standing open at her feet and the promise of hidden treasures below, how could she have turned away?

The passage was rough-edged and narrow, sloping down into the side of the Hill. She stepped inside, stooping a little, and gingerly tested the earth ceiling. To her relief it was dry and firm; from the depths of the tunnel came a cellar scent. Maddy took another step, but One-Eye stayed where he was, watching her, and made no move to follow.

'Well?' said Maddy. 'Are you coming, or what?'

For a moment One-Eye said nothing. Then he slowly shook his head. 'I can't go in there, Maddy,' he said. 'He'd recognize me the moment I set foot in World Below. And he'd know at once why I was there.'

'Who would?' said Maddy.

'I wish I could tell you,' he said. 'But time is short, and there's none to spare for a long tale. The treasure you seek – the Whisperer – is no ordinary piece of loot. It may be disguised as a block of glass, a lump of iron ore – even a rock. It's in its nature to hide – but you'll know it by its colours, which it can't disguise. Look for it in a well or a fountain. It may be buried very deep. But if you call it – it will come to you.'

Maddy looked once again into the passageway – it was dark in there, dark as a tomb, and she remembered One-Eye telling her that there were roads beneath the Hill that led all the way to Death, Dream and beyond . . .

She shivered and turned to him again. 'So, how do we know it's still there? What if someone's taken it?'

'They haven't,' said One-Eye. 'I would have known.'

'But you said there were others. And now—'

'Truth is, Maddy,' he interrupted, 'I'm not sure if he's there at all, or what he means to do if he is. But if I come with you and he's waiting down there with whatever glam he's managed to hang onto—'

'Who is he?' said Maddy again.

One-Eye gave a twisted smile. 'A . . . friend,' he said. 'From long ago. One who turned traitor in the Winter War. I thought he was dead, and maybe he is, but his kind have nine lives, and he always was lucky.'

Maddy started to speak, but he cut her off. 'Listen, Maddy. He's waiting for *me*. He won't suspect you. He may not even notice you. And you can find the Whisperer and bring it to me before he sees what's happening. Will you do it?'

Once again Maddy looked into the Horse's Eye. It yawned darkly at her feet, as if the Horse were coming awake after centuries of sleeping.

'What about you?' she said at last.

The Outlander smiled, but his good eye gleamed. 'I may

be old, Maddy, but I think I can still handle a rabble of villagers.'

And perhaps it was a trick of the light, but it seemed to Maddy that her friend had grown taller somehow, and looked younger, stronger, his colours brighter and more powerful, as if years had been shorn from him – years, she thought, or maybe more. For Maddy knew that the Winter War had come to its end over five centuries ago; demon wolves had swallowed the sun and moon, and the Strond had swollen to the flanks of the mountains, levelling everything in its path.

Nat Parson called it *Tribulation*, and preached of how the Ancient of Days had tired of mankind's evil and sent fire and ice to cleanse the world.

One-Eye called it Ragnarók.

'Who are you?' she said.

'Does it matter?' said One-Eye.

He must have seen his answer in Maddy's face, because he nodded and some of the tension went out of him. 'Good,' he said. 'Now run and find the Whisperer – or let it find you if it can. Stay hidden, and stay alert. Trust no one, whoever they may appear to be, and above all, say nothing – to *anyone* – of me.'

'Wait!' said Maddy as he turned away.

'I've waited enough,' said the Outlander, and without a glance or a farewell gesture he began to walk back down Red Horse Hill.

BOOK TWO
World Below

My name is Untold . . .

Invocations, 9:7

1

The passage was not even, but dipped down at irregular intervals, sometimes crossing water, sometimes narrowing to a cleft through which Maddy had to squeeze to pass through. By inverting the runes she had closed the mouth of the tunnel behind her, and now the rune *Bjarkán* at her fingertips was her only means of penetrating the darkness.

After some minutes, however, she found that the passage-way had broadened a little, and that its earth walls had begun to give way to a hard, almost glassy surface. It was rock, Maddy realized as she moved deeper into the hillside; some kind of dark and shiny mineral, its surface occasionally broken by a crystalline outcrop that shone like a cluster of needles.

After half an hour the floor too had mostly changed to the same glassy rock, and sheets of phosphorescence powdered the walls, so that the way was softly illuminated.

And there were colour-signatures everywhere, like skeins of spider-web, too many to count or to identify. Many of these showed the remnants of magic – cantrips and glamours and workings and runes – as easy to see as wagon tracks on a muddy road.

She cast *Yr*, the Protector, to keep herself hidden, but even so she was sure that among so many workings she must have set off a few alarms. Uncomfortably she wondered what kind of spider might live in such an intricate web, and her mind returned to One-Eye, and to the person – friend or enemy – he feared, and who might be lying in wait at the heart of the Hill.

What was she looking for? she wondered. And what did One-Eye know of any treasure of the Elder Age?

Well, she told herself, there was only one way to find out, and the simple fact of being under the Hill was thrilling enough – for the moment, at least. She wondered how far downwards the passage led; but even as she did so, she felt the ground drop abruptly at her feet, and without further warning the narrow walls at either side of her opened to reveal a huge underground canyon, broadening out far beyond Maddy's field of vision into a labyrinth of tunnels and a vastness of caverns and halls.

For a long time Maddy could do nothing but watch and wonder. The passage had come to a sharp stairway cut into the rock face; this led downwards into a vast gallery, occasionally intersecting with other walkways and cavern entrances set at intervals down the canyon walls, with what seemed to be suspended catwalks, illuminated by torches or hanging lanterns, on the distant far side.

Maddy had expected a single cave; maybe even a single passage. Instead, there were hundreds – no, thousands – of caves and passages. From the bottom of the canyon came a sound of water, and although it was too dark – in spite of the lanterns – to see the river itself, Maddy guessed it to be broad and fast-moving; its voice was like that of a wolf with a throatful of rocks.

Here too there were spells and signatures; there were green fingers of phosphorescence; nuggets of mica studded the walls; and wherever there was a trickle of water against the rock, musky flowers cast their tendrils: the pale, sad lilies of World Below.

'Gods,' said Maddy. 'Where do I start?'

Well, to begin with, more light. Raising her hand, she cast *Sól* – the Sun – so that her fingertips blazed and the tiny crystals embedded in the steps and walls flared with sudden brilliance.

It was not nearly enough to light the vastness ahead, but

even so, she felt a little better, if only because there was less chance of her falling down the stairway. At the same time she thought she caught sight of something at her elbow, something which shrank quickly into the shadows as her light shone out, and, almost without thinking, she cast *Naudr* like a net and pulled it in with a flick of her fingers.

'*You* again!' she exclaimed when she saw what she had caught.

The goblin spat, but could not escape.

'Stop that!' said Maddy, drawing the rune a little tighter.

The goblin pulled a face, but kept still.

'That's better,' said Maddy. 'Now, Smá-rakki' – the goblin made a *Pff!* sound – 'I want you to stay right here with me. No slinking off this time, do you understand?'

'*Pff!*' said the goblin again. 'All this fuss for a nip of ale.' All the same, he did not move, but glared at Maddy with his amber eyes, lips drawn back over his pointed teeth.

'Why were you following me?'

The goblin shrugged. 'Curiosity, kennet?'

Maddy laughed. 'Plus, I know your name.'

The goblin said nothing, but his eyes gleamed.

'A named thing is a tamed thing. That's it, isn't it?'

Still the goblin said nothing.

Maddy smiled at the unexpected piece of luck. She was not sure how long her control over him would last, but if she could have an ally – however reluctant – in World Below, then maybe her task would be a simpler one. 'Now listen to me, Smá-rakki—'

'They call me Sugar,' said the goblin sullenly.

'What?'

'Sugar. You deaf? Short for Sugar-and-Sack. Well? You don't think any of us go round tellin' folk our *real* names, do you?'

'Sugar-and-*Sack*?' repeated Maddy.

Sugar scowled. 'Gødfolk names are like that,' he said. 'Sugar-and-Sack, Peck-in-the-Crown, Pickle-Nearest-the-Wind. I don't go round laughin' at *your* name, do I?'

'Sorry, *Sugar*,' said Maddy, trying to keep a straight face.

'Right. No harm done,' said Sugar with dignity. 'Now what exactly can I do you for?'

Maddy leaned closer. 'I need a guide.'

'You need yer bleedin' head seein' to,' said the goblin. 'The minute the Captain learns you're here—'

'Then you'll have to make sure he doesn't,' she said. 'Now, I can't possibly find my way around this place on my own—'

'Look,' said the goblin, 'if it's the ale you're after, then I can get it back, no trouble—'

'It isn't the ale,' said Maddy.

'Then what is it?'

'I don't know,' she said. 'But you're going to help me find it.'

It took some minutes to convince Sugar that he had no choice. But goblins are simple creatures, and he was not blind to the fact that the sooner Maddy had what she wanted, the sooner she would be out of his way.

However, he was clearly very much in awe of the individual he called the Captain, and Maddy soon realized that it would be best if she did not confront her new ally with too great a conflict of loyalties.

'So who is he, this Captain of yours?'

The goblin sniffed and looked away.

'Oh come on, Sugar. He must have a name.'

'Course he has.'

'Well?'

The goblin shrugged expressively. It was a shrug that began at the tips of his furry ears and went all the way down to his clawed feet, making every link of his chain mail shiver.

'Call him Sky Trekker, if you like, or Wildfire, or Crookmouth, or Hawkeye, or Dogstar. Call him Airy, call him Wary—'

'Not his nicknames, Sugar. His *real* name.'

The goblin made a face. 'You think he'd tell *me*?'

For a while Maddy thought hard. One-Eye had warned her that he might not be the only one with interests under the Hill, and the webwork of glamours she had encountered on her way in confirmed his suspicions. But the goblins' Captain – most likely a goblin himself, or maybe a big cave-troll – could *he* be the one of which her friend had spoken? It seemed unlikely – no goblin had woven those spells.

Still, she thought, it was worth finding out more about this Captain person, and any threat he might represent. But Sugar was annoyingly vague; his attention-span was catlike at the best of times, and as soon as the conversation turned to details of where, why and how, he simply lost interest.

'So, what's your Captain like?' she said.

Sugar frowned and scratched his head. 'I think the word is *volatile*,' he said at last. 'Yeh, that's the word I'm lookin' for. Volatile and *narsty*. Tricky, too.'

'I meant, what does he *look* like?' persisted Maddy.

'Just pray you don't see him,' said Sugar darkly.

'Great,' said Maddy.

In silence, they moved on.

2

According to legend, the world beneath the Middle World is divided into three levels, linked by one great river. World Below is the realm of the Mountain People, the goblins, trolls and dwarves. Beneath that is Hel's kingdom, traditionally given over to the dead, then Dream, one of the three great tributaries of the Cauldron of Rivers, and lastly, at the very door of Chaos, Netherworld, known to some as the Black Fortress, where Surt the Destroyer guards the gate and the gods themselves have no dominion.

Maddy already knew this, of course. One-Eye's teachings had been thorough on all matters concerning the geography of the Nine Worlds. But what she had not suspected was the monstrous *scale* of World Below; the countless passageways, tunnels, alcoves and lairs that made up the underside of the Hill. There were rifts and fissures and crannies and nooks; and dugouts and dens; and side passages, storerooms, walkways and potholes, burrows and warrens and larders and pits. And after what seemed like hours of searching through these, Maddy's excitement at actually being in the fabled halls was starting to fade visibly as she began to understand that, even with Sugar's reluctant help, she was unlikely to be able to cover even the hundredth part of them.

They found goblins only on the top level of the great gallery. Cat-faced, golden-eyed, squirrel-tailed, all dressed in mail and rags and leather, they had paid little attention to Maddy, or to her companion.

They were not the only inhabitants of that level. As she hurried along the crowded passageways, Maddy passed dozens of other creatures, all as busy and incurious as the goblins themselves: Tunnel People, coloured like the clay of their native earth, with great jaws and tiny, lashless eyes; Mountain People; Sky People; Wood People; even a couple of men of the Folk, hooded and furtive, with traders' packs on their shoulders and staves in their hands.

'Aye, miss, there's always some that'll trade with the Gødfolk,' said Sugar when Maddy commented on this. 'You don't think you're the only one what's found their way down here, do yer? Or that the Eye's the only gateway under the Hill?'

Below that there was less traffic, fewer spells. Here were storerooms; vaults; sleeping quarters, food stores. Maddy, who was growing hungry, was tempted to raid these, but goblins are not especially particular about what they eat, and she had heard too many tales to take the risk. Instead, searching her pockets, she found an apple core and a handful of nuts, and made a small, unsatisfying meal of these; a decision she was to regret later.

They moved down towards the river, and here at last were stone lanes packed with spoils and takings. Remembering what One-Eye had told her, Maddy cast *Bjarkán* and searched; but among the webwork of little spells and signatures that crisscrossed the tunnels, among the bundles of feathers, chests of rags, pots and pans and broken daggers and battered shields, she could find no sign of anything resembling a treasure of the Elder Age.

Goblins, of course, are terrible hoarders and, unlike dwarves, will steal anything that comes to hand, regardless of its value. But Maddy was not discouraged. Somewhere in all this, she was sure she would find the Whisperer. Rather an odd name for a treasure, she thought; but then she remembered the Dropper, Odin's ring; his spear, Fear-Striker; and Mjølnir, the Pounder, the Hammer of Thor; and told herself that the treasures of the Elder Age had often borne such mysterious names.

And so she searched on: through old mattresses, dry bones and broken crockery; through sticks and stones and dolls' heads and partnerless shoes and loaded dice and fake toenails and scraps of paper and tasteless china ornaments and dirty handkerchiefs and forgotten love poems and balding oriental rugs and lost schoolbooks and headless mice.

But still, as One-Eye had warned her, she found nothing of value, no gold, no silver, not even a nickel penny.

'There's nowt here.' The goblin had grown increasingly restive as they proceeded deeper into the belly of the Hill. 'There's nowt down here and it's not bloody safe.'

Maddy shrugged and kept on going.

'Now if I knew what you were looking *for* . . .' said Sugar.

'I'll tell you when I've found it.'

'You don't even know what it looks like, do yer?' he said.

'Shut up and watch where you're going.'

'You don't bloody *know*!'

As Maddy followed Sugar deeper and deeper into the Hill, she began to fear that the goblin was right. The Hill was a ragman's paradise, stuffed from seam to seam with worthless trash. There was nothing resembling treasure here; nothing magical, nothing precious, nothing approaching One-Eye's description.

Also it was clear to Maddy that Sugar was as baffled by their search as Maddy was herself. He had repeatedly denied that there was any kind of treasure beneath the Hill, and after consideration she was inclined to believe him. Goblins don't really understand wealth, and are just as likely to steal a broken teapot as half a crown or a diamond ring. Besides, she just couldn't imagine how a treasure of the Elder Age – a thing of such importance that One-Eye could spend years trying to locate it – would remain for long in the hands of Sugar and his friends.

No – the more Maddy thought about it, the less likely it seemed that the Good Folk had anything to do with this. The secret – if it was there at all – lay deeper than the goblins' lair.

In the hours that passed she twice cast *Naudr* on her reluctant companion, with slightly less effect each time. She was very hungry now and wished she had taken advantage of the goblins' food stores; but these were far behind her now and hunger, fatigue and the strain of controlling the goblin, casting and recasting *Sól* and passing unseen through the labyrinth of spells were beginning to take their toll. Her glam was weakening like a lamp fast running out of oil. Soon it would be used up.

Sugar was not unaware of this, and his gold eyes gleamed as he trotted tirelessly down one passage after another, leading Maddy further and further under the Hill, away from the storerooms and into the dark.

Maddy followed him recklessly. The webwork of signatures that had so baffled her on the earliest levels had mostly thinned out and disappeared, leaving her with one single persistently bright and powerful trail that over-whelmed everything else and filled her with curiosity. It was an unusual colour – a pale and luminous violet shade – and it lit the darkness, crossing and re-crossing as if someone had passed there many, many times. Maddy followed – thirsty now and numb with fatigue, but with a growing sense of excitement and hope that blinded her to her own weakening glam as well as to the furtive glint in the goblin's eye.

They were passing through a large high-ceilinged cavern with a chandelier of stalactites that picked up the glow of Maddy's runelight and threw it back at her in a thousand wands of fire and shadow. Sugar trotted ahead, ducking automatically beneath a protruding ledge of stone that brought Maddy up short and gasping. 'Slow down!' she called.

But Sugar did not seem to have heard. Maddy followed him, lifting up her hand to light his trail, only to see him vanish behind an outcrop of gleaming lime.

'I said *wait!*'

As she hurried forward, Maddy realized that she was beginning to see more clearly. There was light coming from somewhere ahead; not runelight, nor a signature, nor the cool phosphorescence of the deep caves, but a warm, red, comforting glow.

'Sugar?' she called, but either the goblin could not hear, or was maliciously ignoring her, because there was no reply but the echo of her own voice – sounding small and very lost – rebounding glassily between the great stalactites.

All at once a shudder went through the ground, and Maddy lurched forward, holding out her hands to steady herself. Dust and stone fragments, dislodged by the upheaval, pattered onto her back. She was just straightening up again when a second tremor struck, and she was flung against the wall as a slab of rock the size of a haunch of beef dropped from the ceiling.

Instinctively Maddy threw herself into a connecting tunnel. Stalactites fell like spears from the roof of the main chamber as the whole mountain seemed to shudder to its roots. But although Maddy was showered with dust and particles of rock, the tunnel roof held, and as the tremor died away – sounding to Maddy like the rumble of a distant avalanche over the Seven Sleepers – she put her head out of the tunnel mouth and looked out.

Maddy, of course, knew all about earthquakes. It was the World Serpent at Yggdrasil's Root – or so Crazy Nan had always maintained – grown too large for Netherworld to contain, shaking out his coils into the river Dream. In time, said Nan, he would grow so large that he would circle the world, as he had in the days before Tribulation, and he would gnaw right through the World Tree's roots, causing the Nine Worlds to collapse one by one, so that Chaos would have dominion over all things for ever.

Nat Parson had a different tale; according to him, the tremors were caused by the struggles of the vanquished in the dungeons of Netherworld, where the wicked (meaning the old gods) lie in chains until the End of All Days.

One-Eye denied this, and spoke of rivers of fire under the earth and avalanches of hot mud and mountains boiling over like kettles; but this seemed to Maddy to be the least likely explanation of all, and she was inclined to believe that he had exaggerated the tale, as he did so many things.

Nevertheless she was sure that an earthquake had caused the tremors, and it was very cautiously that she left the safety of the tunnel mouth. The stalactite chandelier had partly collapsed, leaving a treacherous rubble of shattered pieces in the centre of the chamber. Beyond it was nothing but stillness and silence, apart from the distant after-echo and the dust that filtered from the trembling walls.

'Sugar?' called Maddy.

There was no reply, but she thought she heard a scuffling sound, far away to her right.

'Sugar?'

Once more there was no reply. Stepping out into the hall, Maddy thought she saw him, just for a moment, about a hundred steps ahead, then he dodged beneath a broken archway and was gone.

Quickly she cast *Naudr* again, but her concentration had been broken by the earthquake; the light was failing; her feet suddenly felt too far away; and she realized, too late, as the shadows rushed in, that she had fallen victim to the goblins' oldest trick.

Sugar had never meant to guide her towards anything. Instead, without ever quite disobeying her, he had allowed her to move deeper and deeper into the perilous passages under the Hill, sapping her strength and waiting until her endurance gave way and her power over him failed, and he was able to seize an opportunity to make his escape, leaving her alone, exhausted and lost in the tumbled passageways of World Below.

3

It was lucky for Maddy that she was a sensible girl. Anyone else might have tried to feel their way through the unlit passageways, moving blindly further and further into the tortuous guts of the Hill. Or called for help, bringing who knows what from the darkness.

But Maddy did not. Though she was afraid, she kept her head. Her glam was used up, which was bad enough, but she was almost sure that sleep would replenish it – sleep and (if she could get it) food. The short tunnel in which she had taken shelter seemed safe enough; it was warm and there was a sandy floor. Groping her way, she found it again, and settled there to rest.

She had no idea what time it was. It could be night in World Above, or even morning. But here there were no days, and time seemed to have a life of its own, stretching like a weaver's thread into a loom that wove nothing but darkness.

Tired as she was, Maddy was certain she wouldn't sleep. Every few minutes the floor trembled beneath her; dust fell from the ceiling; and there were other sounds, rustlings and patterings just outside the tunnel mouth that to her overstretched imagination sounded like giant rats, or great cockroaches chittering over the fallen stones. Still, at last, her fatigue got the better of her fears. Curled up on the floor with her jacket around her, she slept.

It might have been three, or five, or even twelve hours later; there was no way of telling. But she felt rested; *Sól* at her fingers shone out without a moment's hesitation, and although she was hungry – and fiercely stiff from lying on the floor – she felt a rush of pleasure and relief as the colours sprang to life around her once again.

Standing up, she looked out from the tunnel's mouth. She could see that the darkness was not complete. There was no phosphorescence in the walls at this lower level, but the red glow from the caves was more noticeable now, like a reflection of fire against a bank of low cloud, and the violet signature she had followed so far was brighter than ever, leading straight towards the distant glow.

Of Sugar there was no sign, except for a signature too dim to be of use. It was likely that on his return he might give the alarm; but that couldn't be helped. No, thought Maddy; the only thing she could do was continue downwards, following the direction of the violet trail, and hope that she might find something to eat – her last frugal meal seemed a very long time ago now.

Beyond the cavern, the passage branched out into two forks, one larger than the second, still lit with that dim, fiery glow. Without hesitation Maddy followed it; it was warmer than in the lower caverns, and as she moved gradually downwards – the incline was small, but unmistakable – she thought she could hear a sound, far below her, like the low *hishhh* in the shells One-Eye brought her from the shores of the One Sea.

Coming closer, she realized that the sound was not constant. It came and went, as if carried on a gusting wind, at intervals of five minutes or so. There was a smell too, which grew stronger as she neared its source; a curiously familiar laundry smell with an occasional whiff of sulphur; and now there was a film of steam on the walls of the passage, and a new slickness to the floor, which suggested that she was approaching its source.

Even so, she must have been walking for almost an hour when the passage came to its end. During that time there had been several small earth tremors, which had caused no damage, the rushing sounds had grown progressively louder, and the air was fugged with steam and fumes. The glow came brighter now – bright as sunlight, but bloodier and less constant – bright enough now to obscure any colours, if there had been any to follow.

Instead, Maddy followed the light, and as the passage opened out, she found herself entering a cavern larger than any she had ever seen or dreamed of.

She guessed it to be close to a mile in width, with a ceiling that soared away into shadow, and a floor of cindery, tumbled rock. A river ran through it – she could see a gully at the far end of the cavern into which the water disappeared; and in the centre, a round pit with a furnace at its heart, clearly the source of the reddish light.

As she stepped into the cavern, there came a rushing sound, and a great plume of steam, like the boiling of a million kettles, erupted from the firepit, sending her scurrying for the safety of the passageway. The laundry smell intensified; sulphurous steam enveloped Maddy in a burning shroud and the fissures and passageways of World Below shrieked and bellowed like the pipes of a giant organ.

It lasted a minute, maybe less. Then it was over.

Cautiously, over half an hour, Maddy crept closer to the pit.

The eruptions occurred at regular intervals – Maddy guessed five minutes or so – and she was soon able to recognize the signs and get under cover when danger threatened. Even so, the going was not pleasant; the air was scarcely breathable, and soon Maddy's shirt and hair were stuck to her skin with steam and sweat. There must be an underground river, she thought – maybe even the river Dream on its way down to Netherworld – meeting the cauldron of fire as it passed, each element fighting to dominate the other until at last they burst forth together in a spume of superheated air.

Still, she never thought of giving up. There was something in the firepit; some force that drew her as surely as a fish on a line. This was no trick, she told herself; nor was its power anything she had encountered before. Whatever it was, it was very close, and Maddy had to curb her impatience as she inched her way forward.

Once more the geyser burst forth. Maddy, now less than twenty feet away, felt the blast in the small of her back and, as soon as it began to die down, crossed the remaining stretch of rocky floor towards her goal. She stepped up onto the lip of the well, and shielding her face with a fold of her jacket, looked straight into the eye of the pit.

It was smaller than she had expected, no wider than a foot across, and as round and regular as a water well. Her eyes had been deceived into thinking it larger by the intensity of the furnace within, and it was lucky for Maddy that she had covered her face, for already her vision was blurred, like that of someone who has looked into the noonday sun.

Jed Smith's forge was a candle in comparison; here, metals and rocks bubbled like soup a thousand or more feet below the lip of the pit, and the stench of sulphur came to Maddy on a column of air so hot that it crisped the hairs in her nose and raised blisters on her unprotected hands.

She bore it for less than five seconds. But in those seconds Maddy saw the heart of the mountain, burning brighter than the sun. She saw the sink through which the river drained, and the meeting of forces within the pit. And she saw something else in that fiery throat; something blurred and difficult to see, but which spoke to her as plainly as the signatures she had followed through the passageways.

The thing was not large – the size of a watermelon – and was roughly rounded in shape. It might have been a lump of glowing rock, suspended by who knew what forces in the gullet of the pit.

Surely there could be little hope of recovering anything from such a hiding place. The most skilled climber could not reach it; even assuming he could somehow withstand the blaze, the geyser would shoot him back out of the pit like a cork from a bottle before he had covered half the distance.

Besides, any fool could see that the thing was caught fast; a flexible webwork of glamours and runes bound it tighter than the strongest of chains.

As she watched, the rock seemed to glow even brighter, like an ember beneath the blacksmith's bellows. A thought as absurd as it was troubling struck her – *it sees me* – and looking down into the pit, she could almost believe she *heard* it now – a strong, soundless call that seemed to drill into her mind.

(*Maddy! To me!*)

'The Whisperer.'

Now she began to move away, breathless and almost fainting from the heat, once more using the rocks and hollows of the cavern for shelter. She could do no more for the present. All she could hope for was to recover her strength and try to think of some kind of plan; or if she could not, to find her way back to the Red Horse and tell One-Eye that, whatever his disappointment in her failure to bring back the Whisperer, he could at least be fairly sure that no one else would ever lay hands on it.

It was cooler at the edge of the cavern, and the air, though noxious, was easier to breathe. Maddy rested there for some time, letting her eyes adjust once more to the gloom. There were smaller caves set into the sides, some barely alcoves, others as large as fair-sized rooms, which might give reasonable shelter from tremors and eruptions.

In one she found a trickle of clean water and drank gratefully, for her thirst had begun almost to equal her hunger.

In another she found a vein of dull-yellow metal almost as thick as her arm running through the wall.

And in the third, much to her surprise, she found a stranger standing with his back against the wall and a loaded crossbow pointing straight into her face.

4

For a second or two she was confused. The figure in the shadows seemed to have no shape, no substance – all she could see was his eyes and a slash of light across his mouth that flickered and glowed. But if her mind was fuddled, her *hands* seemed to know exactly what to do. Impulsively she raised them and, without a moment's hesitation, cast *Kaen* – Wildfire – as hard as she could into the stranger's face.

Why Maddy had chosen that particular rune she could not have told you, but its effect was immediate and devastating. It struck her would-be attacker like a whip, so that he dropped his crossbow with a howl and fell to his knees on the cavern floor.

Maddy was almost as stunned as he was. She had acted on pure instinct, with no anger and no desire to harm. And now that she could see him more clearly, she was surprised to discover that her assailant was not the giant super-goblin she had imagined, but a slim red-haired person not much bigger than she was.

'Get up,' she said, kicking the crossbow out of his reach.

'My eyes,' said the stranger behind his upflung arms. 'Please. My eyes.'

'Get up,' she repeated. 'Show me your face.'

He looked no more than seventeen. His red hair was tied back, revealing sharp but not unpleasant features, now drawn with pain and distress. His eyes were streaming, and there was a vicious welt across the bridge of his nose where the mindbolt had struck, but otherwise – to Maddy's relief – there seemed to be no lasting damage.

'My eyes.' In the light from the distant firepit they were a curious, flaming green. 'Gods, what hit me?'

In all events he was no goblin; but Maddy could tell at once that he was not from the valley, although there was nothing outlandish in his bearing or dress. A little ragged, perhaps, as if he had travelled rough; his leather jacket was deeply stained, and his boots were worn thin at the soles.

Slowly he got to his feet, squinting at Maddy, one hand lifted defensively in case of another attack. 'Who are you, anyhow?' His accent marked him as a stranger – a northerner, from the Ridings perhaps, judging from the colour of his hair. But Maddy, who had initially been alarmed at finding him, was now surprised at the depth of her relief. To see another human being after so many hours alone in the caverns was an unexpected joy, even if the stranger did not share it. 'Who are you?' he repeated sharply.

Maddy told him.

'You're not with *them*?' he said, jerking his head at the upper levels.

'No. Are you?'

'You're a Fury,' he said. 'I can see your glam.'

'A Fury?' Maddy looked at her runemark and saw it glowing dully on the palm of her hand. 'Oh, that. It won't hurt you, I promise.'

She could see the stranger was not convinced. Every muscle in him seemed tensed, as if he were uncertain whether to run or fight, but his eyes stayed fixed upon Maddy's hand.

'It's all right, I won't spell you. What's your name?'

'Call me Lucky,' he said. 'And keep your distance.'

Maddy sat down on a rock by the entrance. 'Is that better?'

'For now, yes.'

For a moment they faced each other. 'Do your eyes still hurt?'

'What do *you* think?' he snapped.

'I'm sorry,' said Maddy. 'I thought you were going to shoot me.'

'You could have *asked* me instead of just belting me in the face.' Cautiously he fingered his damaged nose.

'I know a runecharm that would help.'

'No thanks.' He seemed to relax a little. 'What are you doing here, anyway?'

Maddy hesitated for only an instant. 'I'm lost,' she said. 'I came here through the Horse's Eye and got lost in the tunnels.'

'Why'd you come?'

She hesitated again – and decided on a half-truth. 'Don't you know?' she said. 'The whole Hill's a giant treasure mound. Gold left over from the Elder Age. Isn't that why *you* came here?'

Lucky shrugged. 'I've heard the tale,' he said. 'But there's nothing here. Nothing but trash and goblins.'

He had been hiding out in the tunnels for nearly two weeks, Maddy learned. He had entered World Below from the other side of the mountains, beyond Hindarfell; had evaded capture several times on his way before finally running into a posse of goblins who caught him and took him to their Captain.

'Their Captain?' said Maddy.

He nodded. 'Great big vicious brute. Seemed to think I was some sort of spy. When I told him I was just a glass-blower's prentice from up the Ridings, he flew into a rage and swore he'd starve the truth out of me. Then he shut me up in a hole, and left me there for three days.'

On the third day Lucky had got lucky. In the floor of his cell he had uncovered a grating, once the opening to a drainage tunnel, through which he had managed to escape. Famished, filthy and afraid, he had stolen what he could from the goblins' stores before finding his way to relative safety, where he had been hiding ever since, living on fish and fresh water from the river, plus what was left of his stolen supplies.

'I've been trying to get back aboveground,' he told Maddy, 'but every goblin under the Hill's after me now. They won't come here, though,' he said, looking beyond her at the glowing firepit. 'None of that rabble ever comes this far.'

But Maddy's attention was elsewhere. 'Food?' she said. 'You've got *food* here?'

'Why? You hungry?'

'What do you think?'

For a moment Lucky seemed unsure. Then he came to a decision. 'All right. This way.' And with that he led her out of the cave and along the edge of the firepit cavern until they reached a place where the river, running swift and dark from an opening in the wall, had been partly diverted by a fall of rocks.

'Wait here,' he told Maddy. Then he ran up to the water's edge, leaped up onto a cluster of fallen boulders and vaulted off into the darkness.

For a second Maddy was alarmed – from where she was standing it looked as if Lucky had simply flung himself into the rapids. But she could see him now, standing on a flat shelf about halfway into the stream, white water surging around him. He must have known about the shelf, Maddy thought; even so, it was a dangerous move. Still, any fisherman will tell you that river fish love fast water best of all, and Maddy was not surprised when, a few seconds later, Lucky bent down and pulled sharply at something at his feet.

It was a fish trap, cleverly woven from string or twine. Lucky inspected the contents, hefted the net over his shoulder and returned, moving quickly and deftly over the hidden rocks.

While he was thus occupied, Maddy watched him closely through *Bjarkán* – the magic circle of finger and thumb. She made certain he didn't see her do it; she didn't want to frighten him off. Still, *Trust no one*, One-Eye had said, and she wanted to be sure that this glassblower's boy was all that he appeared to be.

But *Bjarkán* confirmed what she already felt. Lucky cast no colours at all. Her first, fleeting impression – that of someone older, taller, with fiery eyes and a crooked smile – had been nothing but a trick of the light and of her own fears. And as Lucky reached the water's edge, grinning, with his catch over his shoulder, Maddy breathed a sigh of relief, and allowed herself – at last – to unbend.

They shared the catch between them. Lucky showed Maddy how to cook the fish. These were sour-fleshed and bony, with huge, blind eyes; but Maddy ate every scrap of hers, licking her fingers and making hungry little noises of appreciation.

Quietly Lucky watched her eat. The messy business of catching, cooking and eating the fish had broken much of the ice between them, and he had dropped his sullen manner and become quite friendly. Maddy guessed that he was as relieved as she was to find an ally in the tunnels; and the fact that he had survived there alone for two weeks said a lot for his courage and ingenuity.

In that time, she learned, he had found food and a means of cooking it; he had located a source of good drinking water and a place to wash; he knew where the air was sweetest and had found the most comfortable place to sleep. He had been charting the tunnels too, one by one, trying to discover a means of reaching the surface without passing through the great gallery, but so far without success. And all that without even a cantrip to help him.

'What will you do if there's no way out?' asked Maddy when he had finished his tale.

'Risk it, I suppose. They'll drop their guard eventually. But that Captain – I don't want to run into *him* again.'

Maddy looked thoughtful. The Captain – she still felt she was missing something, but couldn't put her finger on what it was.

'So what about you?' Lucky went on. 'How did you find your way down here? And how come you know so much about this place?'

It was a fair question. Maddy considered it, and Lucky watched her, not quite smiling, his eyes flame-green in the firelight. 'Come on,' he said, seeing her hesitation. 'I may not be a Fury, but that doesn't make me a fool. I've seen your glam, and I know what it means. You came here for a reason. And don't give me that old tale of treasure under the Hill, either. There's no treasure here, and you know it.'

So he hadn't believed her tale. On reflection, she wasn't surprised. He was too clever to be taken in. In a way, that reassured her. She could use an ally in the caves, and his knowledge and his resourcefulness might well come in handy.

Trust no one, One-Eye had said. But surely she owed him some explanation, and besides, if the goblin Captain *was* the enemy, then there could be no danger in telling Lucky a few things.

'Well?' There was an edge to his voice. 'Do you trust me or not?'

'It's not that I don't trust you—' began Maddy.

'Yeah, right,' said Lucky. 'I don't have to be a Fury to see what's what. I mean, what have I done to make you suspect me? Apart from fishing for you, that is, and showing you where it's safe to drink, and—'

'Please, Lucky—'

'It's all right for you, isn't it? You're in no danger. You can get out of here whenever you like. Me, I'm here till I get caught. Why should you help me, after all? I'm only a glassblower's boy from the Ridings. Why should you care what happens to me?'

And with that he turned his back on her, and was silent.

Trust no one. Even now the urgency of One-Eye's words rang in Maddy's ears. But One-Eye wasn't there, was he? One-Eye had sent her under the Hill with no warning and no preparation, expecting her to know exactly what to do. But neither of them had foreseen this – and what was she supposed to do now? Abandon Lucky to his fate?

'Lucky,' she said.

He hunched his shoulders. Even in the flickering light Maddy could see that he was shaking.

'You're scared,' she said.

'Well, *duh*,' said Lucky. 'Believe it or not, being dismembered by goblins wasn't on my list of priorities for the week. But if you don't trust me—'

Maddy sighed. 'All right,' she said. 'I'll trust you.'

She just hoped One-Eye would understand.

So Maddy told her tale in full – everything she had meant to tell, and quite a lot she hadn't. She spoke of her childhood; of her father; of Mae; of Mrs Scattergood and the invasion of rats and insects in the cellar – at this point Lucky laughed aloud; of her dreams and ambitions; of her fears. He was a good listener; and when Maddy finally stopped talking, feeling tired and dry-mouthed, it was with the not unpleasant feeling that she had never revealed quite as much to anyone – not even to One-Eye – as she had to this boy.

'So,' he said when Maddy had done. 'You opened the Hill. You found your way here' – for some reason she had not told Lucky about Sugar – 'and now you've found your Whisperer. So what happens next?'

Maddy shrugged. 'One-Eye said to bring it out.'

'That simple?' He grinned. 'And did he give you any idea of how you were going to work it? Magic rope, perhaps, or a cantrip to make you fireproof?'

Silently Maddy shook her head.

'It's a glam, isn't it?' said Lucky. 'It's some bauble from the Elder Age, all bound up in heathen runes. How d'you know it's safe, Maddy? How d'you know it won't just zap you into smithereens the minute you lay your hands on it?'

'One-Eye would have told me.'

'Assuming he knows.'

'Well, he knew it was here.'

'Hm.' Lucky sounded unconvinced. 'It just seems rather odd, that's all. Him sending you down here alone like that.'

'I told you,' said Maddy. 'It was safer this way.'

There was a rather lengthy pause. 'Don't bite my head off,' said Lucky slowly, 'but it seems to me your Journeyman friend knows a lot about this that he hasn't told you. First he says there's gold under the hill, then he says it's a treasure of the Old World, but he won't say what it is, then he sends you in here alone without even a syllable of warning – I mean, didn't you ever hear the tale of Al-Adhinn and the enchanted lamp?'

Maddy began to feel annoyed. 'One-Eye's my friend. I trust him,' she said.

'Your choice.' Lucky shrugged.

'No one *made* me come here, you know.'

'Maddy, he's been feeding you tales of World Below since you were seven years old. I'd say he's got you well trained by now.'

Maddy's fists clenched, just a little. 'What are you saying? That he lied to me?'

'What I'm saying,' Lucky told her, 'is that a man may plant a tree for a number of reasons. Perhaps he likes trees. Perhaps he wants shelter. Or perhaps he knows that some day he may need the firewood.'

Now Maddy's face was pale with anger. She took a step forward, the runemark on her palm flaring suddenly from russet-brown to angry red. 'You don't know what you're talking about.'

'Look, all I said was—'

In an instant Maddy's hand was aflame; a bramble of runelight sprang from her palm. It was *Thuris*, the Thorn, angriest of runes, and Maddy could feel it wanting to bite, to sting, to lash out at the cause of her rage—

Alarmed, she flung it at the wall. *Thuris* discharged harmlessly into the rock, leaving a sharp scent of burned rubber in the air.

'Nice aim,' said Lucky. 'Feel better now?'

But Maddy had already turned her back. Who in the Nine Worlds did he think he was? He was only an accidental player in this game; a bystander; just clever enough to enter World Below, but not enough to get out again; just a glass-blower's prentice with no magic and no glam.

And yet, she thought, *what if he was right?*

She shot him a look over her shoulder and saw him watching her curiously. Serve him right, she thought, if she left him here. Let him rot underground, or be caught by goblins. It would be no more than he deserved. She stood up abruptly and turned to the cave entrance.

'Where are you going?' Lucky said.

'I'm going to get the Whisperer.'

'What, now?'

'Why not?'

Now there was alarm in Lucky's voice. 'You're crazy,' he said, catching hold of her arm. 'It's late, you're exhausted, you haven't got a clue—'

'I'll manage,' she snapped. 'I'm a lot smarter than you give me credit for.'

Now Lucky gave a rueful sigh. 'Maddy, I'm sorry,' he said. 'Me and my mouth. My brother always said I should have it sewn up, do everyone a favour.'

Maddy glared, and would not turn round.

'Maddy. Please. Don't go. I apologize.' Now he even *sounded* sorry, and Maddy found herself relenting. He couldn't be expected to take all this on trust. His world was very different from hers, and it was only natural for him to be suspicious. He had no magic; knew nothing of the Whisperer; and more importantly, she reminded herself, he didn't know One-Eye.

The question remained, Maddy thought – did *she*?

5

The doubts he had awakened were not easily put aside. After a rather silent supper of leftover fish, Maddy found herself tired but unable to rest. While Lucky slept, apparently oblivious, she tried in vain to find a comfortable position on the rock floor, but again and again found her mind going back to the same words.

A man may plant a tree for a number of reasons.

What had been One-Eye's reason? Why had he taught her so much and yet kept so much from her? Most of all, how could he know anything about a treasure that had been lost since the Winter War?

Behind her, Lucky was still asleep. Maddy couldn't see how he *could* sleep in such relentless heat, with the sounds of World Below echoing and rumbling like thunder around them, but there he was, twitching a little, as if at some dream, curled comfortably into a hollow in the rock with his jacket rolled up beneath his head.

Perhaps he was used to the heat, she thought. A glass-blower's prentice has to spend long hours working the ovens, fanning and stoking the fires for the melted glass. Besides, he was unusually resourceful – for a prentice – and he had had time to get used to the unpleasant conditions.

Still, now that she came to think of it, Maddy realized that although Lucky knew a great deal about her, *she* still knew almost nothing about *him*. What was he doing under the Hill? From what he had told her, he had been gone for two weeks or more – a serious breach of his contract of apprentice-ship, for which he would be punished when he returned. Why would a glassblower's prentice come here? More importantly, how had a glassblower's prentice managed to break into World Below in the first place?

A few feet away, Lucky slept, a picture of innocence. Maddy could not believe she hadn't at least questioned him; hadn't even thought of doing so until now. There had been so much else to do – and besides, Lucky had no magic, no glam. *Bjarkán* confirmed it – he left no trail.

But now even that made Maddy uneasy. She tried to recall exactly *what* she had seen as Lucky came back over the rocks with his fishing net. Surely there should have been something, she thought – his colours, at least. Lucky was young and strong and smart; he should have left a good, bright signature behind him. But even with *Bjarkán*, there had been no colours. Not a gleam, not a glimmer.

Could he have hidden them somehow?

The thought was too alarming. It suggested—

Sitting up sharply, she raised her hand and cast *Bjarkán* for the second time, and this time she concentrated as hard as she could, looking into the runeshape for anything – *anything* – out of the ordinary.

The glassblower's prentice slept on, one hand clenched at his side, the other flung out against the rock. Now she could see his signature, a bright and exuberant violet, glowing fitfully as he slept.

Maddy gave a sigh of relief. Just nerves, that's all it was; nerves and her own fears, making her jump at shadows. She lowered her gaze . . .

And then she saw it in his left hand, where, sleeping, he must have relaxed his guard. A trio of runes, like thin trails of coloured fire scrawled across his palm: *Yr* – the Protector,

crossed with *Bjarkán* and *Ós*, a complex charm to shield him
as he slept.

So much for his innocence, Maddy thought. Gods knew
who this Lucky was, or why he had lied, but one thing about
her new friend was clear. He was no prentice, after all.

He was a Fury, just like her.

Most runes can be neutralized, either by reversal or by casting another to combat their effect. Maddy judged that *Tyr*
might break through Lucky's defence, revealing whatever he
was hiding. Of course, it did depend to some extent on
the strength of his glam; but Maddy had the advantage, and
surely now his resistance must be at its lowest.

Taking care not to disturb the sleeper, she stood up and
silently cast the rune. Then, with a sudden push, she set it to
work.

His charm flickered, but did not fail.

Maddy gave another push, and at the same time cast
Bjarkán. The runes vanished; and Maddy was left looking into
a face she had seen once before and which, now that she saw
it in its true colours, seemed unexpectedly familiar.

His Aspect had not been greatly altered. He had much the
same colouring and build, although he was a little taller. But
he was older than he had first seemed, and even in
sleep, there was less innocence in his features, more guile.
There were marks too, which had not been there earlier; a
runemark –

– *Kaen*, reversed, on his bare arm – and now she saw that his mouth was crisscrossed with fine, pale scars, too regular to be accidental.

Maddy dropped her hand to her side. Too late now she understood everything; too late she remembered what Sugar had said; too late remembered One-Eye's words.

A ... friend, he had told her; *turned traitor in the Winter War. I thought he was dead, and maybe he is, but his kind have nine lives, and he always was—*

'Lucky,' whispered Maddy, turning pale.

'That's right,' said Lucky, opening his fiery eyes. 'But you can call me Captain.'

6

He moved fast – very fast for a man just waking from a deep sleep. But to Maddy's surprise he did not attempt to strike at her, but simply leaped towards the mouth of the cave, so that the mindbolt she flung at him smashed against the wall, dislodging a shower of rock fragments as it did so.

She raised her hand again, moving to the cave entrance to block his escape. This time Lucky did not attempt to run but, with a curious rapid flick of his fingers, summoned the rune *Kaen* and cast it – not at Maddy, but at *himself* – and vanished, or so she thought, leaving only a thin gunpowder-trail of fire where he had been standing, a trail that now moved swiftly towards the cave mouth.

The violet signature went with it, and in that instant Maddy summoned *Logr* – Water – and shot it at the fire-trail, stopping it short and charging the air with thick steam.

In a second Lucky was back, soaking wet and gasping.

Logr trembled once more at Maddy's fingertips, ready to strike. Slowly, hands raised, Lucky got up.

'Try that again, and I'll kill you,' she said.

'Hold it, Maddy; I thought we were friends.'

'No friend of mine,' said Maddy. 'You lied.'

Lucky pulled a face. 'Well, of course I lied. What did you expect? You creep up on me, you whack me in the face with something that feels like a combination of a sledge-hammer and a lightning bolt, you interrogate me and then – then you just happen to mention that you're big friends with One-Eye, of all people . . .'

'So I was right,' she said. 'Who are you?'

He had dropped his disguise, standing before her in his true Aspect. Once again Maddy thought he looked familiar, although she was sure she had never met him before. In a story, perhaps, or a picture from One-Eye's books. But she knew him, she was sure of it; she knew those eyes.

'Listen. I know you don't trust me. But there are a lot of things One-Eye hasn't told you. Things I can help you with.'

'Who are you?' she demanded again.

'A friend.'

'No you're not,' said Maddy. 'You're the one I was warned about. The thief. The one who's after the Whisperer.'

'Thief?' He laughed. 'Maddy, I have as much right to the Whisperer as anyone else – more right than some, as a matter of fact.'

'Then why did you lie to me?'

'Ask yourself rather – why did *he* lie to you?'

'This isn't about One-Eye,' she said.

'Isn't it?' Lucky's gaze was difficult to hold; his voice low and oddly persuasive. 'He knew I'd be here,' he said. 'Ask yourself why. And as for the Whisperer – you've still no idea what it is, have you?'

Slowly Maddy shook her head.

'Or what it does?'

Again she shook her head.

Lucky laughed. It was a light and pleasant sound, instantly likeable, irresistibly contagious. Maddy found herself grinning back before she realized the trick. She was being charmed.

'Stop that,' she said sharply, casting *Yr* with her fingers.

Lucky looked unrepentant. Even behind the protection rune there was something in his smile that invited a response.

'I know you,' she said slowly. 'And One-Eye knows you, too.'

Lucky nodded. 'Told you I was a traitor, didn't he?'

'Yes.'

'And that I turned my coat when the war turned against him?'

Again Maddy nodded.

Oh, there was definitely something familiar about him; something she knew she ought to remember. She struggled with the thought, but Lucky was still speaking, his voice soft and compelling.

'All right,' he said. 'Just listen to this. It's something I'll bet old One-Eye *hasn't* told you.' Now his grin was hard and metallic, and in the dark his eyes gleamed fire-green and subtle. 'Get this, Maddy,' he said. 'We're brothers.'

Maddy's eyes grew very wide.

'Brothers in blood, sworn to each other. You know what that means, don't you?

She nodded.

'And yet he was willing to break his oath – betray his brother – for the sake of his cause, his war, his power. What kind of loyalty is that, do you think? And do you really think a man who can sacrifice his brother would think twice about sacrificing *you*?'

Now Maddy felt like she was drowning. The words flowed over her and she found herself drawn in, helpless. But even as she struggled against the charm there came once more that little sting of recognition; the feeling that if only she could remember *why* she knew him, then everything else would fall into place.

Think, Maddy, think.

Once more she drew the protective charm. *Yr* lit at her fingertips, dimming the persuasive glamour of *Kaen*.

Think, Maddy. Think.

That voice. Those eyes. The silvery crisscross of scars over his lips, as if long ago, someone, armed with something very sharp . . .

And now at last it came to her: the old tale of how the Trickster had challenged the Tunnel Folk – the master forgers, Ivaldi's sons – to a test of skill, and had wagered his head in return for their treasures, and lost. But even as they made to cut it off, he had cried, *The head is yours, but not the neck!* – and so, outwitting them, escaped with the prize.

At that the dwarves, enraged at the deception and bent on revenge, had sewn up Loki's mouth, and from that day forth his smile had been as crooked as his thoughts.

Loki. The Trickster. How could she have missed it? She knew him so well by reputation, had seen his face in a dozen books. One-Eye had given her what warning he could; even Sugar had called him Crookmouth. And the biggest clue was right there on his arm.

Kaen. The fire-rune. Reversed.

'I know you,' said Maddy. 'You're—'

'What's a name?' Loki grinned. 'Wear it like a coat; turn it, burn it, throw it aside and borrow another. One-Eye knows; you should ask *him*.'

'But Loki died,' she said, shaking her head. 'He died on the field at Ragnarók.'

'Not quite.' He pulled a face. 'You know, there's rather a lot the Oracle didn't foretell, and old tales have a habit of getting twisted.'

'But in any case, that was centuries ago,' said Maddy, bewildered. 'I mean – that was the End of the World, wasn't it?'

'So?' said Loki impatiently. 'It isn't the first time the world has come to an end, and it won't be the last, either. Thor's beard, Maddy, didn't One-Eye teach you *anything*?'

'But that would make you—' said Maddy, perplexed. 'I mean, the Seer-folk – the Æsir, I mean, weren't they – the *gods*?'

Loki waved his hand dismissively. 'Gods? Don't let *that* impress you. Anyone can be a god if they have enough worshippers. You don't even have to have powers any more. In my time I've seen theatre gods, gladiator gods, even *storyteller* gods, Maddy – you people see gods everywhere. Gives you an excuse for not thinking for yourselves.'

'But I thought—'

'God's just a word, Maddy. Like *Fury*. Like *demon*. Just words people use for things they don't understand. Reverse it, and you get *dog*. It's just as appropriate.'

'What about One-Eye?' said Maddy, frowning. 'If he's your *brother*' – her mouth dropped as she remembered yet another of those old stories – 'then that would make *him*—'

'That's right,' said Loki, with his crooked smile. 'The Allfather. The General. Old Odin himself.'

BOOK THREE
The Whisperer

I speak of a mighty Ash that stands.
Its name is Yggdrasil.

Prophecy of the Seer

1

Ragnarók. The End of the World. According to Nat Parson, it had been a great Cleansing by the Nameless, a single, titanic attempt to rid Creation of evil and to bring Perfect Order to the Worlds, with fire and ice and Tribulation.

Only Noar's line survived, or so the Good Book tells us, and the survivors – the demons and heretics that cheated Death – were flung into Netherworld to await the End of Everything.

One-Eye, on the other hand, had told her of the Prophesy of the Oracle and of the last great battle of the Elder Age; of how Surt the Destroyer had joined with Chaos and marched against the gods in Asgard, while the armies of the dead, in their fleet of coffin ships, sailed against them from the Underworld.

On that final plain the gods had fallen, fathoms-deep in glamours and blood; Odin, the last General, swallowed by the Fenris Wolf; Thor the Thunderer, poisoned by the World Serpent; Tyr the One-Armed; Heimdall of the Golden Teeth; Frey the Reaper; Loki . . .

'But if they were the *gods*,' Maddy had said, 'then how could they fall? How could they die?'

One-Eye had shrugged. 'Everything dies.'

But here was Loki telling her a different story; of how the fallen gods had not been destroyed, but had remained – weakened, broken, lost to themselves – waiting to return even as Chaos swept over the Nine Worlds, taking everything in its wake.

Years had passed; a new Order had come. Its temples were built on the ruins of springs and barrows and standing

103

stones that once were sacred to an older faith. Even the stories were outlawed – *There's nobbut a thread 'tween forgotten and dead*, as Crazy Nan used to say – and at last the march of the Order had trampled the old ways into near-oblivion.

'Still, nothing lasts for ever,' said Loki cheerfully. 'Times change, and nations come and go, and the world has its revolutions, just as the sea has its tides.'

'That's what One-Eye says.'

'A sea without tides will go stagnant,' said Loki, 'just as a world that stops changing will stiffen and die. Even Order needs a little Chaos – Odin knew that when he first took me in, and swore brotherhood between us. The others didn't understand. They were out to get me from the start.'

'Chaos was in my blood, they said – but they were happy enough to use my talents when it suited them. They despised deceit, hated lies, but were content to enjoy the fruits of them.' Maddy nodded. She knew what he meant. To be an outsider – a bad-blood – always blamed and never thanked. Oh, yes. She understood that very well.

'When Odin took me in,' Loki went on, 'he knew *exactly* what I was. Wildfire that cannot be tamed. So what if I slipped my leash a couple of times? I saved their skins more often than any of them knew. No one was grateful. And in the end' – once more Loki gave his crooked, but oddly charming smile – 'in the end, who betrayed whom? Was it *my* fault that I got out of hand? All I ever did was follow my nature. But accidents happen. Something went wrong. High spirits, perhaps; a little understandable friction at a difficult time. And all of a sudden, old friends didn't seem quite so friendly any more, and I began to think it might be good to remove myself until the dust had settled. But they came after me, and meted out their clumsy vengeance. I imagine you've heard the story.'

'Sort of,' said Maddy, who had heard a somewhat

different version. 'But I rather thought – I mean, I heard you'd killed Balder the Fair.'

'I never did,' snapped Loki crossly. 'Well, no one ever *proved* I did. What happened to the presumption of innocence? Besides, he was supposed to be invulnerable. Was it my fault that he wasn't?' Now his face darkened again, and his eyes took on a malevolent gleam. 'Odin could have stopped them,' he said. 'He was the General; they would have listened to him. But he was weak. He could see the end coming, and he needed all his people on his side. And so he turned a blind eye – 'scuse the pun – and delivered me into the hands of my enemies.'

Maddy nodded. She knew the tale – some part of it, anyway: how the Æsir had left him chained to a rock; how Skadi the Huntress, who'd always hated him, had put a snake to drip venom into his face; how their luck had been bad from that day until the End of the World; and finally, how Loki had broken free on the eve of the battle, to play his part in the destruction that followed.

Clearly he had no regrets. He said as much as he told Maddy of the last stand of the Æsir; of the battle One-Eye called Ragnarók.

'Perhaps I could have saved them if they'd stood by me at the end. Who knows, I might even have turned the battle round. But they'd made their choice. *He'd* made his choice. And so the world ended; and here we are, the dregs of us, hiding in caves or peddling cantrips, trying to figure out what went wrong.'

Maddy nodded. One-Eye's voice inside her head warned her that this was Loki – *Loki* – and that whatever else she must not be charmed, flattered or deceived into dropping her guard. She remembered One-Eye telling her that charm comes easily to the children of Chaos, and determined to take nothing of what he told her at face value.

But Loki's tale was dangerously plausible. It explained so many things that One-Eye had refused to tell – although some of it was still hard to digest; and his talk of the gods as if they were human beings – vulnerable, fallible, besieged – was especially difficult to accept. She had grown up with stories of the Seer-folk; had learned to think of them as friends; had dreamed of them in her secret heart, but even in her wildest imaginings had never thought to meet one some day, to talk to one as an equal, to touch a being who had lived in Asgard and have him stand in front of her, with a very human-looking welt across the bridge of his nose – a welt that her own mindbolt had caused . . .

'So . . . are you . . . immortal?' she said at last.

'Nothing's immortal,' he said, shaking his head. 'Some things last longer than others, that's all. And everything has to change to survive. Why d'you think I carry my glam reversed? Or that Odin does, for that matter?'

Maddy glanced at the runemark on his arm. *Kaen* – Wildfire – still gleamed there, violet against his pale skin. A powerful sign, even reversed, and Maddy had used it often enough herself to know that she must respect and mistrust its bearer.

'So how *was* your glam reversed?'

'Very painfully,' he said.

'Oh,' said Maddy. There was a pause. 'Well, what about the Fieries? Fieries, Furies, whatever they are . . .'

'Well, we're *all* Furies now,' he said with a shrug. 'Like anything that's been touched with the Fire. Demons, as your parson might say. Of course, *I* always was – comes of being a child of Chaos – but it can't be easy for the General, who was always so set on Law and Order.' He grinned. 'Must be hard for him to accept that – to the new gods, at least; to the Order – he's the enemy now.'

'The new gods?'

Loki nodded, for once not smiling.

'You mean, all that's real, too? The Nameless, and everything Nat Parson preaches from the Book of Tribulation?'

Loki nodded. 'As real or imaginary as any of us,' he said. 'No surprise your parson's so gloomy about the old ways. *He* knows who the enemy is, all right; and he and his kind will not be safe until ours is cleansed from the Nine Worlds; every tale forgotten, every glam subdued, every Fiery extinguished, to the last spark and flame.'

'But – *I'm* a Fiery,' said Maddy, opening her hand to look at her own runemark, now glowing like an ember.

'That you are,' said Loki. 'No question about it, with that glam you carry. No wonder he kept so quiet about you. You are something quite unique – and that's worth more than Otter's Ransom to him – or to me – or to anyone who can keep you on their side.'

Maddy's runemark was burning now, sending tendrils of thin fire snaking towards her fingertips.

'The Oracle predicted you,' said Loki, watching, fascinated. 'It predicted new runes for the New Age; runes that would be whole and unbroken, with which to rewrite the Nine Worlds. That rune of yours is *Aesk*, the Ash, and when One-Eye saw it on your hand, he must have thought all his Fair Days and Yules had come at once.'

'*Aesk*,' said Maddy softly, flexing her fingers into a cat's cradle of fire. 'And you think One-Eye knew this all along?'

'I should think so,' Loki said. 'It was to Odin that the prophecy was made.'

Maddy thought about that for a moment. 'Why?' she said at last. 'What does he want? And what's this . . . Whisperer he needs so badly? Did the Oracle mention that at all?'

'Maddy,' said Loki, beginning to smile, 'the Oracle *is* the Whisperer.'

2

There was a flask of dark mead hidden in the cave. Loki gave Maddy a sip, and drank the rest as he told his tale.

'The Whisperer,' he said, 'is an ancient power, even older than the General himself, though *he* doesn't enjoy being reminded of that. It's a story that goes back to the very beginning of the Elder Age, to the first wars between Order and Chaos, and – if you ask me – it's one that doesn't reflect too well on either side. Of course Yours Truly was completely neutral at that time—'

Maddy raised a sceptical eyebrow.

'Listen, do you want to hear this story or don't you?'

Maddy nodded.

'All right. In the old, old days of the General's youth, Asgard was a stronghold of perfect Order, and there wasn't a spark of magic there. The Vanir – enchanters from the borders of Chaos – *they* were the keepers of the Fire, and they and the Æsir waged war for years, until at last they realized that neither of them was ever going to win. And so they exchanged hostages as proof of good faith, and the Æsir got Njörd, and his children Frey and Freyja, and the Vans got Honir – nice lad, but not bright – and a wily old diplomat called Mimir, who stole their glam, gave them his counsel and reported back home in secret.

'But the Vans soon realized they had a couple of spies on board; and in revenge they killed Mimir and sent his head back to Asgard. By then, though, the General had already got what he needed. The runes of the Elder Script, the letters of the ancient tongue that created the Worlds.'

'The language of Chaos,' Maddy said.

Loki nodded. 'And Chaos was not best pleased at the theft. So Odin used his new skills to keep the Head alive, and gave it glam to make it speak. Not many folk return from the dead, and what they have to say is usually worth hearing. It gave old Mimir the gift of prophecy, invaluable to the General. But the gift came at a high price. Odin paid for it with his eye. And as for Mimir, or as he called it, the Whisperer' – Loki finished the bottle of mead – 'I don't imagine it cared much for us then, so I wouldn't count too far on its goodwill now. I've tried to talk to it, but it never was fond of me, not even in the old days. And as for getting it out of here—'

'But what do you *want* with it?' said Maddy. 'Why is it so important?'

'Please, Maddy,' said Loki with some impatience. 'The Whisperer's not just some bauble. It's an oracle. It knows things. It predicted Ragnarók, and a number of other things I wish I'd known at the time. If Odin had paid more attention to its prophecy instead of trying to prove it wrong, then perhaps Ragnarók wouldn't have turned out as it did.'

There was a pause as Maddy took in the implications.

'But why go after it now?' she said.

'A second chance?' Loki gave his twisted smile. 'Listen, Maddy, Odin put half of himself into that old glam. Half of the General in his prime; think what he could do with it now. Powers you can't imagine, just waiting to be tapped. Powers from the realms of Chaos.' He sighed. 'But the damn thing has a mind of its own, and it isn't bound to co-operate. Nevertheless there are folk out there who would give anything to lay their hands on it. And others, of course, who would give anything to stop them.'

'Gods,' said Maddy.

'Amen,' said Loki.

He had found the Whisperer on one of his exploring trips,

he said, some hundred years after the end of the war. Everything else was Chaos and slaughter. Many had fallen; some lost for ever, some buried in ice, some consumed by the fires of Chaos. The survivors were thrown into Netherworld, but Loki, slippery as ever, had somehow managed to escape.

'You escaped the Black Fortress?' Maddy said.

Loki shrugged. 'Eventually.'

'How?'

'Long story,' said Loki. 'Suffice it to say that I found . . . alternative accommodation in World Below. And it was there at last that I found the Whisperer,' he went on, 'though I soon realized it was useless to me. It recognized me, of course, but it wouldn't talk except in gibes and insults, wouldn't lend me so much as a spark of glam and certainly wouldn't prophesy. I thought maybe to get it out of the pit, to use it as a bargaining tool with one of the surviving Æsir—'

'The surviving Æsir?' said Maddy quickly.

'Rumours, that's all. I had a feeling Odin might still be around. It would certainly have helped my position if I could have brought *him* the Whisperer. And of course, with the General back on my side, I'd have been safe from any former colleagues with an axe to grind. Or even a hammer.'

Since then, he said, he had tried many times to retrieve the Whisperer from its fiery cradle. But he had not yet found a way to break the glamours that held it in the firepit – glamours left over from Ragnarók, which his reversed and thus weakened glam could not hope to combat.

Failing that, he had made the Hill impregnable, putting together an army of goblins, a webwork of glamours; a labyrinth of passages to hide the Whisperer from the world.

'And maybe it's best left hidden,' he said. 'Unless Odin gave you something to help? A glam, a tool – perhaps a word?'

'No,' said Maddy. 'Not even a cantrip.'

Loki shook his head, disgusted. 'In that case, forget it. Might as well try to catch the moon on a string.'

Maddy thought about that for a while. 'So you think it's hopeless?' she said at last. 'There's really no way of bringing it out?'

Loki shrugged. 'Believe me, I've tried. If the General wants to talk to it, he'll have to come down here himself.'

'Perhaps.' Maddy was still thinking hard.

'You should tell him, you know. Ragnarók's over. And as far as the Order is concerned, we're all of us the enemy. Perhaps we should rethink our allegiances. Bury our grudges. Start again.'

'You betrayed the Æsir,' said Maddy. 'You're crazy if you think he'll ever take you back.'

'The Æsir!' Unexpectedly her words had struck home; for a moment Loki's eyes flared with unfeigned anger. His colours flared too, from ghostly violet to hellfire red. 'All they ever did was use me when it suited them. When there was trouble, it was always; *Please, Loki, think of something.* Then when it was over, it was *Back to your kennel* without so much as a thank you. I was always a second-class citizen in Asgard, and not one of them ever let me forget it.'

'But you fought against them at Ragnarók,' said Maddy, who had begun to feel more sympathy for this dangerous individual than she dared admit.

'Ragnarók,' said Loki scornfully. 'Whose side did they expect me to take? I *had* no side. The Æsir had abandoned me; the Vanir always hated me, and as far as Chaos was concerned, I was a traitor who deserved to die. No one would take me; so I looked after Number One, as always. All right, maybe I settled a few scores on the way. But as far as I'm concerned, that's all history. The General has nothing to fear from me.'

'What are you saying?' Maddy said.

Loki gave his crooked smile. 'Maddy,' he said, 'I've been hiding out in World Below for the best part of five hundred years. All right, it's not the Black Fortress, but it's hardly bliss. It stinks, it's dark, it's overrun by goblins and I'm constantly having to watch my back . . . Besides, if I read the signs correctly, there will come a time very soon when none of us are safe; when even the deepest hole will not be enough to hide us from our enemies.'

'So?'

'So I'm tired of hiding,' Loki said. 'I want to come home. I want to see the sky again. More importantly, I want the General to make it clear to any of the others who might still harbour a grudge that I'm officially back on the side of the gods.'

He paused, and a wistful look came over his face. 'There's a war on the way. I can feel it,' he said. 'I don't need an oracle to tell me that. The Order is already on the march, spreading the Word through the Middle World. Odin knows – according to my sources he's spent the last century or so travelling between here and World's End, charting its progress, trying to learn how much time we have left. My guess is, it just ran out. That's why he needs the Whisperer. As for myself' – Loki grinned and put down the bottle – 'Maddy, I can't help it. It's the Chaos in my blood. If there's a war, I want to fight.'

For a long time Maddy said nothing. 'Then tell him so,' she said at last.

'What, meet him aboveground?' Loki said. 'You must be out of your tiny mind.'

'You really think One-Eye's going to come to *you*?'

'He'll have to,' said Loki. 'If he wants the Oracle. With that on his side there isn't a secret, scheme or strategy that the Order can keep from him. He can't hope to win the war without it. And he certainly can't afford to let it fall to the other side.' Loki grinned. 'So you see, Maddy, he has no choice but to accept my terms. Bring Odin to me, and I'll let him talk to the Whisperer. If not, then frankly I don't rate his chances when the Order gets here.'

Maddy frowned. It all sounded just a little too slick. She had already experienced Loki's charm; but she knew his reputation too, and she knew that his motives were rarely pure. She looked at him, and saw him watching her with a dangerous gleam in his fiery eyes.

'Well?' he said.

'I don't trust you,' said Maddy.

Loki shrugged. 'Few people do. But why not? You're strong. You've already beaten me once before.'

'Twice,' said Maddy.

'Whatever,' he said.

Maddy considered the point for a moment. She realized – rather late – that she didn't actually know very much about Loki's powers. Certainly she had beaten him – or had she? It hadn't been a fair fight. She had taken him by surprise. Or maybe he'd *let* her surprise him, she thought. Maybe that too was part of his plan.

Now Maddy's mind began to race. What did she know of the Whisperer? It was an oracle, Loki had said. A power of the Elder Age; a old friend of One-Eye; an enemy of Chaos. Loki had said it hated him; would not speak except in gibes. But One-Eye had said it would come to *her*, and *could it be*, she thought suddenly, *that Loki somehow knew that too* . . .

Could it be, wondered Maddy, that he had misdirected her? That far from wanting to *rescue* the Whisperer, he was actually trying to keep it from being rescued?

Could it even be possible that it was Loki *himself* who had trapped the Whisperer in the firepit, having failed to make it work for him?

Fire was his element, after all. Could it be that all this was a carefully constructed trap, its aim to lure One-Eye into

World Below, where Loki had had centuries to prepare himself for their eventual showdown?

'Well?' said Loki impatiently.

Well, it was far too late to waste time in questions. *Yesterday's ale is nobbut this morning's piss*, as Crazy Nan used to say, which meant, Maddy supposed, that if anyone was going to get her out of this mess, it probably wasn't the King's Guard.

'Well?'

Maddy sighed. A shadow of a plan was beginning to form in her mind. It was a rather desperate plan, but it was all she could think of at such short notice. 'All right,' she said. 'But first you have to show me.'

'Show you what?'

'The Whisperer.'

3

She followed him back to the firepit hall, taking care not to let him out of her sight. He had agreed to her demand with apparent good cheer, but with a trace of sullenness in his colours that suggested that he was far from pleased. She knew he was tricky – indeed, if he was Loki, he was trickery itself, and if he already suspected what she meant to do, there was no telling how he might react.

They stepped to the lee of the firepit, sheltering behind a spur of rock until the geyser had spent itself. Then, in the brief lull between two ventings, Loki stepped forward and came to stand on the lip of the well.

'Stand back,' he told Maddy. 'This can be dangerous.'

Maddy watched as he stood motionless, his colours flaring with sudden intensity and the first and little fingers of his right hand pronged to form the runeshape *Yr*.

His face was streaming with sweat, she saw; his fists were clenched; his eyes screwed shut as if preparing for some painful ordeal. This part at least was no act, she thought. She could feel the effort he was making; see the trembling of his muscles and the strain in every part of his body as he waited, tensed, for the Whisperer.

Even when the geyser began to reawaken, the low rumble rising to become a muted roar, Loki did not stir, but seemed to wait, regardless of his peril, as patiently as a fisherman snaring a trout.

Two minutes had already passed, and now Maddy could hear the eruption building, like a furious howl in a giant's throat.

Then, almost imperceptibly, he moved.

If Maddy had not been watching very carefully, she would have missed it altogether, for Loki's style of working was very different from hers. Under One-Eye's instruction Maddy had learned to value caution and accuracy above all things; to *coax* the runes, rather than to fling them, to handle them with care, as if without it they might explode.

But Loki was fast. Balancing like a rope-dancer on the edge of the pit as the column of steam came rushing towards him, he raised his head and made a curious quick fluttering movement of his hand. At the same time he shifted to his fiery Aspect, his features just discernible in the twisting flames, and skimmed runes at the column like a handful of firecrackers.

Maddy had scarcely time to read them all. She thought she recognized *Isa*, and *Naudr* – but what was that shuttling rune that spun like a sycamore key into the boiling flow, or the one that broke into a dozen shining pieces as it skimmed the flame?

She had little time to ask herself the question, though, for it was then that the geyser blew. The column of steam punched into the ceiling, hurling fragments of rock into the scorched air. And in the column, suspended for a moment in that massive splurge of cloud and flame, Maddy saw something that popped up like a cork from a bottle, and half heard, half felt its silent call –

(?)

(?)

– as it dropped once more into the pit.

Loki had fled in fiery Aspect, taking refuge behind a slab of rock. Now he returned to his true form. His face was flushed, his hair lank with sweat, and a reek of burning came from his clothes. Nevertheless he seemed exhilarated; in the afterglow his eyes were pinned with weird fire. He turned to Maddy. 'You saw it, then?'

Uneasily she nodded, recalling the quick way it had

bobbed to the surface; and how the light had seemed to shine right through; and how it had *called* to her . . .

'That was the Whisperer. Ouch,' he said, blowing into his scorched hands.

'But it's alive!'

'In a manner of speaking.'

Now Maddy could see just how much this effort had cost him; in spite of his careless words he was shaking, breathless, and his colours were dim. 'It really doesn't like me,' he said. 'Though to be fair, I don't think it likes any of us very much. And as for getting it out of there – you've seen what it's like. If Odin wants to consult the Oracle, then he'll just have to do it the hard way.'

There was a silence as Maddy stared at the firepit and Loki's breathing returned to normal. Then she stood up cautiously. She could feel the next eruption preparing itself; beneath her feet she sensed rather than heard the ripping of fiery seams under enormous pressure.

'What are you doing?' Loki said. 'Didn't you hear what I just told you?'

Maddy stepped up to the firepit. Beneath her, it gargled molten fire. Loki followed, uneasy now, but hiding it well – except for his colours, which betrayed his anxiety and his fatigue. Whatever he had done to the Whisperer, it had already robbed him of much of his glam – an advantage Maddy intended to use.

Now she was standing at the edge of the pit.

'Watch your step,' said Loki casually, 'unless you care for a Netherworld hotfoot.'

'Just a second,' she said, looking down into the fiery throat. The pit was very close to venting. Maddy could smell the burnt-laundry fume; she could feel the fine hairs in her nose begin to crackle. Her eyes stung; her hands were trembling as she too formed the runeshape *Yr*.

'Maddy, be careful,' Loki said.

At the bottom of the pit hot air began to roar as the subterranean river gushed out into the flow of boiling rock. In a second, steam would obscure the pit; then, a second later, the column of flaming gas and ash would erupt.

Maddy just hoped she had timed it right.

Now she was balanced on the very edge of the firepit. The stones beneath her feet were slick with sulphur and the glassy residue of many, many ventings. She tried to recall how Loki had done it – balancing on the rim like a dancer on a rope; his hands shuffling runes so fast that Maddy could hardly see them before they sank into the cloud at his feet.

He was right behind her now; her skin prickled at his closeness, but she did not dare turn – he must not see what she was planning. Inside the pit, the furnace glow brightened from orange to yellow, from yellow to almost white, and as the power began to build, Maddy turned the full force of her concentration on the Whisperer.

If you call it, it will come to you.

She felt it, heard it in her mind –

(?)

And now she called it, not in words, but in glam – what Loki had called the language of Chaos. It was no language she had ever learned; and yet she could feel it linking her with the Whisperer, joining with it like notes in a long-lost chord.

At last she could see in the depths of the pit something like a cat's cradle of light, a complicated diagram in which many, many runes and signatures crossed and re-crossed in strands of increasing complexity.

A net, she thought, and for the second time she felt a response – a glimmer, a cry – from the object in the pit. A net just like the one Loki had used to trap his fish –

(!)

And it was a net that she meant to use against him. But

Loki's runes did not play fair; straining and twisting between her fingers. *Naudr*, the Binder; *Thuris*, the Thorn; *Tyr*, the Warrior; *Kaen*, Wildfire; *Logr*, Water; *Isa*, Ice.

Loki's runes; Loki's trap. Even as she drew them she could feel them moving, turning slyly out of alignment, waiting for her concentration to break.

'Maddy!' said Loki's voice behind her, and she needed no runes now to sense his fear. His hand brushed her shoulder; Maddy swayed, uncomfortably aware of the pit at her feet. *One push*, she thought . . .

She called out again to the thing in the fire and, with a cry that echoed across the cavern, wrenched the net with its catch of glamours up and towards her out of the pit.

It was just then that the geyser blew.

The steam, a great hot hammer of air, came punching out of the narrow gauge. For a second everything went white; the laundry smell filled the cave and Maddy was sheathed in a scalding cloak. But for that second Loki flinched back and at the very same time Maddy cast the net, not at the Whisperer in its fiery column, but directly behind her, in Loki's face.

He had no time to shield himself. The runes of the Elder Script flickered out – *Naudr*, *Thuris*, *Tyr* and *Ós* – *Hagall* and *Kaen*, *Isa* and *Úr*. The net fell, snaring Loki as neatly as any fish, and finally *Aesk*, Maddy's own rune, hurled the Trickster across the cavern as the fiery column burst free, showering them both with ash, sulphur and shards of volcanic glass.

The blast was greater than any thus far. It threw Maddy forward twenty feet, and she fell to her knees, half stunned. Behind her the geyser was reaching its climax: ash and cinders filled the air; flaming rocks fell all around her; something heavy crashed to the ground only yards from where she had been standing.

'Loki?' Maddy's voice resonated flatly against the seeping walls. Half blinded by the scalding steam, she lay behind a flat rock, gasping for breath. The unaccustomed working had all but exhausted her glam. If he were to attack right now, she wouldn't have much more than a cantrip to throw back at him.

'Loki?' she called.

There was no reply.

A minute later the blast had abated; now sulphurous fumes filled the cavern. Maddy risked a glance around; but in the sickly yellow mist there was nothing to be seen.

Then, as the mist cleared and the extent of the damage became apparent, Maddy realized why. The ceiling above them had partly collapsed. A mound of debris obscured the pit; one huge slab of rock, its near side studded with pieces of stalactite, lay atop the mound like a gauntleted fist.

And Loki?

And the Whisperer?

There was no sign of either in the ruined cavern.

4

It was a few minutes more before Maddy could stand. She did so shakily, brushing cinders out of her hair. Her vision was still cloudy from looking into the firepit; her face and hands were sore, like sunburn.

The aftershock was over now, and in its wake the cavern was eerily still. Dust trickled from the broken ceiling onto the giant mound of rocks and rubble, completely obliterating the end of the cavern where Loki and his net had been.

Congratulations, Maddy, said a dry voice inside her head. *Now you're a murderer.*

'No,' whispered Maddy, horrified.

She'd never intended to hurt him, of course. She'd only meant to keep him at bay, to hold him while she claimed the Whisperer. But everything had happened so *fast*. She'd had no time to measure her strength. And if now, by her fault, he was under there – smashed beneath that fist of rock . . .

And now it was not just the fumes from the pit that were making it hard for Maddy to breathe. The mound of stones, so like a barrow from the Elder Age, almost seemed to fill the cavern. Slowly, reluctantly, she moved towards it. A small part of her protested against all hope that Loki might be trapped but unhurt, and fitfully she began to turn over the smaller rocks, searching in vain for a scrap of sleeve, a boot, a shadow—

A signature.

That was it! Maddy could have kicked herself with frustration. Casting *Bjarkán* with a trembling hand, she

121

found his at once; that unmistakable wildfire trail. No two light-signatures are ever the same, and Loki's, like One-Eye's, was unusually complex and alive.

Alive!

A good tracker may tell the age of the wolf he hunts; whether it limps; how fast it was running and when it made its last kill. Maddy was not so skilled a tracker, but she spotted the fragments of the net and traces of the mindrune she had cast.

There had been tremendous power in that final rune; power enough to collapse the ceiling as Maddy dragged the Whisperer out of the pit. Pieces of *Aesk* still littered the floor, like shards from an exploded ginger-ale bottle, and here was where the rune had hit, pinning Loki like a moth as the ceiling collapsed on top of him.

But then . . .

There it was, against all hope, leading away from the mound of stone. Not a backtrail, not a fragment, but a signature, scrawled fleetingly in that characteristic lurid violet against the rock.

She guessed from its faintness that he had tried to hide; but either he was too weak to shield his colour-trail, or the falling rocks had taken up too much of his concentration, because there it was, unmistakably, leading towards the cavern mouth.

It was there at last that Maddy found him. He had fallen behind a block of stone; one arm was up to cover his face, his fingers still pronged into the runeshape of *Yr*, the Protector. He was very still, and there was blood – an alarming amount of it – on the rock behind him.

Maddy's heart did a slow roll. She knelt down, shaking, and held out a hand to touch his face. The blood, she saw, came from a narrow slash just above his eyebrow. A rock must have caught him as he ran, unless it was the fall that had knocked him unconscious. In any case, though, he was alive.

Relief made Maddy laugh aloud; then, hearing her voice rattle eerily across the ruined cavern, she thought better of it.

He was alive, she reminded herself – but as soon as he awoke, doubly dangerous. This was *his* place. Gods knew what resources he might have at his command. She needed to get out, and quickly.

She looked around. The cavern was still acrid with the stench of the firepit, but at least the air was cooler, now that the shower of debris had stopped. It had been a close shave, she saw now: a chunk of volcanic glass the size of a hog's head had flown through the air, missing her by inches, and now lay, still glowing, by her feet.

Thinking fast, Maddy assessed the situation. It looked bad: she had failed; she had lost the Whisperer; her strength was exhausted; and she was buried in the tunnels of World Below with miles and miles of passages and galleries between herself and the surface.

Still, she thought, it had been a good plan. It should have worked. For a second there had been a *contact* between them. The Whisperer should have answered her call. It almost had – but, as Crazy Nan used to say, *Almost never wins the race.*

Maddy looked around in desperation. What on earth was she to do now?

'Kill him,' said a voice behind her.

Startled, Maddy turned round.

'Go on. He deserves it.' It was a man's voice, dry and rather fussily disapproving, like Nat Parson in mid sermon. But there was no one in sight; around her the shadows swelled, red-tinged, as the firepit drew breath.

'Where are you?' she whispered.

'Just kill him,' said the voice again. 'Do the Worlds a favour. You'll never get a better chance.'

Maddy looked left and right, but saw no one.

Had she imagined it? Was she so addled by smoke and fumes? Somewhere at the back of her mind she was conscious of a small, persistent voice telling her to run; that the geyser was about to vent again, that she was already half poisoned from the firepit fumes and that unless she got out into breathable air she would collapse; but none of that seemed very important now. So much easier to ignore it; to close her eyes; to think of nothing.

'Stop that,' said the voice sharply. 'What are you, an imbecile? Look down, girl, look *down*!'

Maddy dropped her gaze.

'Lower.'

'But there's nothing—' began Maddy, then stopped short, her eyes widening as she finally saw – *really* saw – the thing that had crash-landed almost at her feet, still glowing from the heat of its fiery cradle.

'Ah, at last,' said the Whisperer in a weary tone. 'Now, if you can possibly bear a *little* more exertion, you might at least give that bastard a kick from me.'

5

As far as anyone knew, the passages that ran beneath Red Horse Hill had never once been mapped or counted. Even the Captain didn't know them all, for although he had used the place for centuries as a bolt hole and rallying place for goblins, he was not the architect of the Hill, nor the custodian of all its secrets.

Rumour had it that if you went deep enough, you could follow the Strond right down into Netherworld and the Black Fortress that straddled the river Dream, but no one knew that for sure – except possibly the Captain, and any goblin foolish enough to ask *him* for particulars deserved everything he got.

Sugar-and-Sack was no fool. But he was curious – perhaps more curious than was altogether safe – and he had seen a number of peculiar things, which he longed to try to investigate. It had begun with that girl who knew his true name, and her descent into regions where no goblin ventured, but into which the Captain sometimes disappeared, returning in a foul temper and reeking of smoke.

Next had come the developments in World Above. In usual circumstances Sugar would have taken little interest in these. Goblins don't like trouble, unless they are causing it themselves, and the frequent comings and goings on Red Horse Hill – the posses and the parson stirring up the neighbourhood – would normally have kept him safely underground.

But this time he sensed that there was something more afoot than the usual tension between Folk and Faërie. There had been rumours – and a horseman, riding hard on a laden steed, galloping back to the Hindarfell. There was a scent too, like incense and burned stubble; and half an hour ago the Captain had returned from one of his forays with a rag around his head and a nasty gleam in his eye, had put his guard on full alert and had shut himself up in his private quarters, snapping at any goblin who came close.

Sugar knew better than to get in his way. He had done what he always did in similar circumstances: had settled himself in an out-of-the-way place and prepared to acquaint himself with a plum cake, a ripe cheese and a small barrel of mule-kick brandy that he had stashed there several weeks before. He was just getting comfortable when the sound of voices reached him – and one of them, he knew at once, was Maddy's.

His duty was plain – to stop the girl. Those were his orders, clear as kennet, orders from the Captain himself – and the Captain had a way of making himself very unpleasant if his orders were not obeyed.

On the other hand, he told himself, anyone who could make Loki nervous would be more than a match for Sugar-and-Sack. The better part of valour, in this case, would be to lie low and finish the brandy.

It was a good plan; and it would have worked just fine, thought Sugar later, if it hadn't been for his dratted curiosity. The same that had led him to the girl in the first place; and now it got the better of him once again as he crept along in the shadows, trying to hear what the voices were saying.

An argument seemed to be in progress.

It had not taken long for Maddy to discover that the Whisperer was not at all grateful for its release. In the hours following their escape from the cavern, and carrying the object in a sling made from her jacket, she had many opportunities to curse herself for having succeeded so well.

One-Eye had been right, she thought. The Whisperer

looked and felt just like a lump of rock. A chunk of some glassy volcanic stuff – obsidian, perhaps, or some kind of quartz – but looking closer she could see its face: a craggy nose; a downturned mouth; eyes that gleamed with mean intelligence.

And as for its personality . . . It was like dealing with a bad-tempered old man. Nothing pleased it. Not their pace, which was too slow, but which became uncomfortable when Maddy speeded up; nor Maddy's conversation, nor her silence, and especially not the fact that they were going to join One-Eye.

'That war-crow?' said the Whisperer. 'He doesn't own me, never did. Thinks he's still the General. Thinks he can just start giving orders again.'

Maddy, who by now had heard this several times before, said nothing. Instead she tried to concentrate on the path, which was rocky, and filled with holes.

'Arrogant as ever. Who does he think he is, eh? Allfather my—'

'I suppose you'd rather I'd left you in the firepit,' said Maddy under her breath.

'What? Speak up!'

'You heard.'

'Now listen to me,' said the Whisperer. 'I don't think you know what you're dealing with here. I'm not just a rock, you know. In the wrong hands I could explode like a grenade.'

Maddy ignored it and kept on walking. It was hard going. The Whisperer was heavy and awkward to carry, and every time she thought of resting she imagined Loki – angry, recovered, and out for revenge – running up the passage after her. She had done what she could to hide her trail, crossing it at intervals with the runesign *Yr*, or doubling back on her own tracks. She hoped it would be enough to delay or lose him; but she couldn't know for sure.

The Whisperer had not been slow to deplore her compassion. 'You should have killed him when you had the chance,' it complained for the twentieth time. 'He was helpless, unconscious – completely at our mercy. Failing that, you could have left him, and the fumes would probably have finished him off. But what do you do? You *save* him. You drag him into the clean air. You tie a rag around his head. You practically tuck him into *bed*, for gods' sakes – what next, a glass of milk and a runny egg?'

'Oh, give it a rest,' said Maddy crossly.

'You'll regret it,' said the Whisperer. 'He's going to bring us nothing but trouble.'

To give the thing some credit, she thought, it had just cause to resent the Trickster. As they moved towards World Above, it treated Maddy to a centuries-long catalogue of grievances against Loki; beginning with his adoption into Asgard and the havoc he had wrought there, and culminating in his reappearance, some hundred years after Ragnarók, and in the most unlikely place – the catacombs of the Universal City in distant World's End.

'What was he doing there? I don't know. Up to no good – that goes without saying – and weak from his reversed glam. But just as tricky as ever, damn him, and he must have known I'd be somewhere near by—'

'Known?' said Maddy.

'Yes, of course.' The Whisperer hissed. 'There I was, peace at last, sleeping away the centuries, and what does he do? He wakes me, the bastard.'

'But how could he know where you'd be?'

It gave a pulse of angry light. 'Well, given that I'm not what you'd call independently mobile nowadays, I suppose he just searched among the ruins until—'

'Ruins of what?' Maddy said.

'Well, Asgard, of course,' snapped the Whisperer.

Maddy stared. 'Asgard?' she said. Of course she knew that the Sky Citadel had fallen at Ragnarók. And she had heard so many stories about the place that she almost felt she'd seen it herself, with its golden halls and its rainbow bridge that spanned the sky.

The Whisperer laughed. 'What? Didn't Odin tell you? The far side of that bridge was at World's End. The Folk never knew about that, of course. They couldn't cross it, only ever saw it when it was raining and sunny at the same time, and even then they thought it was a natural phenomenon, due to extraordinary weather conditions. But Dogstar knew – that's Loki, to you – and he found me and brought me to this place, a place at the very centre of the Worlds, a place where lines of great power converge, where he bound me with runes and trickery, and swore he'd release me – if I gave him what he wanted.'

'I knew it,' said Maddy. 'But what did he want?'

Once more the Whisperer hissed to itself. 'He wanted his true Aspect back. He wanted his rune unreversed. Failing that, he wanted to use me, to sell me to either the Æsir or the Vanir in exchange for his miserable skin. But he had done his job too well. He couldn't get me out of the pit. The forces that imprisoned me – forces from Dream and Death and beyond – held me fast, and all he could do was stand guard over me, and hope and pray that I never escaped. And so it has been for centuries' – the Whisperer gave its dry laugh – 'and if that doesn't give me a right to revenge, then this New Age of yours is even more pathetic than I thought it was.'

By this time they had reached the upper levels, and Maddy could see increasing signs of goblin activity. Their colours gleamed across her path; their footprints scuffed the red earth floor. When she found she could *hear* them too, she stopped.

This was the most dangerous part. From here on there

would be no place to hide. The long climb to the upper level would leave her visible on the rock stairway for a dangerous length of time. But she knew no other way out; all other paths led into the warren of storage and treasure rooms that honeycombed the Hill; and below there was the river, a crashing darkness in which lay no hope.

'What have we stopped for?' demanded the Whisperer.

'Quiet,' said Maddy. 'I'm thinking.'

'Lost, are you? I should have known.'

'I'm not lost,' said Maddy, annoyed. 'It's just that—'

'Told you you should have killed him,' it said. 'If I were him, I'd get back before us, set up an ambush, have posses of goblins at every corner and—'

'Well, what do *you* suggest?' she snapped.

'*I* suggest you should have killed him.'

'Well, that's a lot of use,' she said. 'I thought you were an oracle. Aren't you supposed to know the future, or something?'

The Whisperer glowed in open contempt. 'Listen to me, girl. Gods have paid – and dearly – for my prophecy. The General gave me his eye, you know – but that was a long time ago, and he got a bargain. As for you—'

'I'm *not* giving you an eye—' said Maddy at once.

'Gods alive, girl. What would I want with that?'

'Then what is it you *do* want?'

The Whisperer glowed brighter still. 'Listen,' it said. 'I like you, girl. I like you and I want to help. But you'll have to listen to me now. Listen, and take notice. Your old friend One-Eye has systematically lied to you to bring you to this point. Over the past seven years he has fed you a careful diet of half-truths and deceptions, all the more heinous for *what you are—*'

'What d'you mean, *what I am?*'

The Whisperer glowed brighter than ever, and now Maddy could see sparks of runelight trapped like fireflies within the volcanic glass. They danced, beguiling, and Maddy's head began to feel pleasantly befuddled, as if she had drunk warm spiced ale. It was a charm, she told herself; and she shook aside the pleasant feeling and pronged *Yr* with her fingers at the Whisperer, which continued to glow – in smugness, she thought – as if it had made some rather clever point.

'Stop that,' she said.

'Merely a demonstration,' said the Whisperer. 'I speak as I must, and cannot be silent. That rune of yours is strong, you know. I predicted such runes before Ragnarók. I imagine that's why One-Eye sent you. Didn't want to risk his own skin.'

For a moment Maddy said nothing. She was cautious of the Whisperer; and yet it confirmed some of what Loki had said. Loki, of course, was not to be trusted; but the Oracle . . .

Could an Oracle lie? she thought.

'He means to start a war,' it said. 'A second Tribulation, to wipe out the Order once and for all. Thousands will die at a single word.'

'Is this a prophecy?' Maddy said.

'I speak as I must, and cannot be silent.'

'What does that mean?'

'I speak as I must—'

'All right, all right. What else do you see?' Now Maddy's heart was beating fast; behind the Whisperer's rocky face, lights and colours danced and spun.

'I see an army poised for battle. I see a General standing alone. I see a traitor at the gate. I see a sacrifice.'

'Couldn't you be a little less vague?'

'I speak as I must, and cannot be silent. The dead will awake from the halls of Hel. And the Nameless shall rise, and Nine Worlds be lost, unless the Seven Sleepers wake, and the Thunderer freed from Netherworld . . .'

'Go on!' said Maddy.

But the Whisperer's colours had suddenly dimmed, and it almost looked like a rock again. And now Maddy was conscious of something nearby; a furtive movement in the shadows, a tiny crunch of pebbles on the floor. She spoke a sharp cantrip – *Nyd byth nearu* – locked her hands together to form the runeshape *Naudr*; then reached into the gloom and dragged out a diminutive figure, furry-eared and golden-eyed and covered in mail from head to foot.

'You again!' she said incredulously.

Sugar's curiosity had finally got the better of him.

'Kill it,' said the Whisperer.

Maddy was looking down at the dazed goblin. 'Spying, were you?'

'Kill it,' repeated the Whisperer. 'Don't let it get away.'

'I won't,' said Maddy. 'Will you stop asking me to kill people? I know this goblin,' she went on. 'He's the one who guided me.'

The Whisperer made a sound of exasperation. 'What does it matter? Do you want it to report us?'

Sugar was squinting cautiously at Maddy. 'Report what?' he said. 'I don't know nowt, and I don't *want* to know. In fact,' he went on in sudden inspiration, 'I think I've lost me memory – can't recall a thing, kennet. So there's no call for you to be worrit about what I've heard – you can be on yer way and I'll just lie here quietly—'

'Oh, please,' said the Whisperer. 'It heard everything.'

Sugar assumed an expression of hurt astonishment.

'I know,' said Maddy.

'Well then? We have no choice. The minute it gets the chance, it will report to its master. Why don't you just kill it, there's a good girl, and—'

'Be quiet,' said Maddy. 'I'm not killing anyone.'

'Spoken like a lady, miss,' said Sugar with relief. 'You don't want to listen to *that* nasty thing. You just get on back nice and safe to the Horse's Eye. No need to be staying here any longer than you have to, kennet?'

'Shut up, Sugar. You're going to lead us back to World Above.'

'*What?*' snapped the Whisperer.

133

'Well, obviously we can't leave him here, and we need to find a safe way out of the Hill. So I thought—'

'Were you listening to *anything* I just said?'

'Well . . .' said Maddy.

'I happen to have just made a major prophecy,' said the Whisperer. 'Have you any idea how privileged you are? Four hundred years in that blasted firepit, with Dogstar at me every day, and I never gave him so much as a syllable.'

'But aren't you supposed to be telling One-Eye all this?'

The Whisperer made a sound very like a snort. 'Look what happened last time,' it said. 'The idiot got himself killed.'

It was just then that they heard the sound. A distant pounding directly overhead, too regular to be accidental, which sent shock waves through the hollow Hill that made the rock walls tremble.

Boom-boom-boom.

Boom-boom-boom.

'What's that?' said Maddy.

'Trouble,' said the Whisperer.

To Maddy it sounded like cannonfire; to Sugar, like the Tunnel Folk at work. Some kind of mining, or digging, perhaps; and now they could hear the sound of falling grit as it filtered down onto the stairway from the ceiling far above.

'What is it, Sugar?'

Sugar gave one of his whole-body shrugs. 'Sounds to me like the Horse's Eye,' he said. 'P'raps it's your lot at it again. Bin a lot of bloody noise among the Folk recently.'

Maddy wondered how long she had spent underground. A day? Two days? 'But we have to get out. Can't we bypass Red Horse Hill?'

'You can, miss, but it's a long way round, nearly as far as the Sleepers, and—'

'Good. It'll be safe, then.'

Safe? thought Sugar. *Safe?* The idea of *safety* and *Sleepers* in the same sentence – even in the same paragraph – made him want to whimper. But there was no denying the hammering sound, and now his sharp ears could make out other sounds too: the sounds of heavy horses, wheels and the occasional clap of metal against metal . . .

'Uh-oh,' said Sugar.

'What?'

'I think they're tryin' to get inside.' His voice was incredulous; in five hundred years of siege (as he saw it) the Folk had never managed to do so much as crack open the front door to World Below, and here they were actually *pounding* their way into the rock.

'The Captain's not goin' to like this,' he said. 'He's not going to bloody like this at all.'

7

In a corner of Little Bear Wood, Loki's head was still aching. Wildfire his name, and wildfire his temper, and in World Below he had given it rein, cursing in his many tongues and breaking a number of small, valuable objects that just happened to be lying around.

He had blundered, that he knew. He had misjudged Maddy not once, which was forgivable, but twice, which was not; he had been careless and complacent; he had been tricked – and by a girl! – and worst of all, of course, he had let her get away with the Whisperer.

The Whisperer. That thrice-damned bauble. It was his pursuit of the Oracle, and not his fear of the Folk on the Hill, that had brought him out of his stronghold, though now he was here, watching the Hill from a suitable tree, he was unsettled to see the numbers of people gathered around the Horse's Eye.

There was the constable; the mayor in his official hat; several hundred men and women, armed with pitchforks and hoes (How rustic, thought Loki); a clutch of assorted brats; some ox-drawn digging machines; and the parson, of course, very smart in his ceremonial robes, with his prentice beside him, riding a white horse and reading aloud from the Book of Tribulation.

All this in itself was not so unusual. Every once in a while there was unrest among the Folk; often after a bad harvest, a cattle plague, or a bout of the cholera. The Faërie tended to get the blame for anything that went wrong, and over the years their legend had built, so that now most of the villagers believed – as Nat Parson did – that the Hill was the abode of demons.

Loki had never discouraged this. On the whole, it was fear that kept people away, and when they did march against him (once in every twenty years or so), waving flags and relics, swearing to burn out the vermin once and for all, they rarely stayed long. A couple of days – and a gaudy glamour or two – was usually enough to cool their evangelism. And besides, the Eye was securely shut. Sealed by runes, it was surely proof against any attempt at entry by the Folk.

Still, this time he could not help feeling a little uneasy. The digging machines were a new development; and in all his years under the Hill he had never seen such a large and well-organized gathering. Something had happened to excite them thus. A raid, perhaps? Some trick carried out by the goblins in his absence? Too late he told himself that he should have paid more attention to what was going on in World Above. The parson, especially, should have been watched. But, as always, there had been the Whisperer to deal with. The thing seemed to have boundless energies, and over the years most of Loki's strength had gone into keeping it subdued. Then Maddy had arrived; and all his attention had suddenly turned towards her.

This – this almighty shambles – was the result.

Loki sighed. Of all the times to lose the Whisperer, this was perhaps the worst. He was not unduly afraid of the Folk. His glam might be reversed, but that didn't make him helpless. Even the machines were not much of a threat; it would take them weeks – maybe months – to reach him.

What he *did* fear, though, was their fanaticism. Left alone, it would burn itself out; but at the right time, and with the right kind of leader – a leader who awakened it, nurtured it, fanned it, fed it on a diet of prayer and Tribulation . . .

He had heard the tales, of course. He employed an efficient network of spies from his stronghold in World Below, and over the past few hundred years the word from

World's End had been getting stronger. Word of the Order, followers of the Nameless, of the conflict building between Folk and Fiery, and of the last, the greatest Cleansing; the holy war that would sweep the Fiery from the faces of all the Worlds.

In World's End, the rumours said, there were cathedrals tall as mountains, large as cities, where the Examiners held court, and their prentices copied out endless invocations on scroll after scroll of illuminated parchment.

In World's End, Order reigned; bad blood had already been mostly erased, and goblins and other vermin were dealt with efficiently and without mercy. In World's End, if a sheep or a cow was born with a ruinmark, then the whole herd was swiftly destroyed, and if – Laws have mercy – it was a human child that bore the mark, then that child would be taken away and given into the guardianship of the Examiners, never to be heard of again.

There were other tales too of hills and barrows once given over to the old gods, now emptied of their original occupants and made holy once again in preparation for the Great Cleansing. And there were other, darker tales of demons caught and bound by the power of the Word; demons who were dragged, screaming, to the scaffold and the pyre; demons who looked like men and women but were in fact the servants of the enemy, and therefore had no souls to save.

In World's End Prayer was compulsory; Sundays were fallow; Mass was twice daily and anyone refusing to attend – or indeed exhibiting unnatural behaviour of any sort – was likely to face Examination and Cleansing if they failed to renounce their ways.

Of course, thought Loki, that was all a very long way from the valley of the sleepy Strond. But his many informants spoke ever more loudly of the coming of the Examiners; and it was whispered on the Roads and reported in World Below that even the Ridings had become infected by rumour and tales.

Tales of the *Word*, that power given only to the highest rank of priests (though Loki could recognize a cantrip sure enough, and as far as he was concerned, their incantations were just cantrips under a new coat of paint). Tales of the Nameless, who, according to the Book of Tribulation, rose from the dead at the End of the World, and will come again at the hour of need to save the righteous and strike down the blasphemers.

Loki was in no doubt that he counted as one of the blasphemers. Reviled by the new gods as a demon, loathed by the old gods as a traitor, his position had never been good. But now he had lost the Whisperer – the single ace in an indifferent hand – without which he would have nothing to bargain with when the time of reckoning came.

He had to get it back, he thought, before it reached the General. The Oracle would have guessed that, of course; and Maddy would be on her guard. Still, he thought, he was not beaten yet. He knew all the exits to Red Horse Hill, and from his hiding place in the wood he could watch out for the fugitives unobserved. In World Below, without knowing their destination, he might lose them among the thousands of tunnels that lined the Hill; but here, in World Above, Maddy's colours and those of the Whisperer would shine out like beacons for miles around. True, so did his own colours; but still, it was worth the risk, he thought. Besides, at the first sign of danger he could open the doorway under the Hill and be safe underground in a matter of seconds.

Loki's sharp eyes travelled all around the valley, from Red Horse Hill to Farnley Tyas, to Forge's Post and Fettlefields and even as far as the Hindarfell, where distant smoke from a hayrick or a cook-fire smudged the horizon into a haze. There was as yet no trace of a signature, but he felt sure

Maddy would show herself soon. He watched and waited, taking his time – it had been decades since he'd last ventured into World Above, and in spite of the urgency of his task he could not help but take pleasure in the feel of the sun and the blue of the sky.

It had been a good falltime; but the season was almost done, and soon would come the long, bleak winter. He could smell it: the wild geese had flown; the fields were bare after that busy Harvestmonth, and the stubble burned in time for the next seeding. Wherever Maddy and Odin were planning to meet, they would surely not venture out of the valley at such a time. So far it was still warm in the afternoon sun, but there was a sharp edge to the air that would soon turn to ice, and a long, slow fivemonth before spring's awakening.

Awakening! The thought came to Loki with sudden certainty, and he froze, his eyes fixing on the hazy sky, the distant pass and the seven peaks that guarded the valley. There were tales about those peaks, he knew. He had spread many of them himself in the hope of discouraging attention from the glacial halls under those mountains, and from the seven deadly inhabitants that slumbered beneath the ancient stone.

The Sleepers.

'No. They wouldn't *dare*.'

In his alarm he spoke aloud, and birds flew cackling out of the scrub at the sound of his voice. Loki scarcely heard them. Already he was sliding down the tree trunk, sending leaves and fragments of bark showering onto the forest floor. Surely, he thought, they wouldn't dare! The General himself had never dared – after Ragnarók, Odin could no longer assume the Sleepers were his to command.

Unless he knew something that Loki did not. Some new rumour; some warning sign, some omen that his spies had failed to read. Perhaps, at last, Odin *had* dared.

Loki's mind raced furiously. If the Sleepers were awake, he thought, then surely he would have known by now. Their presence would have launched echoes and alarms throughout World Below. No reason to panic just yet, then. The General was above all a tactician, and he would not risk unleashing the Sleepers without first ensuring his absolute authority.

But with the Whisperer in his hands . . .

A distant shudder ran through the ground. It must have been the digging machines – though for a second Loki had been almost sure that he sensed something else; a convulsion that passed over the skin of the valley like a tremor on the skin of an old dog.

He shivered.

Surely not! There must still be time . . .

If the Sleepers awoke, he was as good as dead.

Unless he recovered the Whisperer . . .

Now Loki's mind raced furiously. If Maddy was heading for the Sleepers, he thought, then the quickest way was underground. It might take her four hours to reach the place – that gave her quite a lead on him – but Loki knew World Below better than anyone. He had short cuts through the Hill that no one else knew and, with luck, perhaps he could still cut her off. If not, then at least he could be sure that Odin would not have ventured underground. So the General would be travelling overland towards the mountains, which gave him a journey of twice as long – and over some rather rough terrain. Which left Maddy and the Whisperer alone.

Loki grinned. In a fair fight he knew he had no chance; but Loki was not accustomed to fighting fair, and had no intention of starting now.

Well, then –

With a flick of the fingers he cast *Yr* at the ground and prepared to re-enter World Below.

Nothing happened.

The door that should have slipped open at his command remained sealed.

Loki cast again, frowning a little.

Still the doorway declined to reveal itself.

Loki cast *Thuris*, then *Logr*, Water, and finally *Úr*, the Mighty Ox, a rune of brute force, which was his equivalent of kicking the door hard in his impatience.

Nothing worked. The door stayed shut. Loki sat down on the forest floor, angry, puzzled and breathing hard. He had flung those runes with all his glam. Even if the door had been magically sealed, surely *something* should have happened.

It was shielded, then, whatever it was. He cast *Bjarkán* as hard as he could.

Still there was nothing. Not a gleam, not a twinkle. The door was not just sealed; it was as if it had never been there.

That shudder, he thought. He'd taken it for the work of those digging machines. Perhaps it was; but now that he thought about it more carefully, he realized he'd made a mistake. That was the echo of powerful glam – a single working, likely as not – and World Below had shifted accordingly, going into total lockdown against a potential intruder.

He tried to think what kind of assault might have triggered such a response.

Only one thing came to mind.

Now he began to feel afraid. He was locked out of World Below, alone and with enemies on either side. Time was short, the Sleepers might already be awake, and every second lost brought Maddy and One-Eye closer together. The solution was a dangerous one, but he didn't see that he had a choice. He would have to go after them overland.

He uttered a cantrip, cast *Kaen* and *Raedo*, and if anyone had been there to witness it, they would have been amazed to see the young man with the scarred lips and the harried expression dwindle, shrink, shed his clothes and become a small brown bird of prey which looked around for a second or two with bright, un-birdlike eyes before taking wing, circling the Hill twice in a widening arc and soaring away into the thermals and off towards the Seven Sleepers.

Anyone with the truesight, of course, would not have been fooled for a minute. That violet trail was far too distinctive.

8

Nat Parson was enjoying himself. It wasn't just the robes, or the ceremony, or the knowledge that everyone was watching him, majestic on his white horse, with Adam Scattergood standing beside him with the incense pot in one hand and a fat church candle in the other. It wasn't the close attention of the visitor from World's End, who watched him (with admiration, Nat thought) from his position in the Eye of the Horse. It wasn't the noble sound of his own voice as it rolled over the Hill, or the roar of the digging machines, or the smoke from the bonfires, or the Fair Day firecrackers that popped and flashed. It wasn't even the fact that that tiresome girl was for it at last – her and the Outlander too. No, all these things were pleasing, but Nat Parson's happiness ran deeper than that.

Of course, he'd always known he was destined for greatness. His wife Ethelberta had seen it too – in fact it had been her idea to embark on that long and dangerous pilgrimage to World's End, and his subsequent awakening to the stern duties of the Faith.

Oh, there was no denying that he had been dazzled by the sophistication of the Universal City: its abbeys and cathedrals; its solemn passageways; its laws. Nat Parson had always respected the Law – what there was of it in Malbry – but World's End had opened his eyes at last. For the first time he had experienced perfect Order; an Order imposed by an all-powerful clergy in a world where to be a priest – even a country parson – was to command hitherto unimaginable authority, respect and fear.

And Nat had discovered that he *liked* to command

authority. He had returned to Malbry with a craving for more, and for ten years following his return, through sermons of increasing violence and dire warnings of terrors to come, he had built up a growing clique of admirers, devotees, worshippers and prentices, in the secret hope that one day he might be called upon in the fight against Disorder.

But Malbry was a quiet place, and its ways were lax and sleepy. Common crime was infrequent enough; but *mortal* crime – the kind that would enable him to appeal to the bishop, even the Order itself – was almost unheard of.

Only once had he exercised this authority, when a black-and-white sow had been convicted of unnatural acts – but his superiors had taken a dim view of the matter, and Nat's face had been red as beet when he had read the reply from Torval Bishop from over the pass.

Torval, of course, was a Ridings man, and took every opportunity to sneer at his neighbour. That rankled; and ever since, Nat Parson had been on the lookout for a way to settle the score.

If Maddy Smith had been born a few years later, he often told himself, then his prayers might well have been answered. But Maddy had been four years old when Nat returned from World's End, and although it might have been possible to take a newborn child into custody, he knew better than to try it then, just as he sensed that World's End Law would have to be adapted to suit the needs of his parishioners, unless he wanted trouble from the likes of Torval Bishop.

Still, he'd kept his eye on the Smith girl, and a good thing too – this present matter was far too serious for Torval to dismiss, and it had been with a feeling of long-delayed satisfaction that Nat had received the visitor from World's End.

That had been luck indeed for Nat. That an Examiner from World's End should agree to investigate his little parish was cause enough for excitement. But by chance, for that same Examiner (on official business in the Ridings) to have been within only a single day's ride of the Hindarfell pass – well, that was beyond anything Nat could have hoped for. It meant that instead of waiting weeks or months for an official to ride over from World's End, the Examiner had been able to reach Malbry in only forty-eight hours. It also meant that Torval Bishop could not interfere, however much he wanted to, and that in itself was enough to fill Nat Parson's heart with a righteous glow.

The Examiner had had a number of complimentary things to say to Nat: had praised his devotion to duty; had shown a flattering interest in Nat's thoughts on Maddy Smith, the one-eyed peddler who had been her companion and the artefact they called the Whisperer – which Adam had heard them discussing on the hillside.

'And there has been no sign yet of the man or the girl?' the Examiner had said, scanning the Hill with his light-coloured eyes.

'Not a sign,' the parson had replied, 'but we'll find them all right. If we have to raze the Hill to the ground, we'll find them.'

The Examiner had given one of his rare smiles. 'I'm sure you will, brother,' he had said, and Nat had felt a little shiver of pleasure move up his spine.

Brother, he had thought. *You can count on me.*

Adam Scattergood was also enjoying himself. In the short time following Maddy's disappearance he had almost completely forgotten his humiliation at the Witch Girl's hands, and as the frenzy had spread, so had Adam's self-importance. For a young person of such limited imagination, Adam had found plenty of tales to tell, aided by Nat and by his own desire to sink Maddy once and for all.

The result had been far more than either of them could have hoped for. The tales had led to searches, alarums, a visit from the bishop, an Examiner – an *Examiner*, forsooth! – and now this wondrous combination of Fair Day and fox hunt, with himself as the youthful hero and man of the hour.

He shot a quick glance over his shoulder. There were four machines on the Hill now, giant screws made of wood and metal, each one drawn by two oxen. From four drill points, two at each end of the Horse, came forth clots of red clay. Around these points the animals' hooves had made such deep ruts in the earth that the outline of the Horse was barely visible, but even so Adam could see that the entrance was still as closely sealed as ever.

Boom-boom-boom!

Once more one of the drilling machines had hit stone. Still the oxen strained and lowed. Nat Parson raised his voice above the squeal of the machine. A minute passed, and then another. The oxen kept on moving, the drill gave half a turn, and then there was a *crack!* – and the mechanism spun free.

Two men went to the beasts' heads. Another climbed into the hole to inspect the damage to the drill. The three remaining machines went on, inexorably. Nat Parson seemed unmoved by the setback. The Examiner had warned him it might take time.

BOOK FOUR
The Word

Not kings, but historians rule the world.

Proverbs, 19

1

Deep in the tunnels of World Below, Maddy was hungry, tired and at the end of her patience. The passage was featureless; they had been walking for hours; and the steady shuffling lurch of her footsteps in the semi-darkness had begun to make her feel quite seasick.

Sugar had turned sullen as it became clear that he was expected to walk all the way to the Sleepers.

'How far now?' Maddy asked.

'Dunno,' he said dourly. 'Never go that far, do I? And you wouldn't, neither, if you knowed what was there.'

'Why don't you tell me?' said Maddy, containing an impulse to mindbolt the goblin through the nearest wall.

'How *can* it tell you?' the Whisperer said. 'It has nothing but legends and stories to go by. Devices used by the ignorant for the benefit of the foolish and the obfuscation of the credulous.'

Maddy sighed. 'I suppose *you're* not going to tell me either.'

'What,' it said, 'and spoil the surprise?'

And so they shuffled on, through a passageway that smelled sour and unused, for what seemed like leagues (though in fact it was only three or four miles). As they left the Hill, the pounding of the machines receded, although they all heard the peculiar clapping sound that came afterwards, and felt the cold tremor that shivered all along the granite layer above their heads.

Maddy stopped. 'What in Hel was that?'

It was the sound of glam, she thought. That unmistakable aftershock – but so much louder, so much stronger than any mere cantrip she had ever heard.

The Whisperer brightened like an eye.

'You know, don't you?' Maddy said.

'Oh, yes,' said the Whisperer.

'Then what *was* it?'

The Whisperer glowed complacently. 'That, my dear,' it said, 'was the Word.'

2

Nat Parson could barely contain his excitement. He'd heard of it, of course – everyone had – but he'd never actually seen it in action, and the result was more splendid and more terrible than even he could ever have hoped for.

It had taken more than an hour of prayer for the Examiner to prepare himself. By then the Hill had been trembling with it; a deep resonance that seemed to suck silently at Nat's eardrums. The villagers felt it; it raised their hackles, made them shiver, made them laugh without knowing why. Even the oxen felt it, lowing and straining at their harnesses as the machines went on grinding, and the Examiner, his pale face now sheened with sweat, his brow furrowed with exertion, his whole body trembling, stretched out his hand at last and spoke.

No one had actually heard what he said. The Word is inaudible, though everyone said afterwards that they had *felt* something. Some wept. Some screamed. Some seemed to hear the voices of people long dead. Some felt an ecstasy that seemed to them almost indecent – almost *uncanny*.

Loki had felt it from Little Bear Wood but, in his eagerness to seek out Maddy and the Whisperer, had mistaken the vibration – and the crack that followed – for the work of the digging machines on the Hill.

One-Eye had felt it as a sudden rush of memories. Memories of his son Balder, dead of a shaft of mistletoe; of his faithful wife Frigg; of his son Thor – all folk long lost, whose faces seldom returned to his thoughts.

On the Hill there had come a wakening shudder, making Nat's hair stand on end. Then a crack like a thunderbolt.

Laws, that power!

'Laws,' he said.

The Examiner was the only one who had seemed unimpressed by the procedure. In fact Nat thought he had looked almost *bored*, as if this were some everyday routine, somewhat fatiguing, but no more exciting than digging out a nest of weasels.

Then he had forgotten everything and, like the rest of them, had simply stared.

At the Examiner's feet there was now an irregular gash in the ground, some sixteen inches long and perhaps three inches wide. Its shape seemed vaguely significant – it was *Yr*, the Fundament, reversed – although Nat, who was not familiar with the Elder Script, did not recognize its importance.

'I have broken the first of nine locks,' said the Examiner in his flat voice. 'The remaining eight are as yet intact, but this reversal is the most important.'

'Why?' asked Adam, which pleased Nat because it was the question he had wanted to ask, but had not for fear of sounding ignorant.

The Examiner gave a small, impatient sigh, as if to deplore the ignorance of these rustic folk. 'See this mark – this ruinmark. This marks the entrance to the demon mound. Eight more of these locks remain to be broken before the machines can get inside.'

'How do you know there isn't another way into the Hill?' said Dorian Scattergood, who was standing close by.

'There are several,' said the Examiner. He seemed to be enjoying himself, though his voice remained dry and contemptuous. 'However, the enemy's first defence is to close the Hill against all intruders. To dig deep, as a rabbit does when it scents the hawk. And so now, as you see, the Hill has been sealed. No escape from within, no way in from without. However, as any hunter knows, it is sometimes useful to *fill in* smaller rabbit holes with earth before setting the snare at the main burrow's mouth. And when *this* burrow is opened at last' – the Examiner gave a chilly smile – 'then, Parson, we shall dig them out.'

'You mean the . . . Good Folk?' said a voice behind him. It was Crazy Nan from Forge's Post, perhaps the only person, thought Nat, who would have dared speak openly of the Faërie – and in front of an Examiner, no less.

'Call them by name, lady,' said the Examiner. 'What good can possibly come from this evil place? They are the Fiery, Children of the Fire, and they shall be put to the fire, every one, until the Order rules supreme, and the world is Cleansed of them for ever.'

A hum of approval went round the gathering – but Nat noticed that Crazy Nan did not join it, and that several others looked a little anxious. It was easy to see why, he thought; even in World's End such powers as the Examiner's were rare; honours conferred upon the highest and holiest rank of the clergy. Torval Bishop wouldn't have approved; to an oldster like Torval such things would have seemed dangerously close to *magic* – which was, of course, an abomination – but to Nat Parson, who had travelled and seen a little of the world, there could be no mistaking one for the other.

'Not *children*, though,' persisted Nan. 'I mean, goblins, Good Folk, that's all right, but we're not going to Cleanse any *real* children, are we?'

The Examiner sighed. 'The Children of the Fire are *not* children.'

'Oh.' Crazy Nan looked relieved. 'Because we've known Maddy Smith since she were a bairn, and she may be a little *wild* but—'

'Lady, that is for the Order to judge.'

'Oh, but *surely*—'

'Please, Miss Fey,' interrupted Nat. 'This isn't just common business any more.' His chest swelled a little. 'This is a matter of Law and Order.'

3

'The Word?' said Maddy. 'You mean it exists?'

'Of course it *exists*,' said the Whisperer. 'How else do you think the Æsir were defeated?'

Maddy had never read the Good Book, though she knew *Tribulation* and *Penitences* well enough from Nat Parson's Sunday sermons. Only Nat and a handful of prentices (all boys) were allowed to read any part of it, and even then, their reading was restricted to the so-called 'open' chapters of *Tribulation, Penitences, Laws, Listings, Meditations* and *Duties*.

But some chapters of the Book were locked, with silver clips that pinned the pages shut and the key kept on a fine chain around Nat Parson's neck. No sermons were ever preached from these Closed Chapters, as they were called, although Maddy knew some of their names from One-Eye.

There was the Book of Apothecaries, which dealt in medicine; the Book of Fabrications, in which were histories of the Elder Age; the Book of Apocalypse, which predicted the final Cleansing and, most importantly, the Book of Words, which listed all the permissible cantrips (or *canticles*, as the Order preferred to call them) to be used by the special elite when the time of Cleansing came.

But unlike the rest of the Closed Chapters, the Book of Words was sealed with a golden clip, and it was the only chapter of the Book that was closed even to the parson. He had no key to the golden lock, and although he had tried several times to open it, he had always failed.

In fact on the last occasion, when he had taken a leather-worker's awl to the golden lock, it had begun to *glow*

157

alarmingly and to get uncomfortably hot, after which Nat had been careful not to interfere with it again. He knew a charmed lock when he saw one (it was not so very different, in fact, to the runecharm the Smith girl had placed on the church door), and though he was disappointed that his superiors had shown so little trust in him, he knew better than to challenge their decision.

Maddy knew all this because when she was ten years old, Nat had asked her to remove the lock, saying that he had lost the key and needed to consult the Book for parish purposes.

Maddy had taken malicious pleasure in refusing. 'I thought *girls* weren't allowed to touch the Good Book,' she'd said modestly, watching him from beneath her lowered lashes.

This was true; Nat had said so only the week before, in a sermon in which he had denounced the bad blood, disorderly habits and weak intellect of females in general. After that, of course, he could not insist any further, and so the Book of Words had remained closed.

That had done nothing to endear Maddy to Nat; in fact, it was at that moment that the parson's dislike of Maddy had turned to hate, and he had begun to watch out for any sign that might justify an official Examination of Jed Smith's pert, clever daughter.

'But the parson doesn't have the Word,' Maddy said. 'Only an Examiner could have—' She stopped and stared at the Whisperer. 'Examiners?' she murmured in disbelief. 'He's called in the *Examiners*?'

Not kings, but historians rule the world. It was a proverb that One-Eye had often quoted, but even Maddy didn't quite realize how true it was.

The Order of Examiners had begun five hundred years ago, in the Department of Records in the great University of

World's End. It had to have happened there, of course. World's End was always the centre of things. It was the financial capital and the home of the king; the Parleyment was there, and the great cathedral of St Sepulchre, and rumour had it that in the vaults of the Department of Records there was a library of more than *ten thousand* books – poetry and science and histories and grimoires – to which only the *serious* scholars – Professors, Magisters and other senior staff – had access.

In those days the Examiners were simply officials of the university. They were entirely secular, and their Examination procedures consisted merely of written tests. But after Tribulation and the dark time that followed, the University had remained a symbol of Order. Gradually its influence had grown. Histories were written; conclusions drawn; dangerous books hidden away. And quietly, studiously, power had passed. Not to kings or warriors, but to the Department of Records, and the little clique of historians, academics and theologians who had appointed themselves the sole chroniclers of Tribulation.

The Good Book had been the culmination of their work: the story of the world and of its near-destruction by the forces of Chaos; a catalogue of world knowledge, science, wisdom and medicine; and a list of commandments to ensure that in future, whatever else happened, Order would always triumph.

And so the Order was begun. Not quite priests, not quite scholars, though they shared elements of both, over the years they had become increasingly powerful, and by the end of the first century following Tribulation they had extended their authority far beyond the University and into the world beyond. They controlled education, and ensured that literacy was restricted to the priesthood, its prentices and those of the Order. The word 'University' was expanded to make

'Universal City', so that as years passed, folk forgot that once there had been free access to books and to learning, and came to believe that things had always been as they were.

Since then the Order had grown and grown. The king was on the coins, but the Order told him how many to strike; they governed the Parleyment; the army and the police were under their jurisdiction. They were immensely wealthy; they had the power to seize land and possessions from anyone who broke the Law; and they were always recruiting new members. From the priesthood, for the most part; although they also took students from the age of thirteen, and these prentices – who gave up their names and renounced their families – often turned out to be the most zealous of all, working tirelessly up the ranks in the hope that one day they might be found worthy to receive the key to the Book of Words.

Everyone had heard tales; of how some prentice had denounced his father to the Order for failing to attend Prayers, or how some old woman had been Cleansed for decking a wishing well or keeping a cat.

World's End, of course, was used to it; but if anyone had suggested to Maddy Smith that a villager of Malbry – even one as vain and stupid as Nat Parson – would deliberately court the attention of the Examiners, she would never have believed them.

Two hours later, and at last the passageway had broadened out, a faint gleam reflecting dully against mica-spackled walls. The sour cellar smell that suffused the Hill no longer troubled Maddy at all. In fact now that she thought about it, the air seemed sweeter than before, although it was growing perceptibly colder.

'We're getting close to the Sleepers,' she said.

'Aye, miss,' said Sugar, who had been getting more and

more nervous as they approached their goal. 'Not long now. Well, that's my job done, then, and if I could just be on me way . . .'

But Maddy's eye had lit upon something, a point of luminescence too pale to be firelight, too bright to be a reflection on the stone. 'That's daylight,' she said, her face brightening.

Sugar considered putting her straight; then he shrugged and thought better of it.

'That's the Sleepers, miss,' he said in a low voice, and that was when his courage, already tried to breaking point, finally gave way. He could withstand many things; but enough was enough, and there comes a time for every goblin to take the better part of valour and run.

Sugar-and-Sack turned and ran.

Maddy ran towards the light, too excited to think either about Sugar's desertion or about the fact that it didn't really look like daylight at all. It was a cool and silvery light, like the pale edge of a summer pre-dawn. It was faint, but penetrating. Maddy could see that it touched the sides of the passageway with a milky gleam, picking out the fragments of mica in the rock and lighting the plumes of steam that came from Maddy's mouth in the cold air.

It was a cavern. She could see that now. The passage broadened, became funnel-shaped, and then opened out; and Maddy, who had considered herself accustomed to marvels after her time under the Hill, gave a long sigh of amazement.

The cavern was beyond size. Maddy had heard tales of the great cathedrals of World's End, cathedrals as big as cities with spires of glass, and in her imagination they might have been something like this. Even so, the sheer hugeness of the space almost defeated her. It was a bristling vastness of luminous blue ice, its ceiling vaulted in a thousand bewildering swirls and fantails, its height lifted unimaginably by glassy pillars as broad as barn doors.

It stretched out for ever – or so it first seemed – and the light seemed trapped within the ancient ice, a light that shone like a distillation of stars.

For a long time Maddy stared, breathless. The ceiling was open in part to the sky; a thin fragment of moon stood outlined against a patch of darkness. From the gaps in the vaulting, icicles fell, tumbling and plunging hundreds of feet to hang, crystalline, above her head. *If I threw a stone*, thought Maddy with a sudden chill, *or if I were to even raise my voice . . .*

But the icicles were the least of a thousand wonders that filled the cavernous hall. There were strands of filigree no thicker than a spider's web; there were flowers of glass with leaves of frozen gauze; there were sapphires and emeralds growing out of the walls; there were acres of floor smoother than marble, fit for a million dancing princesses.

And the *light*: it shone out from everywhere, clean and cold and pitiless. As her eyes adjusted, Maddy saw that it was made from *signatures*; thousands of them, it seemed, criss-crossing the rapturous air. Maddy had never, never in her life seen so many signatures.

Their brightness left her speechless. *Gods alive*, she thought, *One-Eye's is bright and Loki's brighter but this makes them look like candles in the sun.*

She had been moving, wide-eyed, bewildered, further into the cavern. Every step showed her new marvels. She could hardly breathe – hardly *think* – for wonderment. Then in front of her she saw something that momentarily eclipsed everything else: a raw-edged block of blue ice with thin columns at its four corners. Maddy peered closer – and gave a cry as she saw, embedded deep beneath the ice, something that could only be . . .

A face.

4

In the fields to the west of Little Bear Wood, Odin One-Eye was watching birds. One bird in particular, a small brown hawk, flying fast and low across the fields. Not in a hunting pattern, he thought – although there was surely plenty of prey. No, this hawk flew as if it sensed a predator; though there were surely no eagles this far from the mountains, and only an eagle would bring down a hawk.

A hawk, but what kind?

That was no bird.

He had *sensed* rather than *seen* it almost at once. Its movement, perhaps; or the speed of its course; or its colours scrawled across the sky – half obscured by the setting sun, but as familiar to One-Eye as his own.

Loki.

So the traitor had survived. It came as no great surprise to him – Loki had a habit of beating the odds, and that hawk had always been a favourite Aspect of his. But what in Hel's name was he doing here now? Loki, of all people, should have been fully aware of the recklessness of flaunting his colours in World Above. But here he was in broad daylight – and in too much of a hurry even to cover his tracks.

In the old days, of course, Odin could have brought down the bird with a single mindrune. Today, and at such a distance, he knew better than to try. Runes that had once been child's play to him now cost him an effort he could ill afford. But Loki was a child of Chaos; its harmonies were in his blood.

What could have forced him to leave the Hill? The Examiner and his invocations? Surely not. No single

Examiner could have flushed out the Trickster from his stronghold, and Loki wasn't the type to panic. Besides, why would he leave his base? And why, of all places, make for the Sleepers?

One-Eye left the fields by a gap in the hedge and, skirting the edge of Little Bear Wood, squinted after the fleeting hawk. The western road was completely deserted; the sun's rays shone low across the brindled land, sending his long shadow sprawling behind him. On the Hill a bonfire was lit: the folk of Malbry were celebrating.

Briefly One-Eye hesitated. He was reluctant to leave Red Horse Hill, where Maddy would surely look for him. But Loki's presence in World Above was much too disturbing to ignore.

He took out his bag of runestones and cast his fortune quickly, there on the side of the western road.

He drew *Ós*, the Æsir, reversed –

– crossed with *Hagall*, the Destroyer –

– with *Isa* and *Kaen* in opposition –

– and finally his own rune, *Raedo*, reversed, crossed with *Naudr*, the Binder, rune of the Underworld – rune of Death.

One-Eye, unlike Loki, had always been a natural with weapons. Even so, he could feel his glam weakening; it takes a great deal of power to use a mindsword, and his time was running short. Jan swiped at him again, hitting his right arm with sickening force; the blow that would have speared Jan went astray and hit Matt Law instead, a messy blow right in the midsection.

One-Eye followed up with another strike, this time spearing Jan through the ribs – a clean thrust, and One-Eye had time for a single thought – *You've killed him, you fool* – before *Tyr* guttered and died in his hand.

Then they were on him, seven men with staves, moving together like reapers in the corn.

A blow to the stomach doubled him up. Another to the head sent him sprawling across the western road. And as the blows fell – too many to count; far too many for the crooked fingerings of *Yr* and *Naudr* to disperse – One-Eye had time for one more thought – *This is what you get for helping the Folk* – before one final crashing blow fell across the back of his head and pain and darkness swallowed him whole.

5

Meanwhile Loki was not finding his task quite as straight-forward as he'd hoped. It had been many years since he had approached the Sleepers by this route, and by the time he reached the mountains, it was dark. Beneath him the slopes were blank and featureless in the starlight. A waning moon was rising; small clouds flirted across it from time to time, painting the sky silver.

He flew onto a spar of rock that jutted out above a broad belt of scree. Here he regained his Aspect and rested – his shift to hawk guise had stolen more of his glam than he had expected.

Above him the Sleepers were icebound and forbidding; below was scree and stark rock. Down in the foothills, narrow paths crisscrossed the scrubby brushland; thorn and sloe trees grew; wildcats had their lairs here and sometimes fed on the small brown goats that ran freely across the heather. A few huts had been built on the slopes of these foothills – mostly by goatherds – but as the land grew bare, even these few signs of habitation ceased.

He stood and looked up at the Sleepers. The entrance was maybe two hundred feet above him; a deep, narrow crevasse buried in snow. He'd been through once, but would not have chosen to take the same route again if there had been any other choice.

There was not; and now he stood shivering on his spar of rock and quickly considered his position. The great disadvantage of his type of shapeshifting was that he took nothing with him but his skin – no weapons, no food and, more importantly, no clothes. Already the bitter cold had begun to work on him; much more of it and it would finish him quick.

He thought of shifting to his fiery Aspect, but dismissed the idea almost at once. There was nothing to burn above the snowline; and besides, a fire on the mountain would attract far too much of the wrong sort of attention.

Of course, he could always fly up to the crevasse, sparing himself a long, exhausting struggle up into the icy regions. However, he was aware that his hawk guise made him vulnerable – for a hawk can speak no cantrips, and a hawk's claws are useless if fingerings are required. Loki did not relish the thought of flying blind – not to mention naked – into the Sleepers and whatever ambush might be waiting.

Well, whatever he did, it would have to be fast. He was too exposed out on the blank rock, his colours visible for miles. He might as well have written LOKI WAS HERE across the open mountainside.

And so he regained his bird form and flew to the nearest goatherd's hut. It was abandoned, but in it he managed to find some clothes – little more than rags, but they'd do – and skins to bind around his feet. The skins smelled of goat, and were a poor substitute for the boots he had left behind, but there was a sheepskin jacket, rough but warm, which should keep out the worst of the cold.

Thus attired, he began to climb. It was slow, but it was safe; and over the last five hundred years Loki had learned to value safety more than ever.

He had been climbing for nearly an hour when he met the cat. The moon had risen, scything over the frozen peaks and throwing every rock, every spur into sharp relief. He had passed the snowline. Now his feet crunched against the skirt of a glacier, which looked frilly white from a distance, but which closer inspection revealed to be a grim hardpack of snow, stones and ancient ice.

Loki was tired. He was also aching with cold; the skins and rags he had stolen from the goatherd's hut might have served him well enough on the lower slopes, but did little against the bitter cold of the glacier. He had tucked his hands into his armpits for warmth, but even so they ached viciously; his face was sore; his feet in their skin bindings had long since lost all sensation and he stumbled drunkenly across the crust of snow, hiding his trail as best he could.

Once more he considered reverting to his fiery Aspect, but the cold was already too intense. Shifting to his fire form would simply burn up his glam all the faster, leaving him helpless.

He needed rest. He needed warmth. He had already fallen half a dozen times, and found it harder on each occasion to struggle to his feet. At last he fell and could not stand up again, and he realized that he no longer had a choice: the possibility of his freezing to death by far surpassed the risk of his being seen.

He cast *Sól*, but clumsily, and winced at the pain in his frozen fingers. Shifting to hawk guise was no longer an option; his strength was gone, and he was down to his last cantrips. The rune lit up, but gave little heat.

Loki cursed and tried again. This time the warmth was more focused, a glowing ball the size of a small apple that shone against the dull snow. He held the fireball close, and little by little he felt the life return to his crippled hands. Pain came with it. Loki yelped: it felt like hot needles.

Perhaps it was this cry that alerted the cat, perhaps the glow; in any case it came, and it was *large* – five times larger than a common wildcat, and brindled brown as mountain stone. Its eyes were yellow and hungry; its claws soft-sheathed steel in the shaggy pads of its feet.

Further down the slopes, where prey was plentiful, it would most likely have given Loki a wide berth. But here on the glacier prey was scarce. This human – helpless, on his knees in the snow – seemed like a gift.

The cat moved closer. Loki, who could feel the sensation returning to his feet as well as his fingers, tried to stand up, then fell once more, cursing.

The cat moved closer still, wary of the fireball between Loki's hands, wondering in its dim fashion if this was a weapon that might harm it if it sprang. Loki did not see it and continued to curse as *Sól* sent its knives into his fingers.

He might be big, the cat thought, but he was slow; he was tired; and more importantly he was on the ground, where his size would be of no advantage to him.

All in all, it fancied its chances.

The cat had never attacked a human before. If it had, it would have gone for the face, and would most likely have killed him with a single bite. Instead it leaped onto Loki's back, caught him by the scruff of his neck and tried to roll him over.

He acted fast. Surprisingly fast for a human – though Loki was not *precisely* human, the cat sensed – and rather than try to grapple with his attacker, he hauled himself upright – ignoring the claws that gouged into his ribs – and deliberately flung himself as hard as he could onto his back.

For a second the cat was stunned. Its jaws loosened and Loki broke free, boosting himself away and onto his knees so that now he faced the creature head-to-head, his fire-green eyes reflecting its yellow ones, his teeth bared.

The cat squalled, a terrible, ratcheting sound of rage and frustration. It faced him, ready to spring if he made the smallest move. Such battles of will could last for hours among the cat's own kind, but it sensed that the human's strength would fail him before long.

Loki knew it too. Numbed as he was with cold, it was hard for him to judge the damage done by the cat's claws, but he could feel warmth flowing down his back, and knew he might collapse at any time. He had to act – and quickly.

Eyes still locked on those of the cat, he held out his hand. In it shone *Sól*, fading a little but still alight. Very gently Loki moved from his knees to the balls of his feet, so that now he was squatting on his haunches, the Sun rune outstretched. The cat squalled and bristled, ready to pounce.

But Loki pounced first. With an effort he sprang to his feet, and at the same time, gathering the last of his glamour, he flung *Sól* – now a white-hot firebrand – at the snarling creature.

The cat fled. Loki saw it go, a streak against the glacier's breadth, and heard its cry of defiance as it went. It did not go as far as he would have liked, however, but settled at a distance of about three hundred yards, where the edge of the glacier met a nest of rock.

Here it waited, immobile. It could smell blood – and that made it growl softly with frustrated hunger – but more importantly it could smell weakness. The human was wounded. At some point soon he would relax his guard.

And so it watched; and when Loki began once more to climb, slowly and laboriously, towards the dim blue cleft between the Sleepers, the cat climbed with him, keeping its distance but gradually closing as his steps faltered, his shoulders slumped, and at last he fell, headfirst and senseless, into the moonlit snow.

6

The face was buried deep, half obscured by tiny rosettes of white frost. But it was unmistakably a woman's face, white and remote beneath the ice.

'Who is she?' said Maddy at last. With her hands she had managed to clear some of the frost. Underneath, the ice was dark and clear, like lake water. Beneath it the woman lay, slim as a sword, hands crossed against her breast, her pale, cropped hair fanning out into ice crystals around her.

'See for yourself,' said the Whisperer.

Maddy cast *Bjarkán* with a hand that shook. The runelight seemed to pick out every gleam, every glamour, every rune carved against the surface of the ice block, with a radiance that hurt her eyes.

Through it she found she could see the woman clearly: her face was still and coldly beautiful, with the high cheekbones and full lips that were typical of the northern folk. She wore knee-high boots and a tunic, belted at the waist, and at her belt there hung a long white knife.

But the most startling thing was the woman's signature. It was a chilly, piercing blue, like the ice itself, and although it was sheathed tight around her body in a sleeping pattern it was unmistakably alive. Its gleam was only fractionally less than that of the mark on the woman's right thigh:

The runemark *Isa* – Ice.

Now Maddy could see the glamours that ringed the ice block; a complex chain of runes that strongly resembled the net in which Loki had imprisoned the Whisperer.

'So he told the truth,' said Maddy softly. 'There *are* more of us.'

She realized that she had been afraid to believe it. Now the joy of knowing that she was not alone made her want to scream like a savage.

She did not – remembering that ice cascade poised above her head – but she clenched her fists in fierce delight. And now she could see, further down the hall, more of the ice blocks, their pillars standing out like sentinels in the gleaming hall. Seven of them, all in a line, like four-poster beds, their columns festooned with dripping icicles, their coverlets of frost.

'Who are they?' said Maddy.

'The Sleepers,' said the Whisperer. 'Though not for long.'

Once more Maddy thought of the firepit hall. 'Did Loki do this?'

'No,' it said.

'Does One-Eye know?'

'Oh yes. He knows.'

'Then why didn't he tell *me*?'

'I'm an oracle,' said the Whisperer, 'not a bloody mind-reader.'

Once more Maddy looked at the ice woman. 'Who is she?' she said.

'Ask her,' said the Whisperer.

'How?'

'In the usual way.'

'You mean – wake her up?'

'Why not?' it said. 'You're going to do it eventually.'

Maddy was sorely tempted to try. She remembered the Whisperer's prophecy: how the Sleepers would awake, and Thor be freed from Netherworld – on the other hand she knew it to be devious, and she didn't like its superior tone.

'I'm not doing anything,' she said, 'unless you tell me who they are.'

'They are the Vanir,' the Whisperer said. 'Hidden here since Ragnarók. Surt's shadow had fallen across the Worlds; the Æsir had fallen, one by one. The Vanir, defeated, fell back and hid; and with the last of their glamours they created this half haven, half tomb, in the hope that one day they might be reawakened in the new world, the new Asgard.'

'The new Asgard?' Maddy said. 'What happened to *that*?'

'Prophecy isn't an exact science. It will happen eventually. Though maybe not for your friend One-Eye—'

Maddy gave it a sharp look. '*I see a General standing alone?*'

The Whisperer gave its chilly smile. 'So you *were* paying attention,' it said. 'It's nice to be appreciated. Now wake the Sleepers, there's a good girl, and we can get the rest of my prophecy under way . . .'

'Well . . .' She hesitated. 'I'll need to talk to One-Eye first.'

'In that case you may have a long wait,' said the Whisperer, and its colours glowed in the pattern Maddy had come to associate with smugness.

'Why?' she said. 'What's happened to him?'

So the Whisperer told her of One-Eye's arrest; of the fight with the possemen and of what had followed. There could be no doubt about it, said the Whisperer. It was attuned to the General; it knew his mind; felt every piece of glam he cast.

'He fought them,' it said, 'but they were too many, and he lost. If he were dead, I would have known. Therefore I suppose that they took him to whatever suitable place of imprisonment you may have in the village—'

'The roundhouse,' said Maddy.

'Most likely,' it said. 'And there, we must assume, whoever was using the Word back on the Hill will be more than eager to interrogate him.'

Maddy's eyes were wide with alarm. 'They won't hurt him, will they?'

'Is that a question?'

'Of course!' she said.

The Whisperer smirked. 'Then yes. They will. They will extract every piece of information he possesses, and when they have finished, they will kill him. And after they have killed him they will go after the rest of you. And they will not stop until every last one of you has been wiped out. I hope this addresses your query.'

'Oh,' said Maddy. There was a long pause. 'Is this a . . . professional opinion – or is it an actual prophecy?'

'Both,' said the Whisperer. 'Unless, of course, you do something about it.'

'But what can *I* do?' said Maddy in despair.

The Whisperer laughed, a dry, unpleasant sound. '*Do?*' it said. 'My dear, you'll have to wake the Sleepers.'

7

According to the Book of Meditations, there are nine Elementary States of Spiritual Bliss.

One: Prayer. Two: Abstinence. Three: Penitence. Four: Absolution. Five: Sacrifice. Six: Abnegation. Seven: Assessment. Eight: Arbitration. Nine: Enquiry.

By this definition Nat Parson had reached the seventh Elementary State, and was about to move on to the eighth. It felt good. So good, in fact, that he had begun to wonder if he might soon be permitted to tackle the Intermediary States – those of Examination and Judgement – for which he felt himself to be more than ready.

The Outlander was guilty – no doubt about that. Nat Parson had already Assessed him on more than a dozen counts of common crime – such as theft, vagrancy, corruption and vagabondage – but the real meat was on the *mortal* charges: attempted murder of an officer; conspiracy; conjuration; artifice; and, most promising of all, heresy.

Heresy. Now *that* would be something, Nat Parson thought. There hadn't been a charge of heresy in Malbry for over half a century. World's End was different – more civilized; more particular. Hangings were common in the Universal City. The Examiners were quick to spot heresy as soon as it reared its ugly head, and their tolerance for all things uncanny was short.

Odin One-Eye knew that, of course. He knew a great deal, in fact, that would have made the parson's jaw drop, though to Nat's frustration he had not spoken a word since his arrest.

Well, he would be *made* to talk, thought Nat savagely; and anyway, that ruinmark straddling the scarred socket of the Outlander's blind eye spoke for itself.

It had certainly spoken to the Examiner. If the business on the Hill had left him unmoved, the capture of the Outlander now saw him close to agitated. At first he had shown irritation at being called away from his place on the Hill, but as soon as he saw that ruinmark, and the man lounging insolently against the inner wall of the roundhouse, he lost much of his early aloofness.

'Who *is* this man?' he said in a strangled voice.

'A vagrant,' said Nat, pleased to have found something at last that impressed the World's Ender. Until then nothing had – not his own quick thinking, not the menace under Red Horse Hill, not even Ethelberta's cooking, which was acknowledged to be excellent as far as the Hindarfell and beyond.

In fact the previous night, when Ethelberta had gone to the trouble of cooking the Examiner a meal (and it was one of her best, Nat could have told him – spatchcocked quail and fried mushrooms and honey cakes with almonds), the Examiner had refused all nourishment but bread, bitter herbs and water, reminding both of them of the joys of Abstinence (the second Elementary State of Spiritual Bliss), so that no one had eaten anything much, Ethelberta had thrown a quiet but intense little tantrum in the kitchen, and Nat, in spite of his uncritical admiration of all World's Enders, had felt quite annoyed with the fellow.

Now, in the roundhouse, he felt as if he'd got a little of his own back.

Nat Parson was very pleased with the roundhouse. It was not a large building, barely the size of his kitchen at home, but it was built of good solid mountain granite, and there were no windows. If Matt Law had had his way, there would have been no roundhouse at all – ten years ago there hadn't been, and generations of Laws had used their cellars to lock up the occasional drunk or debtor.

Nat Parson, fresh from his pilgrimage, had put an end to that kind of laziness. He was pleased he had; the Examiner considered them a backward enough lot as it was. Still, he was impressed with their prisoner; and Nat felt a brief swell of pride at the efficiency with which the Outlander had been dealt with.

'A vagrant? By what name?'

'Goes by the name of One-Eye,' said Nat, who was enjoying his moment.

The Examiner's voice was sharp. 'I don't care what he *goes* by,' he said. 'Your true name, fellow,' he snapped at One-Eye, who was still sitting against the wall – in truth, he could hardly do otherwise, given that his feet were chained to the floor.

'I'll tell you mine if you'll tell me yours,' said One-Eye, showing his teeth, and the Examiner's lips tightened, so that his pale mouth almost vanished.

'This man must be interrogated,' he said, fingering the gold key – his only adornment – that dangled from the cord around his neck.

'I'll see to it,' said Nat. 'I'm sure that between us, Matt and myself will be able to provide you with all the answers to—'

But the Examiner cut him short. 'You will not,' he said in his scholarly voice. 'Instead you will follow my instructions to the letter. First, you will have this man fully restrained—'

'But Examiner,' protested Nat. 'How could he—?'

'I said *fully* restrained, fellow, and that's what I meant. I want him chained. I want him gagged. I don't want to see him move as much so a fingertip without my permission. Is that clear?'

'Yes, sir,' said Nat stiffly. 'May I ask why?'

'You may not,' said the Examiner. 'Second, no one will hold any conversation with the prisoner unless I myself give the order. You will not address him, nor allow him to address you. Third, guards will be posted outside the door, but no one is to enter without my permission. Fourth, word is to be sent *at once* to the Universal City, to the Chief Examiner in charge of Records. I shall write the message to be delivered to him with the utmost urgency. Do you understand?'

Nat Parson nodded.

'Lastly, you will call a halt to all activity on the Hill. The machines to be left in place, guards to be posted, but no one to be allowed access to the mound or the earthworks without my express permission. Is that clear?'

'Yes, sir.'

'Oh, and Parson' – the Examiner turned and favoured Nat with a look of distaste – 'make up a room for me in your house. I shall need a work space, a large desk, writing materials, a smokeless chimney, adequate light – I prefer *wax* candles rather than tallow – and complete silence to aid my meditations. I may have to remain here for some weeks, until my . . . my superiors arrive to take charge of the situation.'

'I see.'

Nat's annoyance at being spoken to in such a fashion was only slightly tempered by his excitement. His *superiors,* eh? Nat had only the vaguest understanding of the complex system of ranks and seniorities within the Examining body, but it now seemed that *his* Examiner, lofty official though he undoubtedly was, held only a junior rank in the Order. More officials would come; officials who, if approached correctly, might learn to value the talents of a man like Nat Parson.

Now he thought he understood the Examiner's abrupt manner. The man was nervous, out of his depth. Hiding his ineptitude beneath an arrogant façade, he thought to bamboozle Nat into allowing him to take the credit for all Nat's work. *Well, think again, Mister Abstinence,* thought Nat savagely. *One day I too may have a golden key – and on that day I'll make you sorry you ever called me* fellow.

The thought was so attractive that he actually *smiled* at the Examiner, and the World's Ender, startled by the fierce brilliance of that smile, took half a step back. 'Well?' he said in a sharp tone. 'What are you waiting for? It's six hundred miles to World's End, in case you'd forgotten, and I want that rider long gone before nightfall.'

'Yes, sir,' said Nat, and left the roundhouse with a brisk step, while the Examiner, still shaken by that smile – *The man must be a halfwit, to grin so* – fingered the key to the Book of Words and watched anxiously as the guards chained One-Eye to the roundhouse wall by his neck, feet and fingers.

8

The Examiner's caution had seemed excessive – even cowardly – to the parson. Nat, however, had not the other man's experience, and knew next to nothing about the Children of the Fire. The Examiner, however – who, like all members of the Order, had no name, simply a number branded onto his arm – had met with demons before.

It had been some thirty years since his first sighting. At the time he had been a mere junior prentice, a scholar in the Universal City, and had taken little part in the grim proceedings. But he remembered them well. The interrogation had taken close on fourteen hours, and by then the creature – a weakened thing, with a broken ruinmark – had been quite insane.

Even so it had taken two Examiners armed with the Word and three prentices to restrain it; and when at last they had dragged it, howling, to the pyre, it had cursed them with a force that left three of them blind.

The young prentice had never forgotten it. He had studied hard and joined the ranks of the Order, electing to discontinue his studies in order to work more actively in the field, later spearheading the outreach programme into the Ridings and beyond, to root out such evil wherever he found it.

For this sacrifice he was given the Word. It was not usual for a junior to receive it, especially not a junior who had scarcely finished his twelfth year of study, but exceptions could be made in certain cases; and besides, the field operatives of the Order needed all the protection they could get.

On his pioneering journey from World's End the Examiner had seen maybe two dozen cases worth reporting to the Department of Records. Most of these had turned out to be dud: fraudsters and half-breeds and Outlanders and freaks with no real power worth speaking of. He had come to accept that most of his day-to-day job would consist of digging out goblin infestations, filling in sacred springs, tumbling standing rings and making sure the old disorderly ways stayed dead and buried.

But in a few cases he had seen things – disquieting things – that altogether justified his sacrifice. The one-eyed man from Malbry was one of these; and the Examiner was torn between the hope of having finally discovered something that would merit the attention of the Chief Examiner and the fear of having to deal with the creature himself.

He would have felt much happier if the man had been bound by the power of the Word. But the Examiner had used up much of his self-control on Red Horse Hill, and it would take long meditation for him to dare to use it again.

For the Word was not an everyday tool. Every instance of its use – save in times of war – had to be fully accounted for, and a date written into the heavy ledgers of the Department of Records. It was also unwieldy, sometimes taking hours to prepare, though its effects were immediate and devastating.

And, of course, it was dangerous. The Examiner had used it more than most – one hundred and forty-six times in all his long career – but never without an inward shudder. For the Word was the language of the Nameless. To invoke it was to enter another world, and to speak it was to commune with a power more terrible than demons. Besides, behind the fear lay a deeper and far more dangerous secret, and that was the *ecstasy* of the Word.

For the Word was an addiction, a pleasure beyond any other, and that was why it was given only to those men who had proved themselves able to withstand it. The Examiner dared not use it twice in one day, and never without the proper procedure. For in spite of his abstinence the Examiner was a glutton in matters of the Word, and he worked all the time to keep his appetites secret and under control. Even now, the temptation to use it was almost unbearable. To speak, to see, to *know* . . .

He looked at his prisoner, a fellow who might be fifty or sixty or even older, dressed in journeyman's leathers and a cloak where the patches had long since overwhelmed the original fabric. He *looked* harmless as he looked human; but the Examiner knew that a demon may take on any Aspect, and he was not fooled for an instant by his outward appearance.

By his Mark shall ye know him, said the Book of Apocalypse.

Even more damning was the Book of Words, where all the known letters of the Elder Script and their variants had been set out, along with their several interpretations. From this list the Examiner had made quick work of recognizing *Raedo*, the Journeyman, and his suspicions had quickly become certainties.

It had not, of course, escaped his attention that the Journeyman rune, though clear and unbroken, was nevertheless reversed. The Examiner did not drop his guard on that account. Even a broken glam can be lethal, and a whole runemark – reversed or not – was a rarity indeed. In fact in thirty years he had never made such a capture himself, and he guessed that this man, uncouth though he seemed, might prove to be more than a mere foot soldier in the enemy's camp.

'Your name, fellow,' he said once more. In the absence of the parson he had dared remove the Outlander's gag, though for safety's sake he kept the chains in place. By now the man must have been in acute discomfort, but he said nothing, and simply watched the Examiner from his one, unnaturally gleaming eye.

'Your *name*!' said the Examiner, and made as if to kick the stranger as he lay there so insolently. He did *not* kick him, however. He was an Examiner, not an Interrogator, and he found violence distressing. Also he remembered the demon with the broken ruinmark that had left three of his Order blind, and decided that this was not the time for rash action.

Odin laughed, as if he had read the Examiner's mind. 'My name is Untold,' he quoted maliciously, 'for I have many.'

The Examiner was startled. 'You know the Good Book?'

Again Odin laughed, but made no answer.

'If you do,' said the Examiner, 'then you must know that you are already finished. Why resist us? Your time is done. Tell me what I need to know, and you may at least save yourself some pain.'

Odin said nothing, but simply smiled his unnatural smile.

The Examiner's lips compressed. 'Well,' he said, turning to the door. 'You leave me no choice. When I return, you'll be begging to tell me everything you know.'

Odin closed his one eye and pretended to sleep.

'So be it,' said the Examiner dryly. 'You have until tomorrow to reflect. You may mock *me*, fellow, but I can guarantee that you will not mock the power of the Word.'

185

9

'Is there no other way?' said Maddy at last.

'Trust me. I'm an oracle.'

Once more Maddy looked into the ice coffin where the pale woman lay, her colours shining softly in the cold light. The blue tones of the ice that encased her threw deathly shadows across her features, and her short hair, so light that it was almost lost in her frosty shroud, seemed to float around her face like seaweed.

Casting *Bjarkán*, Maddy narrowed her eyes, and the workings which bound the ice woman leaped into sight. As she had first seen, they resembled those that had held the Whisperer, but they were more numerous, binding the Sleeper's ice coffin into a complex knot of interwoven glamours.

'Be careful,' said the Whisperer. 'There may be traps set into the work.'

There were. Maddy could see them now, designed to spring out at anyone unwise enough to lay hands on the Sleeper. A protective measure – but for whose protection? She touched the runes gently with her fingertips; at her touch they glowed ice-blue, and Maddy could feel them itching, working, struggling to be free.

'Think what they could tell you, Maddy,' said the Whisperer in a silky voice. 'Secrets lost since the End of the World. Answers to questions you never dared ask – questions Odin would never have answered . . .'

It would be easy, Maddy knew. Beneath her fingertips the runes were alive; quickening almost of their own accord. All they needed was a little help. And if in exchange they could give her the answers to questions that had plagued her all her life:

Who was she really?

What was her glam?

And how did she fit into this tale of demons and gods?

Quickly, before she could change her mind, Maddy gathered her strongest runes. She cast them like knuckle-bones, swift and sure: *Kaen, Tyr, Hagall* – and finally, *Úr*, the Mighty Ox, beneath which the block shattered with a sudden almighty *crunch*, and the blue surface of the ice was blasted in a second into a milky crackle-glaze.

The impact threw Maddy backwards, one arm raised to shield her eyes from the ice shards that accompanied it. Then, when nothing else happened, she dropped her arm and moved carefully towards the now opaque block.

Nothing moved. The trembling chandelier of ice above her head made small, shivery sounds in the aftershock of the blast, but no icicles fell, and a chilly silence came once more over the great hall.

'*Now* what?' she said, turning to the Whisperer.

But before it could answer there came a sound: first a distant crunching sound, followed by a rumbling, a tumbling, a slip-sliding and finally an avalanche of frozen material that fell from some distant funnel in the ceiling to thud against the glassy floor.

Maddy moved fast; made for the wall of the cavern and flattened herself against it, as now the balancing icicles began to drop from the vaulted ceiling, spike by spike, like the teeth of some giant threshing machine.

A packet of snow the size of a hay wagon exploded against the ground close by, bringing down with it a jangling necklace of small projectiles and lastly a single large object – no, a *person* – that landed heavily – and with a muffled *ouch!* – on the fallen snow.

10

When Loki collapsed, bleeding and exhausted against the skirts of the glacier, it was with the knowledge that he had made a number of grave – possibly fatal – miscalculations.

What kind of fool puts his head into the wolf's mouth for the sake of curiosity? What kind of fool leaves his citadel to go aboveground, unarmed and unprotected, chasing rumours, when he should have been preparing for a siege? But curiosity had always been Loki's besetting sin, and now it looked as if he was going to pay for it.

But he had always had more than his share of luck. As it chanced, the very spot where he fell hid one of the skylights that opened out into the hollow halls of the mountain below. Snow had formed over it; but it was a brittle frosting, and a man's weight was more than enough to break through.

And so, just as he hit the ground, a fissure opened up beneath him, revealing a ragged hole through which he fell, helpless to prevent himself; through the ceiling of the great cavern with its hanging ice gardens; through filigrees of brittle lace, fashioned by a thousand years of freeze and thaw; and finally through a sickening swatch of empty air before landing – more mercifully than he would have dared to expect – on a thick wad of powdery snow.

Even so, the impact knocked all the breath out of him. For a time he just lay where he had fallen, half dazed and gasping. And when he looked up, shaking the ice crystals out of his hair, it was to see a familiar face staring down at him; a face as merciless as it was beautiful, around which the pale, cropped hair stood out like a frill of sea-foam.

In one hand she carried something that looked like a whip made from runes, a flexible length of barbed blue light, coiled carelessly about her wrist. Now she released it, with a hiss and a crackle, and it slithered to the ground, snapping with glam. The ice woman stared at the fallen Trickster and her lips, still tinted faintly blue, curved in a smile that made him shiver.

From the far side of the cavern, Maddy was watching. She had seen Loki fall, and had recognized him at once by his signature and the colour of his hair. She had seen the ice woman rise, striding confidently across the great hall, apparently oblivious to the fragments and shards that rained from the ceiling.

Now she watched the confrontation, cautiously, through *Bjarkán*, keeping low to the ground behind a table-sized block of unpolished ice.

'Loki,' purred the woman. 'You look terrible.' The glam between her fingers began to uncoil, slowly, like a sleepy snake.

Loki raised his head, not without difficulty. 'I try to oblige.' He pushed himself up onto his knees, keeping a watchful eye on the runewhip.

'Please don't get up on my account.'

'It's no trouble,' Loki said.

'I wouldn't *quite* say that,' said the woman, pushing him down with a booted foot. 'In fact I think I can safely say that you're in rather a lot of it.'

'That's Skadi,' said the Whisperer.

'The Huntress?' said Maddy, who knew the tale. A part of it, anyway: how Loki had tricked Skadi out of her vengeance against the Æsir, and how, at last, she had made him pay.

'The same Skadi who hung the snake—?'

'The very same,' said the Whisperer.

That, thought Maddy, complicated things. She had been counting on the fact that the reawakened Sleeper would be both friendly and eager to help. But this was Skadi, the Snowshoe Huntress, one of the Vanir by marriage to Njörd. Her hatred of Loki was legendary; and from the look of things, five hundred years had done nothing to abate it.

'What about Loki?' Maddy said.

'Don't worry,' said the Whisperer indifferently. 'She'll kill him, I expect, and then we can get on with business again.'

'*Kill* him?'

'I would think so. Why do you care? He wouldn't lift a finger to help you, you know, if your positions were reversed.'

Maddy glared. 'You knew this would happen.'

'Well, of course I did,' said the Whisperer. 'Have you ever known Loki to keep his nose out of anything that might be interesting? And Skadi always had a special grudge against him above all, you know, ever since the Æsir killed her father Thiassi of the Ice People, warlord of the Elder Age. The Æsir killed him, but Loki arranged it. I'd keep out of her way if I were you.'

But Maddy was already moving. Using the ice block as cover, she edged closer to the two opponents, *Bjarkán* crooked between her fingers. Across the hall Skadi looked down at Loki and gave her chilly smile.

'Come on, Skadi,' said Loki, working to recover a little of his glam. 'I thought we were past all this by now. It's been how long – five hundred years? Don't you think it's time we—'

'*That* long?' she said. 'It seems only yesterday that you were in chains with a snake over your head. Those were the days, eh, Loki?'

'Well, *you* haven't changed much either,' said Loki, bringing one hand slowly behind his back. 'Still as *perilously* attractive as ever,' he went on, 'and still with the same delightful sense of humour—'

And at this he moved, with the same uncanny speed that

Maddy had seen before, and as he threw himself out of range of Skadi's glam, he flung a rune into her face.

Maddy had time to recognize *Yr*, just as Skadi countered it with a blow of her runewhip. The coil struck once, like blue lightning, casually pulverizing *Yr*, then slammed home, the barbed runes that made up its length biting into the frozen ground.

Loki dodged – but only just. The runewhip opened up a crevice in the ground where he had been and swept a dozen icicles off a hanging buttress twenty feet above as it snapped back into the light-crazed air.

Loki tried for another rune, but before the fingering was even complete, *Tyr*, the Warrior, was blasted from his hand with a force that left his fingers numb. And now he was cornered, his back to the wall, one arm thrown up to cover his face as Skadi stood over him, runewhip raised. Maddy could see him forking runes at the Huntress, but his glam was burned out; not a glimmer remained.

'Now, Skadi,' he said, 'before you do anything hasty—'

'*Hasty?*' she said. 'Not a chance. I've been looking forward to this for five hundred years.'

'Well, yes. Nice to see you've kept your strength up,' said Loki. 'But *before* you cut me into little pieces—'

'Oh, Loki, I wouldn't do *that*.' She gave a laugh that rattled the icicles all the way to the frozen vault. 'That would be over far too quickly. I want to see you suffer.'

Now Loki played his final card, his crooked smile beginning to show. It was a desperate move, to be sure, but he had always been at his most inventive in time of crisis.

'I don't think you do,' he said.

'And why's that?' said Skadi.

Loki grinned. He'd never felt less sure of himself, but it was his last card, and he played it with style. 'I've got the Whisperer,' he said.

There was a very long pause.

Slowly the runewhip was lowered to the ground.

'You've got it? Where?'

Loki smiled and shook his head.

'*Where?*' In Skadi's hand, the runewhip stirred threateningly, its tip reaching for him like the fangs of a snake.

He waved it away with an impatient gesture. 'Oh, please. The minute I tell you that, I'm dead.'

'Good point,' said Skadi. 'So. What do you want?'

11

Maddy had frozen the moment Loki mentioned the Whisperer. In her anxiety over One-Eye, it had not occurred to her how dangerous it was to have brought it with her into the hall of the Sleepers.

Now it did, and Maddy cast about wildly for a place to hide it. Fortunately, she realized, the ice cavern was perhaps the only location in World Below where such a thing was possible; for the light-signatures that stitched the air were so bright and so numerous that among them even a powerful glam like the Whisperer might pass unnoticed for a time.

Cautiously she edged back behind the block where she had first taken cover. By scraping at the base with the edge of her knife, Maddy found she could dislodge just enough of the frozen material to make a gap large enough in which to fit the Whisperer. Sealing it with *Yr* and a few handfuls of packed snow, she inspected the result and decided it might pass.

It would have to pass, she told herself. Time was short, One-Eye was a prisoner, and although Loki was hardly a friend of hers, she wasn't going to stand by and watch him be slaughtered. And so Maddy stood up and began to walk calmly towards the two deadlocked adversaries.

So far, so good. He'd bought himself some time.

Of course it was the worst kind of ill chance to have happened upon Skadi, of all people – Skadi in her full Aspect, angry, alert and as strong as ever, *Isa* having no reverse position – besides which Loki had never been much of a fighter, even in the old days, relying on wits rather than weaponry.

That runewhip of hers, he thought darkly. Doubtless some glam of the Elder Days, when they still had time and power to spend on such fancy work. It had not struck him directly – if it had, it would probably have taken his hand off – but even so it had felt like being hit over the knuckles with a cudgel. His whole arm hurt; his right hand was still numb; and his chances of being able to work even the simplest fingering within the next hour were poor indeed.

But he *was* alive, against all expectation, and that was enough to cheer him for the present. At least . . .

Skadi had her back turned, and the first she knew of Maddy's approach was the look of sudden anguish that flashed through Loki's eyes. She turned, and saw a young person not more than fourteen years of age walking steadily towards them.

'Skadi,' she said. 'Nice to meet you. I see you and Loki have been catching up.'

Loki swallowed. For the second time that day he found himself at a loss, and did not enjoy the feeling. He was only too aware that a single word from Maddy could condemn him. And who could blame her? They'd hardly parted on the most friendly of terms.

Still, he thought, there's always hope. Already his quick mind was sifting plans and possibilities. 'Skadi,' he said. 'Meet Maddy Smith.'

Of course, if the girl was still carrying the Whisperer, then he was lost. And if she refused to play along, there again, he was lost. Perhaps they both were; for though Maddy was undoubtedly strong, Skadi was old and battle-trained, and with that deadly glam at her fingertips, Loki didn't rate their chances if it came to a fight.

Maddy, however, seemed cheerful enough. 'I'm glad to see you, Skadi,' she said. 'I imagine Loki told you why we're here.'

'Actually – no,' said Loki. 'We were . . . discussing old times.'

'Well, it's like this,' said Maddy, reaching down to pull him to his feet. 'They've got One-Eye. And they're using the Word.'

BOOK FIVE
The Sleepers

And there shall come a Scarlet Horse . . .

Apocalypse, 9:8

1

'When?' demanded Loki.

'This afternoon.'

'Then they may not have used it yet,' he said.

Skadi looked at him. 'Used what?'

'The Word, of course.' Shivering, he began to pace, his bare feet soundless on the glassy floor.

'What Word?' said the Huntress with suspicion.

'Gods,' said Loki in disgust. 'This just gets better and better, doesn't it? Maddy, where's the General?'

'The roundhouse, I think.'

'How well guarded is it?'

Maddy shrugged. 'Two men. Maybe.'

'Then we'll have to move fast. We can't let the Order interrogate him. If they find out who he is and what he knows . . .' He shivered once again at the thought.

'What Word?' repeated Skadi. 'What is this Word, and where is the Whisperer?'

Loki looked impatient. 'Look, dearie, things have changed a bit since Ragnarók. There have been some quite significant developments in the fight between Order and Chaos, and if you hadn't been asleep under the mountains for the past five hundred years—'

'That wasn't my idea,' Skadi hissed.

'Convenient, though, wasn't it? Nice of old Njörd to count you in, even if you're not technically a Van. No Examiners, no reversals, no Black Fortress—'

The Huntress's eyes lit dangerously. 'Hold your tongue, Dogstar, or I'll relieve you of it.'

'Hey,' said Loki. 'What did I say?'

'Please,' interrupted Maddy. 'We don't have time. One-Eye needs help—'

Skadi looked at her in scorn. 'You want *me* to help *him*?'

'Well, yes,' said Maddy. 'Isn't he the General?'

Skadi laughed, a cheerless sound. 'To the Æsir, perhaps. But not to the Ice People. Not to my folk. Whatever alliance we once had, it ended with the war. As far as I'm concerned, he and the rest of you can all go to Hel.'

For a moment Maddy was at a loss. Then she had a sudden inspiration. 'He's got the Whisperer,' she said.

The Huntress froze. '*Has* he?' she said, staring at Loki.

'Has he?' said Loki, genuinely startled.

Skadi raised her runewhip again. 'I should have known you were lying,' she said

'I wasn't,' said Loki. 'I said I knew where the Whisperer *was*. I didn't say I had it on my person. For gods' sakes, Skadi, give me some credit. Why would I bring it here, of all places? Would I really be that stupid?'

Maddy glanced uneasily over her shoulder to the ice block behind which she had hidden the Whisperer. 'Would that be very stupid, then?'

'Very,' he said.

Meanwhile Skadi was watching Maddy. 'So you were the one who woke me,' she said.

Maddy nodded. 'I thought you'd help. The Whisperer said to wake the—' She stopped short, realizing her mistake.

But it was too late. Skadi's eyes had widened. 'It *spoke* to you?'

'Well . . .' said Maddy. 'Only once.'

'Did it make a prophecy?'

'Well, it told me to wake you,' said Maddy, who was wishing she hadn't got into this. 'Look, are you going to help or not?'

'I'll help,' said the Huntress with a chilly smile. 'But I'm taking *him* with me. We'll fly out together, find the General, pick up the glam, and if for some reason it isn't there—'

'Why shouldn't it be there?' said Loki.

'Let me guess,' said Skadi. 'Perhaps some lying, conniving person thought he might be able to get me out of the way by sending me on a wild-goose chase while he and his little friend weaselled off with the Whisperer – you know, something like that. This way we can all rest easy. Don't you think?'

Maddy glanced at Loki. 'I'll go.'

'You can't.' He spoke reluctantly, as if weighing heavy odds. 'The Hill is sealed from the Horse's Eye. You can't use the tunnels. Anyway it would be suicide to go aboveground in this snow – as well as taking more hours than we can afford. No. She's right. Whoever goes will have to take bird form to reach the village – an hour's flight, if all goes well.'

Demon blood, Vanir blood, meant the power to shift from one Aspect into another. Loki and Skadi both shared that skill. Too late Maddy saw that her attempt to help had simply placed One-Eye in greater danger than before.

Loki knew it too – being basically dishonest himself, he had no great trust in Maddy's story, and the prospect of facing Skadi again – this time after an hour-long flight and with One-Eye as his only chaperone – filled him with dread. 'My dear Skadi,' he said, 'it's not that I don't *want* to come with you – I mean, there's nothing I'd like better than to risk my life for the General again, but—'

'No buts. You're coming.'

'You don't understand.' Now there was desperation in his voice. 'My glam's used up. I'm tired. I'm hurt. I'm frozen stiff. There was a mountain cat the size of a— Honestly, I couldn't light a *fire* in this state, let alone tackle an Examiner armed with the Word.'

'Hm,' said Skadi, and frowned.

Loki was right. She saw that now. His colours were weak, and, using *Bjarkán*, she could read his distress there as clearly as footprints in snow. He couldn't shift; he couldn't fight; she was only surprised he could still stand.

'I need food,' said Loki. 'Rest.'

'No time for that. We leave at once.'

'But *Skadi* . . .'

Skadi had already turned away. Leaving Maddy and Loki together, she seemed to be searching around the vast cavern, inspecting the walls, the floor and the ice sculptures that rose out of it – here an oliphant, there a waterfall, a giant table, and beyond that a ship that gleamed in the moonlight, its every surface clustered with brilliants.

'Maddy, please. You've got to help me.' Loki's voice was soft and urgent. 'I promised her the Whisperer. When she finds out I don't have it—'

'Trust me,' said Maddy. 'I'll think of something.'

'Really? That's good. Forgive me if I don't fall at your feet with gratitude *just* yet . . .'

'I *said* I'll think of something.'

For a second Skadi seemed to pause, then she moved on, still searching, her pale hair shining eerily as she went. 'What are you doing?' Maddy called, seeing the Huntress move deeper and deeper into the Hall of Sleepers.

'Getting help,' came the sardonic voice. 'For our poor, exhausted friend.'

'Oh, no,' said Loki.

'What now?' said Maddy.

'I think she's going to wake someone else.' Loki put his face in his hands. 'Gods,' he said. 'That's all we need. *More* people after my blood.'

2

More people after my blood, he'd said, but the second woman who came strolling out of the Hall of Sleepers was as different to the icy Huntress as cream is to granite.

This second woman was round and soft and golden; flowers gleamed in her long hair and *Ár*, the green rune of Plenty, shone out from her forehead. Her gaze fell on Maddy, and it was wide and trusting and slightly perplexed, like that of an infant who wishes to please.

And such was the charm of this strange and childlike woman that even Maddy, who had plenty of reason to dislike a certain kind of cowslip-haired beauty, felt the air of the cavern thaw a little at her presence, and seemed to smell the scent of distant gardens and ripe strawberries and fresh honey straight from the comb.

Skadi walked behind her at some distance, as if unwilling to get too close to something so unlike herself.

Loki too recognized her; as the smiling woman made her way towards him, Maddy saw in his face a mixture of relief and what might have been embarrassment.

'Who is it?' whispered Maddy.

'Idun,' he said. 'The Healer.'

'Here he is,' said Skadi curtly. 'Now get him moving, and fast.'

Idun peered at Loki, wide-eyed. 'Oh, dear. What have you been up to this time?' she said.

He pulled a face. 'Me? Nothing.'

'*Do* be polite, Loki, or you won't get your apple.'

Idun, thought Maddy. The keeper of the magical fruit that cures sickness and heals Time. According to the tales, the fruit were golden apples stored in a golden casket, but the fruit that Idun held out to Loki was small and yellow and wrapped in foliage, more like a crab apple than anything else, though its scent, potent even in the frosty air of the cavern, was all green summer and creamy Harvestmonth crammed into a handful of withered leaves.

'Eat it,' said Skadi as Loki hesitated.

Loki did, looking none too pleased. For a moment nothing seemed to happen; and then Maddy saw his signature brighten suddenly from its dim bruise-colour to a vibrant gleam. It had been fading; now it hummed with power that crackled from his hair and his fingertips and shimmered briefly across his entire body like St Sepulchre's fire.

The effect was immediate. He straightened; breathed deeply; tested his ribs and his injured hand and the gouges from the cat's claws and found them mended.

'Feeling better?' said Idun.

Loki nodded.

'Good,' said Skadi. 'Let's go. And Loki . . .'

'What?'

'In case you were thinking of pulling a fast one—'

'Who, *me*?'

'I'll be watching you.' She smiled. 'Like a hawk.'

It would take them an hour to cross the valley. Ten minutes later, an eagle and a small brown hawk were on their way to the village of Malbry. Without wings, Loki said, it was pointless to follow – and yet Maddy hated the thought of leaving One-Eye at the mercy of the Huntress when she realized (as she inevitably would) that she had been deceived.

Idun, as she soon discovered, was no help. She listened attentively enough to Maddy's story, but seemed to feel no sense of urgency or danger at all.

'Odin will think of something,' she said, and appeared to feel *that* ought to reassure her.

But Maddy was not reassured. 'There must be some way,' she said. 'It's my fault. *I* took the Whisperer . . .'

Idun was sitting on a block of ice, singing to herself. At the mention of the Whisperer she stopped, and a look of mild anxiety crossed her features.

'*That* old glam?' she said. 'Best leave it alone. It never did give us anything but bad news.' She pulled a comb from her hair and examined it, then began to sing again, her voice a thin filament of sweetness in the chilly air.

It was clear to Maddy that whatever powers Idun possessed would be of little use to her in their present situation. Wild thoughts of mindblasting her way out of the cavern were attractive, but impractical, and she knew that however much she tried, she could never walk to the village in time.

One solution remained, and as she examined it from all angles, weighing the benefits and disadvantages, she became more and more convinced that it was her only hope.

'There's no choice,' she said at last. 'I'll have to wake another Sleeper.'

Idun smiled vaguely. 'That would be nice, dear. Just like old times.'

Maddy had a feeling that reviving old times was the last thing they needed right now, but she didn't see any alternative. The question was, whom to wake? And how could she be sure that waking someone else wouldn't just make matters worse?

With a heavy heart, and with *Bjarkán* gleaming at her fingertips, Maddy went over to the remaining Sleepers. Idun followed her through the caverns like a lost child, singing to herself and wondering at the lights and colours. Maddy noticed that wherever Idun went, the ice melted briefly, reconfiguring itself into frost flowers and ice garlands in her wake. More than once she looked anxiously at the chains of icicles suspended above their heads and tried not to think of what might happen if Idun stopped moving for too long.

Instead she concentrated on the Sleepers. There they lay in their beds of ice, still and gleaming beneath the bindwork of runes. Five remained of the original seven – four men and one woman – and for some time Maddy went from one to the other and back again, trying to determine which one to choose.

The first was a man of powerful build, with shaggy hair and a beard that curled like foam. His signature was ocean-blue; he wore the rune *Logr* beneath a tunic of something that looked like close-linked scale, and his feet, which were large and shapely, were bare.

Maddy had no difficulty recognizing him from One-Eye's accounts, and decided at once that there was no question of waking him. That was Njörd, the Man of the Sea, one of the original Vanir and one-time husband of Skadi the Huntress. Their marriage had failed, due to irreconcilable differences, but all the same Maddy felt it wiser to keep Njörd out of the situation for the moment.

The second Sleeper was like Njörd, with the fair skin and pale hair of the Vanir, though Maddy sensed a warmth coming from him that had been absent in the Man of the Sea. He too was a warrior, with the rune *Madr* on his chest and a spyglass around his neck. It took Maddy some time to decide who he was, but she finally made up her mind that he was golden-toothed Heimdall, messenger of the Seer-folk and wakeful guardian of the rainbow bridge; even beneath the ice his bright-blue eyes remained open and fiercely aware.

Maddy passed him by with a shiver of unease. She knew from her stories that Heimdall, though loyal to Odin and to the Æsir, hated Loki with a passion, and was unlikely to be sympathetic to anyone trying to help him.

The third was Bragi, husband of Idun. A tall man with the rune *Sól* on his hand and a crown of flowers around his head. He looked gentle (Maddy knew him mainly as a champion of songs and poetry) and she would have liked to have chosen him, but Bragi, she knew, was no friend of Loki's, and she didn't like the idea of having to explain his role – or indeed, her own – in what was becoming a very tortuous mess.

The fourth Sleeper was armoured in gold; his long hair gleamed with it; the rune *Fé* shone out from his brow and a broken sword lay at his side.

Next to him, close enough to touch, was the last Sleeper, a woman of bright and troubling beauty. *Fé* adorned her; her hair was fretted and woven with gems, and a necklace of twisted gold circled her throat, catching the light even through the ice. She bore a striking resemblance to the Sleeper beside her, and Maddy knew them at once to be Frey and Freyja, the twin children of Njörd, who had joined the Seerfolk with him in the time of the Whisperer.

With her hands Maddy swept the loose snow from the face of the last Sleeper. Freyja slept on, beautiful and impassive, giving nothing away.

Dared she wake her? Could she even be certain that Freyja – or *any* of the Vanir – would be any more helpful than Skadi or Idun? Of course Skadi was only one of the Vanir by marriage; she came from the Ice People of the north, a savage race with whom the gods had held an uneasy truce. Surely it had been pure bad luck that Skadi should have awoken first; and surely the other Vanir would be keen and ready to rescue their General.

Rapidly Maddy went over in her mind all that she remembered about Freyja. The goddess of desire; Freyja the fair; Freyja the fickle; Freyja the falcon-cloaked—

Ah. That was it.

Sudden hope surged through Maddy. Now she could see a glimmer of hope – not much, but enough – that once more set her heart beating.

The runes felt familiar now, kindling quickly beneath her fingers. Here too the net that contained them seethed with impatience; the bindings itched; the glamours shone out with an imperious light.

Maddy reached for them with one hand; a bunch of coloured ribbons like those on a maypole. She pulled –

– and the whole assembly came loose with a ripping and tearing and a great flare of colours and hues.

This time the ice did not shatter, but instead melted away, leaving the Sleeper damp but unharmed, dabbing at her eyes and yawning delicately.

'Who are you?' she enquired when the operation was complete.

Maddy explained as quickly as she could. One-Eye's capture; Skadi's awakening; the Examiner; the Whisperer; the Word. Freyja listened, her blue eyes wide, but as soon as Maddy mentioned Loki's name, they narrowed again.

'I'm warning you now,' said Freyja stiffly. 'I have . . . certain issues . . . with Loki.' (Maddy wondered briefly whether there was anyone in the Nine Worlds who *didn't* have issues with Loki.)

'Please,' she urged. 'Lend me your cloak. It's not as if I'm asking you to come with me.'

Freyja looked Maddy over with a critical eye. 'It's my only one,' she said. 'You'd better not damage it.'

'I'll be *really* careful.'

'Hm. You'd better.'

Moments later it was in Maddy's hands; a cloak of tricks and feathers, light as an armful of air. She pulled it around her shoulders, feeling the delicious whispery warmth of the feathers against her skin, and at once it began to *shape* itself to her form.

The thing was alive with glamour, it seemed. Runes and bindings stitched it through. Maddy could feel them, delving, painlessly taking root in her flesh and bone; transforming her into something other.

It was blissful; it was terrifying. In seconds her muscles lengthened; her vision sharpened a thousandfold; feathers sprouted from her arms and shoulders. She opened her mouth in astonishment, but nothing emerged except a harsh bird-cry.

'There. It quite suits you,' said Freyja, leaning over to inspect the result. 'Now, when you want to take it off, just cast *Naudr* reversed . . .'

How? thought Maddy.

'You'll manage,' said Freyja. 'Just make sure you bring it back.'

It took her a few minutes to become accustomed to her new wings. For an agonizing time she fluttered wildly, confused by the altered perspective and half panicked by the enclosed space. Then at last she found the skylight and shot through like a flung projectile into the night.

Oh, the freedom, she thought. *The air!*

Below her the valley hung like a silver-stitched tapestry; the glacier; the road twining down along the Hindarfell pass. The sky was all stars; the moon was dazzling; and the joy, the exhilaration of flight was such that for an indeterminate length of time she simply let it take her, shrieking, into the illuminated sky.

Then she remembered the task at hand and, with an effort, took control. With her enhanced vision she could see about a mile ahead of her the hawk and the eagle – Loki and Skadi – streaking towards Malbry.

Below them the fields were beginning to turn, moving from Harvestmonth yellow to Year's End brown. In Malbry a few lights still shone, and the smell of smoke from the bonfires hung over the land like a banner. Somewhere among those lights, she knew, her father would be awake, drinking beer and watching the sky. Her sister would be dreamlessly asleep on her bed of boards, a lace cap tied around her cowslip curls. Crazy Nan Fey would be sitting in her cottage talking to her cats.

And One-Eye? What was he doing? Was he sleeping? Suffering? Hopeful? Afraid? Would he be grateful to see her, or angry at how badly she'd handled the situation? Most important of all, would he play along? And if so, with whom?

3

Midnight. A potent hour.

The church clock tower struck twelve, then, a minute later, struck twelve again. In a small bedroom under the eaves of the Parsonage the visiting Examiner, who had been waiting for just that signal, gave a tiny smile of satisfaction. All the rituals had been performed. He had bathed; prayed; meditated; fasted. Now it was time.

He was hungry, but pleasingly so; tired, but not sleepy. Once more he had refused the Parsons' offer of a home-cooked meal, and the resulting slight feeling of light-headedness had been more than compensated for by a renewed intensity of concentration.

On the bed at his side the Book of Words lay open. Now at last he allowed himself to study the relevant chapter, with the familiar shiver of pleasure and fear. *That power*, he thought dimly. *That intoxicating, indescribable power*.

'Not mine, but yours, o Nameless,' he murmured. 'Speak not *in* me, but *through* me . . .'

And now he could feel it already at his fingertips, moving through the parchment to illuminate him: the ineffable wisdom of the Elder Days; the desire; the knowledge; the *glamour*—

Tsk-tsk, begone! The Examiner banished temptation with a canticle. *Not mine, but yours is the power of the Word.*

That was better. The feeling of delirium subsided a little. He had a job to do, and an urgent one: to identify the agent of Disorder, the one-eyed man with the ruinmark on his face.

That ruinmark. Once more he considered it, with a tremor of unease. A potent glam, even reversed – the Book of Words

211

said so – and there were verses in the Book of Fabrications –
obscure verses, couched in terms so archaic as to be almost
impossible to understand – that hinted at some dark and
perilous connection.

By his Mark shall ye know him.

Aye. That was the crossroads.

If only the Examiner had completed his studies, stayed on
at the Universal City for another ten years or so, then he
might have been able to trust in his gut. As it was, he was still
a novice in so many ways. A novice, and alone – but if *Raedo*
meant what he thought it did, then he badly needed the
support of his Magisters, and quickly.

A horseman riding as far as the Universal City might take
weeks to bring help. Time aplenty for the Outlander to regain
his strength and to contact his minions. All the same, the
Examiner had held back until now. The Book of Words was
not to be used lightly at any time, and the canticles of greatest power – Bindings, Summonings and Executions – were
especially restricted. Even more so was the Communion; a
series of canticles through which, at a time of great need, a
member of the Order could convey a message to the rest. It
was a ritual of great power; a merging of minds and information; a mental link with the Nameless itself.

But Communion was dangerous business, he knew. Some
said it drove the user insane; others spoke of bliss too terrible
to describe. He himself had never used it before. He'd never
had to; but now, he thought, perhaps he must.

Once again his eyes slid back to the Book of Words, open
now at the first chapter, the chapter of 'Invocations'. One
canticle headed the first page – underneath, a list of names.

The Examiner read: *A named thing is a tamed thing.*

He read on.

Fifteen minutes later he had made up his mind. The
decision could no longer be delayed; whatever the risk to his

sanity or his person, he had to invoke Communion with the Order.

Some part of him regretted this – for the present the Outlander was his alone, and to involve the Order would be to lose that independence – but mostly it was a blessed relief. Let someone else take charge, he thought. Let someone else make the decisions.

Of course, there was always the chance that he might have misread the signs. But even *that* might be a relief. Better the ridicule of his peers than the terrible responsibility of having allowed the enemy to slip through his untrained fingers.

He considered the Book. It had to be done according to the correct process, he reminded himself. His mind would be wide open during the time of Communion, and he wanted to be sure that no taint of vainglory marked it. It took him ten minutes to achieve the required state of tranquillity, and five more to summon the courage to utter the Word.

The rune Ós vibrated at untold length; an unheard note of piercing resonance that cut through the dark. All over the valley, dogs pricked up their ears; sleepers awoke; trees dropped their remaining leaves and small animals cowered in burrows and nests.

Maddy felt it in a pocket of turbulence that tumbled and turned her.

Loki saw it as a ripple of deeper darkness that flickered over the land.

Skadi neither heard nor saw it, all her attention being fixed on the little hawk ahead of her.

For a moment the Examiner sensed their presence. For that moment the Examiner was *everywhere*: soaring in the air; crawling on the ground; imprisoned in the roundhouse; buried under the Hill. Power surged within him, terrible and astonishing. With his mind he reached further; touched World's End and the tangle of minds awaiting him; was

213

suddenly *there* – in a study, a library, a cell – linking, touching, Communing with every soul in the Order without the need for any words.

For a time it was a babel of minds, like voices in a crowd. The Examiner struggled to keep the link; struggled to keep his own mind from foundering. He could make out individual voices now – Magisters, Professors. The Council of Twelve – the high seat of the Order, where all decisions are made, all information regulated.

Then, suddenly, all fell silent. And the Examiner heard a single Voice that addressed him by his true name.

Elias Rede, intoned the Voice.

The Examiner took a sharp breath. It had been close on forty years since he'd heard his name; had given it up, as all prentices did, for his safety and anonymity within the Order. For practical purposes he'd been given a number instead – 4421974 – which had been branded onto his arm during his initiation.

Hearing his name after so long filled him with an inexplicable fear. He felt exposed; alone; utterly vulnerable beneath the scrutiny of some immensely superior mind.

I hear you, Magister, he thought, fighting the urge to run and hide.

The Voice – which was not quite a Voice, but an illumination that shone directly into his secret self – seemed to chuckle softly.

Then tell Me what you see, it said, and at once the Examiner felt the most terrible, most agonizing sensation: that of something moving relentlessly through the pages of his mind.

It did not hurt, but it was anguish nevertheless. It was secrets thrown open; foibles exposed; old memories brought out to shrivel beneath that merciless light. There was no question of resisting it; beneath that scrutiny Elias Rede gave up his soul – aye, to the last scrap – every memory, every ambition, guilty pleasure, little rebellion, every thought.

It left him empty, sobbing his confusion. And now he was aware of a new horror: that of the Order watching and sharing. Every prentice, every Professor, every Magister, every scrub. All were present; all judged him in that moment.

Time stopped. From the depths of his misery the Examiner was conscious of a debate going on in the chambers of World's End. Voices boomed around him, raised in excitement. He didn't care. He wanted to hide, to die; to bury himself deep under the earth where no one could ever find him.

But the Voice had not finished with Elias Rede. Now it shuffled through the past few hours, going over in relentless detail the business on the Hill, the arrival of the parson and the capture of the Outlander – especially the Outlander – sifting and checking every feature, going over every nuance of every word the man had spoken.

More, it said.

The Examiner faltered. *Magister . . . I—*

More, Elias. Give me more.

Please! Magister! I've told you everything!

No, Elias. You see more.

And in that moment he realized he did. It was as if an eye had opened within his mind, an eye that saw *behind* the world into some other, fabulous place of lights and colours. His eyes grew wide.

Oh! he gasped.

Look well, Elias, and tell me what you see.

It was a revelation. Forgetting his misery, he drank it greedily. Everything around him had a *life*, he saw: behind the trees, colours; behind the houses, signatures. Even his own hand, crooked into a circle with the thumb and forefinger joined together, cast a trail of brightness, gleaming against the dark air. Surely the Sky Citadel itself could not have been more beautiful than this—

Stop your gawping and look outside.

Forgive me, Magister, I—

Outside, I said!

He opened the window and leaned out, once more peering through the circle of his fingers. The night too was stitched with patterns; fading trails of many colours, most of them dim, but some like meteors crossing the sky. And above the roundhouse a brightness shone; a kingfisher trail that shot sparks into the starry sky.

At last, in that moment, Elias Rede knew the man with the scarred face, and hid his own face with trembling hands.

Well done, Elias, said the Voice. *The Nameless thanks you for your work.*

The link was fading, its many voices growing unruly as the One Voice grew faint. Elias Rede felt his mind contract; the Communion was nearing its end. And yet the visions – the wondrous visions – remained, though slightly dimmed; as if, once seen, they could never be quite unseen.

A gift, said the Voice. *For loyal service.*

The Examiner reeled. Now that his mind was mostly his own again, he began to understand the outstanding honour that had been given to him. *A gift,* he thought, *from the Nameless itself . . .*

O Nameless, he cried, *what must I do?*

Without words, it told him.

And as the church clock struck half past twelve, Elias Rede – Examiner Number 4421974 – lay on the floor of the Parsons' guest bedroom with his arms wrapped around his head and shivered and wept with terror and joy.

4

Meanwhile, in the roundhouse, everything was quiet. Two duty guards stood at the door, but there had been no sound from inside the oven-shaped building since the Examiner's departure, just before dark.

Even so, the guards – Dorian Scattergood, from Forge's Post, and Tyas Miller from Malbry village – had been left with very strict, very specific orders. According to Nat Parson, the Outlander was already responsible for two near-fatalities, and they had been strictly warned against any lapse in concentration.

Not that he *looked* to be much of a fighter. Even if he were, the Examiner had left him chained hand and foot, with his fingers strapped together and with a hard gag between his teeth to prevent him from speaking.

This last measure had seemed a little excessive to Dorian Scattergood – after all, the man had to *breathe* – but Dorian was just a guard, as Nat Parson had pointed out, not paid to ask questions.

At any other time Dorian would have had no hesitation in pointing out that he wasn't actually being paid *at all*, but the presence of an Examiner from the Universal City had made him cautious, and he had returned to his post without a word. Which didn't make him any happier. The Scattergoods were an influential family in the valley, and Dorian didn't enjoy being ordered about. Perhaps that was why he decided to check on the prisoner – in spite of his orders – just as midnight rang from the church tower.

Entering the roundhouse, he found the prisoner still awake. Not surprising, really – it was hard to imagine anyone being able to sleep in such a position. The prisoner's one eye glittered in the light of the torch; his face was drawn and motionless.

Now, Dorian Scattergood was an easy-going fellow. A pig farmer by trade, he valued the quiet life above all, and he didn't like unpleasantness of any kind. He was, in fact, Adam's uncle, but had little in common with the rest of the family, preferring to mind his own business and let them get on with theirs. He'd moved out to Forge's Post some years ago, leaving Malbry, Nat Parson and the rest of the Scattergoods behind him. Unbeknownst to everyone but his mother, he also had a ruinmark on his right forearm – a broken form of *Thuris,* the Thorn, which she had obscured as best she could with a hot iron and soot – and although he had never shown any evidence of unnatural powers, he was known in the valley as a sceptic and a freethinker.

Unsurprisingly this had not endeared him to Nat Parson. Tension had built up between them, and then, ten years ago, Nat had found out that one of Dorian's sows – Black Nell, a good breeder, with a broken ruinmark and a vicious temper – had eaten a litter of her own piglets. It happened occasionally – breeding sows were funny creatures, and old Nelly had always been temperamental – but the parson had made a great meal of the whole affair, calling in the bishop, for Laws' sakes, and practically implying that Dorian had been involved in unnatural doings.

It had cost Dorian some business – in fact there were still folk in the valley who refused to deal with him – and it had left him with a great mistrust for the parson. Lucky for Odin it had, of course; for it meant that Dorian, of all the villagers, was the most inclined to disobey his orders.

Now he peered at the prisoner. The fellow certainly *looked* harmless enough. And that gag must hurt, forced between the Outlander's teeth and held in place with a bit and a strap.

He wondered why Nat had thought it so necessary that he be gagged at all. Just plain old meanness, more than likely.

'Are you all right?' he asked the prisoner.

Understandably Odin said nothing. Through the gag his breath came in shallow gasps.

Dorian thought he wouldn't treat a plough horse to a bit like that, let alone a man. He moved a little closer. 'Can you breathe?' he said. 'Just nod if you can.'

Outside the roundhouse Tyas Miller was getting nervous. 'What's wrong?' he hissed. 'You're supposed to be keeping watch.'

'Just a minute,' said Dorian. 'I don't think he can breathe.'

Tyas put his head round the door. 'Come on,' he urged. 'You're not even supposed to be in there.'

When he saw Dorian, his face dropped. 'The parson said not to go near him,' he protested. 'He said—'

'The parson says a lot of things,' said Dorian, leaning over to release the gag from the prisoner's mouth. 'Now, you stay outside and watch the road. I'll not be a minute in here.'

The strap was stiff. Dorian loosed it then cautiously drew the gag from between the prisoner's teeth. 'I'm warning you, fellow. One word and it goes back.'

Odin looked at him but said nothing.

Dorian nodded. 'You'd like a drink, I dare say.' He pulled out a flask from his pocket and held it to the prisoner's lips.

The Outlander drank, keeping his eye on the gag in Dorian's hand.

'I'd leave it off all night if I could,' said Dorian, seeing his look, 'but I'm under orders. Do you understand?'

'Just a few minutes,' whispered Odin, whose mouth was bleeding. 'What harm can it do?'

Dorian thought of Matt Law and Jan Goodchild, and looked uncertain. He wasn't sure he believed half of what the parson had told him, but Tyas Miller had seen the mindsword with his own eyes; had seen it cut through flesh like steel.

'Please,' said Odin.

Dorian shot a glance over his shoulder to where Tyas was standing guard outside the door. The fellow was chained fast enough, he thought. Even his fingers were fastened tight. 'Not a word,' he said.

The prisoner nodded.

'All right,' said Dorian. 'Half an hour. No more.'

For the next thirty minutes Odin worked in near silence. His glam was still weak, and even if it had been stronger, the straps on his hands would have made the fingerings of the Elder Script almost impossible.

Instead he concentrated on the cantrips; those small uttered spells that require little glam. Even so, it was hard. In spite of the water, his throat was still parched dry, and his mouth hurt badly enough to make speech difficult.

He tried it anyway. *Naudr*, reversed, would have loosened his hands, but this time it died, barely raising a spark. He tried it again, forcing his cracked lips to form the words.

'*Naudr gerer naeppa koste*
Noktan kaelr i froste.'

It might have been his imagination, but he thought the straps on his left hand slackened a little. Not enough, though; at this rate he would have to cast a dozen cantrips in order to free just one finger. After that he might be able to try a working – if there was time, and if his glam held, and if the guard—

The clock tower struck. Half past twelve. Time.

220

5

Meanwhile, less than a mile away, Maddy was closing steadily on the eagle and the hawk. She'd kept high above the other two, well out of their line of vision, and she was almost sure she hadn't been seen. Now she veered a little to the right, still keeping very high, and surveyed the village with her falcon's gaze.

She could see the roundhouse, a squat little building not far from the church. A guard stood outside it; another seemed to be looking inside. *Only two of them. Good*, she thought.

Elsewhere it seemed fairly quiet. There was no sign of a posse, or any other unusual activity. The Seven Sleepers Inn had closed for the night, and only one light shone from inside, where no doubt Mrs Scattergood had found some other poor soul to do her clearing up.

In the street behind the Seven Sleepers a couple of late revellers were walking home, their gait uncertain and their voices raised. Maddy recognized one of them straight away – it was Audun Briggs, a roofer from Malbry – but it took her a few moments more to recognize the second.

The second was her father, the smith.

That was a shock – but Maddy flew on. She couldn't afford to be delayed. She only hoped that if there was trouble, Jed would have the sense to keep well clear. He was her father, after all, and she would prefer him – indeed, she would prefer *all* the villagers – to be well out of the way when the sparks began to fly.

She was reaching the outskirts of Malbry now. In front of her, less than a hundred yards ahead, the hawk and the eagle were beginning their descent.

Maddy stooped, falling steeply from her superior height. She made for the church tower, dropping down behind its stubby spike, and fluttered to a landing, gracelessly, in the deserted churchyard.

The feather cloak proved simple to release. A shrug, a cantrip, and it fell to the ground, leaving Maddy to bundle it up as best she could and thrust it into her belt. Unlike the others in their Aspects, she had retained her clothes underneath the falcon cloak. Good. That gave her a little more time.

She looked around. There was no one about. The church was dark, and so was the Parsonage. Only one light shone from under the eaves. Good, thought Maddy again. She found the path – mourning the loss of her bird's night vision – and began to run quietly down it towards the village square, now deserted as the church clock struck half past the hour.

It was time.

In the sky above Malbry, Loki's time was running out. He had been thinking furiously throughout his flight, but as yet no solution to his particular problem had presented itself.

If he tried to get away, the eagle would catch him, ripping him apart with her talons.

If he stayed, he faced one (or both) of two enemies, neither of whom had any reason to love him. His hold on Skadi, he knew, would last just long enough for her to realize that he'd lied to her once more. As for the General – what mercy could he expect from him?

Even if he managed to get away – during the scrap, perhaps, or in the confusion – how long would he last? If Odin escaped, he'd soon come after him. And if he didn't, the Vanir would.

It didn't look good, he thought as he began his descent. His only hope was that the girl Maddy would take his side.

That didn't seem likely. Then again, she could have killed him twice. She had chosen not to. What that meant he couldn't say, but perhaps—

Behind him the eagle gave a harsh cry of warning – *Hurry up, you* – and Loki obediently entered his dive.

6

The night was aflame with secret stars. So the Examiner told himself as he stepped out into the cold air and, in the magic circle of his finger and thumb, saw the light-trails of a thousand comings and goings spring into life around him.

So this is what the Nameless sees, he thought, looking up into the illuminated sky. *I wonder – however does It stay sane?*

He staggered a little beneath his new awareness. Then he saw something that made him draw sharp breath. Two light-trails, one violet, one icy blue, streaking like comets towards Malbry. *More demons,* he thought, and drew the Good Book even tighter to his thin chest. *More demons. Better hurry.*

He reached the roundhouse minutes later. He was pleased to see that the guards were still alert, though one of them gave him an anxious look, as if expecting censure.

'Anything?' he said in a sharp voice.

Both guards shook their heads.

'Then you are dismissed,' said the Examiner, reaching for the key. 'I won't be needing you again tonight.'

The anxious guard now looked relieved and, with the sketchiest of salutes, went on his way. The second – Scattergood, if the Examiner recalled the name – seemed inclined to loiter. His colours too seemed somehow wrong, as if he were nervous, or had something on his mind.

'It's a little late,' he said, politely enough but with a question in his voice.

'So?' said the Examiner, who was not used to having his decisions questioned.

'Well,' said Dorian, 'I thought—'

'I can do my own thinking, I'll thank you, fellow,' said the Examiner, making the sign with his finger and thumb.

Now Dorian's colours deepened abruptly, and the Examiner realized that the man was not nervous, as he had first assumed, but actually *angry*. This did not trouble him, however. He had dealt with a good many rustics in his time, and he was aware that such folk often resented the work of the Order.

'*Fellow?*' said Dorian. 'Who d'you think you're calling *fellow?*'

The Examiner took a step towards him. 'Out of my way – *fellow*,' he hissed, holding his gaze, and smiled as the guard's colours flickered from angry red to uncertain orange, then finally to muddy brown. His eyes dropped; he muttered some commonplace; and then he was gone with a single backward glance of resentment, furtive, into the night.

The Examiner shrugged. *Rustics*, he thought.

Little did he know that for Elias Rede – otherwise known as Examiner Number 4421974 – he'd used that word just once too often.

Odin looked up as the door opened. He was far from close to breaking free, but by working and needling at the straps that bound his right hand he had managed to slip three fingers loose. It was not enough, but it was a start; and thanks to Dorian Scattergood it was to take the Examiner completely by surprise.

He'd entered the roundhouse boldly, the Good Book tucked comfortably beneath his arm. He had already quite forgotten the misery of Communion; that feeling of worth-lessness and the knowledge that the most trivial and intimate part of his secret self had been peeled open for the casual scrutiny of something immeasurably more powerful . . .

Now he felt *good*. Strong. Masterful.

Armed with his new awareness, he saw now that what he had taken for the compassion in his soul was in fact a deep, unworthy squeamishness. He had been arrogant enough to believe that he knew the will of the Nameless.

Now he knew better. Now he saw that he had spent the past thirty years as a rat-catcher who thought he was a warrior.

Today, he thought, *my war begins. No more rats for me.*

Still trembling with the exaltation of his noble task, he turned to his prisoner. The man's face was in shadow, but the Examiner saw at once that his gag had been removed.

That stupid guard! He felt a surge of annoyance, but no more; the prisoner's hands were still behind his back, and his colours reflected his exhaustion. Across the ruin of his left eye, *Raedo* shone weirdly, a butterfly blue against his weathered skin.

'I know you,' said the Examiner softly, opening the Book. 'And now I know your true name.'

Odin did not move. Every muscle protested, but he remained quite still. He knew he would have one chance, and one chance only. Surprise was on his side, but confronted with the power of the Word he had few illusions as to his success. Still, he thought, if he could only get the timing right . . .

Hands still behind his back, he worked at the runes, aware that his glam was almost out; that if he missed, there could be no second try; but that sometimes a flung stone can be just enough to turn aside a hammer blow.

Beneath his fingers, with aching slowness, the rune *Tyr* had begun to take shape. *Tyr* the Warrior, which had once adorned a mindsword of such power that it made him well-nigh invincible in battle – now reduced to a sliver of runelight no bigger than his fingernail.

But it was sharp. Beneath its small curved blade a fourth finger worked free of its bindings, then a thumb. Odin flexed his right hand, rubbing his palm softly with his middle finger like a spinner rolling a thread.

The movement was too small for the Examiner to see. But he saw its reflection in One-Eye's colours; a darkening of purpose that made him narrow his eyes. Was the fellow planning something?

'I see you'd like to kill me,' he said, watching the blue of the prisoner's glam take on the glossy purple of a swollen thundercloud.

Odin said nothing; but behind his back his fingers worked.

'So you won't talk?' said the Examiner, smiling. 'I assure you, you will.' In his hands the Book of Words lay open at chapter one: 'Invocations'.

In other words, *Names*.

227

7

It takes a superior kind of courage to torture a man, reflected the Examiner. Not everybody has it, nor are many called to the task. Even he, in spite of his brave talk, had never been required to deal with anything much higher up the scale of being than a ruinmarked nag, or a warren of rabblesome goblins.

And now he must cast the Word on a man.

The thought made him feel slightly sick – but not with horror, he realized. With excitement.

Of course, he already knew its effects. He'd first seen them in action thirty years ago, when he was just a scrub. It had sickened him then: the creature's hate, its curses; and at the end, when the final invocations had all been made, the near-human bewilderment in its pain-filled eyes.

Now he felt a surge of righteous joy. This was to be his moment of glory. For this task he had been granted a power that Magisters waited years in vain to receive; and he would prove himself worthy – aye, if he had to wade through rivers of unnatural blood.

Around him the Word began to take shape as, in a steady voice, he began to read aloud.

> '*I name you Odin, son of Bór.*
> *I name you Grim and Gan-glari,*
> *Herian, Hialmberi,*
> *Thekk, Third, Thunn, Unn.*
> *I name you Bolverk, Grimnir, Blindi, Harbard;*
> *Svidur, Svidri—*'

At this point Odin could leave it no longer. With a sharp

movement he brought his hand from behind his back and flung *Tyr* with all his strength at the Examiner. At the same time he tore his left hand free of its bindings and cast *Naudr*, reversed, to release the chains that held him.

The weapon was small but its aim was true. It snickered through the air, bit deeply into the Examiner's thumb and sliced across the pages of the Good Book before punching into the Examiner's side.

It lodged there, sadly not deep enough to kill the man, but able to tap his blood in such abundance that for a moment Odin had the upper hand. He leaped at the Examiner, not with glamours now but with his own strength, knocking the Book out of his hands and driving the man against the wall of the roundhouse.

The Examiner, no fighter, gave a cry of alarm. Odin closed in. And he might even have managed to take the man if at that very moment the roundhouse door had not been flung open, and three men appeared in the doorway.

One was Audun Briggs. The second was Jed Smith. And the third was Nat Parson, his face flushed with unholy fire.

229

8

Meanwhile, above the roundhouse, Loki had spotted the Examiner's trail. He'd seen it before; it was a strange greenish colour, bright but somehow *sickly*, glowing like St Sepulchre's fire.

He saw the parson too, with his couple of henchmen; though both of them were far too preoccupied with what was happening in the roundhouse to pay any heed to the small brown bird that landed on the hedge, not far from them. Quickly Loki shrugged off his bird Aspect. A glance over his shoulder told him that Skadi had come to rest not far away, also clad only in her skin, but with her runewhip already in hand.

Here goes, he thought. *Death or glory*. Of the two, he wasn't sure which he feared most.

Odin saw the three men enter. Instinctively he turned to fight – and straight away caught Jed Smith's crossbow bolt straight through the shoulder. It pinned him to the wall, and for a few seconds he was caught there, one hand pressed against the missile's shaft, trying vainly to wrench it out.

'*Examiner!*' Nat ran towards the fallen man. The Examiner was pale, but still conscious; his reddened hands clasped over his belly. At his feet the Good Book lay open, sliced almost in two by the mindbolt that had struck him.

Impatiently he waved the parson away. 'The prisoner!' he gasped.

Nat felt a twinge of resentment. 'He's safe, Examiner,' he assured his guest.

'Secure him!' gasped the Examiner again, groping for his Book. 'Secure him – gag him – while I invoke the Word!'

Nat Parson gave him a sideways glance. Oho, so the Examiner was asking for his help now, was he? *Polite as ever, eh, Mister Abstinence? But not so cool with that hole in your gut!*

Nevertheless he raced to obey the order, joining Audun Briggs in half dragging Odin to the far side of the roundhouse while Jed Smith kept the prisoner covered, a second crossbow bolt ready.

He had no need of it, however. There was no fight left in the Outlander. Once more bound and gagged, he could do nothing but watch as the Examiner, lurching to his feet (with the parson's help), prepared to complete the canticle.

'I name you Thror, Atrid, Oski, Veratyr . . .'

And now Odin could feel the Word closing on him . . .

'Thund, Vidur, Fiolsvinn, Ygg.'

His curse was stifled by the gag; his entire will now struggled against that of the Word. But his will was failing; his blood soaked into the hardpack floor. He remembered the Examiner saying to him *Your time is over* and was suddenly conscious – amid his rage and sorrow – of a feeling of deep and undeniable relief.

9

Something was definitely going on inside the roundhouse. Maddy could feel it – *see* it – as *Bjarkán* teased out the signs from the cool night air. She could see two signatures – Skadi and Loki – approaching from the opposite side of the square. They had not yet seen her, and silently Maddy made for the roundhouse's only door, keeping to the broad crescent of moonshadow that skirted the building.

At her side her hand began to curl into the familiar shape of *Hagall*, the Destroyer.

Less than a dozen feet away the Examiner was preparing to unleash the Word.

The Word itself is entirely soundless.

Nat had learned that already, on Red Horse Hill. The Word is *cast*, not spoken, although in most cases it is preceded by all manner of verses and canticles designed to give it greater power.

His eye flicked back to the Book in the Examiner's hands. The Book of Words, unlocked in his presence for the first time. The list of names on the butchered page filled nine verses, and their effect on the prisoner had been dramatic. Now he slumped, glaring, on the roundhouse floor, his single eye blazing defiantly, the ruinmark on his face glowing with unnatural light.

The Examiner too looked exhausted; his hands fumbled blindly at the open Book.

'Let me hold it,' said Nat, reaching to take it.

The Examiner did not protest; he surrendered the Book into the parson's hands without even seeming to hear his words.

'Now answer me.' The Examiner's voice was hoarse with exertion. His eyes fixed the prisoner; his bloody hands shook. 'Tell me this, and tell me true. Where are the Seer-folk? Where are they hiding? What are their numbers? Their weapons? Their plans?'

Odin snarled beneath the gag.

'I said, where *are* they?'

Odin writhed and shook his head.

Nat Parson wondered how the Examiner expected to get a confession of any sort from a man who was so securely prevented from speech. 'Perhaps if I removed the gag, Examiner—'

'Be quiet, fool, and stand aside!'

At this, Nat jumped as if stung. 'Examiner, I must protest . . .'

But the Examiner was not listening. Eyes narrowed like a man who can almost – but not quite – grasp the thing he seeks, he leaned forward, and the Word rang soundlessly into the air.

All over the village, hackles raised; cupboard doors swung open; sleepers turned over from one uncomfortable dream into another.

'*Where are the Seer-folk?*' he hissed again, making a strange little sign with his finger and thumb.

And now the parson was sure he could see a kind of coloured light that surrounded prisoner and Examiner like an oily smoke. It peacocked around them in lazy coils, and with his hands the Examiner fretted and teased the illuminated air like a seamstress combing silks.

But there was more, the parson thought. There were *words* in the colours. He could almost hear them: words fluttering like moths in a jar. Not a word came from the prisoner on the floor; and yet somehow the Examiner was making him speak.

And now Nat realized with mounting excitement that

what he had taken for colours and lights were actually *thoughts* – thoughts drawn directly from the Outlander's mind.

Of course, Nat knew perfectly well that he should not have been watching this at all. The mysteries of the Order were jealously guarded, which was why the Book of Words was closed. By rights he knew his duty: to stand back, eyes lowered, well out of range, and let the Examiner perform his Interrogation.

But Nat was ambitious. The thought of the Word – so close he could practically touch it – eclipsed both caution and sense of duty. Instead he stepped closer, made the same strange sign he had seen the Examiner make – and in a second the truesight enveloped him, spinning him for a moment into a maelstrom of lights and signatures.

Could this possibly be . . . a *dream*?

If so, it was the first one Nat Parson had ever experienced.

'O beautiful!' he breathed, and moving closer, unable to help himself, for a second he held the prisoner's eye and something – some intimacy – passed between them.

The Examiner felt it like a rush of air. But the parson was in his way, damn the fool, and in the half-second it took to push him aside, the precious information was lost.

The Examiner gave a howl of anger and frustration.

Nat Parson stared at the prisoner, his eyes wide with new knowledge.

And at that moment the roundhouse door slammed open on its hinges and a bolt of deadly blue light shot into the room.

I'm going to die, the parson thought as he cowered on the floor. He was vaguely conscious of Audun and Jed doing the same; at his side the Examiner lay, already stiffening, hands outstretched as if to ward off annihilation.

There was no doubt in Nat's mind that the man was dead – the bolt had ripped him almost in two. The Good Book lay on the floor beside him, its pages scattered and scorched by the blast.

But even this had not killed his curiosity. As the other two hid their eyes, he looked up, made a circle with his finger and thumb and saw his attackers: a woman, quite naked and almost too beautiful to look at in her caul of cold fire, and a young man in a state of similar undress, with a crooked smile that made the parson shiver.

'Get him,' said Skadi.

'Hang on,' said Loki. 'I'm freezing to death.' Briefly he surveyed Audun, Nat and Jed, still lying shivering on the roundhouse floor. 'That tunic should do,' he said to Audun. 'Oh, and the boots.' And at that he rapidly relieved him of both, leaving the guard in his underthings. 'Not exactly a *perfect* fit,' said Loki, 'but in the circumstances—'

'I said, *get* him,' snapped Skadi with mounting impatience.

Loki shrugged and stepped over to the prisoner. 'Stand up, brother of mine,' he said, forking a runesign so that the chains dropped off. 'Here comes the cavalry.'

Odin stood up. He looked terrible, thought Loki. Good news at any other time – but today he had been rather counting on the General's protection.

Skadi moved forward and raised her glam. The runewhip hissed; its tip forked like a serpent's tongue. 'And now,' she said, 'give me the Whisperer.'

10

Loki considered shifting to his fiery Aspect, then rejected the thought as a waste of glam. Skadi was standing over him, *Isa* at the ready; and fast as he was, he feared she was faster.

'Of course I'll keep my end of the bargain,' he said, not taking his eye away from the runewhip that crackled and hissed like bottled lightning. 'Eventually.'

Skadi's expression, habitually cold, grew icy. 'I warned you,' she said in a low voice.

'And I told you straight. I promised you the Whisperer. You'll get it, don't fret' – he glanced at Odin – 'when we're all out of this safely.'

Now, One-Eye was weak, but he had lost none of his mental agility. He knew Loki well enough to understand the game he was playing, and to play along – for the time being. He could be lying – he probably was – but whether or not he had the Whisperer, now was not the time to dispute it.

'That wasn't the deal,' said Skadi, coming closer.

'Try to think,' said Odin calmly. 'Would either of us have brought it here, like some valueless bauble? Or would we rather hide it in a safe place, a place where no one would ever find it?'

Skadi nodded. 'I see,' she said. Then she turned and raised her glam. 'Well, Dogstar, I think that concludes our business,' she said, and brought the runewhip down with a head-splitting crack. It missed Loki – just – and gouged a four-foot-long section out of the wall where he had been standing.

Nat, Jed and Audun, who had all three been lying low in the hope of being overlooked, tried to press themselves further into the roundhouse floor.

Loki shot Odin a look of appeal. 'I don't know if you noticed, but I just saved your life.'

'You think that matters?' Skadi said. 'You think that pays for what you've done?'

'Well, not exactly,' Loki said. 'But you may still need me one of these days . . .'

'I'll take that risk.'

She raised her glam. Barbed *Isa* fretted the air.

But now it was Odin who stepped forward. He looked old now, his face drawn, his shirt drenched with fresh blood, but his colours blazed with sudden fury.

Skadi found him in her way, and stared at him in astonishment. 'You can't be serious,' she said. 'You're giving him your protection now?'

Odin just looked at her steadily. To Nat, who was watching, his colours seemed to envelop him in a cloak of blue fire.

'No,' said Skadi. 'I've waited too long.'

'He's right. I may need him,' Odin said.

'After what happened at Ragnarók?'

'Things have changed since Ragnarók.'

'Some things never change. He dies. And as for you . . .' She fixed Odin with her cold gaze.

'Go on.' His voice was very soft.

'As for you, Odin, my time with the Æsir is done. I have no quarrel against you – yet. But don't imagine I'm yours to command. And don't you *ever* stand in my way.'

Behind her, Nat was mesmerized. The door stood open, not six feet away, and he knew he ought to take his chance to flee before these demons remembered his presence. And yet it held him; their dreadful fascination, their startling *glamour*.

They were the Seer-folk, of course. He'd guessed that at once, as soon as the Examiner cast the Word. *That makes them gods*, he thought in excitement. *Gødfolk or demons; and with that power, who cares?*

Now the three Seer-folk faced each other. To Nat they

looked like columns of flame, sapphire, violet and indigo. He wondered how he could see them still, now that the Examiner was dead, and he remembered the moment of contact between himself and the Outlander, the moment he had looked into the man's eyes and seen . . .

What, exactly, had he seen?

What, exactly, had he *heard*?

The Seer-folk were arguing. The parson vaguely understood why: the ice woman wanted to kill the red-haired man, and the Outlander – who was no Outlander but some kind of Seer warlord – meant to stop her.

'Take care, Odin,' she said in a low voice. 'You left your sovereignty in the Black Fortress. Now you're just another used-up has-been with delusions of godhood. Let me pass, or I'll split you where you stand.'

And she would too, thought Nat Parson. That thing in her hand was all rage. The Outlander, however, seemed unmoved. He was trying to call her bluff, thought Nat; not a move he himself would have considered.

'Last chance,' she said.

And then something that looked like a small firework of great intensity and spectacular power whizzed soundlessly over Nat's head and hit the ice woman in the small of the back, pitching her abruptly into the Outlander's arms.

Nat turned and saw the newcomer, engulfed for the present in a fabulous blaze of red-gold light. *A woman*, he thought – *no, a girl* – clad in a man's waistcoat and a homespun skirt, her hair unbound, her arms outstretched, a sphere of fire in each of her hands.

Laws, he thought, *she makes the other one look like a penny candle* – and then he caught sight of the girl's face and gave a hoarse cry of disbelief.

It's her! Her!

For a second Maddy looked at him, her eyes filled with

dancing lights. Nat almost swooned; and then she was past him without a word. The first thing she did was check the Outlander. 'Are you all right?'

'I will be,' said Odin. 'But I'm out of glam.'

Now Maddy knelt beside the stricken Huntress and found her alive, but still unconscious. 'She'll live,' said Odin, guessing her thoughts. 'But I knew those skills of yours would come in useful.'

Loki, who had dived to the ground the moment the mind-bolt had shot through the door, now dusted himself off with a good show of carelessness and gave Maddy his crooked grin.

'Nice timing,' he said. 'Now to get rid of the Ice Queen . . .' And he raised his hand, summoning *Hagall*, the Destroyer.

'Don't,' said Maddy and Odin together.

'What?' said Loki. 'The moment she comes round she'll be after us.'

'If you touch her,' said Maddy, summoning *Tyr*, 'I'll be the one after you. And as for the rest of you,' she said, turning to Nat and the other two, 'there's been enough violence here already. I wouldn't like to see any more.'

She looked at Jed Smith, who was watching her with horror in his eyes, and her voice trembled, but only once.

'I'm sorry, Dad,' she told him softly. 'There are so many things I can't explain. I—' She stopped there, conscious of the absurdity of trying to tell him that the daughter he'd known for fourteen years had turned into a total stranger. 'Look after yourself,' she said at last. 'Look after Mae. I'll be all right. And as for *you*' – this was to Nat and Audun Briggs – 'you'd better be off. You don't want to be here when Skadi wakes up.'

That was enough for the three men. They left in haste, only Jed daring to look once more over his shoulder before he vanished into the night.

Loki made to follow them. 'Well, folks, if that's all—'

'It isn't,' said Odin.

'Ah,' said Loki. 'Look, old friend, it's not that I don't appreciate this reunion. I mean, it's been a long time, and it's great that you've kept going and all, but—'

'Shut up,' said Maddy.

Loki shut up.

'Now listen, both of you.'

Both of them listened.

11

In the tunnels beneath Red Horse Hill Sugar-and-Sack was trying vainly to avert a rebellion. In the absence of the Captain, and with the growing crisis in the Horse's Eye, things had begun to fall apart, and it was only Sugar's conviction that the Captain was – firstly – still alive and – secondly – liable to blame *him* for all this upset that kept him from joining the rabble in looting, destroying and running amok.

'I'm tellin' yer now,' he told his friend Pickle-Nearest-the-Wind. 'When he gets back and finds this mess—'

'How's he goin' to *get* back?' interrupted a goblin called Able-and-Stout. 'The Eye's closed. They've reversed the Gate. We're down to tunnelling like rabbits to get into World Above, and when we do make it out there, there's guards and posses and whatnot all over the place. I say pack up, take what's worth taking, and get the Gødfolk out of here while we still can.'

'But the Captain—' protested Sugar.

'Let him rot,' said Able-and-Stout. 'Ten to one he's dead anyway.'

'Done,' said Pickle, scenting a bet.

Sugar looked nervous. 'I really don't think—' he began.

'Don't yer?' said Able, grinning. 'Well, I'll give you odds, if you're game. A hogshead of ale says he's dead. All right?'

'All *right*,' said Pickle, shaking his hand.

'All right,' said Sugar, 'but—'

'All right,' said a pleasant – and rather familiar – voice behind them.

'Ah,' said Sugar, turning slowly.

'It's Sugar-and-Spice, isn't it?' said Loki.

Sugar made a strangled noise of protest. 'We was just talking about you, Capten, sir, and sayin' as we knew you'd be back in time – *hem!* – so to *h*ensure that everythin' was ready, and *h*anticipatin' your requirements we – *hem!* . . .'

'Sugar, do you have a cough?' said Loki, looking concerned.

'No, sir, Capten, sir. We just thought, didn't we, boys . . .' He turned to the others for support, and saw, to his astonishment, that they had already fled.

It had taken their combined forces to reverse the runes and break open the Hill. As it was, the aftershock had blown apart the Horse's Eye, which now stood permanently open, a tunnel of darkness leading into World Below.

Loki had not wanted to take them there. But Maddy had convinced him otherwise. In any case One-Eye in his weakened state was not capable of shifting his Aspect, and they could not expect to go far with only one feather cloak between the two of them.

No, she had said, the only thing that made sense was to hold World Below for as long as they could and explore the possibilities of their new partnership.

'Partnership?' She could tell Loki was as uncomfortable with the idea as One-Eye had been. But he was far from being a fool, and with Skadi on the warpath he had been quick to see the advantage of staying together.

Now they sat in his private rooms, with food and wine (provided by Sugar), and talked. No one ate much except Maddy, who was ravenous; Odin drank only a little wine and Loki sat to one side looking edgy and uncomfortable.

'We have to stay together,' Maddy said. 'Settle our differences and work as a team.'

'Easy for you to say,' said Loki. '*You* weren't killed at Ragnarók.'

'*Killed?*' said Maddy.

'Well, as good as,' admitted Odin. 'You know, they don't usually let you into the Black Fortress of Netherworld if you're still alive.'

'But if you were killed, then how—?'

'It's a long tale, Maddy. Perhaps one day—'

'In any case, we're finished now,' said Loki, interrupting. 'The Order on our trail, the Sleepers awake—'

'Not all of them,' said Maddy quickly.

'Oh no? And how long d'you think it'll take Skadi to wake the others?'

'Well,' said Odin, 'at least they haven't got the Whisperer.'

Maddy examined her fingernails very closely.

'They haven't, have they?'

'Well – not as such.'

'Why?' Now his voice was sharp. 'Maddy, is it safe? Where did you leave it?'

There was a rather uncomfortable silence.

'You hid it *where?*' howled Loki.

'Well, I thought I was doing the right thing. Skadi would have killed you if I hadn't thought of something.'

'She'll kill me anyway,' said Loki. 'And she'll kill you for helping me. And as for the General – she'll kill *him*.' He glanced at Odin. 'Unless you've got some fabulous trick up your sleeve, which I rather doubt . . .'

'I haven't,' said Odin. 'But I do know that if the Vanir are awake, then there is really only one thing we can do.'

'What? Surrender?' said Loki.

Odin gave him a warning look.

Loki put a finger to his scarred lips.

'Some of the Vanir are loyal to me,' said Odin. 'The rest may yet be brought around. We can't afford to oppose each other. We'll need all the help we can get if we're to go into battle against the Order.'

Loki nodded. His smile was gone; now he looked eager, almost wistful, as he had by the firepit, when he'd told Maddy there was a war coming. 'So you think we will?'

'I think we must.' Odin's voice was heavy. 'I've known it since I found her, seven years old, savage as a wolf cub, with that mark on her hand. How she got there I couldn't say; but all the signs were there from the beginning. An unbroken runemark – *Aesk*, no less – an innate ability to throw mindrunes, even her *name*—'

'My name?' said Maddy. Both of them ignored her.

'She never suspected,' Odin went on. 'I fed her tales, half-truths in readiness. But I knew from the start. It was in her blood. You can't imagine all the times I've wanted to tell her – all the times I've wanted to give in to her demands and take her back to World's End with me.'

'Tell me *what*?' said Maddy, beginning to lose patience. 'What's in World's End? One-Eye, what is it you haven't told me?'

'But I knew she was safe,' said Odin, ignoring her. 'As long as she lived in this valley, by the Red Horse, I knew she'd come to no real harm. A little unpleasantness from the other children, perhaps—'

'A *little* unpleasantness!' cried Maddy, thinking of Adam Scattergood.

'Aye, a *little*,' snapped Odin. 'It isn't easy being a god, you know. You have to take responsibility. It isn't all about golden thrones and castles in the clouds.'

Maddy was staring at him, mouth slightly open. 'A *god*?'

'Seer, demon, whatever.'

'But I'm a Fiery,' said Maddy. 'You said so yourself.'

'I lied,' he said. 'Welcome to the clan.'

Maddy just stared at both of them. 'You're crazy,' she said. 'I'm Jed Smith's daughter from Malbry village. A runemark, a few glamours – that doesn't make me one of the Seer-folk. It doesn't make me one of *you*.'

'Oh but it does,' said Loki, grinning. 'This was predicted centuries ago. But you know what they say – never trust an oracle. Their talent is all misdirection. Sounds prophetic, but makes no real sense until the thing's already happened.'

'So who am I?' cried Maddy.

'You haven't guessed? All those clues and you haven't guessed?'

'Tell me, Loki,' she snarled, 'or I swear I'll blast you, whether you're a relative or not.'

'All right,' said Loki. 'Keep your fur on.'

'Then tell me,' said Maddy. 'If I'm not Jed Smith's daughter, then *who am I*?'

Odin smiled. A real smile, which gave his stern face a kind of tenderness. 'Your name is Modi,' he said at last. 'You're my grandchild.'

BOOK SIX
Æsir and Vanir

In the beginning there was the Word.
And the Word begat Man
And Man begat Dream
And Dream begat the gods
After which you may find things getting
just a tiny little bit more complicated . . .

Lokabrenna, 6:6:6

1

Outside the roundhouse Nat Parson stood up on legs that felt like wet string. Audun Briggs had almost passed out – whether from fear or from too much ale he could not say – but Jed the smith was sober enough, and grasped the implications of what he had just seen with commendable agility.

'Did you see her?' demanded Nat. 'Did you see the girl?'

Jed nodded.

Nat felt some of his agitation recede. He was aware that Maddy had been in his thoughts rather often in the past few days, and had secretly feared that his obsession might have clouded his mind. Now he felt vindicated. The girl was a demon; and there could be nothing but praise for the man who brought her to justice.

That he himself should be that man was never in doubt. With the Examiner dead, Nat Parson unilaterally proclaimed himself in charge, and appointed Jed Smith (for want of anyone else) his second-in-command. Besides, thought Nat, Jed had every reason to want an end to the bad blood that shamed his family, and when the reinforcements from World's End finally arrived, he would want to make it clear that his loyalties had been with Law and Order from the very beginning.

He turned to Jed, who had moved back towards the roundhouse building, and was watching the fallen Huntress through the open door. Jed had never been a perceptive man, being blessed with more muscle than most but somewhat less brain, and it was clear from his expression that events had left him at a loss. Examiner dead; lawman injured; and here they were, outside a building wherein lay a demon who might awaken at any time.

Jed's eyes found his crossbow, which had fallen to the ground during his flight. 'Shall I go in and finish her?'

'No,' said the parson. His head was spinning. Ambitions that had once seemed as distant as the stars now lay almost within reach. He thought fast, and saw his chance. He would have to be quick. And it would be dangerous, aye – though the rewards could be great. 'Leave me here. Get clothes for the demon woman. You'll find some in my house – borrow one of Ethelberta's gowns. Take Briggs home and sober him up. Don't speak of this to anyone. Either of you. Understood?'

'Aye, Parson. But will you be safe?'

'Of course I will,' said the parson impatiently. 'Now off you go, fellow, and leave me to my business.'

Skadi awoke, and found herself in darkness. The roundhouse door was shut, the Æsir were gone, she was mysteriously clothed, and she had a headache. Only the runes she carried had prevented it from being worse – her attacker had taken her quite unawares.

She snarled a curse and raised her glam; and in the sudden flare of light she saw the parson sitting there, looking pale but quite calm and watching her through the spyhole of the rune *Bjarkán*.

In a second she had reached for her glam; but even as it took shape in her hand, the parson spoke. 'Lady,' he said. 'Don't be alarmed.'

For a second Skadi was astonished at the fellow's presumption. To imagine that she feared him – *him*! She gave a crack of laughter like splitting ice.

But she was also curious. The man seemed so singularly unafraid. She wondered what he had seen, and whether he could identify the person who had knocked her down. Most of all she wondered why he had not killed her when he'd had the chance.

'Did *you* put this on me?' She indicated the gown she was wearing; a blue velvet with a bodice of stitched silver. It was one of Ethelberta's best; and although Skadi despised a lady's finery, preferring the skins of a wild wolf or the feathers of a hunting hawk, she was aware that someone, for some reason, had attempted to please her.

'I did, lady,' said Nat as the Huntress slowly lowered her runewhip. 'Of course, you have every reason to be suspicious of me, but I assure you, I mean you no harm at all. Quite the reverse, in fact.'

Using the truesight, the Huntress looked at him once more with curiosity and contempt. Surprisingly his signature – which was a strangely mottled silver-brown – showed no attempt to deceive or betray. He genuinely believed what he was telling her; and although she now saw him to be wildly excited beneath his appearance of calm, she perceived astonishingly little fear.

'I can help you, lady,' he said. 'In fact I think we can help each other.' And he held out his hand, wherein lay a key, its teeth still red with its master's blood.

Now, the parson had always been an ambitious man. The son of a potter of modest means, he had decided at an early age that he had no wish to follow in his father's footsteps, and had become a parson's prentice at a fortunate time, taking over from his erstwhile master just as the old man was growing too feeble for the task.

He'd married well – to Ethelberta Goodchild, the eldest daughter of a rich valley horse-breeder. To be sure, she was nine years older than Nat, and there were some who considered her a trifle muffin-faced; but she came with a handsome settlement and excellent connections, and her father, Owen Goodchild, had once had high hopes of promotion for his new son-in-law.

But years passed, and promotion never came. Nat was already thirty-one years old, Ethelberta was childless, and he told himself that unless he took matters into his own hands, the chance of achieving something more than a simple parish in the mountains seemed distant indeed.

It was at this point that Nat began to consider the Order as a possible career. Knowing little about it except that it was for the spiritual elite, he set out on a pilgrimage to World's End – officially to replenish his Faith, in reality to discover how he might access the secrets of the Order without having to devote too much of his time to study, abstinence or prayer.

What he found in World's End filled Nat with excitement. He saw the great cathedral of St Sepulchre, with its glass spire and brass dome, its slender columns, its painted windows. He saw the Law Courts, where the Order dispensed justice; and the Penitents' Gate, where heretics were led to the gallows (though sadly the Cleansings themselves were not open to the public, for fear the canticles might be overheard). And he frequented the places where the Examiners went; he walked in their gardens, ate in their refectories, drank in their coffee houses and spent hours watching them in the streets, black gowns flapping, discussing some element of theory, some manuscript they had studied; waiting for his moment to discover the Word.

But of the Word itself he received no sign. The elderly Professor to whom he finally voiced his ambition told him that a prentice must study for a full twelve years before reaching the level of Junior in the Order, and that even at Examiner level it was by no means certain that a member would ever be granted the golden key.

His hopes dashed, Nat had returned to his parish in the mountains. But the image of the key had never left his mind. It became an obsession; the symbol of all that life had denied him. And when Maddy Smith had refused to break the charm upon the golden lock . . .

Nat looked at the key in his hand and smiled – and Skadi wondered briefly how such a fatuous smile could also appear so wolfish.

'*You*? Help *me*?' She began to laugh, an unsettling sound.

The parson watched her patiently. 'We can help each other,' he said. 'The Seer-folk have something both of us want. You want revenge against those who attacked you. I want the Smith girl brought to justice. Each of us has something the other needs. Why not co-operate?'

'Gods,' said the Huntress. 'I'll give you this: I haven't laughed so much since I hung the snake above Loki's head. If you never make it as an Examiner, there's a career in comedy waiting for you. What in the Worlds could you have that I need?'

Nat indicated the ravaged Book, pages scattered on the roundhouse floor. 'Everything we need is in this Book. Every name, every canticle, every invocation of power. With your knowledge and the words in this Book, we could bring down every one of the Seer-folk, we could make them do whatever we want . . .'

Skadi picked up one of the scorched pages.

So, this Word was a kind of glam – a series of cantrips and incantations available even to the Folk. Loki had known of it, she recalled. He had feared it too, she told herself, although the Huntress could not imagine any magic of the Order being more powerful than that of the Ice People.

She scanned the page, expressionless, then dropped it back onto the ground. 'I need no books,' she said.

It was then that Nat had an inspiration. Something in her eyes, perhaps; or the contemptuous way she had said *books*, or the way she'd held the page upside-down . . .

'You can't read, can you?' he said.

Skadi faced him with eyes like knives.

'Don't worry,' the parson said. 'I have the key. I can read

for the both of us. Your powers combined with those of the Word – together we could succeed where the Order has failed. And then they'd *have* to take me in – I'd be an Examiner, maybe even a Professor . . .'

Skadi's lip curled a little. 'I have no use for a book or a key. But if I did, what's to stop me from taking them both – and then killing you, just for fun – like *this*?' And she grasped hold of the parson's hand and forced the fingers back one at a time. The key fell; there was a sound like that of a small twig snapping—

'Please! You need me!' Nat Parson screamed.

'Why?' she said, moving in for the kill.

'Because I was *there*!' the parson cried. 'I was there when the Examiner cast the Word on the one-eyed journeyman!'

The Huntress paused. 'So?' she said.

'So I've seen *inside the General's mind* . . .'

The Huntress stood as if transfixed, her eyes shining like distant glaciers. Next to her, Nat nursed his broken finger, whimpering a little in pain and relief. He had told her everything – not quite in the way that he'd envisaged it (over sherry, in the Parsonage), but in a scrambling, squealing way, in terror for his life.

Lucky for him that she had believed his tale. But glam, as she knew, is volatile – and the fellow's description of what had happened left her in no doubt. He had trespassed into the path of the Word, and in doing so had glimpsed Odin's thoughts – thoughts and plans regarding the Æsir.

Coldly the Huntress considered the Æsir. Though she had joined them for strategy's sake, she felt no loyalty to Odin's clan. Her father and brothers had died at their hands, and Odin himself, who had promised her full recompense, had somehow managed to renege on his deal; to trick her into marriage with Njörd, when Balder the Fair had stolen her heart; and to rob her of her revenge on Loki, who had lured her kinsman to his death.

The Vanir were no better, she thought, following blindly where Loki led. Skadi's allegiance was still to the Ice People, in spite of her marriage to the Man of the Sea, and she'd always been happiest in the Ice Lands, living alone; hunting; taking eagle form and soaring over the dazzling snow.

If war were to be declared, she thought, then this time there would be no alliance. The General had betrayed her, Loki was her sworn enemy, and Maddy Smith – whoever she was – had planted her colours in the enemy camp.

She turned to Nat, who was watching her, his broken finger in his mouth. 'So what did you see?' she asked him softly.

'First your word. I want the girl – and the power in that Book.'

Skadi nodded. 'Very well,' she said. 'But at the first sign of treachery, or if I even suspect you of trying to use your book against me . . .'

The parson nodded.

'Then we have a deal. What did you see?'

'I saw *her*,' he said. 'I saw Maddy Smith. When the Examiner asked, *Where are the Seer-folk?* – that's what I saw in your General's mind. That's what he was trying to hide. And he was ready to die rather than give up her name —'

'Name?' said Skadi.

'Modi,' said the parson. 'That's what he called her. Modi, the Lightning Tree, first child of the New Age.'

255

2

Meanwhile, under Red Horse Hill, Maddy was thinking furiously. One-Eye and Loki had left her alone; One-Eye to sleep and regain his strength before setting off to recover the Whisperer, Loki on some nefarious business of his own. The hall was lit only by a branch of candles, and Maddy's shadow pranced and sprang against the stony walls as she paced repeatedly up and down.

Her initial reaction to One-Eye's disclosure had been an immediate and overwhelming feeling of anger. That he could have kept such a secret from her for so long, only now revealing the truth at a time when battle lines were already drawn, with Maddy – like it or not – firmly on his side.

She hated the deceit of it; and yet, she thought as she paced – hadn't a part of her longed for this? To have a purpose, a clan – a *family*, for gods' sakes? Hadn't the signs been there from the start? Hadn't some part of her always known that Jed Smith and Mae were none of her blood, and that Odin, for all his strangeness, was?

She did not hear Loki enter the hall. He had changed the clothes he had stolen from Audun Briggs for a fresh tunic, shirt and soft-soled boots, and it was only when he touched her arm that she realized he was there at all. By then her agitation was so great that she almost hit him before she recognized who he was.

'Maddy, it's me,' he protested, seeing *Tyr* half formed between her fingers.

Listlessly she banished the rune. 'I don't feel like talking, Loki,' she said.

'Can't say I blame you.' Loki sighed. 'Odin should have told you the truth. But try to see it from his point of view . . .'

'Is that why he sent you? To argue his case?'

'Well, of course he did,' said Loki. 'Why else?'

Maddy couldn't help feeling a little disarmed at his unexpected frankness. She smiled – then remembered his legendary charm.

'Forget it,' she said. 'You're as bad as he is.'

'Why? What did *I* do?'

Maddy gave an angry sniff. 'Everyone knows what's going on except me,' she said. 'What am I, a child? I'm sick of it. I'm sick of *him*. And I'm sick of being treated as if I don't matter. I thought he *liked* me.' She sniffed again, more fiercely than before, and wiped her nose with the sleeve of her shirt. 'I thought he was my friend,' she said.

Loki gave his crooked smile.

'So what does he want? A war with the Order? Is that why he needs the Whisperer?'

Loki shrugged. 'I wouldn't be surprised.'

'But he doesn't have a chance!' she said. 'Even with the Vanir on our side, it would still be the ten of us against *all* of the Order, and anyway' – she lowered her voice – 'the Whisperer practically *told* me he'd lose.'

Loki's eyes widened. 'You mean it made a prophecy? It made a prophecy and you didn't think to tell anyone about it?'

'Well, it didn't make sense,' said Maddy awkwardly. 'I don't even know if it was a prophecy at all. It just kept saying things like, *I speak as I must, and—*'

'Gods,' said Loki, disgusted. 'It made a prophecy. To *you*. After all these years I've been trying to persuade it to say something – *anything*.' Eagerly he leaned closer. 'Did it mention me at all?'

'It wanted me to kill you. Said you'd turn out to be nothing but trouble.'

'Ah. That figures. What else did it say?'

'Something about a terrible war. Thousands dead at a single word. Something about waking the Sleepers . . . a traitor . . . and a General – a General standing alone . . .'

'And when were you planning to tell him all this?'

Maddy was silent.

'Well?'

'I don't know.'

Loki began to laugh softly. But Maddy was scarcely paying attention. Dry-mouthed, she recalled the Whisperer's words; struggled to remember the exact phrasing. It sounded more like verse to her now, bleak verse in the language of prophecy.

I see an army poised for battle.
I see a General standing alone.
I see a traitor at the gate.
I see a sacrifice.

And the dead will awake from the halls of Hel.
And the Nameless shall rise, and Nine Worlds be lost,
Unless the Seven Sleepers wake,
And the Thunderer freed from Netherworld . . .

'It's coming true,' she said at last. 'The Sleepers are awake. The Order is coming. It said the Nine Worlds would be lost . . .' Maddy swallowed, feeling sick. 'And I can't help thinking it's all my fault. *I* was the one who woke the Sleepers. I was the one who recovered the Whisperer. If I'd left it in the firepit—' She broke off and frowned. 'But why is the General standing alone? Why aren't we with him?' Once more Maddy began to pace up and down in the dark hall. '*This isn't what I wanted!*' she yelled.

'Believe it or not,' said Loki sourly, 'I'm not altogether thrilled to be here, either. But I have no choice – without Odin

I'm already dead. The fact that I have a very good chance of ending up dead anyway doesn't *exactly* fill me with enthusiasm.'

'Then *tell* me,' said Maddy urgently. 'Tell me the truth. Who am I really? And why am I here?'

Loki watched her with a little smile across his scarred lips. 'The truth?' he said.

'Yes. *All* of it.'

'The General won't like that,' he said.

All the more reason to tell her, he thought, and deep in his stomach, Loki grinned.

3

'So who am I?' she said. 'And what's my part in all this?'

Loki helped himself to wine. 'Your name is Modi,' he began. 'And the Oracle predicted your birth, long before Ragnarók, though it turns out it wasn't entirely accurate on genders. But one thing it was certain of: Modi and his brother Magni are the first children of the New Age; born to rebuild Asgard and to overthrow the enemies of the gods. That's why you carry that rune on your hand. *Aesk*, the Ash Tree: symbol of renewal and of all the Worlds.'

Maddy looked down at her hand, where *Aesk* shone blood-red against her palm. 'I have a *brother*?' she said at last.

'Or a sister, maybe. If they've been born yet. Like I said, the Oracle hasn't been all that accurate.'

'And my . . . parents?'

'Thor, the Thunder Smith, and Jarnsaxa – not *exactly* his wife, but a warrior woman from the other side of the mountains. So you see, little sister, you *do* have demon blood in you, on your mother's side at least.'

But Maddy was still reeling from the new information. She tasted the names on her tongue – Modi, Magni, Thor, Jarnsaxa – like some fabulous, exotic dish.

'But if *they* were my parents—'

'Then how come you were born to a couple of rustics from the valleys?' Loki grinned, enjoying himself. 'Well, remember when you were little, how you were always told that you shouldn't ever dream, that dreaming was dangerous, and that if you did, the bad nasty Seer-folk would come out of Chaos and steal your soul?'

Maddy nodded.

'Well,' said Loki. 'It turns out they were almost right.'

Maddy listened in near-silence as Loki told his tale. 'Let's start at the good bit,' he said, pouring more wine. 'Let's start at the End of Everything. Ragnarók. The doom of the gods. The fall of Æsir and Vanir alike, the triumph of Chaos, and all that jazz. *Not* a comfortable time for Yours Truly, what with being killed – and by that pompous do-gooder Heimdall, of all people—'

'Hang on,' said Maddy. 'You said that before. You were actually *killed* at Ragnarók?'

'Well,' said Loki, 'it's not that simple. One Aspect of me fell there, yes. But Death is just one of the Nine Worlds. Some of the Æsir found refuge there, where even Surt has no power. But some of us were not so lucky. Some of us were thrown into Netherworld – what your folk would call Damnation—'

'The Black Fortress. What was it like?'

Loki's expression darkened a little. 'Nothing prepares you for Netherworld, Maddy. It was beyond anything even I had known. I'd seen the insides of dungeons before, and until then I had thought a prison was simply a place of walls, bricks, guards – familiar trappings, the same in all worlds.

'But in Netherworld, Disorder rules. So close to Chaos, almost anything becomes possible: the rules of gravity, perspective, sense and substance are bent and shifted; hours and days have no meaning; the line is erased between reality and imagination. What was it like? It was like drowning, Maddy; drowning in an ocean of lost dreams.'

'But you got out.'

Darkly he nodded.

'How?' she said.

'I made a deal with a demon.'

'What deal?'

'The usual,' said Loki. 'A favour for a favour. I was a traitor to both sides, so they decided to make an example of me. I was locked in a cell with no windows and no doors, no up and no down. Nothing could reach me – or so they thought. But the demon offered me a means of escape.'

'How?' said Maddy

'There's a river,' he said, 'at the far edge of Hel. The river Dream charges towards Netherworld iron-clad and at a gallop, churning with all the raw mindstuff of the Nine Worlds. To touch the water is to risk madness or death – and yet it was through Dream that I escaped.' Loki paused to refresh himself. 'I almost lost my mind in the struggle, but at last I found my way into that of an infant, an infant of the Ridings folk.'

Somewhat ruefully he indicated his person. 'I've done what I could with this Aspect,' he said. 'But frankly I used to be much better looking. Still, it's an improvement on Netherworld – which is why I've adopted such a low profile over the past few hundred years. Don't want Surt to get any ideas about checking up on old friends, eh?'

But Maddy's thoughts were racing like winter clouds. 'So you and One-Eye escaped through Dream. Doesn't that mean that others could too?'

Loki shrugged. 'Perhaps,' he said. 'It's dangerous.'

Maddy watched him, a gleam in her eyes. 'But that's not where *I* came from, right? I wasn't part of the Elder Age . . .'

'No, you're new. A new shoot from the old tree.' Loki gave her a cheerful grin. 'A brand new Aspect – no previous owner – just the way the Oracle said. It's people like you who are going to rebuild Asgard after the war, while Odin and I end up as compost. And I'm sure you'll understand if I'd prefer that to be later rather than sooner.'

She nodded. 'I see. Well, I've got an idea.'

'What?' said Loki.

She faced him, eyes bright. 'We'll go and find the Whisperer. Right now, before One-Eye wakes up. We'll bring it back to Red Horse Hill. And we'll put it back into the firepit. That way, no one will have it, and things can go back to the way they were.'

Loki watched her curiously. 'You think so?'

'Loki, I have to try. I can't stand by and let One-Eye get killed for some stupid war he can't possibly win. He's tired. He's reckless. He's living in the past. He's so fixated on the idea of the Whisperer that it's made him think he has a chance. And if he loses, *everyone* loses. All the Nine Worlds, the Oracle said. So you see, if you help me get it back—'

Loki gave a mocking laugh. 'Impeccable logic, as always, Maddy.' He turned away in seeming regret. 'I'm sorry. I'm not getting involved.'

'Please, Loki. I saved your life . . .'

'And I'd like to keep it, if that's all right with you. The General would tear me limb from limb—'

'One-Eye's asleep. He'll be out for hours. Besides, I wouldn't let him hurt you.'

Loki's eyes flashed fire-green. 'You mean you'll give me your protection?' he said.

'Of course I will. If you'll help.'

Loki looked thoughtful. 'Swear it?' he said.

'On my father's name.'

'It's a deal,' he said, and finished the wine.

And so keen was Maddy's excitement, and so eager was she to begin their search that she quite failed to see the look in the Trickster's eyes, or the grin that slowly formed across his scarred lips.

4

In the Hall of Sleepers there was confusion among the Vanir. All were now fully awake; all were present except for Skadi, but neither Idun – who had spoken to the Huntress – nor Freyja – who had not – were able to give a satisfactory account of what had actually occurred.

'You *said* Loki was here,' said Heimdall through his golden teeth.

'So he was,' said Idun. 'He was in a bad way.'

'He'd have been in a worse way if I'd been there,' muttered Heimdall. 'So what's he up to, and how is it that Skadi let him live?'

'And who was the girl?' said Freyja, for the third or fourth time. 'I tell you, if I hadn't been so sleepy and confused, I would *never* have lent her my feather dress—'

'Nuts to your feather dress,' said Heimdall. 'I want to know what Loki's doing in all this.'

'Well,' said Idun, 'he *did* mention the Whisperer . . .'

Five pairs of eyes fixed upon the goddess of plenty.

'The Whisperer?' said Frey.

So Idun told him what she knew. The Whisperer at large; Odin imprisoned; Loki possibly in league with him; and rumours of the Word; not to mention a mysterious girl who could unlock the ice and who had gods knew what glamours of her own . . .

'I say we get out while we still can,' said Frey. 'We're too exposed here if an enemy tries to mount an ambush.'

'I say wait for Skadi,' said Njörd.

'I say go after Loki,' said Heimdall.

'What about the General?' said Bragi.

'What about my feather dress?' said Freyja.

Idun said nothing at all, but simply hummed to herself.

And in the passageway leading into the cavern, two figures standing in the shadows exchanged glances and prepared to put their plan into action.

Loki cast *Yr* and held his breath. So far, so good – he and Maddy had reached the Sleepers without incident, and, more importantly, without alerting the Vanir to their intention.

From the Hall of Sleepers he could already hear a rumour of voices – and through the rune *Bjarkán* he could glimpse their colours: gold, green and ocean-blue. He noted with satisfaction that the Huntress was not among them. Good.

Now for the tricky part; the part that would place him in most danger. They needed a diversion – something to draw the Vanir and to give Maddy the chance to recover the Whisperer. In other words, bait.

And so Loki took a deep breath and began to walk, quickly but casually, towards the entrance to the Sleepers' Hall.

It was gold-armoured Frey who saw him first, and for a few moments he squinted through the daze of glamours that crisscrossed the cavern, trying to decipher the intruder's colours.

There were none that he could see, and that in itself was enough to make him a little wary. However, the figure that stood at the cavern's mouth looked very small to be the cause of alarm. As the others turned to look, the intruder (a little girl of three or four) raised a face of such innocent entreaty in their direction that even Heimdall was taken aback.

'Who are you?' he snapped, recovering quickly.

The child (barefoot and clad only in a man's shirt) smiled prettily and held out her hand. 'I'm Lucy,' she said. 'Do you want a game?'

For a moment the Vanir watched her in silence. It was clear to them all (except perhaps for Idun) that this was some trick: a reconnaissance; a diversion; maybe a trap. Warily they scanned the hall: there was no sign of anyone else, just the curly-headed infant standing alone.

Heimdall bared his golden teeth. 'That's no child,' he said softly. 'If I'm not very much mistaken, that's—'

'You're It,' said Loki, grinning.

And before Heimdall could react, he slipped his disguise, shifted at speed to his wildfire Aspect, and fled for his life across the open hall.

The Vanir wasted no more time. In less than a second the air was shot through with mindbolts, flying daggers of rune-light, flung nets of barbed blue fire. But Loki was fast, using the frills and crannies of the ice cavern to dodge, feint and bewilder his attackers.

'Where is he?' yelled Heimdall, squinting through the runelight.

'Peekaboo,' said Lucy from behind a pillar of ice at the other side of the cavern.

Isa, cast from four different angles, shattered the pillar into a drift of diamonds, but by then the Trickster was already gone. In wildfire Aspect he led them towards the far side of the hall, dodging glamours and runes, twice more reappearing as Lucy from behind one of the fabulous constructions of ice. As the Vanir closed in on all sides, he pretended to falter, turning an expression of anguished appeal onto the group of angry gods.

'Got him!' said Frey. 'There's no way out—'

'Tig,' said Lucy, and shifted again, to bird form this time, and made straight for the ceiling and its colossal central chandelier. At the hub, the small opening made by Loki's fall gaped palely at the approaching dawn.

Too late the Vanir saw his plan.

'After him!' yelled Frey, and shifted into a harrier hawk, rather larger than Loki's bird Aspect. Njörd became a sea eagle, white-winged and dagger-clawed; and Heimdall shifted into a falcon, yellow-eyed and fast as an arrow. The three of them made straight for Loki, while Freyja shot missiles at the gap in the roof and Bragi took out a flute from his pocket and played a little saraband that peppered the air with fast, deadly notes, scorching Loki's feathers and almost bringing him down.

Loki spun in midair, lost control for a moment, then recovered and made for the sky. The sea eagle saw its chance and closed in, but its wingspan was too large for the cavern; it dodged a volley of semi-quavers, wheeled round and clipped an ancient column of ice, shattering its core before flying out of control into the nest of icicles that made up the main part of the ceiling. The frozen chandelier trembled, shook, and finally began to disintegrate, throwing down shards of ice that had hung intact for five hundred years into the Hall of Sleepers.

For a time confusion reigned. A cataract of frozen pieces, some knife-edged, others as large as bales of hay, had begun to tumble, slowly but with increasing momentum, from the bright vaulting. Some smashed onto the polished floor, flinging up fragments that were as sharp and deadly as pieces of shrapnel. Others pulverized before they reached the ground, snowing steely particles into the air.

It was so sudden, so cataclysmic, that for a few crucial seconds the Vanir lost interest in the winged fugitive and scattered to the far corners of the Hall of Sleepers in their various attempts to escape the avalanche:

Bragi played a jig so merry that the ice melted into gentle rain long before it reached his head.

Freyja flung up *Yr* and created a mindshield of golden light against which the falling fragments rebounded harmlessly.

Idun simply smiled vaguely and the particles of ice turned into a shower of apple blossom that drifted quietly to the ground.

Heimdall, Njörd and Frey beat their wings in angry confusion, trying to dodge the falling ice as their prey vanished, with no more injury than a few scorched feathers, through the grinning gap.

And in all the confusion Maddy simply strolled into the hall, quietly retrieved the Whisperer from its hiding place under the loosened snow, then calmly strolled out again – unobserved and unsuspected – into the tunnels of World Below.

5

Now Loki was flying for his life. He'd bought himself some time, of course; the three hunters had been slowed down, both by the collapse of the ice chandelier and by their greater size, which had made it less easy for them to leave through the small gap in the roof.

As it was, he had fifteen minutes on them before he spotted his three pursuers: the falcon, the sea eagle and the harrier hawk, circling the valleys in a hunting pattern, searching for him in the early morning sunlight.

At once Loki dropped his hawk Aspect and came to rest behind a small copse just outside Forge's Post; here stood a tiny log cabin, with a line of washing behind it, and an old lady dozing in a rocking chair on the porch.

The old lady was Crazy Nan Fey, the nurse of Maddy's younger days. She opened one eye as the hawk came to land, and she watched with some interest as it became a naked young man, who proceeded to ransack Nan's washing line in search of something to wear. Nan supposed she ought to intervene – but the loss of an old dress, an apron and a shawl seemed a small price to pay for the spectacle, and she decided against it.

Two minutes later a second old lady, barefoot and with a thick shawl over her head, was walking at a suspiciously athletic pace towards Malbry village. Closer observation might have shown that her left hand was oddly crooked, though few would have recognized the runeshape *Yr*.

Some birds flew overhead for a time, but as far as she saw, they did not land.

Maddy and Loki had arranged to meet by the big old beech in Little Bear Wood. Maddy reached it first, having taken the road through World Below, and she sat down on the grass to wait, and to settle things once and for all with the Whisperer.

Their conversation was not a comfortable one. The Whisperer was resentful at having been left in the Cavern of the Sleepers 'like a damned pebble', as it put it, and Maddy was furious that it had hidden the truth about her Æsir blood.

'I mean, it isn't something you just forget to mention,' she snapped. 'Oh, and by the way, you're Allfather's grand-daughter. Didn't it occur to you that I might be interested?'

The Whisperer glowed in a bored kind of way.

'And another thing,' said Maddy. 'If I'm Modi, Thor's child, and according to the prophecy I'm supposed to rebuild Asgard, then presumably whichever side I'm on wins the war. Right?'

The Whisperer yawned lavishly.

Now Maddy blurted out the question that had been burning the roof of her mouth since Odin had first told her who she was. 'Is that why One-Eye found me?' she said. 'Is that why he taught me what he did? Did he just *pretend* to be my friend so he could use me against the enemy when the time came? And how would he do it? I'm no warrior . . .'

She had a sudden, vivid memory of Loki in the caves saying: *A man may plant a tree for a number of reasons* – and though it was warm in the little wood, Maddy could not suppress a shiver.

The Whisperer gave its dry laugh. 'I warned you,' it said. 'That's what he does. He uses people. He used me when it suited him, then abandoned me to my fate. It'll happen to you, if you let it, girl – to him you're nothing but another step on the road back to Asgard. He'll sacrifice you in the end, just as he sacrificed me, unless—'

'Is this another prophecy?' Maddy interrupted.

'No. It's a prediction,' the Whisperer said.

'What's the difference?'

'Predictions can be wrong. Prophecies can't.'

'So you don't actually know what's going to happen either?' said Maddy.

'Not exactly. But I'm a good guesser.'

Maddy bit a fingernail. '*I see an army poised for battle. I see a General standing alone. I see a traitor at the gate. I see a sacrifice.*' She turned to the Whisperer. 'Is that me?' she said. 'Am I supposed to be the sacrifice? And is One-Eye the traitor?'

'Couldn't say,' smirked the Whisperer.

'*The dead will awake from the halls of Hel. And the Nameless shall rise, and Nine Worlds be lost, unless the Seven Sleepers wake, and the Thunderer freed from Netherworld—* Freed from Netherworld?' Maddy said. 'Is that even possible?'

Within the Whisperer's glassy shell, fragments of rune-light sparkled and spun.

'I said, is it possible?' repeated Maddy. 'To free my father from Netherworld?'

Loki had thought her childish and irrational. In fact, ever since she had heard the tale of his escape from Netherworld Maddy had been thinking very clearly indeed. She had gambled on his willingness to help – not because she trusted in Loki's better nature, but because she expected him to lie. She was sure he had no intention of allowing her to throw the Whisperer back into the firepit; but the task of retrieving it from the Hall of Sleepers was a two-man job, and rather than let it fall into the hands of the Vanir, she was sure that Loki would be ready to humour her – at least until they reached World Below, where he would deliver Maddy and the Whisperer safely into Odin's hands. For a price, of course.

Well, two could play at that game.

On her way from the Hall of Sleepers Maddy had been

doing some serious thinking. Part of her wanted to run to One-Eye with her questions, as she had always done as a small child – but the Whisperer's prophecy had made her wary, not least because, if she read it correctly, One-Eye's defeat could lead to the end of the Worlds.

She wished she'd never heard of the Whisperer. But now that she had, there was no going back. And although it was a poor substitute for her old friend's counsel, at least a prophecy could not lie.

She knew what One-Eye would think of her plan, and it hurt her to deceive him; but there was nothing she could do. *I'd be saving him from himself*, she thought. *I'd be saving the Worlds*.

'Just as long as Loki agrees to help . . .'

'Don't worry about that,' said the Whisperer. 'I can persuade him. I'm very persuasive.'

Maddy gave it a long look. 'Last time I knew, you wanted him dead.'

'Even the dead have their uses,' it said.

It was half an hour later that Loki arrived, footsore and dusty in Crazy Nan's skirts.

'Oh *look*,' said the Whisperer in its nastiest voice. 'Dogstar's taken to wearing a dress. What next, eh? Tiara and pearls?'

'Ha ha. Very funny,' said Loki, untying the shawl that covered his head. 'Sorry I'm late,' he said to Maddy. 'I had to walk.'

'Never mind that now,' said Maddy. 'What matters is that we have the Whisperer.'

The Trickster looked at her curiously. He thought she looked flushed, in excitement or fear, and there was something in her colours, some brightening, that made him feel uneasy.

'What's wrong?' he said.

'We've been talking,' said Maddy.

Loki looked uncomfortable. 'What about?'

'I have an idea,' she told him.

And then she began to outline her plan, hesitantly at first, then with growing confidence as beside her Loki's face went paler and paler, and the Whisperer glowed like a clutch of fireflies and smiled as if it might explode.

'Netherworld?' he said at last. 'You want me to go to *Netherworld*?'

'You heard what the Oracle said!'

'Poetic licence,' snapped Loki. 'Oracles love that kind of thing.'

'*The General will stand alone*, it said. *The Nameless shall rise. Nine Worlds will be lost.* War, Loki. A terrible war. And the only way of stopping it is to free my father from Netherworld. You promised you'd help—'

'I said I'd help you recover the Whisperer,' said Loki. 'I never said anything about saving the Worlds. I mean, what's so wrong with a war anyway?'

Maddy thought of the Strond valley, and the fields and houses scattered all the way from Malbry village to Forge's Post, and all the little roads and hedges, and the smell of burning stubble in the fall. She thought of Crazy Nan in her rocking chair, and of market day on the village green, and of Jed Smith, who had done his best, and of all the soft, harmless people of the valley with their little lives and their silly conviction that they were at the centre of the Worlds.

And for the first time in her life Maddy Smith understood. The lectures; the bullying; the signs forked in secret behind her back. The hundred small cruelties that had sent her running for Little Bear Wood more times than she could remember. She'd thought they hated her because she was different; but now she knew better. They'd been afraid. Afraid of the cuckoo in their nest; afraid that one day it would grow and bring Chaos upon their little world.

And she had, Maddy thought. She'd started this. Without her, the Sleepers would not have awakened, the Whisperer would still be safe in the pit, and the war might be fifty years away, or a hundred years, or even more . . .

She turned to Loki. 'It can be done. You said so yourself.'

Loki gave a sharp laugh. 'You've got no idea what you're suggesting. You've never even so much as set foot outside your valley before, and now you're planning to storm the Black Fortress. Bit of a leap, don't you think?'

'You're afraid,' said Maddy, and Loki gave another crack of laughter.

'Afraid?' he said. 'Of *course* I'm afraid. Being afraid is what I'm good at. Being afraid is why I'm still here. And speaking of being afraid' – he glanced at the Whisperer – 'have you any idea what the General would do to me if— No, *don't* answer that,' he said. 'I'd rather not know. Suffice it to say that we both go and see him now, give him the damn thing, let him negotiate with the Vanir, yadda yadda yadda . . .'

'When Odin and Wise Mimir meet, Chaos will come to the Nine Worlds.' That was the Whisperer, speaking almost idly, but with its colours flaring like dragonfire.

Loki turned. '*What* did you say?'

'I speak as I must, and cannot be silent.'

'Oh no.' Loki held up his hands. 'Don't even think of making a prophecy right now. I don't want to hear it. I don't want to know.'

But the Whisperer was speaking again. Its voice was not loud, but it commanded attention, and both of them listened, Maddy in bewilderment, and Loki in growing disbelief and horror.

'I see an Ash at the open gate,' said the Whisperer. 'Lightning-struck, but green in shoot. I see a meeting at

Nether's Edge, of the wise, and of the not so wise. I see a death ship on the shores of Hel – and Bór's son with his dog at his feet—'

'Oh, gods,' said Loki. 'Please don't say any more.'

'I speak as I must, and cannot be—'

'You were silent enough for five hundred years,' protested Loki, who had gone even paler than before. 'Why break the habit now?'

'Hang on,' said Maddy. 'Bór's son – that's one of Odin's names.'

Loki nodded, looking sick.

'And the dog?'

Loki swallowed painfully. Even his colours had turned pale, shot through with silvery threads of fear. 'Forget it,' he said in a tight voice.

Maddy turned to the Whisperer. 'Well?' she said. 'What does it mean?'

The Oracle glowed in the pattern she had come to recognize as amusement. 'All I do is prophesy,' it said sweetly. 'I leave the interpretation to others.'

Maddy frowned. 'The Ash. I suppose that's me. The green shoot from the lightning tree. The wise – surely that's the Whisperer. Bór's son on a death ship – with his dog at his feet . . .' Her eyes came to rest on Loki's face. 'Ah,' she said. 'Dogstar. I see.'

Loki sighed. 'So it means I die. Do you *have* to repeat it?'

'Well, it doesn't *necessarily* mean you die—'

'Oh, really?' snapped Loki. 'Me, on Hel's shore? What else do you think I'd be doing there?' He began to pace, tucking his skirts into his waistband, his shawl flying. 'Why couldn't you have told me all this before?' he demanded of the Whisperer.

The Oracle smirked and said nothing.

Loki put his face in his hands.

'Come on,' said Maddy. 'You're not dead yet. In fact—'
She stopped for a moment, her face brightening. 'Let me get this right,' she said. 'According to the Whisperer, if Odin dies, then you do too.'

Loki made a muffled sound of despair.

'And when Odin and Mimir meet, then Chaos will come – Odin will fall . . .'

Loki's eyes turned to hers.

'*Unless* we free Thor from Netherworld – in which case the war won't happen at all, the General won't be die, Nine Worlds will be saved and my father . . .'

There was a long silence, during which Loki stared transfixed at Maddy, Maddy's heart raced even faster and the Whisperer shone like a chunk of star.

'So you see,' she said, 'you have to come. You know the way into Netherworld. The Whisperer said it could be done – and if we keep hold of the Whisperer, then Odin won't meet it, and there won't be a war, and—'

'Listen, Maddy,' interrupted Loki. 'Much as I'd love to save the Nine Worlds while committing suicide, I have a much simpler plan. The Oracle saw me dead in Hel. Right? So as long as I stay *away* from Hel—'

He broke off suddenly, aware of a small but vicious stabbing pain just above his left eyebrow. For a second he thought something had stung him. Then he felt the Whisperer's presence, like a sharp object raking his mind. He took a step back, and almost fell.

Ouch, that hurts!

He sensed it catch his thoughts, like a fingernail snagging silk. It was an uncomfortable feeling, but when Loki tried to close his mind to it, a second lance of pain, more acute this time, slammed through his head.

'What's wrong?' said Maddy, seeing him falter.

But Loki was in no position just then to explain. Eyes

closed, he took another drunken step. Below him the Whisperer sparkled with glee.

What do you want? he said silently.

Your attention, Dogstar. And your word.

'My word?'

In silence, if you value your life.

With an effort, Loki nodded.

I know what you're thinking, said the voice in his mind. *You are afraid, because I can read your thoughts. You are surprised at how my powers have grown.*

Loki said nothing, but gritted his teeth.

And you are wondering whether I mean to punish you.

Still Loki said nothing.

I ought to, said the Whisperer. *But I'm giving you a chance to redeem yourself.*

Redeem myself? said Loki, surprised. *Since when did you care about saving my soul?*

In his mind he felt the Whisperer's amusement. *It's not your soul I care about. Nevertheless you will do as I say. Go with the girl to Netherworld. Take me with you as far as Hel. Free the Thunderer – avert the war—*

And why would you want to go to Hel? What's your plan, you old fraud?

A last, tremendous bolt of pain went rocketing through Loki's head. He fell to his knees, unable to cry out, as the voice in his mind delivered its warning.

No questions, it said. *Just do as I say.*

And then the alien presence was gone, leaving him shaking and breathless. Once more he wondered at how much stronger it had grown; his struggle to contain the thing, centuries earlier, had lasted for days, exhausting them both and causing devastation in World Below, but today it had brought him to his knees in seconds.

Now it shone with a warning gleam, and Loki heard its

whispering voice, faint but commanding at the back of his mind.

No trickery. Do I have your word?

All right. He opened his eyes and took slow, deep breaths.

'What happened?' said Maddy, looking concerned.

Loki shrugged. 'I fell,' he said. 'Bloody skirts.' And with those words he picked himself up and turned the full force of his scarred smile at Maddy. 'Now,' he said. 'Are we going to Netherworld or not?'

6

It was a most unholy alliance. On the one side the Huntress, royally clad in Ethelberta's blue velvet; on the other, the parson, with his golden key. It was two in the morning when they repaired to the Parsonage and, to Ethel's bewilderment and displeasure, went immediately to Nat's study and locked themselves in.

There, Nat told the Huntress all he knew – about Maddy Smith, the one-eyed journeyman who had been her friend, and most especially about the Order and its works – and he read to her from the Good Book, and recited some of the canticles in the lesser of the Closed Chapters.

Skadi watched and listened with cold amusement to the little man's efforts to master the glamour that he called the Word. As the hours passed, however, she began to grow curious. He was clumsy and untrained, but he had a spark; a power she did not quite understand. She could see it in his colours; it was almost as if there were *two* light-signatures there instead of one: a normal signature of an undistinguished brown, and a brighter thread that ran through it, as a silver skein may be woven into a cheaper silk. Somehow, it seemed, Nat Parson, for all his conceit and self-indulgence, had powers that might be of value to her – or might threaten her, if allowed to grow untrained.

'Now light it.' They were sitting at Nat's desk, an unlit taper in a candlestick between them. *Kaen*, the fire-rune, gleamed, a little crookedly, between the parson's fingers.

'You're not concentrating,' said Skadi impatiently. 'Hold it steady, focus your thoughts, say the cantrip and light the taper.'

For several seconds Nat frowned at the candlestick. 'It doesn't work,' he complained at last. 'I can't work these heathen cantrips. Why can't I just use the Word?'

'The *Word*?' In spite of herself, Skadi laughed. 'Listen, fellow,' she said as patiently as she could. 'Do you use an oliphant to plough your garden? Would you burn a forest to light your pipe?'

Nat shrugged. 'I want to get to the things that matter. I'm not interested in learning *tricks*.'

Once more Skadi laughed. You had to give it to the man, she thought – at least his ambitions were vast, if his intelligence wasn't. She had entered their pact with the intention of humouring him for just as long as it took for her to gain the secrets of the Order, but now her curiosity had been aroused. Perhaps he could be useful, after all.

'Tricks?' she said. 'These *tricks*, as you call them, are your apprenticeship. Despise them, and our alliance is over. Now stop complaining and light the taper.'

Nat made a sound of disgust. 'I can't,' he muttered angrily, and at that very moment, with an angry *whoosh!* the taper leaped into violent flame, scattering papers, bowling over the candlestick and sending a jet of fire so high towards the ceiling that it left a black soot-stain on the plasterwork.

Skadi raised a dispassionate eyebrow. 'You lack control,' she said. 'Again.'

But Nat was looking at the blackened taper with an expression of wild exhilaration. 'I did it,' he said.

'Poorly,' said the Huntress.

'But did you *feel* it?' said Nat. 'That *power*—' He paused abruptly, bringing one hand to his temple as if he had a headache. 'That power,' he repeated, but vaguely, as if his mind were on something else.

'Again, please,' said Skadi coolly. 'And this time try to exercise a little restraint.' She righted the candlestick – which was still hot – and placed a fresh taper on the spike.

Nat Parson smiled almost absently. The rune *Kaen*, less crooked this time, began to take shape between his fingers.

'Steady,' said the Huntress. 'Give yourself time.' *Kaen* was burning brightly now, a nugget of fire in the parson's hand. 'That's too much,' said Skadi. 'Bring it right down.'

But either Nat didn't hear her, or he didn't care; for *Kaen* brightened once again, now glowing so intensely that Skadi could feel it, like a lump of molten glass radiating fierce heat.

Now Nat's eyes were pinpoints of eager fire; before him on the desk, scattered papers began to curl and crisp. The candle itself, standing unmarked in its holder before him, began to drool and melt as the heat increased.

'Stop it,' said Skadi. 'You'll burn yourself.'

Nat Parson only smiled.

Now Skadi was beginning to feel unaccountably nervous. *Kaen* across the desk from her was the shrunken heart of a furnace; its yellow had veered to an eerie blue-white.

'Stop it,' she said.

Still there was no reply from Nat Parson. Skadi cast *Isa* with her fingers, meaning to freeze out the fire-rune before it could escape and cause damage.

Then Nat looked at her. Across the desk of charring papers, blue *Isa* and fiery *Kaen* faced each other in a deadlock, and once again Skadi felt that sense of peculiar, nagging unease.

This wasn't supposed to happen, she thought. The fellow had no training, no glam – so where was he getting this influx of power?

In her hand *Isa* was beginning to fail. She cast it again, harder this time, putting the force of her own glam behind it.

On Nat's face the smile broadened; his eyes closed like those of a man in the throes of delight. Skadi pushed harder—

And suddenly it was over; so quickly that she had difficulty in believing it had ever been. *Kaen* broke apart, frozen by *Isa*, and a dozen fragments snickered into the far wall, leaving tiny flecks of cinder embedded in the plasterwork. Nat goggled at these with a bewilderment that might have been comic in any other circumstance, and Skadi let out a sigh of relief – which was absurd, as surely she could not have expected any other outcome.

And yet, hadn't she felt something as she faced him across the desk? As if some power – maybe even a *superior* power – had lent itself to his, or some gaze of unspeakable penetration had flitted briefly over their struggle of wills?

In any case, it was gone now. Nat seemed awakened from a kind of daze, observing the marks of his working against the ceiling and walls as if for the first time. Once more Skadi noticed that he rubbed his forehead with the tips of his fingers, as if to ward off an approaching headache. 'Did I do it?' he enquired at last.

Skadi nodded. 'You made a start. Tell me,' she said. 'How did it feel?'

For a moment Nat thought about it, still rubbing at his temple. Then he gave a tiny, puzzled smile, like that of a man trying to recall the excesses of a night of distant revelry. 'It felt good,' he said at last. His eyes met hers, and she thought she saw in their silvery pupils a reflection of his earlier delight. '*Good,*' he repeated softly, and for the first time since the End of the World, the icy Huntress shivered.

7

She had planned to introduce her new ally to the Vanir without delay. Now she began to think again. After all, the Vanir were not her people – except through marriage, and that had been a mistake. The Old Man was still fond of her, of course, but their natures were too different for the marriage to last. Njörd's home by the sea had proved unbearable to her; her place in the mountains equally so to him. The same went for Frey and Freyja: their loyalties were with their father, not her, and she knew that her pursuit of Odin and his grandchild might not meet with unanimous approval.

Of course, if she'd managed to lay her hands on the Whisperer, then things might have been different. But as things stood at the moment, she was likely to meet with some opposition – Heimdall, at least, would stay loyal to Odin – and she had no desire to find herself at odds with the Vanir. So far Odin held all the cards: the Oracle and, more importantly, the girl. The Vanir knew the prophecy as well as he did. None of them would knowingly oppose Thor's child; and though Skadi had no love for Asgard herself, she guessed that the others would give a great deal for the chance to regain the Sky Citadel.

And so, that morning, after breakfast with the parson, she returned in bird form to the Hall of Sleepers. She flew right over Loki's head; but by then he was already on his way on foot to the meeting place in Little Bear Wood, and it never occurred to the harrier hawk that the old lady it saw on the Malbry road might be the Trickster in disguise.

As Skadi dressed – in the same tunic and boots she had left behind – she gave the Vanir a carefully edited account of the night's work. Odin and Loki were working together, she said, along with a girl – whose identity, she told them, was still unknown. They had the Whisperer; they had foiled the Examiners; and, in spite of her vigilance, had managed to escape.

She did not mention her promise to Nat Parson, or her plans for Maddy Smith.

'So why didn't Odin wake us himself?' said Heimdall when she had finished.

'Perhaps he was afraid,' said Skadi.

'Afraid? Of what?'

Skadi shrugged.

'Obviously he's planning something,' said Frey.

'Without telling us?' said Bragi, offended.

'Why not?' said Skadi. 'It's Odin's way. Secrets and lies were always his currency—'

'Untrue,' said Heimdall. 'He's loyal to us.'

Skadi looked impatient. 'Oh, please. Let's face it, Goldie. The General's *always* flirted with Chaos. *More* than flirted – and now we find he's thick as thieves with Loki again – *Loki*, of all people. What more do you need? If he wanted *you*, he'd have wakened you, wouldn't he?'

Now the Vanir were looking uneasy. 'The world has changed,' Skadi went on. 'There are new gods, *powerful* gods, working against us. Why do you think he took the Whisperer? Why do you think he left the Vanir sleeping?'

There was a lull. 'Perhaps he's working on an alliance,' said Frey doubtfully.

'You think so?' said Skadi. 'With whom? I wonder.' And she told them what she knew of the Examiners of World's End; of the Nameless, of the Word. They listened in silence – all but Idun, who seemed oblivious – and when Skadi had finished, even fickle Freyja was looking grim.

'Their Word is more powerful than any of ours,' said Skadi. 'They can defeat us – they can control us – they can make us their slaves. They are the Order. Who knows what deal Odin may have cut with them to save himself?'

'But you said he was their prisoner,' said Bragi.

'A trick,' she said, 'to lure me to the village.' And she explained how, at the very moment at which she was about to release Odin, they had turned against her, striking her down with a foul blow and making their escape – with the Whisperer – into the Hill.

'Why you?' said Heimdall, still suspicious.

'Because,' said Skadi, 'I'm not one of you. All you Vanir – you've been with him too long. You've started thinking of him as one of your own. He isn't. His loyalties are with the Æsir first and the Vanir second – if there *is* a second. But to save the Æsir, don't you think he'd sacrifice you if he had to? Do you think he'd hesitate, even for a moment?'

Heimdall frowned. 'You think he made a deal?'

Skadi nodded. 'I think they forced him to it,' she said. 'His own life in exchange for ours. But his plan went wrong. I killed the Examiner. I got away, and the Order lost its chance. That doesn't mean it intends to give up.' She began to pace across the shining floor, her ice-blue eyes gleaming. 'We must assume they are coming after us with reinforcements. We must assume they know where we are. And *who*.'

It was enough. The seeds had been sown. Little by little, Skadi watched them grow in the eyes of the newly awakened Vanir. Heimdall bared his golden teeth; Frey's eyes grew colder; kindly Njörd darkened like the edge of a cloud just veering towards rain. Bragi sang a sad song; Freyja wept; and Idun just sat on a block of ice and smiled, her face as unlined and serene as ever.

'Very well,' said Heimdall, turning to Skadi. 'Let's assume

for the moment you're right.' He squinted keenly at the Huntress, as if he perceived something in her signature that the others did not – some shift in her colours, some wrongness in the light. 'Let us assume that Odin has some plan which may not be to our advantage. That's *all* I'm willing to assume,' he said as Skadi seemed about to protest, 'but I do understand the need for caution.'

'Good,' said Skadi.

'All the same, we outnumber them,' said Heimdall. 'Seven of us to the three of them – assuming we're counting the girl, of course . . .'

'Plus the Whisperer,' Skadi reminded him.

Heimdall looked thoughtful. 'Yes, of course. They do have the Oracle. And the Oracle has no cause to love the Vanir. After all, we're the ones who cut off Mimir's head in the first place.'

The others exchanged glances. 'He has a point,' said Frey.

'But Odin controls the Whisperer,' objected Njörd.

'Perhaps not,' said Heimdall.

'Then what do we do?' asked Freyja. 'We can't just hang around here for ever – I say we talk to Odin.'

Skadi shot her a look of contempt. 'Are *you* volunteering for the job?'

Freyja looked away.

'What about you, Goldie? Do you want to walk into whatever trap he's set for you, and find out what he's planning the hard way?'

Heimdall scowled and said nothing.

'Well, what about you, Bragi? You've usually got more than enough to say for yourself. What do you suggest?'

Njörd interrupted her. 'What's your solution, Huntress?' he said.

'Well, as it happens . . .' she began.

She told them as much and as little as she dared. She

spoke of Nat Parson and his ambitions – playing them down as the impossible dreams of a vain and foolish man. She stressed his potential usefulness as an ally; told of his links with the Order and the Church; told them how he had already helped them by giving them access to the Good Book.

Of his newly acquired powers, and of the uneasy feeling those powers gave her, the Huntress said nothing. The man had a glimmer – that was all. But it was unstable power – and that barely more than a spark. Nothing to feel threatened by. And he might prove useful.

'Useful how?' said Heimdall.

Skadi shrugged. 'In these new times we need new allies,' she said. 'How else are we to fight the Order? Besides, the Nameless *has* a name. I'd like to know it before it comes to war.'

Grudgingly Heimdall conceded the point. 'So what does he want, this parson of yours?'

Skadi smiled. 'He wants revenge against a renegade of the Folk. In exchange, he will give us information that will arm us against the Order and the Word. All he wants is the girl – I'd say he's offering us a bargain.'

'The girl?' said Bragi. 'But who is she?'

'No one,' said Skadi. 'You know what Odin's like: he's always had a soft spot for the Folk. I imagine he's been using her as a spy, or something.'

Once more Heimdall gave her a searching look. 'Freyja said she had glam,' he said.

'So what if she does?' said Skadi sharply. 'I told you, she's of no importance. What matters is that Odin's deceived us. And our first priority is to find out why.'

There was a long pause as the Vanir considered Skadi's words.

'All right,' said Frey at last. 'But first we meet with the

General. We get things straight with him once and for all. And
if he's betrayed us—'

'Which I know he *has*—'

'Then,' said Frey, 'we'll give your churchman his revenge.'

8

The passage they had chosen was low and very tight; half blocked with rock-rubble in some parts and with a low stone roof that projected sharply at intervals, threatening to scalp them if they raised their heads. Its entrance was hidden in Little Bear Wood, and the way down was much longer and more tortuous than if they had taken the Horse's Eye.

But, as Loki said, it was safer this way; the few light-signatures Maddy sensed were very dim and very old, which meant that One-Eye would have difficulty locating their trail, even if the runes they'd left failed to hide it entirely.

Loki, however, was taking no chances. He worked methodically to hide their trail with little glamours and runes of concealment, and Maddy would have been impressed by his attention to detail if she had not known that it was entirely motivated by self-interest. Their journey was a dangerous one; and for the first time in his life the Trickster was concerned for the safety of others – namely that of Odin, who, if he managed to follow them, might find himself caught up in the perilous wheels of a prophecy that Loki devoutly (and selfishly) hoped would never be fulfilled.

'He may prove useful after all,' the Whisperer told Maddy as Loki scouted further ahead. 'I can take you through World Below. But after that comes the Land of the Dead, where for all my knowledge I cannot guide you. *He*, on the other hand, has a connection.'

'What connection?' Maddy said.

'A family connection,' said the Whisperer.

Maddy stared. 'A *family* connection?'

'Why, yes,' said the Whisperer. 'Didn't you know? The prodigal father's coming home.'

It could have been worse, Loki thought. The going was hard, but safe; and before long they would reach the honeycomb galleries of World Below, where he would be able to find them food and clothing (he was getting very tired of Crazy Nan's skirts), and from which they would be able to pursue their descent unnoticed and undisturbed. Beyond that the risk – at least the risk of being followed – would decrease a little; after all, who would expect them to go willingly into the very throat of Chaos? As for any other risks they might encounter he could not say; but so far his luck had not failed him, and he was inclined to trust it a little further.

Behind him he could sense, rather than hear, the Whisperer. Not so much *words* as *thoughts* that assaulted his wits and undermined his concentration. He would have to be careful, he thought. Even in the firepit on some occasions, the force of its will had been almost more than he could bear. Now, at close quarters, it made his head ache, and the idea that it could look into his mind whenever it wanted did nothing to allay his discomfort.

What makes you think I'm interested in your mind? scoffed the Whisperer. *Beats me how you can live in that snake-pit anyway.*

Loki shook his aching head. There was no point getting into a flyting match with the thing; insults only made it laugh, and as Chaos grew nearer, he would need all his glam for what was to come.

Shut up, Mimir, he hissed between clenched teeth.

Four hundred years in that pit of yours, and you think I'm interested in your comfort? You have a lot to atone for, Dogstar. Just be grateful we have a common interest. And don't even think *of double-crossing me.*

Loki wasn't about to try – at least, not until he knew what he was dealing with. Long acquaintance with the Whisperer had made him wary, and its sudden desire to be taken to Hel troubled him immensely. Maddy believed it was helping the gods – but Loki was infinitely less trusting, and he knew that the Whisperer wasn't in the habit of doing favours.

It wanted something – *What, old friend?*

What do you care? We have a deal.

Loki knew he should leave it be. The more he spoke, the more he listened to the Whisperer, the greater its hold over his mind. For the moment he could still tune it out; for all its power it had not managed to penetrate his deepest thoughts. That suited him fine. And yet . . .

Why help the Æsir? What's your plan?

In his mind, the Whisperer laughed. *I might well ask the same of you. Since when did you care about saving the Worlds? You're only interested in saving your skin, and if I had any choice right now, you'd be chained to a rock in Netherworld, having your guts pecked out by crows.*

Loki shrugged dismissively. *Sticks and stones may break my bones—*

They'll do worse than that in the Black Fortress.

They'll have to catch me first, said Loki.

Oh, they will, said the Whisperer.

They travelled in silence after that.

9

Meanwhile, in World Below, Odin One-Eye was awake at last. His time in the roundhouse had left him vulnerable, and although he was a quick healer, he needed time to recover his glam. As a result it was past midday before he awoke to discover that Maddy and Loki had disappeared.

No one seemed to know where they had gone; certainly not the goblins, who in the absence of their Captain seemed to have lost any control they might once have had, and were deserting Red Horse Hill in droves, taking what loot they could carry with them.

He intercepted and questioned a number of these fugitives, but could make little of what they told him. Rumours were flying like wild geese. The Order was marching on the Hill; the Nameless had risen; the World Ash had fallen; Surt the Destroyer had crossed over from Chaos, and was even now on his way to devour the world.

There were other, more plausible rumours as well: the Captain was dead (Odin put this down to wishful thinking); World Below was overrun; any treasure, food and ale was therefore free to all comers – this at least was true enough, as Odin discovered on entering the food cellars, although most of the goblins he found there were too drunk to make any sense.

By contrast, in World Above an ominous quiet reigned. The digging machines were abandoned in the open Eye; in the fields only a few people came and went. It felt like a Sunday, but the church bells were silent and even the farmers, who had good reason to be busy, seemed to have forsaken their business. Watching the world from the rune *Bjarkán*,

Odin wondered at the eerie stillness, while over the Hill the wild geese flew, and storm clouds gathered sullen over the valley of the Strond.

Something was stirring, he could sense it clearly. It shivered through World Below, rattling bones and blowing through doorways. It had a voice – seven voices, in fact – and Odin had no need of truesight or oracle to know from where that wind was blowing.

The Sleepers.

Well, he thought, it was inevitable. Once Skadi had awakened, rousing the others was simply a matter of time. And without the Whisperer he could not know for sure what they knew or what they were planning. Did *they* have the Whisperer? Were they responsible for Maddy's disappearence? And where was Loki? Was he still alive? And if so, what was his game?

It was crooked, of course – *that* went without saying – but the one thing of which Odin was still sure was that the Vanir would oppose any partnership with the Trickster. If Skadi had convinced them that Loki and Odin were together again, then he would have to approach them with the greatest of care.

And approach them he must, if he was to have the answers to his questions.

Casting his gaze on the Horse's Eye, he had found their summons in the form of a white-headed crow bearing a message. It sat on the big stone on top of the Hill, cocked its head and spoke.

Craw.

One-Eye liked crows, and knew their language from all the times he had taken their shape. He drew close to the bird, and through the rune *Bjarkán* assured himself that this was indeed a common crow, and not one of the Vanir in bird Aspect.

Vanir, it said. *Parley. No trick.*

One-Eye nodded. 'Where?' he said.

Parson house.

'When?'

Tonight.

Thoughtfully Odin scattered a handful of scraps for the crow, which flapped down and began to peck at the food. *No trick*, they had said. But the parson's house seemed a strange place to meet – could they be thinking of an alliance with the Folk? – and in today's world, he knew, even old friends were not to be trusted.

Damn them, damn them. He was getting too old for diplomacy. His shoulder was still on fire from Jed Smith's crossbow bolt; he was worried about Maddy, suspicious of the Vanir and distressingly weakened by the power of the Word.

The Word. Oh, he'd known of its existence for many years; but he had never encountered its effects first-hand. Now that he had, he feared it more than ever. A single Examiner had bled him helpless. One man – not even a Magister – had come within inches of breaking his mind.

Imagine an army primed with the Word. The Book of Apocalypse didn't seem quite so far-fetched now he'd seen what the Word could do. And the Order was strong – in purpose as well as in numbers – while he and his kind were scattered and in conflict. But what could he – what could any of them do against the Nameless? Alone, he might gain a few years' reprieve – ten, twenty if he was lucky – before the Order finally tracked him down. Together – if he managed to win back the Vanir at all – what could they hope for but defeat?

Perhaps the Examiner was right, he thought. *Perhaps my time is over.* And yet the thought did not fill him with the despair he might have expected. Instead he was conscious of a strange sensation, a kind of lightening of the spirit, and in that moment he recognized the feeling. He'd felt it before, in the days before Ragnarók, with worlds colliding and the forces of Chaos waiting their time. It was the joy of a gambler throwing down his last coin; the knowledge that everything stands or falls on the turn of a card.

Well, what is it to be? he told himself. *A few years' reprieve, or a merciful death? A sliver of hope or a bolt from the blue?*

His chances were poor, he knew that already. The Vanir mistrusted him; Skadi had sworn vengeance on him; Loki had fled, Maddy was lost, the Whisperer missing, the Hill wide open and the Folk on his trail. And without the Oracle the chances of his being able to talk, cajole, negotiate or outright lie the Vanir into obedience were small indeed.

But Odin was a gambler. He liked those odds. They appealed to his sense of the dramatic. And so once more, as the sun tipped westwards, he picked up his staff and his battered old pack and made his way down Red Horse Hill.

10

In Skadi's absence Nat Parson had slept, exhausted after his night's work. But his sleep had not refreshed him, punctuated as it was with itchy, uncomfortable dreams that left him feeling edgy and dissatisfied.

He woke past noon with an aching head; dizzy with hunger, and yet the thought of eating made him feel sick. Most of all he was terribly afraid that the newly acquired powers he had demonstrated to the Huntress might somehow have seeped away.

To his relief, however, the power of the Word remained undimmed. If anything, he thought it had actually *increased* as he slept, like some fast-growing creeper feeling its way through his brain. He lit the altar candles on his first try, almost without thinking, and the colours that had so overwhelmed him before now seemed familiar, almost commonplace.

How this had happened he did not know; but somehow, as he'd stepped forward at the very instant the Examiner summoned the Word against One-Eye, their minds had meshed. By accident or design? Had he been *chosen* to receive this power? With the Order, of course, anything was possible. Perhaps it *was* simply chance – the aftermath of Communion combined with some more random element – Chance or Choice, who knows? – but whatever it was, Nat Parson meant to keep it.

He hardly spoke to his wife at all, except to demand the loan of her second-best dress. Her best was already lying discarded somewhere out on Red Horse Hill, and Skadi would need another when she returned from the Sleepers in bird form.

Ethelberta was quite naturally reluctant to part with the cream of her wardrobe in this way, and there was a small unpleasantness, from which Nat escaped to the sanctuary of his study before his desire to use the Word on Ethelberta became too strong to resist.

Meanwhile the Huntress had returned. It had taken some hours to bring the Vanir around to her way of thinking, and it was early afternoon by the time she reached the village. By then her quarry was already gone: Maddy and Loki into World Below, and Odin into World Above, to observe the Parsonage and to check the area for a possible ambush.

He did not observe Skadi as, in the guise of a white she-wolf, she explored the intricacies of Red Horse Hill, sniffing out its passageways, calculating its defences, searching for a fresh trail. Briefly she caught Loki's scent, but it was faint and soon ran cold, and she could find no trace of Maddy Smith.

Well, that could wait, she told herself.

Today she hunted bigger game.

She turned her attention once more to the Hill. A natural fortress, in normal circumstances it could have withstood a siege of a hundred years or more. But now, with its gates in ruins and its troops deserting, the fortress might yet become a baited trap. *Naudr*, the Binder, angled just so against the catch of a door, might be set like a snare for an unsuspecting rabbit, to snap shut on whomever passed that way, while the rune *Hagall* could be left like a powder charge, to explode in the face of the unsuspecting victim.

She entered through the ruins of the Horse's Eye, and spent the best part of the afternoon setting as many of these snares as she could. She dropped them at crossroads and corner stones; at tunnel mouths and around dark bends. She worked the rune *Naudr* into a net, and stretched it across a darkened doorway, and she fashioned the rune *Tyr* into a cruel barb that would hook the victim like a fish.

It might well work, the Huntress thought. A man on the run – or even a girl – might well be taken unawares. An unguarded moment; a careless step – and the quarry would be caught or wounded, weakened, helpless; easy prey.

It was nearly four of the town clock when Skadi returned to the Parsonage in her wolf Aspect. Ethelberta, who had vowed that this time she would not submit so easily to the woman's demands, found herself quite at a loss when the Huntress arrived, and soon Skadi was clad in sumptuous white velvet (which would *never* brush clean, thought Ethel), while Ethel herself was giving orders to prepare the house for six more guests, and hoping that they, at least, would arrive decently clothed.

Skadi, however, had other concerns. She had sown some suspicion among the Vanir – and Loki's involvement had done the rest – but Heimdall and Frey, at least, remained loyal to the General. If Odin had the Whisperer, and if Maddy was really Thor's child, then he might yet be able to talk them round. Of course, if there were to be a *casualty* . . .

Coolly Skadi considered the Vanir. Not Heimdall, not yet – he was too powerful to lose. Not Frey, for the same reason. Not Idun – she was not as helpless as she first appeared, and besides, they might need a healer in times to come. Bragi? Njörd? She owed him nothing, she told herself. They were no longer married – and yet she was loath to sacrifice the Man of the Sea. He might be useful, after all. Freyja, on the other hand . . .

Skadi considered the goddess of desire.

Oh, she had some powers. She wasn't *useless*. She was annoying, however, and Skadi admitted to herself that of all the surviving Vanir, Freyja was the one she would miss the least. Not because of her beauty – everyone knew Skadi despised such things – or even because of their conflicting natures; but because of the discord she spread in her wake. With Freyja around, arguments broke out; friends quarrelled; the most peaceable folk turned green-eyed and crotchety. Besides, she and Odin—

But Skadi bit off that thought before it could take proper shape. This was no personal grudge, she told herself. This was a tactical choice, taken for the greater good. The fact that Freyja and Odin had always enjoyed more than a passing intimacy did not enter into her calculations at all. Freyja's death might grieve him, of course. It might even *wound* him in a place even the Word could not reach. Should she let that affect her decision? She thought not. Loki might have *caused* her father's death, but it had been Odin who *ordered* it; Odin who afterwards had bought her silence with a few compliments and a strategic marriage. And over the years she had begun to realize how he'd manipulated her; how he'd used her to make a much-needed peace with the Ice People; how long and how cleverly he had misdirected her anger, making her believe that Loki, and he alone, was to blame . . .

And now the brothers were together again.

Skadi clenched her fists against the white velvet of Ethelberta Parson's second-best gown. No amount of ironing would remove those creases; but Skadi's thoughts were far away. In her mind clouds gathered; blood spilled; and Revenge, long-deferred but all the sweeter for that, opened its sleepy eyes and smiled.

Isa is the only rune of the Elder Script to have no reverse position. As a result Skadi had lost none of her powers in the wake of Ragnarók. She considered herself a match for almost any of the Vanir, even Frey or Heimdall – but against the six of them together she knew she could not prevail. Unless, of course . . .

It had been a long time since she'd had leisure or inclination to create a new weapon, and this one, she knew, must be foolproof. Not large, no; but every thread picked over with runes of concealment; a weapon of elegance – a weapon of stealth.

If she'd had time, she might have fashioned a shirt – even a cloak, barbed in every stitch with runes of ice and poison – but time was short, and instead she made a tiny handkerchief, edged with ribbon lace so fine that you could hardly even see it; so intricate that the glamours that warped and wefted it were hidden between the love-knots and the embroidered flowers; so deadly that a single cantrip would be enough to unleash its working. And on it, in plain, bright script, she placed the rune *Fé*:

Freyja.

Skadi was pleased. Normally she disdained the homely art of needlework, but as a daughter of the Ice People she was skilled in it nevertheless. Carefully she folded the tiny handkerchief and put it into a drawer of the elegant escritoire. The Vanir would be here before nightfall. Smiling, the Huntress awaited their arrival.

Odin saw them coming from his vantage point beneath a stand of trees, half a mile from Malbry village. It was six o'clock in the evening, and against the last of the sunset he could just make out their signatures moving across the fields, arching into the smoky sky. Skadi's colours were not among them – but it was possible that she might be hiding in ambush nearby, using the others as bait to draw him in. Of Maddy and Loki there was no sign; and only now did he admit to himself how much he had been hoping to see them there.

He cast *Yr* and ducked behind a hedge. There they were: the Reaper, the Watchman, the Poet, the Healer, the Man of the Sea and finally the goddess of desire, trailing far behind.

Why had they chosen to come on foot? What was their business at the Parsonage? And exactly how much did they know?

Through *Bjarkán* he tried to detect the Whisperer. There was no sign of it; nor could he hear its voice as yet. But that didn't mean it wasn't there. He moved in closer along the hedge, circling in behind the little group so that he stood the least chance of being spotted. It felt so wrong, to be hiding thus from his friends; but the world had changed, and not even old friendships could be taken entirely on trust.

Njörd was speaking. 'I know she's reckless – maybe even a little wild—'

'A *little* wild!' That was Freyja, her long hair shining like frost, the links of her necklace catching the light. 'She's an *animal*, Njörd – all that prowling around as a wolf and a hawk . . .'

'She was always loyal. At Ragnarók—'

Frey said: 'We were at war then.'

'If Skadi's right, we're at war *now*.'

'With the Folk. With the Order, perhaps,' said Heimdall. 'But not with our people.'

'The Æsir are *not* our people,' said Njörd. 'We might all do well to remember it.'

Behind the hedge Odin frowned. So *that* was where the land lay; of course, Njörd was the oldest of the Vanir, father to the twins, and it was understandable that his allegiance should belong to the Vanir first and the Æsir second. Besides, he'd long suspected that Njörd still felt tender towards his estranged wife, and as Odin knew, there could be no reasoning with a lover. He himself was not immune: there had been times – quite a few of them – when even Odin the Far-Sighted had shown himself as blind as the next man . . .

He glanced at Freyja, still dragging behind, her blue dress black to the knees with mud. 'How far now?' she wailed. 'I've been walking for hours, I've got a blister, and just *look* at my gown—'

'If I hear any more about your gown, or your shoes, or your feather dress . . .' muttered Heimdall.

'We're nearly there,' said Idun gently. 'But I can give you some apple if your foot hurts—'

'I don't want an *apple*. I want some dry *shoes*, and a clean *dress*, and a *bath*—'

'Oh, shut up and use a cantrip,' said Heimdall.

Freyja looked at him and sniffed. 'You don't have a clue, do you, Goldie?'

From his hiding place, Odin smiled.

11

In World Below Maddy and Loki had hit trouble. Trouble in the form of a vertical shaft slicing down through the levels – no path downwards, no alternate route, and a hundred-foot leap to the far side.

It lay at the end of a long, low passage, through which they had half crawled, half clambered for close on three laborious hours. Now, looking down into the axe-shaped rift and listening to the tumbling water some four hundred feet below, Maddy was ready to wail with despair.

'I thought you said this was the best way down!' she said, addressing the Whisperer.

'I said it was the *quickest* way down,' it replied waspishly, 'and so it is. It's hardly my fault if you can't handle a little climb.'

'A *little* climb!'

The Whisperer glowed in a bored way. Once more Maddy looked down; below them the river churned like cream. It was the river Strond, Maddy knew, swollen with the autumn rains, probing and battering its way between the rocks towards the Cauldron of Rivers. It seemed to fill the chasm completely, and yet as her eyes became accustomed to the deeper gloom, she saw a break in the rock on the far side – just visible across the gap.

She gave a long, exhausted sigh. 'We'll have to double back,' she said. 'Find some other route down.'

But Loki was looking at her with a strange expression. 'There isn't another route,' he said. 'Not unless you want to share it with a couple of thousand goblins. Besides . . .'

'Besides,' said the Whisperer, 'we're being followed.'

'What?' said Maddy.

'*He* knows.'

'Knows *what*?'

Loki glared at the Oracle. 'I spotted a signature an hour ago. Nothing to worry about. We'll lose them further down.'

'Unless he's leaving some kind of trail.'

'A trail?' said Maddy. 'Why would he do that?'

'Who knows?' it said. 'I told you he was trouble.'

Loki gave a hiss of exasperation. 'Trouble?' he said. 'Listen, I'm already risking my skin. It happens to be rather a *nice* skin, and I'm in no hurry to see it damaged. So why would I want to leave a trail? And why in Hel's name would I want to slow us down?'

Maddy shook her head, abashed. 'It's just that the thought of turning back—'

Once more he gave her a puzzled look. 'Who said anything about turning back?'

'But I thought—'

'Maddy,' he said, 'I thought you understood. Chaos blood on your mother's side, Æsir on your father's. Did you really think that *climbing* down that cliff was the best option?'

Maddy thought about that for a moment. 'But I don't know any glamours—' she began.

'You don't need to *know any glamours*,' said Loki. 'Glamour is a part of you, like your hair or your eyes or the fact that you're left-handed. Did Odin have to teach you to throw mindbolts?'

Frowning, Maddy shook her head. Then she remembered Freyja's feather dress and her face lit up. 'I could use Freyja's cloak,' she suggested.

'No chance. No bird could carry the Whisperer. And besides – I'm getting tired of losing my clothes.'

'Well, what do you suggest?' she said – and then she saw how it might be done. A rope – a *thread*, even – woven from runes, stretching from the top of the gully to the cave entrance. *Úr*, the Ox, would make it strong. *Naudr*, the Binder, would hold it in place. It would need to last a moment only – just long enough for them to swing down safely – and then it could be banished as quickly and easily as a spider's web. She thought it might work; and yet, looking down into the seething water, she began to feel afraid. What if it didn't? What if she fell, like a fledgling too eager to leave the nest, and was swept away into the Cauldron of Rivers?

Loki was watching her with amusement and impatience. 'Come on, Maddy,' he said. 'This is child's play compared to what you did by the firepit.'

Slowly she nodded; and then she opened her hand and looked at *Aesk* inscribed on her palm. It was glowing dully, but as she watched, it brightened, as the embers of a fire may brighten when air is blown over them. Closing her eyes, she began to *tease* out the runes to suit her purpose, as she had once teased the raw wool of newly shorn lambs, thread by thread, around a spindle. She could see it now, growing at her finger-tips, a double skein of runelight that was as strong as steel-linked chain and as light as thistledown; and she spun it into the dusky air as a spider spins a web, until it reached the ground by the river's edge and was securely anchored to the rock.

She carefully tested the line with her weight. It held. It felt like cornsilk between her fingers. Now for the Whisperer. Tucked into her jacket, it was heavy, but not unbearably so, and she found that with a little adjustment she could carry it against her chest as she grasped the line with all her strength and jumped into the darkness.

Loki was watching her with a curious, half-admiring expression on his sharp features. In truth, he was feeling very uneasy. It was a simple working, to be sure; but untutored as she was, Maddy had been very quick to find the technique. He wondered how long it would be before she discovered her *other* skills, and how much power she carried in that seemingly inexhaustible reservoir of glam. He himself was growing weak from the effort of resisting the Whisperer's intrusions into his thoughts. And as Loki in his turn grasped the line, he thought he could see trouble ahead—

And why would that be? said a voice in his mind.

Loki flinched at its unexpected presence. With the distractions of their downward journey he had found it harder and harder to keep his thoughts his own. Below him the river seethed and spat, and he suddenly wished that he was carrying the Whisperer – as it was he was too helpless, he thought, strung out in the air like a bead on a thread. The thing in his mind caught his discomfort and grinned.

Get out of my head, you old voyeur.

What's wrong? Guilty conscience?

Guilty what?

Silently it laughed. To Loki its laughter felt like dead fingernails scraping the inside of his skull. He began to sweat. Maddy had reached the far side of the river, but Loki was barely halfway there, and already the runes were beginning to fail. His arms hurt; his head ached; and he was all too aware of the drop below. And the Whisperer was aware of it too, amused and merciless, watching him squirm . . .

Seriously, Mimir. I'm trying to concentrate.

Seriously, Dogstar. What's your plan?

Loki tried to re-cast the runes, but the Whisperer's presence was too strong, making him writhe like a worm on a line.

Hurts you, doesn't it? it said, tightening its grip more cruelly—

And in that moment, as the Whisperer reached out in its unguarded glee, Loki saw something that made him catch his breath. For as his mind and the Oracle's touched, he had caught a glimpse of something more – something buried so deep in the Whisperer's mind that only its shadow was visible.

(!)

In that instant the Whisperer fled.

Then it was back, its playfulness gone, and Loki sensed its lethal intent. A fearsome bolt of pain went through his body, and he fought the Whisperer with all his strength as it plundered his mind for what he'd seen.

Spy on me, would you, you little sneak?

'No! Please!' Loki howled.

One more sound, and I'll take you apart.

Loki clamped his scarred lips shut. He could see Maddy below him, holding out her hand across the last stretch of water, the rune *Naudr* stretched out almost to breaking point between them.

That's better, the Oracle said. *Now, about that plan . . .*

For a second longer its hold increased, wringing him like a wet dishcloth. His fingers cramped; his vision blurred; one hand left the disintegrating line to cast runes of strength into the darkness—

And it was at that moment that the line gave way, pitching Loki towards the racing Strond. He leaped for the other side, casting feather-light runes with both hands, and landed, one foot in the water, on the rocky far side of the churning gulf, and found, to his relief, that the Oracle was gone. Pale and shaking, he hauled himself out.

'What's wrong?' said Maddy, seeing his face.

'Nothing. Headache. It must be the air.'

He stumbled on, carefully keeping his mind a blank. That little glimpse had been bad enough; but he knew that if the Whisperer guessed the full extent of his knowledge, then nothing – not even Maddy – could save him.

And that was how they crossed the river that marks the edge of World Below and the beginning of the long, well-travelled road to Death, Dream and Damnation.

12

Hawk-eyed Heimdall never slept. Even at his moments of lowest ebb he kept one eye open, which was why he had been chosen as the watchman of the Æsir in the days when such things as watchmen were still necessary. That night, however, none of the Vanir *dared* to rest – except Idun, whose trusting nature set her apart, and Freyja, whose complexion needed its eight hours. Instead they sat uneasy; waiting for Odin.

'What makes you think he'll come at all?' said Njörd at last, looking out of the parlour window. The moon was rising; it was eleven, maybe twelve, and nothing had stirred since just after nine, when a fox had run across the open courtyard and vanished into the shadows at the side of the Parsonage. There had been a moment of uncertainty then, as the Vanir fell over themselves to make sure the creature was just an ordinary fox; and then, for hours, silence – a tense, awkward silence that oppressed their senses like fog.

'He'll come,' said Skadi. 'He'll want to talk. He'll have got our message, and besides—'

Heimdall interrupted her. 'If you were Odin, would *you* come?'

'He may not come alone,' said Bragi.

'Yes, he will,' said Skadi. 'He'll want to negotiate. He'll try to buy you back into his service using the Whisperer as bait.' She smiled as she said it; only she knew that Odin had nothing with which to bargain. Loki's trail led under the Hill; and she had every reason to believe that *he* had the Whisperer, sure as rats run. 'But he's tricky,' she warned. 'He can't be trusted. It would be just his style to lead us into a trap—'

'Stop it,' said Heimdall. 'We've heard your opinion. We understand the risk. Why else would we be here, making bargains with the Folk?' He sighed, looking suddenly tired. 'I see no honour in this, Huntress, and if you ask me, *you're* taking a damn sight too much pleasure in it.'

'Very well,' said Skadi. 'Then I'll let you do the talking. I'll keep my distance, and only intervene if there's trouble. All right? Is that fair?'

Heimdall looked surprised. 'Thanks,' he said.

'All the same,' said the Huntress, 'perhaps the parson should be here. If Odin comes armed . . .'

But on that the Vanir were united. 'The six of us can deal with him,' said Njörd. 'We don't need the preacher fellow, or his Word.'

Skadi shrugged. By the end of that night she was quite certain that they would think otherwise.

Odin came an hour later, in the silvery glow of a false dawn. In full Aspect – a vanity that must have cost him the greater part of his remaining glam – tall, blue-cloaked, spear in hand, his single eye shining like a star from beneath the brim of his journeyman's hat.

In wolf guise Skadi watched him from the outskirts of the village, knowing that he would have come prepared for this meeting. His signature glowed; he looked relaxed and rested – all part of the act, of course, but she had to admit that it was impressive. Only her wolf's acute senses were able to discern the truth beneath the glamour – the faint scent of anxious sweat, of dirt, of fatigue – and she snarled a smile of satisfaction.

So she'd been right, then. He *was* bluffing. His glam was at low ebb; he was alone, and the only advantage he still possessed – their enduring loyalty – was about to be taken away.

She raced him back to the Parsonage and, entering through the half-open side door, made her way rapidly to awaken Nat. 'He's here,' she said.

Nat replied with a curt nod. He did not seem at all confused by his sudden awakening – in fact Skadi wondered whether he had been asleep at all. He stood up, and she saw he had slept in his clothes. His eyes gleamed in the moonlight; his teeth grinned; his colours showed nothing but excitement and one hand went without hesitation to the Good Book at his bedside, while the other clutched at the golden key on its leather thong.

'You remember what to do?' she said.

Silently he nodded.

Ethelberta had shrieked to see the white wolf at her bedside, then shrieked even louder as Skadi had resumed her natural form. Neither the Huntress nor Nat himself had paid her the slightest attention.

Now, lying in bed in her nightgown, she was trembling. 'Nat, please,' she said.

Nat didn't even look at her. In fact at that moment he didn't look much like Nat at all, standing next to the bed in his shirt and trousers, his long shadow brushing the ceiling, and a *glow* – she was sure it was some sort of glow – coming from his eager eyes.

Ethelberta sat up, still mortally afraid but struggling to express her outrage, her fury at this shameless creature – this naked *harpy* – that had seduced her husband into madness and worse. She knew herself she'd never been a beauty, not even in her younger days. And even if she had – May Queen herself couldn't hold a candle to the demon he called the Huntress. But Ethelberta loved her husband, vain and shallow as he was, and she was not about to stand by and watch him consumed.

'Please,' she repeated, clutching at his arm. 'Please, Nat – just send it away. Send them *all* away, Nat. They're demons, they've stolen your mind . . .'

Nat only laughed. 'Go back to bed,' he said, and in the darkness his voice seemed to have a resonance that it had not possessed in daylight. 'This is no concern of yours. I'm here on the Order's business, and I'll not have you interfering in it.'

'But Nat, I'm your *wife* . . .'

He looked at her then, and his eyes were pinwheels of strange fire. 'An Examiner of the Order has no wife,' he said.

And collapsed.

He was out for only a few seconds. Skadi revived him with a sharp pinch while Ethelberta sat with eyes brimming and her hands clapped tightly over her mouth.

An Examiner of the Order has no wife.

What was that supposed to mean? Ethel Parson was no more regarded for her intellect than for her beauty – everyone knew she'd bought her rank with her father's money. Nor was she much of an independent thinker. No one had ever encouraged her to speak for herself. It was enough, she was told, to do one's duty; to be a good daughter of the Church; a good mistress; a good hostess; a good wife. She'd also hoped to be a good mother – but that joy had never been granted her. Nevertheless Ethel was no fool, and now her mind raced to comprehend what was happening.

An Examiner of the Order has no wife . . .

What did that mean? Ethel, of course, had no illusions regarding her husband's devotion to her. An ugly girl rarely marries for love. And money, unlike beauty, often increases with age. Still, to be rejected in such a crude way, and in front of *her*—

This is no time for self-pity, Ethelberta. Remember who you are.

The inner voice that spoke these words was harsh, but

somehow familiar; Ethelberta listened to it in growing surprise. *Why, that's* my *voice*, she thought. It was the first time she had ever really considered such a thing.

She looked at her husband, still lying on the floor. She was conscious of a number of feelings: anxiety; fear; betrayal; hurt. She understood all of those. But there was something else too; something she finally recognized – with some surprise – as contempt.

'Ethel . . .' said Nat in a weak voice. 'Bring me water, and some clothes. My boots from the scullery, and a gown for my lady. Your pink silk will do well enough, or perhaps the lilac.'

Ethelberta hesitated. Obedience was in her nature, after all, and it felt terribly disloyal to stand by and do nothing while her husband was in need. But that inner voice, once heard, was difficult to ignore. 'Fetch it yourself,' she snapped, and gathering her dressing gown about her shoulders, she turned and strode out of the room.

Her departure did not particularly trouble Nat. He had other things on his mind – matters of importance, not least what had occurred just before he passed out: that rush of energy, that certainty of purpose, that overwhelming feeling of being someone *else*, not just a country parson with nothing on his mind but tithes and confessionals, but someone quite different.

He reached for the Good Book by the side of his bed, strangely comforted by the small familiar weight of it in his hand, and by the warmth and smoothness of the well-worn cover. Then, taking the golden key from around his neck, Nat Parson opened the Book of Words.

This time the rush of power barely slowed him down. And the words themselves – those alien, terrible canticles of power – made more sense to him now, scrolling off the page, as easy and familiar as the rhymes he'd learned at his mother's knee. It made Nat feel a little light-headed; that what only yesterday had seemed so new and intimidating should have become so quickly, so hauntingly *familiar*.

Skadi was watching him, closely and with suspicion. What had happened? One moment he was lying on the floor, giving orders to Ethel and calling for his boots, the next he was simply . . . *different*. As if a light had been lit, or a wheel spun that had turned him from the soft, rather vain individual he'd been into another creature altogether. And all that in the batting of an eyelash. The Word, perhaps? Or simply the thrill of anticipated action?

It was a matter she would have liked to explore more fully, but there was no time. Odin was on his way and for the moment she needed this man – and his Word – if her plan was to succeed. Afterwards she would see. The parson was expendable, and when he had served his purpose, Skadi would have no regret in terminating their arrangement.

As a matter of fact, she thought, it might even be a relief.

13

In the old days, thought Heimdall, they would have held their counsel in Bragi's hall. There would have been mead and ale, laughter and song. Now, of course, just thinking about those days depressed him.

He looked out of the window. Odin was waiting in the courtyard, no longer a bent old man, but standing taller than any human, clad in the light of his true Aspect. To Heimdall he looked as if he were *made* of light; and if any of the Folk had dared to look, they would have seen it, that signature blue, blazing from the face of the one-eyed beggar, streaming from his fingertips, crackling through his hair.

'I'll go,' said Heimdall.

'We'll all go,' said Frey. He looked around at the remaining Vanir. They too were in Aspect, filled with the light: Idun and Bragi in summer gold; Njörd with his harpoon; and Freyja – Freyja . . .

Hastily he turned away. It is never wise to look directly upon the goddess of desire in her true Aspect, not even for her own brother. He murmured, 'I wonder, sister, whether it's entirely prudent—'

Freyja laughed – a sound halfway between the clinking of coins and the last chuckle of a dying man. 'Dear brother,' she said. 'I have my own issues with Odin One-Eye. Believe me, I wouldn't miss this meeting for the world.'

There was a bottle of wine on the table beside them. Bragi picked it up. By the laws laid down in the oldest days, where food and drink have been shared, there can be no bloodshed. Bragi's hall might be dust, but the laws of honour and hospitality still stood, and if Odin wanted to parley – well.

Whatever was done would be done according to the law.

For a moment they faced each other. Six Vanir and One-Eye, gleaming like something out of legend, like mountains in the sun.

Odin offered bread and salt.

Bragi poured wine into a goblet.

One by one the Seer-folk drank.

Only Skadi did not, of course; she was in the house with Nat Parson, watching from the bay window. The time was close – she could feel it in every sinew. In her hand she held a scrap of gossamer lace, inscribed with *Fé*, the rune of Wealth. And at her side Nat Parson clutched the Book of Words and stared. And unknown to either of them, unknown even to the gods whose fates lay so dangerously entwined, a third person was watching the meeting with horror and mounting outrage as she stood, hidden and shivering, in the doorway of the house.

When the last of them had honoured the ancient law, Odin allowed himself to relax. 'My friends,' he said. 'It's good to see you. Even in these evil times, it is very good.' His one eye travelled over the assembled Vanir. 'But someone is missing,' he said quietly. 'The Huntress, I think?'

Heimdall showed his golden teeth. 'She thought it better to keep away. You've already tried to kill her once.'

'That was a misunderstanding.'

'I'm glad,' said Heimdall. 'Because Skadi was under the impression that you had betrayed us. That Loki was free, and that you and he were together again, just like in the old days, as if nothing had happened. As if Ragnarók were simply a game we lost, and this was just another round.' He looked at Odin through narrowed eyes. 'Of course, that's where Skadi got it wrong,' he said. 'You'd never do that, would you, Odin? You'd never do that, knowing what it would mean to our friendship and our alliance.'

For a time Odin remained silent. He'd anticipated this. It was Heimdall, of all the Vanir, who most detested Loki, and of all the Vanir, fierce, loyal Heimdall was the one Odin valued most. On the other hand, he valued Maddy; and if she had taken the Whisperer . . .

'Old friend,' he said.

'Cut the crap,' said Heimdall. 'Is it true?'

'Well, yes, it is.' Odin smiled. 'Now before you jump to any conclusions . . .' Heimdall had frozen in astonishment, mouth gaping mid-word. 'Before *any* of you jump to any conclusions,' repeated Odin, still smiling at the circle of Vanir that now enclosed him, 'I'd like you to hear my side of the tale.'

And as Allfather began to speak, no one saw a tiny creature – a common brown mouse – dart out from behind one of the Parsonage outbuildings and cross the yard. No one saw the trail it left and no one saw the thing it carried, very carefully, in its teeth – a scented scrap of something light as spider-gauze, pretty as a primrose – and dropped not a foot away from where Odin was standing. Dropped on his blind side and left on the ground, shining ever so slightly among the glamours and dust, just waiting to be picked up and admired; a dainty thing, a trifle – an object of desire.

'To you, my friends,' Odin began, 'Ragnarók was yesterday. But many things have changed since then. The gods of Asgard are almost extinct; our names forgotten; our territories lost. We were arrogant enough to think that the Worlds would end with us at Ragnarók. But an age is simply one season's growth to Yggdrasil, the World Ash. To the Tree, we are simply last year's leaves, fallen and waiting to be swept up.'

Frey spoke up. 'Five hundred years, and that's the best news you can give us?'

Odin smiled. 'I don't mean to sound negative.'

'*Negative!*' said Heimdall.

'Heimdall, please. I have told you the truth – but there are other things you need to know. Skadi may have told you of the Order' – scurrying back through a hole in the fence, a brown mouse stopped and raised its head – 'but she, like you, has slept since Ragnarók. I, on the other hand, have made it my business to study and to understand the Order ever since it was first begun.'

Heimdall gave him a suspicious look. 'And your findings?'

'Well. At first sight it seems simple. Throughout the history of the world there have been gods and their enemies, Order and Chaos existing in balance. The world needs both. It needs to change, as the World Tree drops its leaves in order to grow. When we were gods, we understood that. We valued the balance of Order and Chaos, and took care to preserve it. But this Order sees things differently. It seeks not to maintain, but to *destroy* the balance of things, to wipe out anything that is not of itself. And that doesn't just mean a few dead leaves.' He paused again and looked round at the Vanir. 'In short, my friends, it wants summer all year round. And if it can't have it, it will cut down the tree.'

He stretched then, and finished the wine, spilling the last few drops onto the earth as an offering to any old gods that might be around. 'Now I don't know quite what Skadi has told you, or what deal she thinks she has made with the Folk, but I can tell you this: *the Order doesn't make deals.* All its members think as one; it has powers I'm only just beginning to appreciate; and if we are to stand a chance against it, then we need to stand united. We can't afford to nurse grudges, or to plot revenges, or to get judgemental about our allies. Our position is simple. Anyone who isn't a member of the Order is on our side. Whether they know it – whether they *like* it – whether *we* like it – or not.'

A very long silence followed Odin's speech. Bragi lay on his back and looked up, turning his face towards the stars. Frey closed his eyes. Njörd smoothed his long beard. Heimdall cracked his knuckles. Idun began to hum to herself, and Freyja ran her fingers over the links of her necklace, making a sound like a dream of avarice. Odin One-Eye forced himself to wait quietly, staring out into the darkness.

Finally Heimdall spoke up. 'I made an oath,' he said. 'Regarding the Trickster.'

Odin gave him a reproving look. 'As I recall, you fulfilled it at Ragnarók. How many more times do you have to kill him?'

'Once more should do it,' said Heimdall, between his teeth.

'Now you're being childish,' said Odin firmly. 'Like it or not, we need Loki. And besides, there's something I haven't told you yet. Our branch of the tree is not as dead as we thought. A new shoot has grown from the World Ash. Its name is Modi, and if we get this right, it will build us a ladder to the stars.'

Inside the Parsonage Skadi heard Odin's words and smiled.

Nat, at her side with the Book of Words open and ready, turned to her with an enquiring look. He looked pale, and feverish, and half mad with impatience; at his fingertips the Word crackled like kindling.

'Is it time?' he asked.

Skadi nodded as she spoke the tiniest of cantrips, and at Odin's feet there was a gleam of response. The handkerchief she had dropped seemed to come into focus: a lovely thing, fashioned with care; embroidered with rosettes and forget-me-nots and edged with cobweb lace. As she'd planned, the rune *Fé* caught his eye; he picked up the scrap of embroidered lace and, for a second, held it out, uncertain, before taking a long step forward to make his bow, the handkerchief held between his fingers, at the elegant feet of the goddess of desire.

'Now,' said Skadi, and at her side Nat began to read from the Book of Invocations.

And in the doorway of the Parsonage, a third watcher drew a deep breath and took a first, faltering step out of the shadows.

Ethelberta Parson had had much to bear during the last twenty-four hours. In that short time she had seen the over-throwing of her household, the plundering of her wardrobe, the ransacking of her cellars and the apparent seduction of her staid husband by a band of degenerates who were even now preparing to return to the Parsonage and raid what was left of her wine cellar.

She could deal with this, she told herself firmly. All it would take was a little common sense. Now was the time to *take charge* – to oust these interlopers from her home – and if Nat didn't like it, then he could join them as far as she was concerned, but they would not step inside her house again, nor would she let them take so much as a rag of hers – no, not if the Nameless himself ordered her to.

Her first step was unsteady as she left the shadow of the doorway arch. It took her into a circle of light – not moon-light, she thought, for the moon was down. Ahead of her the one-eyed pedlar stood, head bent, in front of the flax-haired jade who had stolen Ethel's green silk dress (and the fact that it suited Freyja far better than it had ever suited her made Ethel gnash her teeth with unladylike violence), and from them both, that strange, unseasonal light shone, making giants of the beggar and of the harlot, making them more beautiful, more radiant, more terrifying than any mortal has a right to be.

And as Ethel took another step, her mouth hanging open now in wonder and fear, the pedlar held out his hand to the whore, and there in his palm was a scrap of something, a webspun, tantalizing wisp of lace and moonlight, which he offered to the woman in the green dress saying, 'Yours, my lady?'

This was the moment Nat had awaited. 'He'll give her the handkerchief,' Skadi had said. 'At that moment – and at that moment only – may you unleash the Word. A second too soon, and all will be ruined. A second too late, and we'll lose the bastard. But if you get it right, Parson, then vengeance will be ours – and with the blessing of the Vanir as recompense.'

Of course, Skadi thought, the loss of Freyja would hit them hard. Her lip curled as she considered it – in her estimation it showed very poor taste – but she was sure that they would take some consolation in the pursuit of their revenge.

Try forging an alliance with them after that, she thought, and growled with pleasure in her throat as at her side Nat Parson waited, trembling now but filled with the Word; teeming with it, glowing with it.

It was a marvellous feeling: his blood felt volatile, as if every vein and artery had been filled with hot brandy. He was not quite himself, he knew – he was maybe even a little insane – but why should he care, if it felt like this?

And then Ethelberta stepped out into the light.

'That's my wife,' said Nat in surprise.

Skadi cursed and flung her glam.

'*Now!*' she repeated, cursing again, for Ethel was in the way, damn her, Ethel was between them, snatching at the thing in Freyja's hand and shouting, *No more, lady, not even a rag!* – while the Vanir watched, some smiling, still unaware of their peril, and now Skadi cursed again, more fiercely this time, in a demon tongue, because the Word – the canticle that should have frozen Odin to the spot as the Vanir watched and Freyja fell lifeless to the ground – the Word had failed her, Nat had failed her, saying, *That's my wife*, in that numb, stupid voice as the glamour shot from his fingertips, missed Odin by a gnat's wing and went on to freeze a bird from the sky three miles from the village, while in the courtyard of the Parsonage the following things all happened at once:

In a second the circle of Vanir broke apart.

Heimdall threw himself to one side, mindbolts at his fingertips.

Bragi sang a song of protection.

Frey drew his mindsword and made for the house.

Freyja shifted into the form of a red-tailed falcon and soared out of the danger zone, leaving Ethelberta's green silk dress empty.

And such was the riot of glamours, movement and noise that for a time no one noticed the parson's wife lying dead on the ground, or the fact that somehow, in the confusion, Odin One-Eye had disappeared.

Inside the house Skadi flung *Isa* at Frey, freezing him where he stood. She turned to Nat. 'Can you do it?' she demanded. 'Can you stop them all?'

Nat hesitated. 'Ethel,' he said.

'Forget her,' said Skadi. 'She got in the way.' She grabbed Nat by the arm and forced him to look at her. 'Now tell me, Parson, *can you do it?*'

For a moment he stared at her. The Huntress in Aspect is a fearsome sight, even to the gods. Nat felt sick. The Word and the feelings it had conjured inside him had evaporated; it might return, he told himself, but he would need time to recapture it, time to prepare . . .

'*Magister*,' he whispered.

'What?' she said.

'*A gift*,' said the parson. '*For loyal service*.'

Skadi cursed and flung another mindbolt into the night. This was what came of dealing with the Folk, she told herself fiercely. She'd thought him different, the more fool she. The man was weak, his mind was wandering, and any second now the Vanir would finally understand who had betrayed them, and come running.

Once more she cast *Isa* into the courtyard. Njörd froze, one hand on his harpoon. But it would not last. Without the Word to immobilize them and make them helpless, the Vanir outclassed her by a long way.

One last time Skadi turned to the parson. He was pale and sweating. Shocked, perhaps, by the death of his wife, but looking into his haunted eyes, Skadi didn't think so. She had seen trances that looked like this in men who had worshipped her in the distant past. After the ecstasy, the horror. She saw it in Nat Parson's eyes, a gaping, empty horror, and knew then that they had lost. Odin was gone, and in seconds the Vanir would be upon them.

Till next time, then, the Huntress thought. She put her hands on the parson's shoulders.

'Listen to me, fellow,' she said.

Slowly his eyes turned towards her. '*Don't . . . call . . . me . . . fellow*,' he whispered.

Ah. At last, a reaction. Good, she thought. 'If you want to live, then do as I say. *Do* you want to live?'

Wordless, he nodded.

'Then come with me, Parson, if you can. Take your Book. Follow me. And *run*.' And with that she shifted into her snow-wolf form, shot through the open back door, her pads soundless on the hard ground, and vanished like smoke into the night.

14

In less than a minute – at a single word – the life Nat had always known was over. Gone was the Parsonage; gone wife, flock, comfort, ambitions. Now he was a fugitive.

Ahead of him the snow wolf raced towards the safety of Red Horse Hill. The air was sharp and clean; the ground underfoot brittle with frost. Dawn was approaching; birds sang and a pale green light bled the violet from the sky. It occurred to Nat suddenly that it had been years since he'd watched the sun rise.

Now he could watch it whenever he pleased.

The knowledge was suddenly so overwhelming that he laughed aloud; the snow wolf paused briefly, snarled and padded on.

Nat ignored her. Freedom at last; freedom to do what he'd always yearned for; freedom to use his talents, his *power*—

Tsk-tsk, begone!

Nat frowned. Whose words were those?

He shook his head to clear it. He'd been under some stress, he told himself. It was only natural that there should be a little confusion, a little disorientation in his mind. After all, he'd lost his wife—

An Examiner of the Order has no wife.

The words came unbidden into his mind, and now he remembered them, as in a dream; remembered saying something of the kind to Ethelberta as he collapsed, exhausted – and the voice had spoken – to him – *through* him . . .

It was the same voice. Mournful now, but a voice of authority nevertheless – soft, precise and with a trace of arrogance – and now he thought it was almost familiar, haunting as a tune forgotten since childhood and overheard years later, unexpectedly, from a distance.

'Who are you?' whispered Nat, his eyes widening. 'Are you a demon? Am I possessed?'

In his mind there came a sigh no louder than a breath of air.

He hears me, it sighed. *At last, he hears me.*

'What are you?' he repeated sharply.

A man, it said. *A man, I think . . .*

'What man?' said Nat.

Elias Rede, whispered the voice. *Examiner Number 4421974.*

For a time Nat Parson stood transfixed. The dawn had turned out to be a disappointment. No sun shone; the day's promise was lost under a pall of cloud and suddenly Nat Parson was bursting for a piss, but to relieve himself in the nearby bushes now felt somehow indecent with this interloper in his mind.

'You're supposed to be dead,' he said at last.

Perhaps, said the Examiner, *but I'm still here.*

'Well, go away then,' said Nat. 'Go join the Nameless, or the Hordes of Hel, or wherever you're supposed to go when you die.'

You think I haven't tried? said the Examiner. *You think I wanted to be stuck inside your mind?*

'It's not my fault if you got stuck.'

Oh, isn't it? said the Examiner. *Who got in my way when I spoke the Word? Who stole power from my final casting? And who's been using the Book of Words without control, without any kind of authority – not to speak of fasting, meditation, or indeed any of the Advanced, or even the Intermediary States of Bliss – ever since?*

'Oh,' said the parson. 'That.'

There was rather a long silence.

'I meant well,' he said at last.

No you didn't, said the Examiner. *You meant to seize power.*

'Then why didn't you stop me?'

Ah, said the Examiner.

There was another silence.

'Well?' said Nat.

Well, as an Examiner in life I had certain duties, certain restrictions – protocols to be observed, fasting, preparation – and now . . . It paused, and Nat felt its laughter inside his head. *Do I really need to explain, Parson? You've tasted it – you know how it feels* . . .

'So all that stuff – about using the Word without authority – all that was just to make me feel inferior, was it?'

Well – let's face it, you are only a parson, and—

'Only a parson! I'll have you know—'

My good fellow, I—

'And *don't* call me fellow!'

And at that he turned, unbuttoned, aimed for the bushes and watered them, luxuriantly and at length, as Examiner 4421974 spluttered and protested in his mind and Skadi, in wolf form, caught the scent of their prey and began to run, heedless of the little drama being enacted on the road behind her, towards the Horse's Eye.

The posse on the hilltop saw them coming. A small posse – a group of four, posted there by Nat with orders to report any unusual activity to or from the Horse's Eye. There had been none – much to their relief – save a few scuttling things at around midnight that might have been rats (but were probably goblins).

Now the men were dozing under the wheel of one of the silent machines, while Adam Scattergood, who had bravely volunteered for the safest duty, sat cross-legged on a stone, eating a smoked sausage and watching the road.

He jumped from his perch at once when he saw Nat.

'Mr Parson! Over here!'

As he'd intended, his cry alerted the sleeping men. (His uncle had promised him a shilling if he would stay awake.)

Dorian Scattergood opened one eye. At his side Jed Smith and Audun Briggs were already stirring. By the time the parson reached the foot of the Hill, all three looked as if they had been alert for hours.

It was then that they saw the white wolf. She had run ahead of the parson, breasting the Hill on the blind side, and so was upon them before they knew what was happening. A white snow-wolf, brindled with grey; dark muzzle folded in a velvet snarl displaying teeth as sharp and white as a row of icicles.

They panicked. Wolves were rare in the Strond valley, and it was the first time any of them but Dorian had seen one so close. That experience saved his life; instinctively he faced it, spreading his arms with a loud cry, and Skadi veered away, catching the scent of an easier prey, leaped at Audun, who had gone for his pack (a knife dangled uselessly from his belt), and took out his throat as neatly as a boy bobs an apple.

It had been a trying night for the Huntress. The frustration of her plans, the weakness of her companion, the escape of her quarry and the cumulative effect of having spent so much time in animal skin – all these things conspired to strengthen her wolf's instincts, to urge her to hunt, to bite, to seek relief in blood.

Besides, she was hungry. She shook her quarry energetically, though by then Audun was almost certainly dead, and having sniffed delicately at the blood, she began to feed.

The other three stared in disbelief. Jed Smith, sagging with shock, went for the crossbow at his side. Dorian began to back away, very carefully, down the far hillside, without taking his eyes for one moment from the feeding wolf. (This too was to save his life.)

Adam, no hero, was violently sick.

And it was at this point that Nat reached them.

326

'Mr Parson,' said Jed in a low voice.

Nat ignored him. He stood in a trance, head slightly lowered, eyes fixed on the opening in the Hill. The feeding wolf looked up for a second, bared its teeth and returned to its kill. The parson seemed hardly to notice.

Adam Scattergood, who had never been given to fanciful thoughts, found himself thinking, *He looks dead*.

In fact Nat had never felt so much alive. The sudden discovery in his mind of Examiner 4421974 had unexpectedly put things into perspective for him. He was not mad, as he'd feared. The voice was real. His initial terror and outrage at his mind's invasion had settled; now he realized that there was nothing to be afraid of. His was the power. He was in control. And wasn't it fine – wasn't it *right* – to wield such power over the fellow who had snubbed him?

Your wolf is eating that man. I thought you should know.

Nat glanced at Skadi. Her muzzle, ruff and forelegs were illuminated with blood. 'Leave her,' he said. 'She has to eat.'

Jed Smith, his crossbow raised, overheard and stared in horror. Since the roundhouse he'd been glad to give Skadi a wide berth; but tales of her powers had been whispered afar, and he was in no doubt that this was the same demon woman who had killed the Examiner and taken hold of the parson's mind.

'Mr Parson?' he said.

Eyes that seemed unnaturally bright fixed Jed in their gaze.

Jed swallowed. Turning, he saw that Dorian had fled; only he and Adam remained on the Hill. 'She'll need some clothes,' the parson said. 'The other man's are bloody.'

Jed Smith shook his head. His hand was trembling so much that the crossbow was a blur. 'Don't let her kill me,' he said. 'I won't say a word.'

Interesting, thought Nat Parson. He'd always thought Jed a lumpen fellow, good for hitting things and not much else. But here he was, showing signs of real intelligence. Of course, it was obvious; Nat could not expect even the most fervent of his flock to acquiesce to the murder of a villager. Without witnesses it would be clear that Audun had fallen victim to a prowling wolf. But if Jed talked . . .

Nat pondered with some surprise how easy it was to kill a man. Perhaps it was Ethel's death that had hardened him to the fact; perhaps the Examiner's experience in the field. A week ago Nat Parson would no more have contemplated murder than he would have held Mass stark naked; but now he did, and realized with astonishment that he didn't much care.

Good, said the Examiner. *It takes courage to do what needs to be done.*

'Then there is—' Nat broke off, consciously turning over the words in his mind. *Then there is no sin attached to such an act?*

Of course not, came the immediate reply. *The only sin is to fail in one's duty.*

We think alike, said Nat in surprise.

Perhaps that is why our minds meshed as they did.

For a moment Nat was lost in thought. Was that the reason for what had happened? A meeting of like minds at a crucial moment, both striving for the same goal?

He smiled at Jed. 'Very well,' he said. 'But I'll need your clothes. Come, quickly, man. I don't have all day.'

'Promise?' said Jed, who was still shaking so violently that he could hardly untie his bootlaces. 'Promise you won't let her kill me?'

'I promise,' said Nat, still smiling at Jed, who, reassured, began once more to unlace his boots.

It was almost the truth, after all, he told himself as he spoke the relevant canticle and Jed Smith fell heavily to the ground. Besides – he staggered a little as the aftershock of the Word slammed through the Hill – why should Seer-folk have all the fun?

BOOK SEVEN
Netherworld

The dead know everything, but they don't give a damn.

Lokabrenna, 9:0

1

Many roads lead to Hel. In fact it could be argued that *all* roads lead eventually to Hel, the frictionless pivot between Order and Chaos, where neither holds sway, and nothing – and no one – ever changes.

True Chaos, like Perfect Order, is mostly uninhabited. The many creatures that exist within its influence – demons, monsters and the like – are simply satellites, basking in Chaos as the earth basks in the warmth of the sun, knowing full well the dangers of over-familiarity. Even Dream – which has its laws, though they are not necessarily the laws of elsewhere – is far too near Chaos for comfort, which is why so few dare stay there long. And as for Netherworld – you'd have to be mad to even think about it.

Loki had been pondering this with increasing unease as he and Maddy followed the long, well-travelled road to Hel. Not a difficult road, for obvious reasons, though less worn than you might have expected. The dead leave fewer tracks than the living, but even so, the passageway was deeply rutted and its stone walls had been polished to a mirror-like glaze by the passing of a million million – perhaps more – world-weary travellers.

Not that Hel was to be their final destination. That, thought Loki, would have been far too easy. No, beyond the Underworld lay Netherworld, not so much a land in itself as an island among the many that spread out across the vast river that marks the boundary between World Below and World Beyond; the greatest, the Cauldron of all Rivers: eternal; lethal even to the dead.

The Whisperer had been mercifully silent as they drew ever closer to the Underworld. But Loki sensed its excitement – as it sensed his fear – persistent enough to tax him to the limits as he struggled ahead. And it *was* a struggle; Loki's glam was not at its strongest, and it was no comfort to him to know that the Whisperer could reach into his mind anytime it liked and twist it like a wet rag.

So far, however, it had left him alone; and Loki guessed that behind its silence lay a wariness that had not been present at the beginning of their expedition.

He had read something in its thoughts – or it believed he had – and he could sense that although it enjoyed its power over him, it was wary of what he might see there next – and of what he might tell Maddy. And so it said little to either of them, and there was no repetition of the incident at the river crossing, but even so, Loki's head ached, as if a storm was on its way.

They had stopped to sleep after the river. Three hours' sleep, a mouthful of bread and a sip of water and they had set off again, looking only ahead and never to the side, speaking only when they needed to. They had left World Above at eleven o'clock of the previous morning, and if anyone had told Maddy that barely twelve hours had passed since then, she would never have believed them.

And yet she moved on without complaint. And Loki, who half expected her to have turned back by now, watched in growing disquiet as they embarked on the final stretch.

By now the path was quick with the dead. A hundred dead per cubic foot; crammed all together into the fetid space, moving sluggishly onwards, downwards as far as the eye could see. Which wasn't actually very far: their misty presences distressed the air; their stink – which was worse than any midden or slaughterhouse or garbage dump or field hospital you've ever smelled or imagined – enveloped everything, sinking loamy fingers into their lungs, tainting their food, their drink, the air they breathed.

The dead themselves feel nothing, of course. But they *do* sense; and as the travellers passed through them like ships through thick fog, the legions of the dead shifted instinctively closer to the warmth of the living, dead fingers plucking at their clothes, their hair, dead mouths moving in soundless entreaty.

Men, women, warriors, thieves; stillborn children and drowned sailors; vassals, heroes, poets, kings; ancients, murderers, desperadoes and sellers of fake remedies against the plague; lost loves, old gods, scruffy schoolboys, spurious saints. All dead, existing now as shadows – *less* than shadows – of their living selves, and yet each with his or her own mournful colours, so that Maddy and Loki were close to drowning in their collective despair, and even the Whisperer was silent.

'You're sure you want to do this?' said Loki as Maddy trudged ahead. 'I mean, what are you actually trying to prove? And who are you trying to prove it *to*?'

Maddy looked at him, surprised. It had been so long, it seemed, since she had even asked herself the question *why* – and the thought that she might even now have a choice . . .

Who am I doing this for? she thought. *The gods? The worlds? My father?*

She tried to see her father's face – red-bearded, slow-witted, good-natured Thor, known to her from so many tales that she was sure she'd know him anywhere – and yet when Maddy thought of the words *my father*, it was not the Thunderer, or even Jed Smith, that she pictured in her mind's eye. It was One-Eye: clever, sarcastic, devious One-Eye, who had lied to her, and maybe worse . . .

And yet, for all that, she missed him terribly, and if she hadn't been certain that to involve him in this would be to put him in the most terrible danger . . .

I wonder if he's looking for me.
I wonder if he misses me.
And if he knew – would he be proud?
'There's only one way to find out,' she said.
Doggedly she moved on.

How long now? Impossible to tell. So close to the edge of Chaos, the laws that bind the Worlds are already warped beyond recognition. Logic tells us that such a journey to such a place cannot possibly exist; but Maddy and Loki were travelling *between* possibilities, to places where Logic, the first servant of Order, cannot pass.

The trick, like magic, is not to think too hard about what you're doing, to pass through the world as if in a dream, untrammelled by ideas of what is possible and what is not. And so they cast *Naudr* to open the way, and moved impossibly down into the Underworld, and when morning came (not that they knew it *was* morning), they found themselves standing on a craggy cliff looking down onto a subterranean landscape of stagnant mists and slow dark rivers, a long plain lit from all around with a wan light the colour of an old bruise, and knew they were looking at Hel itself.

Hel is cold, but not freezing. To freeze implies a kind of action; but Hel is a place of inaction, and its chill is the coldness of the empty hearth, of the silent earth, of the grave. And so Loki and Maddy were cold, but not unbearably so, and they were tired, but reluctant to sleep. Most of all they were hungry and thirsty, for their small supplies were running out, and they dared not touch the foul water of Hel. They took turns to carry the Whisperer (on Loki's insistence, to Maddy's surprise), but even so their progress was slow as they trudged towards a sullen horizon that never seemed to get any nearer.

'Does it go on for ever like this?' said Maddy as they stopped once more to rest.

Loki glanced at her and shrugged. 'For some people it goes on for ever. For others – well, it takes the time it takes.'

'That doesn't make sense,' Maddy said. 'Distances don't change depending on who you are.'

'They do here,' Loki said.

Wearily they trudged on.

There aren't many rules in the Underworld, but those that exist are rarely broken. Death is a place in permanent balance, a place of no movement, no progress, no change. Of course, living, moving, changing people were never *meant* to visit Hel. A few have tried (they always do), but little good ever comes of it, and most, if they come back at all, come back mad or broken.

Even the gods had made a point of avoiding the Underworld as often as possible. It's a dreary place; and although many have tried to bargain with its Guardian – to plead for aid, to negotiate the return of one, single, very special soul – such a pact has always ended in tears, failure, lingering death or a bit of all three.

For Hel's safe balance comes at a price. No one raises the dead without disturbing that balance; and so close to Netherworld, the consequences could be disastrous. As a result, Hel's Guardian had a reputation for being cranky and disobliging, and no one had left the Underworld alive since Mother Frigg returned alone after pleading for the release of Balder the Fair, before the end of the Elder Age.

Loki was well aware of this. On the other hand, he had reason to believe that the Guardian of the Underworld might deign to make an exception in his case. Evidently the Whisperer believed it too, which suited Loki just fine, because that belief was what had kept him alive so far.

Now he sensed the thing's impatience.

You said she would be here, it said.

She will, thought Loki, hoping it was true.

It had better be true, because if you've lied . . .

'Don't worry. She'll come,' he said aloud. 'As soon as she knows I'm here, she'll come.'

'Who?' said Maddy, looking at him.

'The Guardian of the Underworld,' he said. 'Half-Born Hel. My daughter.'

2

As Maddy and Loki were entering Hel, the Vanir above-ground were losing no time. The ambush at the Parsonage had alerted them to Skadi's betrayal, but the murder of Ethel Parson suggested that there was another dimension to the business. Had it been an accident? Was the woman a bystander, caught in the crossfire? Or was she a sacrifice, sent out to make them believe that no treachery was intended on the part of the Folk?

'Of course there was treachery,' Frey had said. 'They lured us out there with promises of parley, then tried to use the Word on us. What other reason could there be?'

'But what about Odin?' That was Bragi, looking shaken, combing dust out of his hair. 'He wanted to talk. He broke bread with us – he wanted peace with the Vanir—'

'Oh, grow up,' snapped Frey. 'He was hardly going to wear a sign saying *This is a trap*, was he? I say we waste no more time. Go after him now. Make him talk.'

Freyja was looking thoughtful. 'A poison handkerchief,' she said. 'It doesn't really seem like Odin's style.'

'And what about Skadi?' Bragi said. 'If she'd wanted to do us harm, she could have done it in the Hall of Sleepers, when we were helpless. Why turn against us now?'

'Perhaps she was waiting for something,' said Frey.

'I don't believe she means us harm.' Njörd was looking stubborn now, his sea-blue eyes shining dangerously.

'No, really?' said Heimdall, losing his temper. 'You old idiot, what does she have to do to make you believe? She could have her hands round your throat and you'd still think it a sign of affection.'

'That's ridiculous.'

'*You're* ridiculous. You think that because you were together once—'

'You leave my marriage out of this.'

'Your marriage was over before it began . . .'

As discussion erupted once more among the Vanir, Idun, who had taken no part in the battle, wandered over to its only casualty. Ethel Parson was lying in the yard, face-down in her night dress, the wisp of glamours that had been the handkerchief already dissolving in the first rays of dawn. Her hair had come unpinned, there was a smudge of earth on her cheek, and she looked small and discarded, just a footnote to the real business in hand.

Kneeling quietly beside her, Idun considered, with pity and some wonderment, the mysterious resilience of the Folk. Such frail creatures they were, she thought; with such short lives and such a depth of misery to endure. And yet a blow that might have annihilated a goddess had failed to extinguish the life in this woman. Oh, she was dying – but there was some spark in her yet, and when the Healer touched her face, her eyelids moved, just a little.

Some distance away the remaining Vanir were still arguing. The cause of the argument did not interest Idun. Too many people seemed dissatisfied too much of the time and, for the most part, for a trivial cause. Death alone was not trivial. She glimpsed its mystery in Ethel's blurry eyes and wondered whether she should let it come. The woman was troubled and in pain. Very soon she would be at peace. And yet she fought it – Idun sensed this very strongly – with every particle of her being.

Passive she had always been; obedient to her husband, dutiful to her father; modest and self-effacing throughout her life. Such a woman facing Death submits quietly, without a struggle. But there was steel in Owen Goodchild's daughter.

She wanted to live – and so Idun reached into the pouch at her waist and brought out a tiny sliver of dried fruit. It was no larger than her little fingernail; but it was the food of the gods, and she laid it under Ethelberta's tongue and waited.

A minute passed. Perhaps it was too late, thought Idun; not even the apples of youth could save her if her spirit had already been accepted into Hel's domain. Very gently she turned Ethelberta onto her side, pushing away the soft brown hair to uncover her face. It was a plain face, to be sure; and yet Death had given it a kind of dignity, a stillness that was almost regal.

'I'm sorry,' murmured Idun. 'I tried to save you.'

And it was at that very moment that the dead woman opened her eyes; that her colours came to life once more, flaring from autumn-brown to pumpkin-orange; that she leaped up with her hair wild and the colours flying in her cheeks and announced in a ringing voice to Freyja: *'I'll be taking my dress back now, my lady!'*

3

Odin had fled the moment his meeting with the Vanir had begun to go wrong. Red Horse Hill was the nearest refuge, and, skirting Adam and the sleeping possemen, he made it inside fifteen minutes ahead of the Huntress and the parson, but in his haste he forgot to check his path, and ran straight into one of Skadi's traps.

At any other time he would have seen it: a thin band stretched across the tunnel mouth, ready to snap shut on any trying to pass through. This time he didn't; and the trap – a primitive thing, but primed with *Hagall* – caught him straight in the face, and he went out like a light.

Coming to his senses a few seconds later, Odin found himself in darkness. He cast *Sól* to light his way, but no light shone from his fingertips, and not even the faintest gleam of phosphorescence came from the tunnel's rocky walls. It was not an absence of glam, he thought; there was plenty of power in him still, and it was only when he tried the rune *Bjarkán* that, reluctantly, Odin conceded the truth. There must have been more to Skadi's trap than a simple device to wound or kill.

He was blind.

In haste Odin considered his options. Certainly he could not stay where he was. He had not seen the outcome of the fight at the Parsonage, but he guessed that the Huntress would be on his trail. He had to assume that Loki had fled. Maddy, who might have helped him, was gone. The Whisperer was lost. And it went without saying that any further contact with the Vanir was out of the question – at least until his sight returned.

If it returned.

For now he needed to get away. Skadi could track him in wolf form, and his first concern was to throw her off the scent.

His shirt was still bloody from Jed Smith's crossbow bolt; carefully he took it off, and felt his way down the tunnel until he came to a narrow crossroads, trailing the shirt behind him. He took it some distance down the left-hand passageway and abandoned it there, wedged under a rock. Then, retracing his steps, he took the right fork, walked thirty paces, flung the rune *Hagall* at the roof hard enough to collapse it in part, and ran down the passage as fast as he could.

Blind as he was, he tripped and fell, though luckily out of range of the falling roof. He hoped the rockfall had blocked the tunnel: acrid dust fretted the air, and if his ruse worked, then at least it would slow the Huntress down, or at best send her off on a false trail while Odin found refuge under the Hill. Even so, she would have caught up with him, if the instinct to stop and feed had not been so strong; but as it was, she lost precious minutes, and by the time she entered the Hill the trail was blurred and the true quarry fled.

Now, Odin was nothing if not resourceful. He was blind, but not helpless, and as he fled towards the Strond, he began to rediscover skills he had not used for centuries. The passageway was obstacle-free, the few loose rocks that littered the ground easy to kick aside; and he had his staff to help him along, tapping first one side of the wall and then the other, probing ahead to warn him of anything on the ground that might trip him or stand in his way.

He found that he could tell when the passage forked; could tell from the movement of the air – its temperature, its dampness or otherwise, its sweetness or foulness – which direction he ought to take, which passage led up, which led down, which passed over water and which was a dead end.

Exploration of the rock at his fingertips proved equally fruitful. Damp, porous rock indicated a good air supply;

smooth, well-polished rock suggested a well-travelled route; the patterns of dust on the ground, the distribution of rock litter, the sound made by his staff as he rapped against a hollow wall – all these showed him things that might not have been apparent to a man accustomed to relying upon the evidence of his eyes. In these passages, at least, he was not so much at a disadvantage.

Then there was the truesight. The injury to his good eye had not affected his inner vision; with *Bjarkán* he could still see the colours, the footprints of magic and the muted glow that indicated the presence of life.

In this way, and quite by accident, Odin discovered the Whisperer's trail. He had reached the heart of Red Horse Hill at about the same time as Loki and Maddy crossed the Strond, and found no recent sign of them there. But as he approached the central chasm from one of the tunnels leading down, his truesight showed him a fugitive gleam and he caught his first scent of the Whisperer.

Someone had tried to erase it, he saw; but its signature was very strong, and in places it overwhelmed the workings, spilling out at intervals along the passage. Once it was joined by a faint signature of a familiar violet; another time by a bright fragment that was unmistakably Maddy's. They were moving fast, Odin could tell. And they were heading straight for the Underworld.

But why would they risk the Underworld? Hel had no reason to welcome Loki – in fact she was more likely to kill him on sight or, better still, hand him over to Netherworld, where Surt the Destroyer still kept the Æsir captive, and would be more than interested to learn how one of his prisoners had managed to escape.

Unless he had something to bargain with, thought Odin. *A weapon, perhaps? A glam?*

In the darkness he smiled grimly. Of course. He was not the only one to covet the Whisperer. Surely Hel could have little use for such a glam, but beyond Hel's world, where the balance was set, in Netherworld, or even beyond—

For a moment he stopped. Could *that* be Loki's aim? he thought. To use the Whisperer as a bargaining tool – not with the Æsir, or the Vanir, or even with the Order, but with the very Lords of Chaos?

Odin's mind reeled at the thought.

That power combined with the power of Chaos, destabilizing the Worlds, rewriting reality . . .

It could mean, quite simply, the world's unmaking. Not another Ragnarók, but a final dissolution of all things, a breakdown in the laws of Order and Chaos, a terminal upsetting of the balance.

Surely even Loki would not dare to set in motion such a chain of events. But if not, then what exactly did he expect to gain? And even if he was innocent of malice, then did he *really* understand the risk he was taking – not only with his own life, but with the whole of existence?

4

Above him, at last, the hunt was on. Three hunters, to be exact: a woman, who was a Fury, a goddess and also a wolf; a man who was two men in a single body; and Adam Scattergood, who was beginning to think that even death at the wolf woman's hands might be more merciful than the terror of these endless passages with their sounds and their smells.

Skadi had wanted to kill him at once. Reverting to her natural form, she had levelled her ice-blue gaze at Adam and given a wolfish – and still bloodstained – smile.

But Nat had other plans for Adam. And here he was now, miles below the demon mound, carrying the parson's Book and pack. Fear had made him surprisingly docile; and although the pack was heavy, he made no complaint. In fact, thought Nat, it was easy to forget him altogether, and he did, for long periods, as they followed the white she-wolf deeper into World Below.

They stopped for supplies some way down, and while Nat rested, Adam packed as much food and drink as he could carry. Bread; cheese; dried meat – lots of this, in the silent hope that the wolf woman might prefer it to fresh boy. Adam himself was not at all hungry. Nat ate sparingly, and studied the Good Book, and seemed to *argue* with himself in a way that Adam found very disturbing. Then they walked – Skadi in her natural shape, wearing Jed Smith's cast-off clothes and cursing at the elusive trail – and then they slept for an hour or two; and when Adam awoke from a terrifying dream, he was not really surprised to find that his present reality was far, far worse.

There must have been a thousand roads leading out from under the Hill. Even with Skadi's wolf senses, finding the trail was a difficult task. She did find it, however: it ran alongside their own path, in a small lateral tunnel to which they had not, as yet, gained access. But they were close; once they had even *heard* their quarry tapping its way quietly along the tunnel at their side, and the white wolf had howled with frustration at finding itself so near, with only a span of rock between themselves and their prey.

But the wolf form tired Skadi if she kept to it for too long, and often she was obliged to shift to her human Aspect, eating ravenously every time she did so. Adam found her human Aspect even more intimidating than her wolf form. At least with a wolf he knew more or less what he was dealing with. And when she was a wolf, there could be no spells or glamours; no sudden explosions, mindblasts or conjurings. Adam had always hated magic; only now was he beginning to realize quite how much.

Better to deny it all, he thought. Better to tell himself that it was all a dream from which he would soon awake. It made sense. Adam had never been a dreamer, and so it was natural that this – this exceptionally long and troubling dream – should have unnerved him. But a dream was all it was, he thought; and the more he told himself that it was just a dream, the less he thought of his aching back, or the wolf woman at his side, or the impossible things that came to him out of the dark.

By the time they reached the river, Adam Scattergood had come to a decision. It didn't seem to matter any more that he'd seen two men die; that he was far from home in the company of wolves; that he had blisters on his feet and rock-dust in his lungs; or even that the parson had gone insane.

He was dreaming, that was all.

All he had to do was wake up.

Meanwhile, on the trail of the hunters, the Vanir had made less headway than they would have liked. Not that the trail was difficult to follow – Skadi was making no attempt to shield her colours – but by now the six of them were so little in sympathy with each other that they could hardly agree to anything.

Heimdall and Frey had wanted to shapeshift at once and follow the Huntress in animal guise. But Njörd refused to be left behind, and his favourite Aspect – that of a sea eagle – was hardly practical underground. Freyja refused to shift at all, protesting that there would be no one to carry her clothes for when she returned to her true Aspect; and all of them found it impossible to make Idun understand the urgency of their pursuit, as she stopped repeatedly to marvel over pretty stones or veins of metal in the ground, or the black lilies that grew wherever water seeped through the walls.

Frey suggested shapeshifting Idun, the way Loki had once turned her into a hazelnut to flee the clutches of the Ice People. But Bragi wouldn't hear of it, and finally they proceeded on foot, rather more slowly than they would have wished.

All in all, it had been a long, quarrelsome descent for the six of them; Heimdall maintaining stubbornly that Odin could not have betrayed them; Freyja complaining about the dust; Bragi singing cheery songs that got on everyone's nerves; Njörd impatient, Frey suspicious and Idun so lost to any sense of peril that she had to be closely watched at all times to keep her from wandering away. Nevertheless they crossed the Strond barely an hour after the Huntress; for Skadi had her own problems, in the shape of Nat Parson and Adam Scattergood, both of whom had slowed her down considerably.

On the far side of the Strond, someone else had also been following a trail. It was an easy trail to follow, if you knew where to look; the Captain had shielded his colours, of course, but had left small cantrips at every turn he took, embedded in the tunnel walls or hidden beneath the stones of the path, to show where he was heading.

Not that Sugar had any doubt where he was heading – and only the Captain could be mad or bad enough to believe that any such as he could ever return from such a destination.

But he *was* the Captain; and Sugar had long since learned not to question his orders.

He'd caught up with Sugar in the food stores, where the goblin was about to settle down with a suckling pig and a yard of ale. At first Sugar hadn't recognized him, dressed as he was in Crazy Nan's skirts, looking filthy and hunted and close to exhaustion – but Loki had soon got his attention, binding him to obedience with threats and runes, and giving instructions in a low, hurried tone, as if afraid of being overheard.

'Why me?' had said Sugar desperately.

'Because you're here,' Loki had said. 'And because I really don't have a choice.'

Sugar wished he *hadn't* been there. But Loki's instructions had been quite clear; and so the goblin followed his trail, picking up the spent cantrips as he went, and occasionally checking the pouch around his neck – the pouch the Captain had given him, with orders on how to use it if it became necessary.

The Captain was in trouble – that was for sure. Sugar didn't need any glam to tell him *that*. In trouble deep – and heading deeper – but still alive, though for how long Sugar could not say.

Every half-hour he checked the pouch. What was inside looked like a common pebble, but Sugar could see the runes on it – Ós, for the Æsir, Bjarkán, and Kaen, the Captain's own sign – all cleverly put together to make a sigil that was unmistakably Loki's.

'This runestone will show you what to do,' he had said, cramming clothes and supplies into a pack. 'Follow me close – and don't be seen.'

Follow him where? Sugar hadn't dared to ask. In fact he hadn't needed to – the Captain's expression already told him more than he wanted to know. Loki was going to Hel, of course – a place Sugar didn't even like to hear about in *stories* – and he was taking Maddy with him.

'If the stone turns red,' the Captain had said, 'then you'll know I'm in mortal peril. If it turns black' – his scarred lips tightened – 'then you'll know I'm beyond reprieve.'

Sugar almost wished the stone *would* turn black. He'd been following the trail for what seemed like days; he was hungry, thirsty, tired and getting more and more worried at every step. There were rats deep down in the lower tunnels; rats and roaches as big as he was. There were freezing waters and hidden pits; there were geysers and sulphur pits and limestone sinks. But Sugar continued to follow the trail, though even he wasn't sure any more whether it was fear, loyalty or simply that fatal curiosity of his that kept him going, step by step.

The stone had been red for nearly an hour. And it was getting darker.

5

In a silent chamber boxed within a multitude of silent chambers, Hel the Half-Born was still debating what to do. Nothing happened in the Underworld without her knowledge, and it had not taken her long to realize that a couple of intruders had penetrated her domain.

Normally she might just have ignored the pair. Death's territory is endless, and most trespassers either turned back, or died slowly out in the wastes. Either option suited Hel; it had been centuries since she'd granted an audience to anyone living, and even then, her visitor had returned alone. Hel was not generous, nor was she given to fierce emotions, but now, as she sensed the approach of warm blood, she was aware of a sensation almost of surprise.

Of course, she'd forced them to wait for her. Just long enough to punish them a little, and to teach them some of the patience of Hel. Time has no meaning to the dead. And a day in Hel seems like weeks to the living. And so Loki and Maddy measured their time in gulps of water, slices of sleep and bites of bread so hard that they might have been stones. And when their small supplies ran out, they measured it in the long, looping, staggering steps they took across the endless sand, and the times they fell, and stood up, and fell, and wondered if she would ever come.

Now Hel opened one eye, and closed the other. Her living eye was a bright green, not unlike her father's in colour, but with a coldness in its lack of expression that made even the living side of her face look dead. The dead eye saw further, though it was blind; and its gaze was like an empty skull's.

For Hel was two women merged into one: one side of her face was smooth and pale; the other side was pitted and grey. A sheaf of black hair fell over one shoulder; on the other, a twist of yellow twine. One hand was shapely; the other a claw. The rune *Naudr* marked her throat; the same rune was on the binding rope in her hand. One withered foot gave her a lurching gait.

Not that Hel was in the habit of *walking*; she spent the centuries in a half-doze, dead eye open to acknowledge the thousands that poured, day and night, second by second, into her realm.

Among those thousands, few had ever caught her interest. *The dead know everything but don't give a damn*, as the saying goes, and a dead prince in all his regalia is no less dead than a dead street-sweeper, sewage worker or maker of novelty spoons. There isn't a lot of variety among the dead, and Hel had long since learned to ignore them equally.

But this was different. Two trespassers deep in her domain, their signatures visible to her living eye like two columns of coloured smoke far across the plain. That in itself was enough to arouse her curiosity – and that violet trail was strangely familiar. But there was something else with them – something that tantalized her vision like sunlight on a piece of glass . . .

Sunlight? Glass? Yes, Hel remembered the light of the sun. She remembered how *they* had robbed her of it, how they had sent her to this place where nothing changed or lived or grew, where day and night were equally absent in the eternal corpse-light of the dead.

But who were *they*? The Æsir, of course. The Æsir, the Fiery, the Gødfolk, the gods. They'd promised her a kingdom fit for a queen, and this – *this* – was what she'd got.

Of course, that had been many centuries ago, and she'd thought the Æsir long gone.

But unless her warm-blood sight deceived her, two at least remained; and it was with something close to eagerness that she stood now, the rope of glamours in her living hand, and crossed the endless desert with a word.

It was Maddy who saw her first. Awakening from troubled dreams in her shelter among the rocks, she sensed a chilly presence and, opening her eyes, found herself looking at a woman's profile, green-eyed, high-cheekboned, with hair that gleamed like crows' feathers. She had only a moment to gasp at this woman's beauty, and then she turned, and the illusion was gone.

Hel looked at Maddy's expression and, for the first time in five hundred years, she smiled. 'That's right, little girl,' she said softly. 'Death has two faces. The one that inspires poets and lovers; the one for whom warriors lose their heads . . . And then there's the *other* one. The grave. Worms. Rot.' She gave a mocking curtsey, lurching on her withered foot.

'Welcome to Hel, little girl.'

Loki was wide awake. He'd sensed Hel's watchful presence at once, and had hidden the Whisperer, wrapped up in Maddy's jacket to make a pack, sealed with runes, under an outcrop of weathered rocks. Now he emerged from his hiding place, with a smile that was half insult, half charm, and announced, 'I'd forgotten what a dump this place was.'

Very slowly Hel turned. 'Loki,' she said. 'I hoped it was you.' She gave him a look that made Maddy's flesh crawl. 'I imagine you must have some purpose here.'

'Oh, I do,' said Loki.

'It must be important,' she said. 'To come, unprotected, into my realm is not without a certain risk, even for you. And as for *her* . . .' She squinted at Maddy. 'Who is she, anyway? I can smell her Æsir blood from here.'

'No one you'd know. A relative.'

'Really?' said Hel. Certainly there was something about the girl that looked familiar. Something in the eyes, perhaps. Hel searched her extensive memory; but Death's hospitality is vast, and she could not find the clue she sought.

She smiled at Maddy. 'I'm sure you must be hungry, my dear.' She gestured with her living hand, and suddenly a table appeared, broad as the Strond, bright and gleaming and mountain-ridden with silver, glassware, fine bone china, damask napkins, fruit, mead, wine; pastry pies with lids like cauldrons; tureens of soup like fairy coaches; frosted grapes piled high on platters; roasted piglets with apples in their mouths; and honeyed figs, and fresh young cheeses; slashed pomegranates, peaches, plums; olives in spiced oil; and baked salmon with their tails in their mouths, stuffed clams, rolled herring, sweet cider, plump almond rolls, cinnamon buns, muffins like clouds and bread – oh, bread of a thousand kinds: soft, white, poppy-seeded, plaited, round loaves and square loaves and loaves dark and dense with fruit . . .

Maddy stared, remembering perhaps the last time she had eaten, the last time she had felt hunger, real hunger, in this dead world. Stretching her hand towards the laden table, mouth watering, craving to taste—

'Don't touch it,' Loki said.

'Why not?' said Maddy, with her hand on a plum.

'You don't eat the food of the Underworld. Not a bite, not a sip, not a seed. That is, if you ever want to leave.'

Hel faced him, deadpan. 'None of my guests have ever complained.'

He laughed at that. 'She gets her sense of humour from her father's side,' he told Maddy. 'Now come on, let's go. That hall of yours has to be somewhere around here, right?'

Hel half smiled. 'As you say,' she said, and dismissed the feast – and then just as suddenly it was there: a bone-white palace straddling the desert, spires and turrets and

gargoyles and minarets and skeleton outcrops of Gothic and
neo-Gothic architecture with flying buttresses and fleurs-
de-lys and rows of bishops, priests, Examiners, cardinals,
shamans, mystics, prophets, witch-doctors, soothsayers,
Magisters, saviours, demigods and popes standing in their
niches along the façade.

'Nice,' said Loki.

Hel led the way.

Maddy had never seen such a place as this, not even in
dreams. Of course, she was aware that none of it was quite
real – that is, assuming the word *real* had any meaning so
close to the shores of Dream. But it was impressive: long
white walkways of cool alabaster; ivory hangings; intricate
vaulting; tapestries faded almost to transparency; and fluted
columns of delicate glass. They passed through silent halls
of stone, through mirrored rooms as pale as ice, through
chambers in which dead princesses waltzed alone, through
funeral chapels and deserted hallways soft with dust.

'She's your *daughter*?' whispered Maddy as they went.

Loki nodded. He seemed unconcerned, though Maddy
guessed that he was playing a game. And a dangerous one, she
told herself; there was clearly no love lost between Hel and her
father. 'I wasn't much of a parent,' he said. 'Then again, neither
was her mother. Quite mad, but alluring – like all demons –
though in the end we should never have had children. Too
much Chaos in both of us. Hel's actually pretty normal-
looking, compared to the rest of the clan. Aren't you, Hel?'

Hel did not reply, though her living shoulder stiffened in
rage. Maddy wondered anxiously whether it was entirely
wise for Loki to bait Hel on her own ground, but the Trickster
seemed quite unconcerned.

'Do you know, Loki,' said Hel, stopping abruptly. 'I've
been trying to work you out. This is my realm, the realm of

the dead. In it, I am all-powerful; what comes here belongs to me. And yet here you are, unarmed and unprotected. You seem very sure I'll let you live.'

Loki looked amused. 'What makes you think I'm unprotected?'

Hel raised an eyebrow. 'Don't bullshit me, Trickster,' she said. 'You're alone.'

'Quite alone,' agreed Loki comfortably.

'What *exactly* do you want?'

Loki smiled. 'An hour,' he said.

'An hour?' said Hel.

'In Netherworld.'

Hel's other eyebrow went up. 'Netherworld?' she said. 'I suppose you mean Dream?'

Loki shook his head. 'I mean Netherworld,' he said, smiling. 'More specifically, the Black Fortress.'

'I always knew you were mad,' said Hel. 'You escaped, didn't you? And you want to go *back*?'

'More importantly,' said Loki, 'I want to be sure I can get out again.'

Hel's eyebrow went down again. 'Now *that's* humour,' she said, straight-faced. 'It's almost worth waiting another five hundred years for the punchline.'

Loki shook his head impatiently. 'Come on, Hel. I know you can do it. You can't be so close to the Black Fortress for so many years without getting a few – let's say, unauthorized insights about how it works.'

Hel gave a half-smile. 'Maybe so,' she said. 'But it's a dangerous game. Open the fortress, even for an hour, and who knows what might escape from there – into Dream, into Death, perhaps even into the Middle Worlds. Why should I do it? What's in it for me?'

'One hour,' said Loki. 'One hour inside. After that, I'm out of your hair, all debts paid, for ever and ever.'

Hel's eyes narrowed. '*Debts?*' she said. Her rage seemed to freeze Maddy to the bone.

'Come on, Hel. You know you owe me.'

'Owe you *what*?'

Loki smiled. 'Don't be demure. It doesn't suit you. How *is* Golden Boy these days, anyway? Still as charming? Still as beautiful? Still as dead?'

The bones of Hel's dead hand ground audibly together.

Maddy looked anxiously at Loki.

'You'll like this, Maddy,' he said, still grinning. 'It's a roller-coaster love story through space, death and time. Boy meets girl – *she* loves him madly, but *he* doesn't even notice her, being too busy charming the hell out of everyone he meets; and besides, she's not what you'd call a looker, plus she lives in a bad part of town. So she makes a deal. I do her a little favour. She gets Golden Boy *all* to herself for a slice of eternity, and I get a favour in return. Which favour I'm calling in. Right here, right now.'

'You really are a bastard, Loki,' Hel said in a flat voice.

'I hate to be bitchy, sweetheart, but you weren't exactly born in wedlock yourself.'

Hel sighed. She didn't need to – she hadn't actually *breathed* in centuries – but somehow Loki brought out the worst in her every time. Still, they'd had a deal, she'd sworn an oath, and an oath of any kind, however foolish, was sacred to one who lived and worked at the balancing point between Order and Chaos.

Bitterly she considered her oath. She'd been younger then (not that *that* was any excuse); inexperienced in the ways of World and Underworld. Blind enough and foolish enough to believe in love; arrogant enough to believe that she might be the exception to the rule.

And Balder *was* beautiful. The god of spring blossom; the golden-haired; the good, the kind, the pure in heart.

Everybody loved him; but Hel, from her silent kingdom, longed for him most of all. She came to him at first in dreams, weaving her most seductive fantasies for his pleasure, but Balder recoiled, complaining of nightmares and troubled sleep; grew anxious, pale and fearful, until Hel realized that he hated her as fiercely as he loved life itself, and her cold heart grew colder still as she planned how she could make him hers.

It takes a certain cunning to kill a god. Loki had it; arranged it so that the guilt fell on another, and when Mother Frigg reached out with her glamours, entreating the Nine Worlds to plead for Balder's return, Loki alone did not beg, so that Balder remained for ever at Hel's side, a pale king to her dark queen.

But the victory was bitter. She'd dreamed of having Balder all to herself; had heard stories, in fact, of a previous Guardian of the Underworld who'd gained a similar prize by means of guile and a handful of pomegranate seeds. But Balder dead had none of the charm of Balder in life. Gone was his light step, his merry voice, the sunshine gleam of his golden hair. He was cold now, cold and expressionless; speaking only when conjured to do so, animated only by Hel's own glamours. Dead was dead, it seemed, even for gods. And now she would have to pay the price.

'So,' Loki said. 'Do we have a deal?'

For a timeless time Hel walked on in silence. They followed her through plague-white gates; through crypts and repositories of bone; across mosaics fashioned from human teeth and sepulchres vaulted with varnished skulls. They moved down; and here at last were the catacombs, stretching to infinity in every direction; festooned with the lace of a million spiders.

She paused along an avenue of stone; on either side there

were archways, beneath which a multitude of narrow chambers lay.

'Don't look,' said Loki quietly.

But Maddy couldn't help it. The chambers were dark, but lit as they passed, and inside Maddy saw the dead, some sitting, some standing as they had in life; some with half-familiar faces turning towards the unaccustomed warmth, then turning away as the visitors passed, the chamber dimming once more into the dead half-light of Hel.

Hel gestured with her dead hand, and a chamber to the right of them brightened and lit. Within it Maddy saw two young men, both pale and red-haired and bearing such a strong resemblance to Loki that she caught her breath.

'They killed us,' said one of the pale young men. 'They killed us both because of you.'

Hel's half-smile broadened to ghastly effect.

Loki said nothing, but averted his eyes.

They went on apace. Once more Hel raised her dead hand, and in a chamber to her left a sad-looking woman with soft brown hair turned her face towards the light.

'Loki,' she said. 'I waited for you. I waited, but you never came.'

Loki said nothing, but his expression was unusually grim.

A few minutes later Hel stopped again, and in front of her, a chamber lit. Within it Maddy saw the most beautiful young man she had ever seen. His hair was gold, his eyes blue, and though he was pale with the colours of death, he seemed to shine like a fallen star.

'Balder,' said Loki. He made it sound like a curse, somehow.

'I'm waiting for you,' Balder said. 'There's a place at my side for you, my friend. No man is clever enough to cheat Death; and I can wait – it won't be long.'

Again Loki swore and turned away.

Hel smiled again. 'Had enough?' she said.

Wordlessly Loki nodded.

'And what about you?' she said to Maddy. 'Any old friends *you'd* like to see?'

Loki put his hand on Maddy's arm. 'Maddy, don't look. Just keep on going.'

But Hel had already lifted her hand: another room lit; and inside it Maddy saw a woman with cowslip curls and a bearded man whose face was as familiar to her as her own.

'*Father?*' she said, taking a step.

'Ignore them. Ha'ants. Don't talk to them.'

'But that was my—'

'I *said* ignore them.'

But Maddy had taken another step. Shaking off Loki's restraining hand, she made for the chamber, where Jed and Julia Smith sat side by side in a stillness that might have seemed companionable in anyone other than the dead. Jed looked up as she came in; but with no curiosity; no welcome. He seemed to speak, lips moving silently in the semi-darkness, but no sound came but that of the wind and of the sifting dust.

'This is just glamour, right?' said Maddy in a small voice.

Hel gave her grisly half-smile.

'But he can't be dead. I saw him just a while ago.'

'I can make him speak to you,' suggested Hel in a silky voice. 'I can even show you what happened, if you'd like.'

'Don't,' said Loki tonelessly.

But Maddy could not look away from the room, now lit with an inviting glow. The folk inside were clearer now: Jed and Julia, their faces animated by the flickering light. She knew that they were not her real parents, and yet something inside her still longed for them – for the mother she had never known; for the man she had called Father for fourteen years. It made her feel suddenly very small, very insignificant; and for the first time since she and One-Eye had opened Red Horse Hill, Maddy found herself on the verge of tears.

'Was it my fault?' she said to the shade of Jed Smith. 'Was it something *I* did that brought you here?'

'Leave her alone,' said Loki sharply. 'Your business is with me, not her.'

Hel raised her living eyebrow. The chamber darkened; the ghosts disappeared.

'An hour,' said Loki in a harsh voice. 'One hour inside. After which I swear you'll never see me here again.'

Hel smiled. 'Very well. I'll give you an hour. Not a minute – not a *second* – more.'

'Do I have your oath?' Loki insisted.

'You have my *oath*, and furthermore you have my promise – assuming you survive this latest antic of yours, which I doubt – that next time your path crosses mine, father or not, you'll be a dead man. Understood?'

They shook on it, his living hand in her dead one. Then, with one dead finger, Hel drew a window in the air, and suddenly they were looking out over the river Dream, a vastness of water that no eye could hope to comprehend; wider than the One Sea and ten thousand times as turbulent. Islands dotted its surface like dancers in skirts of pale foam; rocks and skerries too many to count; treacherous sandbanks; cliffs that vanished into cloud; peaks and pinnacles and stovepipe stacks.

'Gods,' said Maddy. 'There are so *many* . . .'

Loki shrugged. 'The islands of Dream come and go,' he said. 'They're not designed to last for long. The fortress, however . . .'

Briefly he considered it. The Black Fortress of Netherworld, its head lost in a pile of cloud, its feet drowned ten fathoms deep. Its shape was uncertain: one moment a great castle barbed with turrets; the next a great pit with a fiery heart. Nothing keeps to a single Aspect so close to Chaos; this was part of what made the fortress impregnable. Doors and gateways came and went; that was why he needed Hel to keep the way open.

He did not doubt that she would do it. Hel's oath was legendary – the balance of her realm depended on it – although he did not doubt her promise either.

For a moment he thought of the Whisperer; its ancient cunning and its intent. Why had it wanted to come to Hel? What had he seen when their minds had crossed? What had he missed in his careful planning, for the Oracle to seem so smug?

I see a meeting at Nether's edge – of the wise, and of the not so wise.

Wise? In all his life the Trickster had never felt less so.

And now for the last time Hel raised her hand, and sketched *Naudr*, reversed, across the newly created window. All at once Maddy could feel the wind on her face; she could hear the *hissh* of the floodwater against the rocks, she could smell its ancient stench . . .

'You have an hour,' said Half-Born Hel. 'I suggest you make the most of it.'

And at that she was gone, and her hall with her, and Loki and Maddy were standing on a rocky turret in the middle of the river Dream, with the Black Fortress of Netherworld gaping at their feet.

6

The Vanir had been gone more than an hour. Ethel Parson had watched them leave with a feeling of peculiar detachment and a sudden certainty that they were gone for good. She felt very strange; very calm; and sitting at her dressing table, looking into the mirror, she tried to make sense of what she had seen.

Over the past twenty-four hours Ethel had seen more than she had in her entire life up until that moment. She had seen gods in battle; women who were wild beasts; her husband possessed by an unholy spirit; her house invaded; her property requisitioned; her life left hanging by a thread.

She knew she should feel *something*. Fear, probably. Grief. Anxiety. Relief. Horror at the *unnaturalness* of it. But Ethelberta felt none of these. Instead she scrutinized her face in her dressing-table mirror. She was not in the habit of doing so often. But today she felt compelled to look – not out of vanity, but more out of *curiosity*, to see if she could find any visible sign of the change she felt within.

I feel different. I am different.

She had changed into a dress of plain brown flannel – not inexpensive, but not good enough to tempt the Faërie woman – and had washed and brushed her long hair. Her face was clean and free of rouge, which made her look younger; her eyes – unremarkable when compared with Freyja's or Skadi's – were a clear and thoughtful golden brown. She was not a beauty – but neither was she the same muffin-faced Ethel Goodchild who had almost ended up on the shelf in spite of all her father's money.

How very strange, thought Ethel calmly. And how strange it was that the Gødfolk had healed her. Perhaps that made *her* unnatural too; marked, in some way, by their passing. Certainly she did not feel the revulsion she knew she ought to feel; instead she felt something like gratitude. Strangely like joy.

She was just about to go out, thinking that perhaps a morning walk would help to calm her spirits, when a knock came on the front door, and, opening it, she saw Dorian Scattergood, dishevelled, wild-eyed, red-faced and close to tears in his eagerness to tell his tale to someone – anyone – who might believe him.

He had run, he told her, all the way from Red Horse Hill. Lying low until he was sure it was safe, he had at last returned to find the dismembered bodies of Audun Briggs and Jed Smith lying beside the open Eye. Of the parson and Adam there was no sign, although he had seen the six Vanir moving fast along the Malbry road, and had hidden under a hedge in a field until the demon folk passed by.

'There was nothing I could do,' said Dorian wretchedly. 'I ran – I hid . . .'

'Mr Scattergood,' said Ethel firmly, 'I think you'd better come in for a while. The servants are due at any moment, and I'm sure you could take a drink of tea to calm your nerves.'

Tea, thought Dorian in disgust. Nevertheless he accepted, knowing that if anyone in Malbry was likely to believe him, Ethelberta would.

She did. Urging him on when he faltered, she took in the whole tale: the wolf woman; two murders; Nat's possession by spirits unknown; the disappearance of Adam Scattergood.

When he had finished, she put down her teacup in its china saucer and added a little more hot water to the pot. 'So where do you think my husband has gone?' she asked.

Dorian was puzzled. He'd expected tears; anger; perhaps

some kind of hysterical outburst. He'd expected her to blame him for running away – certainly he blamed himself – and the need to confess it to someone had been a part of his reason for coming to the Parsonage in the first place. Dorian had never had much time for Nat Parson, but that didn't mean he should have abandoned him to his fate. The same was true of the others, he thought. And as for Adam – his own *nephew*, for Laws' sakes . . . He was deeply ashamed at having run.

'They went into the Hill, lady,' he said at last. 'No doubt about it. Your husband too. They were tracking someone—'

'The Smith girl,' said Ethel, pouring tea.

'Aye, and her friend. The one who escaped.'

Ethel nodded. 'I know,' she said. 'I'm going after them, Mr Scattergood.'

'*After* them?' Now he knew that she was mad. In a way it reassured him; her strange calm had begun to make him uneasy. 'But Mrs Parson—'

'Listen to me,' said Ethel, interrupting. 'Something happened to me today. Right here, in the courtyard. It was done in a flash; like a bolt from the blue. One moment alive, the next slipping away into darkness. I've seen things, you understand. Things you'd scarcely warrant, not even in dreams.'

'Dreams?' said Dorian. Dreaming was not a pastime respectable folk admitted to in Malbry. He wondered whether Ethel Parson had received a knock on the head, and wished he hadn't called on her. 'Perhaps you *were* dreaming,' he suggested. 'There's funny things – dangerous things – can happen in dreams, and if you don't happen to be used to it—'

Ethel made an impatient noise. 'I was *dead*, Mr Scattergood. Dead and halfway to Underworld before the Seer-folk brought me back. Do you think I'm afraid of a few bad dreams? Do you think I'd be afraid of *anything*?'

By now Dorian's unease had deepened into anxiety. He'd never had much experience with mad women and, being unmarried himself, had little idea of how to deal with one now.

'Er – Mrs Parson,' he said feebly. 'Naturally you're distraught. Perhaps a rest, and some smelling salts?'

She fixed him with a pitying look. 'I was dead,' she repeated gently. 'People talk around the dead. They say things they shouldn't. They pay less attention. I don't pretend to understand all of what's happening here. The affairs of the Seer-folk are not our affairs, and I wish none of us had been caught up in them, but it's too late for wishes, I'm afraid. They healed me. They gave me my life. Did they really think that I would return to it as if nothing had happened? Needlework, cooking, and the kettle on the hob?'

'What are you saying?' said Dorian Scattergood.

'I'm saying,' said Ethel, 'that somewhere in World Below, my husband and your nephew are still alive. And that if we are to find them again—'

'*Find* them?' said Dorian. 'We're not talking about a piece of lost knitting here, Mrs Parson—'

Once more she chilled him with a look. 'Do you own a dog, Mr Scattergood?'

'A *dog*?'

'Yes, Mr Scattergood. A dog.'

'Well – no,' he said, taken aback. 'Is it important?'

Ethel nodded. 'By all accounts there are hundreds of passageways under the Hill. We'll need a dog to find their trail. A tracking dog with a good nose. Otherwise we may spend the rest of our lives wandering about in the dark, don't you agree?'

Dorian stared at her, astonished. 'You're not mad,' he said at last.

'Far from it,' said Ethel. 'Now, we'll need a dog, and lamps and supplies. Or I will, if you'd rather stay here.'

Dorian protested less than she'd expected. For a start he welcomed the opportunity to redeem himself for his behaviour on the Hill; secondly, whether Ethel was mad or not, she was clearly determined, and he could hardly let her go alone. Borrowing the parson's horse and trap, he left her to get ready – hardly daring to hope she would change her mind – and returned within the hour with two packs containing food and essentials, and with a small black pot-bellied sow on the seat beside him.

Ethelberta regarded the black sow with some uncertainty. But Dorian was adamant: pigs were his livelihood and he'd always believed in their superior intelligence. Black Nell, the pot-bellied sow that had caused the scandal years ago, had been a famous truffler in her day, faithful and clever, guarding the farm as well as any dog.

This new sow was descended from Nell herself, though Dorian had never mentioned the fact, or declared the broken ruinmark that adorned her soft underbelly with a patch of white. Instead he had used pitch to conceal the mark (as once his own mother had used a hot iron and soot to conceal the mark on her new baby's arm), and he had never regretted it.

'Lizzy'll lead us right,' he said. 'She's the best tracker I've ever had. She can sniff out a potato at a hundred yards; a truffle in a mile. No dog can match her. Take my word for it.'

Ethel frowned. 'Well, if that's the best you can do . . .'

'Lizzy's the best. No doubt about it.'

'Then in that case,' said Ethel, 'we mustn't waste time. Show her the trail, Mr Scattergood.'

Ten minutes later, plus several bribes of apple and potato and many sniffs of Nat Parson's discarded overcoat, and Fat Lizzy was fairly straining at the leash. Her eyes gleamed; her snout twitched; she gave little barking grunts of excitement; it was the closest Dorian had ever seen to a talking pig.

'She scents the trail,' Dorian said. 'Listen, Mrs Parson. She's never let me down. I say we follow her, and if I'm wrong—'

'If you're wrong, then my husband and your nephew may be wolf-meat before long.'

'I know that.' He looked at the pot-bellied sow, who was practically dancing with excitement. 'But I know my Lizzy. She's no ordinary pig. She's one of Black Nell's line, and I never had a pig from that brood that wasn't twice as smart as any other. I say we give her a chance – it's more chance than we have without her, anyway.'

And so it was that Ethel Parson and Dorian Scattergood followed Fat Lizzy down the road and across the fields to Red Horse Hill, and that before noon they had already entered World Below and, lighting a lamp to show their way, had set off along the sloping path into the unknown.

7

On the threshold of another world, Loki and Maddy were facing the shortest hour of their lives. All around them lay the river Dream, a vastness so broad that neither side could be clearly seen, but dotted with islets and skerries and rocks, some drifting, some static, the largest of which housed the Black Fortress of Netherworld.

Above them, purple clouds were gathering like wool on a spindle.

And at their feet lay the Black Fortress, which, Maddy now saw, was no fortress at all, but a huge crater, lipped with steel, from which a thousand thousand galleries dropped and yawped, each gallery lined with barred doors, cells, oubliettes, chambers, dungeons, stairwells, forgotten walkways, dank grottoes, flooded passageways, cavernous spaces and colossal engines of excavation, for Netherworld is the sink of every evil thought, every submerged terror and neurosis, every war crime, every outrage against what is hopeful and good – and it is always expanding its territory, going deeper and deeper into the dark heart of the world towards an inexhaustible mother lode of sickness.

From the crater, the sounds of those engines was like an army of giants cracking boulders with their teeth; above it the voices of the countless dead made a sound like Jed Smith's forge, but infinitely greater.

'Gods,' Maddy said. 'It's so much more than I ever imagined . . .'

'Yes, and you don't even have all that much imagination,' said Loki, putting his hands in his pockets. 'Try to picture how *I* saw it, in the days after Ragnarók – if you think it looks bad from up here, you should try going in deeper – let's say, twelve hundred levels or so – believe me, down there, things begin to get *seriously* imaginative—'

'I don't understand,' said Maddy.

But Loki appeared to be searching for something, and with what looked like increasing anxiety. He searched in the unfamiliar pockets, in his belt, around his wrists, and cursed as he failed to find what he sought.

'What is it?' said Maddy. 'What have you lost?'

But Loki was grinning now with relief. He reached into his shirt and drew out what looked like a watch on a chain around his neck.

'This,' he said. 'It's a timepiece from Hel. Time here doesn't follow the normal rules – minutes here could mean hours, or even days outside – and we'll need to be sure how long we've got.'

Maddy looked at it curiously. It looked a little like a fob watch, though it was no timepiece that she'd ever seen. There were no hours marked on the black dial, and the hands, which were red, showed only the minutes and the seconds. Complex machineries turned and spun behind the glass-and-silver casing.

'What kind of a watch is it?' said Maddy.

Loki grinned. 'A deathwatch,' he said.

The deathwatch was already counting down. Maddy found herself unable to look away as the red hands ticked away the hour. She said, 'Do you really think Hel will keep her word? What's to stop her from leaving us here?'

'Hel's word is what keeps Hel in balance. To break it would mean abandoning her neutral position, and here, at the brink of Chaos, that's the last thing she can afford to do.

Believe me, if she tells us we've got an hour . . .' Loki glanced at the face of the deathwatch again. The countdown now read fifty-nine minutes.

Maddy was looking at him curiously. 'You look different,' she said.

'Never mind that,' said Loki.

'But your face – your clothes . . .'

Maddy struggled to express what she saw. It was like watching his reflection over water as it clears. As she watched, he seemed to come into focus; still recognizably Loki with his fiery hair and scarred lips, but Loki as drawn by some otherworldly artist in colours unknown to Nature's palette. 'And your glam,' she said, with sudden realization. 'It isn't reversed any more.'

'That's right,' said Loki. 'That's because I'm here in my true Aspect, not in the form I was obliged to take when I re-entered World Above.'

'Your true Aspect?' said Maddy.

'Look, this is Netherworld,' said Loki with impatience. 'It's not a place you can visit in person. In fact, as we speak, our bodies are in Hel, tethered to life by the thinnest of threads, awaiting our return. And may I suggest that if we want to rejoin them—'

'You mean *this* – this isn't me?' Maddy looked down at herself and was startled to see that she too was different. Her hair was loose instead of being sensibly braided, and in the place of her usual clothes she now wore a belted chain mail tunic of what she judged to be immodest length. Of her other clothes, her jacket and her pack there was no sign.

'Our packs!' she exclaimed in sudden dismay. 'The Whisperer!'

In Hel's domain she had forgotten it; now the thought filled her with alarm. She realized that she had not felt its call since Hel had joined them in the desert. Loki had been carrying it then; but she could not recall having seen him with it at any time since they entered Hel's halls.

She turned on him with a sudden suspicion. 'Loki,' she said, 'what did you do?'

Loki looked hurt. 'I hid it, of course. Why? You think it would have been safer here?'

He did have a point, Maddy thought. Still, it continued to trouble her. If Odin had followed them there somehow—

'Come on,' said Loki impatiently. 'Just *being* here causes massive disruption, and the longer we stay, the greater the chances of attracting the wrong sort of attention. Now *please*' – once more he checked the deathwatch around his neck – 'you *really* don't want to be here when our time – now fifty-seven minutes – runs out.'

He was right, Maddy thought. Why should she mistrust him? He'd risked his life to bring her this far. And yet there was something in his colours; colours so bright that she no longer needed the truesight to show her his thoughts. Maybe it was a part of being in Aspect, but everything seemed brighter here; brighter and clearer than anywhere else. Squinting at Loki, she could see his fear, that silvery streak in his signature; and running alongside it, something else: a thread of something dark and indistinct, like a thought that even he seemed reluctant to face.

And though it was far too late to turn back, Maddy's heart grew cold with misgiving. For she recognized that hazy thread – she'd seen it so many times before, in Adam Scattergood and his friends; in Nat during his sermon; in poor Jed Smith. It was a most familiar sign, but to see it now, in Loki's glam, meant that something was already terribly wrong.

The darker thread was a sign of deceit.

Whatever the reason, the Trickster had lied.

8

Space doesn't work here as it does elsewhere, Loki had said, and now Maddy could see what he'd meant. She had time only to realize that they were falling before realizing that what she had taken for a giant crater dropping down towards the centre of the earth was actually no such thing, and that the idea of *downwards*, which she had hitherto taken for granted, was also and at the same time *sidewards*, *upwards*, and even *inwards*, with herself at the hub of a great living wheel of space, a vortex intersected at every spoke with galleries, craters and crevices leading off in every imaginable direction into the dark.

'How can this be?' she called to Loki as they fell.

'How can what be?'

'This world. It's just not possible.'

'It is and it isn't,' said Loki over his shoulder. 'In the Middle World, where Order rules, it's not possible. Where Chaos rules, you haven't seen the half of it.'

They were *not* falling, Maddy now saw; although there seemed to be no other word to describe the trajectory that she and Loki were following. Most of the time travel follows a set path; there are rules regarding space and time and distance: one step leads to another like words in a sentence, telling a tale. But how she and Loki travelled was quite different. Not quite falling, nor running, nor standing, nor swimming, nor even flying, they covered no ground; and yet they moved quickly, as in a dream, scenes flicking past them like pages turned at increasing speed and at random in some book of maps of places no one sane would ever want to visit.

'How are you doing it?' shouted Maddy over the noise.

'Doing what?' said Loki.

'This place – you're altering it somehow. Moving things around.'

'I told you before. It's a dream place. Haven't you ever had a dream in which you knew you were dreaming? Haven't you ever thought, *I'll do this, I'll go there*, and in your dream you made it happen?'

A thousand maps, every one a thousand thousand deep in caverns, canyons, caves, catacombs, dungeons, torture chambers, cells. Squinting, Maddy could see them, the prisoners, like bees in a hive, their colours like distant smoke, the buzzing of their voices like flakes of ash rising into the apocalyptic sky.

'Hang on,' said Loki. 'I think I've got something.'

'What?'

'Dreamers.'

Now, with a keenness beyond *Bjarkán*, Maddy discovered that she could focus in on individual prisoners and their surroundings. She found she could see their faces clear, regardless of the distances between them; faces glimpsed at random through a spinning sickness; screaming faces; slices of nightmare; machines that crunched bone; carpets woven from human gristle; dreams of fire and dreams of steel; dreams of hot irons and of slow dismemberment; dreams of blood-eagles and being eaten alive by rats; dreams of snakes and giant spiders and headless corpses that still somehow lived and of lakes of maggots and plagues of killer ants and of sudden blindness and of terrible diseases and of small sharp objects pushed into the soles of the feet and of familiar objects developing teeth—

'Fifty-three minutes to go,' said Loki. 'And for gods' sakes, stop gawping. Don't you know how rude it is to look into other people's dreams?'

Maddy screwed her eyes shut. 'All these are dreams?' she said faintly.

'Dreams, ha'nts, ephemera. Just don't get involved.'

Maddy opened her eyes again. 'But Loki – there must be millions of people here. Millions of prisoners. How are we ever going to find my father?'

'Trust me.'

Easier said than done, she thought. She held more tightly to Loki's hand, trying not to think of what would happen if he decided simply to abandon her here. His face was set, all merriment gone. His violet signature, always bright, was now so fiercely blinding that Maddy could barely see him for the glare.

The magic-lantern show of Netherworld flickered all around them. Worse visions now – creatures with their guts on the outside of their bodies, dripping poison from bloated sacs; fields of carnivorous plants that crooned and sang in the fiery breeze; machines with oiled and interlocked tentacles, each one tipped with a metal prong that sliced and razored—

'Uh-oh,' said Loki at her side. 'Hang on, Maddy, we're being followed.'

And before Maddy could look round (not that she knew which direction to look in) he put on an extra burst of speed and the scenes around them blurred and flickered.

'Followed by *what*?'

'Just don't look.'

Of course, that was exactly what Maddy did; a second later she regretted it.

'Damn it,' said Loki. 'What did I say?'

The creature was beyond scale. Huge as a building, Maddy guessed, with a raw eel head and rows of teeth – a dozen rows at least, she thought – circling the cavernous throat. It moved in silence, like a projectile; and in spite of its very real-looking teeth, its body (if that *was* a body) seemed to be made up of nothing but strands and whips and signatures of light.

'Gods, what is it?' Maddy breathed.

'Not *it*. *They*.'

'*They*?'

'Ephemera. Don't look.'

'But it's gaining on us.'

Loki groaned. 'Don't look at it, don't think of it. Thinking only makes it stronger.'

'But how?'

'Gods, Maddy, didn't I tell you?' He cast an urgent glance at the thing that was following them. 'This is a place where all things are possible. Dreams, fevers, imaginings. We make them so. We give them their strength.'

'But we're ghosts. Surely. In some kind of dream. Nothing can harm us – not really—'

'Not *really*?' Loki gave a crack of laughter. 'Listen to me, Maddy. Reality as you know it just doesn't apply in Netherworld. We're not ghosts. It's not a dream. And they *can* harm us. *Really*.'

'Oh.'

'So keep going.'

Now, each step was an aeon deep, taking them further and deeper into the pit of Netherworld. Maddy looked back at the thing that followed them, and saw a tunnel ringed with lights and lined with concentric rows of knife-edged metal that churned and gulped and circled and gnashed like living machinery.

It took her a second or two to realize that the tunnel was the thing's mouth.

'It's catching up,' she said. 'And it's getting bigger.'

Loki swore. They seemed to be moving more slowly now, and Maddy could almost see what he was doing as he leafed through Netherworld like pages in a book. A yellow sky raining sulphur onto creatures that writhed on a bare rock floor. A woman suspended by her hair above a pit of knives. A man drinking from a river of acid that ate away at his lips and chin, stripping his skin and revealing bone – and still he drank; a man whose feet were swollen to the size of olifants'; small, leggy, many-limbed creatures like articulated trees that crept and chittered along a metal corridor lined with doors in the shape of demon mouths.

'Still there, is it?'

Maddy shivered.

'Slow it down,' Loki said. 'I'm trying to concentrate.'

'Slow it down? What with?'

'You've got weapons, haven't you? Use them.'

Weapons? Maddy looked down at her empty hands. Well, she supposed she had mindweapons, of a kind – but surely nothing to halt the moving mountain at their back. Loki had stopped now; the scene, a broad square passageway flagged with large flat stones. In each stone was set a tiny grille of black metal. From some of these apertures sounds came – cries, groans, screams – only some of them human.

The thing – or things – that pursued them filled the corridor. Once more the size had changed to accommodate the space, and now Maddy could see that it was indeed made up of thousands of creatures, breaking apart and re-forming in constant movement. *Ephemera*, Loki had called them. Maddy saw them as thin filaments of animated light, parasites wriggling through the spaces between the worlds. If even one of them touched her, she knew, they could sever flesh from bone; they would unmake her, burrowing under her fingernails, moving through her bloodstream, eating through her pores, working their way into spine and brain. And there were millions of them.

What could she do?

The ephemera seemed to sense her hesitation. The illusion

of a single creature had dissolved and they were everywhere now, in front of them and behind, filling the corridor from floor to ceiling, writhing like deadly maggots towards them.

Glancing at Loki, Maddy could see that he was casting runes, casting them very fast and urgently in his deft and fluttering style – as she watched, she saw the corridor change shape slightly, its colour veer from iron-grey to the grey of a thundercloud; the metal grilles of the openings set into the stone change shape slightly, from square to oblong—

'Got it,' he said. He dropped to his knees above one of the openings, felt with his fingertips for the edge of the grille.

The approaching ephemera seemed to understand; their movement increased and they began to swarm towards him, the filaments breaking into tiny particles, hopping like fleas across the bare stone.

Loki flinched, but kept working. 'Keep them off me,' he hissed at Maddy, without taking his attention away from the grille.

Maddy opened her mouth to protest, but an image stopped her – she saw those creatures pouring into her mouth, down her throat, filling her like a waterskin with their rotten-meat stench – and she shut her mouth again tight.

How? she thought silently. How did you stop a monster that could be anything, take any shape?

This is a place where all things are possible.

All things? thought Maddy.

Once more she looked down at her weaponless hands. Less than a spear's-length away, the air was thick with ephemera. They were even closer to Loki; sensing his pupose, gathering over his head like a wave . . .

Maddy took a deep breath, focusing all of her glam for the strike. It brightened, veering from reddish brown to brilliant orange, crackling with energy from fingertips and palms. She sought for a rune that might slow down her attackers. *Yr,* the

Protector, was closest to hand; holding its image in her mind, she closed her eyes against the wave of ephemera and flung the rune as hard as she could.

There was a crack like a whip and a smell of burning.

Opening her eyes, Maddy saw that a dome of red light some six feet in diameter had appeared around Loki and herself, against which the ephemera crawled and slithered. It was thin, its surface as delicate and as iridescent as a wash-day soap-bubble, but for the moment it held, and Maddy could see that wherever the ephemera touched it, their airy bodies crackled and dissolved, leaving a residue of soapy scum over the surface of the shield.

'It worked,' she said in disbelief. 'Did you see that? Did you . . . ?'

But Loki wasted no time in congratulations. Using *Tyr* to prise open the grille, he had finally managed to lift it aside. Below him a dead blackness yawned. Sliding his feet rapidly into the hole, Loki prepared to let himself drop into the void.

'Is my father down there?' said Maddy.

'No,' said Loki.

'Then what are we—?'

'That shield won't last,' said Loki grimly. 'And unless you want to be here when it fails, then I suggest you shut up and follow me.'

And with that he pushed himself into the hole and vanished from sight. There was no sound as he fell. Below him there was nothing but darkness.

'Loki?' she called.

No one replied.

In that moment Maddy was frozen with fear. Had Loki tricked her? Had he fled? She peered down into the empty hole, half expecting to see a wave of ephemera surging out of the pit at her feet.

Instead there was silence. *Trust me*, he'd said. But he'd lied to her. And now Maddy remembered the Oracle's words: *I see a traitor at the gate.*

Was Loki the traitor?

There was one way to tell.

Closing her eyes, Maddy jumped.

There was no sense at all of falling. Maddy passed from the corridor to the cell below in a single step, and for long seconds remained in utter darkness, with nothing at her feet and nothing above her, and no clue – not even an echo – as to what she might now expect.

'Loki?' she whispered in the dark.

Then she cast *Sól*, the Bright One, and the space lit up in brilliant light.

Relief filled Maddy as she saw that Loki was still there. They were standing on a narrow ledge, looking across at a slab of rock roughly the size of a barn door, apparently suspended from nothing at all over a gulf that swallowed the light of *Sól* and gave back nothing but emptiness in return. The rock was revolving slowly in mid air some fifty feet away from them, and now Maddy could see that there were chains set into the underside of the stone, from which a set of shackles dangled empty.

But it was the creature that clung to the rock's surface that really caught Maddy's attention. A huge snake, its scales gleaming in every imaginable shade of black, its eyes like electricity, its coils chained twice around the circling rock and dropping down into darkness.

It caught sight of Maddy and opened its jaws; even at such a distance the stench of its venom was enough to make her eyes water.

'It's all right,' said Loki. 'It can't move from the rock.'

Maddy stared. 'How do you know that?'

'Trust me. I know. Hang around the locals for a year or two, and you tend to pick up that kind of information.'

He narrowed his eyes at the circling snake. 'Imagine it, Maddy, if you can. To be chained to that rock, upside-down, with that thing . . .' He shivered. 'You can see why I'd be willing to do pretty much anything to free myself, don't you, Maddy?'

As if it had heard, the snake gave a hiss.

'I know, I know,' Loki said. 'But really – I had no choice. I knew I could escape alone – Netherworld's a big place and it might have taken them centuries to find out I was missing – but if I'd tried to free *you* as well—'

'Excuse me,' said Maddy. 'But are you talking to the snake?'

'That's not just any snake,' said Loki. 'Maddy, allow me to introduce Jormungand. Otherwise known in polite circles as the World Serpent, Thor's Bane or the Dragon at Yggdrasil's Root. My son.'

9

Far away in World's End, in a secure chamber of the Universal City, an earnest discussion was under way. The Council of Twelve had been in debate for a number of hours now, following the disquieting news from distant Upland.

As a result of this disturbing information the Council had been convened with a haste that seemed to many unseemly. In normal circumstances there would have been several pre-Council discussion meetings, a week of prayer and fasting, a lengthy meditation on the Elementary, Intermediary and Advanced States of Bliss and, finally, a gathering of elders armed with the Word, from whose learned ranks would be chosen the twelve members who would invoke the Nameless.

This present gathering had been assembled in a matter of days, which, in the opinion of its spokesman, Magister Emeritus Number 369 (a tiny octogenarian in scarlet robes, whose giant throne of office dwarfed him to the size of a small monkey), showed a rashness of purpose that was both dangerous and undignified.

However, the others had not agreed, and as a result there had been as little ceremony as possible as the twelve members – all high-ranking officials of the Order – had been chosen by lot for the privilege of Communion.

Among them were: the Magister Emeritus himself; his colleague Magister 73838, a mere Junior at seventy-five; and a number of other Magisters of varying seniority, including the Order's oldest member, Magister Number 23.

All had fasted, prayed and purged; all had spoken the relevant canticles and meditated deeply on the Word. Now, at last, they were gathered in the Council Chamber, a large auditorium at the centre of the Universal City, where a dozen rows of empty pews encircled one single large conference table of heavy carved oak.

Like many of the Order's most secret ceremonies, Communion with the Nameless was not an especially interesting spectacle. Anyone watching would have found it dull in the extreme – just twelve old men in red robes sitting around a table with the Good Book on a reading stand in the centre. Several of them looked asleep; it might have been a dull seminar, with the reader slumped over his lectern in the dusty afternoon sun.

Even the Word, uttered an hour later by every man at the table simultaneously, might not have been easily detectable to a spectator. It came as a shiver in the air, as if a small child had skimmed a stone across the reflection of the world, causing a series of widening ripples that went all the way to the far side.

Magister Number 23 felt it first. He was the most senior member of the Council of Twelve, a man as dry and shrunken as a winter apple who, it was rumoured, could trace his parentage right back to the childhood of the Order.

O Nameless, he said, and a tremor went through the members at the table as each man – all of whom had experienced Communion at least two dozen times in their lives – struggled with the same sensation that had so nearly broken Elias Rede.

Of course, these men were Elders of the Order. That made a difference; and yet even Magister 23 felt the burden heavy on his shoulders as the chill presence of the Nameless filled his mind.

I HEAR YOU, said a Voice that resonated through every mind in the Council of Twelve, and sent a shiver up the spine of every Magister, Examiner or scrub in the Order itself.

Magister Number 23 felt the weight of that Voice like a mountain upon him. At the back of his mind he seemed to glimpse the far distant shore of the Nameless's domain; a place where Perfect Order ruled supreme and perfect bliss was served out to such of the faithful who could endure it.

The Magister wondered whether he *could* endure it. Even after his long meditations he feared his mind was all Chaos; and the fear he had so assiduously hidden during all his career as a Magister bobbed to the surface like a rotten cork.

O Nameless, he thought. *Forgive my doubts. And forgive this delay in contacting You on a matter that concerns You closely. One colleague has already died – we sensed it in Communion—*

There was irritation in the Voice. *What, did you think to gain immortality in My service?*

Forgive me, said the Magister. *But our colleague had taken a prisoner. A man he was sure was a General of the enemy – Odin himself, whom we had thought long dead. But our colleague was killed before this man could be Interrogated, and we have not yet managed to identify the enemy's associates, although we believe that one of them may be his half-brother Loki—*

I know this, interrupted the Voice. *I presume that you have not entered Communion with Me simply to give Me information I already possess. How does it proceed?*

O Nameless, said the Magister. *A development has occurred.*

A development?

There was a pause that lifted the hairs on the Magister's neck. Then, hesitantly, he began to explain. How a parson of the Folk had acquired the Word in Communion with Elias Rede; how they had formed an alliance with the Faërie, and were even now in pursuit of their enemy as he worked his way towards Netherworld—

But it's all right, said the Magister hastily. *Our agent has it under control. The enemy will be stopped in time. He will* —

Be silent!

Another pause, during which all twelve members of the Council felt their thoughts being rifled by a presence immeasurably superior and entirely without compassion. Elsewhere in World's End the ripples were felt: heads ached, stomachs griped, eyes crossed and a sensation of icy rage swept through every member of the Order as its Founder searched – with increasing urgency – for the information It sought.

Half-seen images flickered through their minds – images that might be visions, prophecies or dreams: a woman in wolf-skin; a woman with two faces; a Hill that led to Netherworld; a girl . . .

I see him not. It is unclear. The Lands of Chaos cloud My sight—

The images stopped. Then came a moment of eerie calm . . .

I see him. Yes. And—

Now came another of those tantalizing images –

– a symbol written in dark red. They sensed it as a glyph of power; but even Magister 23 hesitated to identify it. The Nameless, however, was quick to react.

In a moment a sudden terrible blast tore through the minds of the Council of Twelve. Eleven of them collapsed outright; Magister 23 suffered a massive stroke and died on the spot; Magisters 73838 and 369 suffered permanent brain damage; and all the Council members developed gushing nosebleeds.

Trickery! hissed the Nameless. *Trickery, incompetence and lies!*

Throughout the Order, people collapsed; heads ached and elderly Magisters lost bowel control as the Voice of the Nameless vented Its displeasure in full. Then It seemed to calm a little. Its fury ebbed from homicidal rage to a glacial lull.

Magister 262 – the one member of the Council of Twelve who had remained conscious – pressed both hands to his spouting nose. *What is it, o Nameless?* he thought desperately. *What does it mean?*

There was a long, ominous silence. Then the Voice in his mind dropped to a purr.

It matters not, the Nameless said. *I have planned for this too.*

Once more the Magister shivered as the Nameless shuffled minds throughout the Order as if they were nothing more to It than a pack of cards. Images flickered into his mind, too many to identify: faces familiar and unfamiliar; landscapes from nightmare.

When it was over, the Voice spoke again, and this time it addressed the Magister by his true name.

Fortune Goodchild, it said, and every man in the Order heard his own true name spoken, and shivered. *Too long have you sat in comfort and complacency here in your fortress of World's End. Too long have you nursed your little empire, forgetting who really rules the world. Now is the time to prove your loyalty. The Seer-folk have shown themselves at last. I knew they would; I feel their presence. The battleground is chosen, the lines drawn. We march today.*

Today? whispered the Magister.

Do you have some criticism of My strategy, Fortune Goodchild? said the Nameless.

No, no, said Fortune hastily. *Of course not, o Nameless. It's simply – ah – it's a month's hard march to the valley of the Strond.*

By the time we get there—

We're not going to the valley of the Strond.

Then where do we march? said the Magister, thinking, *Oh, you fool, you had to ask.*

The Nameless caught his thought, and for a second Fortune Goodchild cringed under the weight of Its terrible amusement.

Where else? It said. *To Netherworld.*

10

'Your son?' said Maddy. 'Gods, Loki, is there anyone here you're *not* related to?'

Loki gave a sigh. 'You know, I was once . . . involved . . . with a demon called Angrboda. She was a changeling, a child of Chaos, and she liked to experiment. The results were sometimes – *exotic*, that's all.'

The giant snake flexed its jaws. It smelled worse than anything Maddy had ever encountered before; a leaden stench of venom, oil and charnel house. Its eyes were like pockets of tar; its body as thick as a man's.

Legend had it that the World Serpent was once so large that only the One Sea could contain it, and that it had grown to encircle the Middle World, moving down towards Yggdrasil to feed upon its roots. In fact it was smaller; but it was still the largest snake that Maddy had ever seen, and there was a disquieting intelligence in those evil eyes.

'It looks as if it understands,' she said.

'Well, of course he understands,' said Loki. 'You don't think they'd put a *stupid* creature to guard me, do you?'

'To guard you?' said Maddy. 'Do you mean when you were a prisoner here?'

'Quick, aren't you?' said Loki irritably. 'We've got forty-eight minutes left,' he said, reading from the deathwatch Hel had given him, 'and if I have to go through every little detail a dozen times—'

'All right, I'm sorry,' said Maddy. 'It's just that . . . if it's your *son*, then why—?'

'That's just their idea of humour,' said Loki. 'To have me tormented by my own son – not that I was much of a father, I'm afraid—'

Once more the World Serpent flexed its jaws.

'Oh, do shut up,' Loki told it. 'I'm back here now.' He turned to Maddy. 'His coils go all the way down to the river Dream,' he said, indicating the snake's long body. 'Haven't you ever dreamed of snakes? Yes? That was Jormungand, or some Aspect of him, slithering through the dreamworld into your mind. That's how with his help I reached the river and made my escape, in my fiery Aspect, into Dream and from there, at last, into living flesh.'

'The snake doesn't seem too pleased about it,' said Maddy.

'Yes. Well. I . . .' Loki looked embarrassed. 'I believe he's annoyed because – well – I promised I'd free him when I made my escape.'

'Free him?' said Maddy. 'But I thought you said he was guarding you.'

'That's the clever bit,' said Loki. 'Remember, all this is a fortress of dreams. Nothing in Netherworld has a definite shape; everything you see comes from the minds that are imprisoned here. That includes our friend . . .' Loki indicated the World Serpent. 'Now, you and I both know that I'm not fond of snakes. And this being Netherworld, and nightmares being more or less coin of the realm, what could be more natural than to appoint a snake – and not just any snake, but the World Serpent – as my guard? And so, in a way, I brought him here – or at least I summoned this Aspect of him. And until I free it – back into the real world – then he's just another prisoner. Here for ever. Just like the rest of them.'

As he spoke, the snake gave a louder hiss, and droplets of venom clouded the air.

'Oh, stop it,' said Loki. 'I mean, did you really think I was going to let you loose after what happened last time? Last time,' he told Maddy, 'not only did he change the tides of the One Sea, flood the Middle World, swallow the Thunderer, hammer and all, but by the time they got him under control the whole Nine Worlds were full of his worm-holes, with the armies of Chaos passing through like mice through a piece of Ridings cheese . . .' He levelled his devastating smile at the World Serpent. 'Still, Jormungand, old son,' he said brightly. 'Or can I call you Jorgi for short? I like Jorgi. It sounds cheerful and unthreatening. Friendly, even. What do you say?'

Across the dizzy space that separated them the World Serpent spat a stream of venom that missed Loki, but took a chunk out of the rock wall.

Loki gave Maddy a nervous grin. 'He's fine.'

'Look,' said Maddy. 'Fascinating though this tour of your relatives may be, I thought we were here to rescue my father . . .'

'And so we are, with Jorgi's help.'

Maddy looked at the giant snake as it circled, still chained to its rock. 'You thought *that* would help us?'

'He helped me. If we can get him into Dream—'

'Dream?' said Maddy in surprise. 'But *I* thought—'

'Well, he can't escape through Hel,' he said. 'You'd need a body for that, of course, and as far as I know we don't have a spare.'

'Oh.' For a moment Maddy was at a loss. She'd focused so strongly on the idea of rescue that such practicalities had never occurred to her.

Loki knew it; had counted on it, in fact, in his dealings with the Whisperer. Thor freed into Dream was one thing; but Thor, re-embodied, and out for revenge – *that* he could definitely do without. Still, first things first, he told himself. It was a long way out of Netherworld, and even Dream was not without risk.

He gave Jormungand his cheeriest smile. 'Better late than never,' he said.

The creature gave a silent hiss.

'But you can't free it,' protested Maddy. 'Quite apart from the damage it could do, ripping holes between the Worlds, won't it rip *you* apart the moment you—'

'Thanks for that,' said Loki dryly. Even in Aspect, his face was pale. 'Don't think it hasn't crossed my mind. But with' – he glanced at the deathwatch around his neck – 'forty-three minutes left to go, I'm running short of good ideas. As for damage, I'm hoping that can work to our benefit.'

'How?'

'Well, for a start we could use a diversion. Netherworld isn't going to sit quiet for ever, you know, and as soon as it senses the disruption we've caused it's going to send some-thing – some*one* – to investigate. I'm hoping that by the time that happens, Jorgi here will have covered our tracks. If I'm right, it should at least buy us a little time.'

'I see,' said Maddy. 'And if you're not?'

'If I'm not,' he said, 'it shouldn't trouble either of us for long. Now take my hand.'

Maddy took it and felt his fingers clamp down on hers. There was a brief sensation of *sidestepping*—

'Don't let go,' Loki warned. 'You're not going to want to be around when Jorgi gets loose.'

On the circling rock the World Serpent writhed and tore at its chains. The stench of its venom redoubled; the air was mulled with its secretions.

And then, quite suddenly, the chains weren't there.

It was almost comic. For a second Jormungand struggled against thin air, its jaws arcing into nothingness, its leaden coils slipping into the pit . . . And then its eyes fixed on Loki. It opened its jaws, seemed to stiffen – and then it struck.

It struck repeatedly, knocking slabs from the rock wall as

big as olifants to drop and circle into the gulf. The air swam with venom; crackled with electricity. In seconds the ledge on which they had been standing was nothing but a nubbin of rock overlooking the void. Nothing else was left alive. Nothing could have survived that strike; nothing remained but the World Serpent in the dark, deserted cell.

11

'Of course, you know he's following us,' gasped Loki, out of breath.

'Wasn't that the plan?'

'What plan?'

They were running hand-in-hand down a broad passage-way lined with doors, lit now with a lurid phosphorescence that seemed to come from everywhere. Except that *running* wasn't quite the word; and the ground beneath them felt insubstantial, as in dreams, and as they ran, the scenery changed, the doors shifting from Gothic oak monstrosities to lead-panelled archways, to holes in the wall vaulted with bones.

'How far now?' said Maddy.

'We're almost there. Just making sure . . .'

The light too was changing fast, now red, now green, and there was a sound – a sound that pressed like a thumb onto their eardrums – the sound of a million dreamers locked inside a million dreams.

'How did you do that?' shouted Maddy above the din.

'Do what?'

'You know. Get out of the cell.'

'Short cut,' he said. 'An Aspect-shift I picked up from Jorgi. Now hang on . . .' He stopped at a door that was red and black and studded all over with glamours and runes. 'You might find this a bit . . . upsetting.'

Maddy looked at him. 'My father?'

Loki nodded. He looked tired behind his Aspect; much of the brightness had gone from his colours. Around his neck

Hel's deathwatch indicated that they had thirty-eight minutes left.

He flung a handful of runes at the door; the inscription upon it brightened, but the door stayed shut.

'Damn.' Loki steadied himself against the closed door and took a couple of deep breaths. 'I'm nearly done,' he said. 'You'll have to do it.'

Maddy studied the locked door. *Thúris* should move it, she decided, and hit the door as hard as she could. It trembled, but did not yield. Once more she hit it – with *Ós* and *Tyr* – once more it trembled, and the passageway trembled with it, shaking beneath their feet.

'It's coming,' said Loki.

'Yes,' she agreed. 'One more hit and I think I'll—'

'I wasn't talking about the *door*.'

He was looking beyond her; and for a second Maddy didn't understand. Then she looked up and saw what was coming, and in that same instant hurled *Hagall* at the door as hard as she could while Loki, with what remained of his strength, flung *Isa* in the path of the World Serpent, which seemed to fill the passage some fifty yards behind them.

Isa froze in mid air, creating a solid barrier against which Jormungand hurled itself in a frenzy. It held, though the first blow cracked the ice; clearly it would not hold the serpent long. But it was enough: in front of Maddy the door did not open; it simply vanished and, with another of those sickening sidesteps, they were inside.

12

From the other side of the river Dream Hel was watching the proceedings with interest. The deathwatch served a number of purposes – not least to keep her suitably informed – and now, in a room deep in her bone-white citadel, she watched the progress of the two trespassers through the darkened mirror of her dead eye.

How odd, she thought. How very odd. Of course, Loki was never entirely predictable, but this was the last place she would have expected him to return. She felt reluctant curiosity as to what his plan might be. She *assumed* he had a plan – whatever else he was, he was no fool – though she wasted no anxiety over his probable fate. Hel would weep no tears if Loki fell – in fact, she thought, to witness his destruction might give her the first true fleeting twinge of pleasure she had felt since Balder's death, centuries before.

Not that it lasted – nothing did. And yet Hel, incurious as she usually was, watched rapt as the seconds ticked by. Her dead eye saw Netherworld, churning with dreams; and her living eye was fixed upon the two figures lying side by side on the shore of the river, their physical bodies linked to their Netherworld counterparts by a skein of runelight finer than silk.

To sever the skein was to cut short their lives – but she had promised them an hour inside, and such an oath, even to Loki, must not be broken. Still, she was intrigued – not least by the glam he had left behind. A powerful glam – some relic of the Elder Days – that gleamed and shone like a forgotten sun. She couldn't imagine why Loki had brought it – or why he had pretended to hide it away, knowing that she would spot it at once.

And now it was *calling* to her from its place in the desert, in a soft and coaxing voice that seemed – almost, but not quite – familiar.

It's a trap, thought Hel. *Whatever it is, he wants me to take it.*

Through her living eye she observed the Trickster. He looked asleep; occasionally he twitched and frowned, as if in the throes of some nightmare. She could see the thread that joined him to his dreaming self; a transparent wisp of violet light. She fingered it delicately, and smiled to think that in another world she was sending a shiver down Loki's spine.

Could it be a trap? she thought. It wasn't like Loki to be so obvious. And yet – if he *didn't* want her to take the thing, then why had he left it so patently?

Loki wasn't obvious. Loki was subtle. And so, whatever he was planning, the obvious answer must be false. Unless he'd known she would think this way. In which case the obvious answer *was* the right one. Unless—

Unless, she thought, *he had no plan.*

Unless the carelessness was a bluff designed to make her think he had something clever up his sleeve. Some kind of protection, some backup in case of a hostile reception. But what if he hadn't? What if, as she'd first suspected, he was running on nothing but wits and bravado?

If so, then he was at her mercy. And the glam he carried – that tantalizing bauble – was hers for the taking.

With a word she summoned it. The glam was hiding in his pack, so bright now that she could almost see it through the worn leather. She lifted it out, and the Whisperer's light blazed out, almost blinding Hel with its intensity.

Hel had never seen the Whisperer. Mimir's time was before her birth, and the Æsir had never been generous with their secrets. But she knew a glam when she saw one, and now she held it in her hands, feeling its energy run through her, its voice deafening in her mind.

Kill them, said the Whisperer. *Kill them both.*

13

A problem shared is a problem solved, or so the saying goes. Fortunately for Sugar-and-Sack, he was quite unaware that he now shared the problem of his journey to Hel with Odin, the six Vanir, the Huntress, Nat Parson, a dead Examiner, Adam Scattergood, the parson's wife, a farmer from the valley and a pot-bellied pig; and even if he *had* known, it is doubtful whether the knowledge would have cheered him.

He'd been checking the runestone every five minutes or so, and either his imagination was working overtime, or in that short time it had darkened still further. Sugar didn't think it was his imagination. And he knew what he was supposed to do.

'The Underworld,' he muttered feverishly. 'He must be madder than I thought. Wants me to go to Underworld, eh? Wants me to find a Whisperer? What's a Whisperer? I sez. And all *he* sez is—'

Don't let me down.

The goblin shuddered. It looked bad – but the Captain, he knew, had a knack for getting himself out of tight corners. And if he did, and Sugar betrayed him . . .

He stared half hypnotized at the runestone, noting the way its colour deepened from vermilion, to crimson, to ruby.

The stone would show him the way, the Captain had assured him. Sugar had seen such stones before, although he'd never used them. Rune magic was for Seer-folk, not goblins; and Sugar felt uncomfortable just *touching* the stone, let alone using it.

But it *had* shown him the trail so far: every broken cantrip, every signature. And now at last the trail had run out, and it would open up the way to Hel – a road that no one living should take – not if they wanted to stay that way.

If it turns red, I'm in mortal peril.

He cast the stone against the ground, just as the Captain had told him to. And a passageway that had not been there a moment before forked out like lightning at his feet. It was dark in the passage; steps that seemed to be made of black glass staggered down into the gap; and below it, he knew, lay the final stretch – to the Underworld, and the Whisperer.

He looked down once more at the Captain's charm, which had darkened once more from ruby to ox-blood, and now to the midnight gleam of a very good claret.

If it turns black . . .

Gods, he thought.

And whimpering with fright, Sugar pocketed the stone and set off once again at a brisk trot down the narrow steps and along the path to the Land of the Dead.

It had been almost three days since Odin had entered World Below on the trail of the fugitives. In that time he had moved gradually and carefully downwards, favouring the smaller passageways and always keeping the river between himself and his pursuers. In this way he had crossed the Strond twice, approaching the Underworld by an oblique route that he hoped would put Skadi and her parson off his scent.

In that time he had barely eaten, barely slept. He still travelled in darkness, but found that his sense of direction had improved beyond measure, and that his reading of colours had become honed to a degree of accuracy he had not known since before the war.

He had sensed the presence of the Vanir in World Below, as he had sensed the presence of the Huntress. It was tempting to try to contact them, but in his present condition he dared not approach. Later he would, in full Aspect, once the

Whisperer was his again – that is, *if* the Whisperer was ever his again.

Till then he concentrated on reading the signs – and there were many, stretching across World Below like the strings of a harp, tuned to exquisite pitch. It took concentration; it took glam; but at every new sign his foreboding grew.

Finally he cast the runes. He cast them blind, but it didn't matter; their message was clear enough. First he drew *Raedo*, reversed. His own rune, crossed with *Naudr*; the rune of Death.

Then *Ós*, the Æsir; *Kaen*, reversed; *Hagall*, the Destroyer; and finally *Thuris*, rune of Victory –

– *but for whom?* Odin thought. *For Order or Chaos? And on whose side do the Æsir stand?*

So it begins, Odin thought. Not aboveground, as he'd imagined, but deep in the belly of Chaos itself. Not the war – surely not yet – but war would follow as winter follows fall. Loki was part of it – Maddy too. What had started the chain of events? The waking of the Sleepers? The discovery of the Whisperer? Something else? He could not tell. But he knew this. He had to be there.

Someone else who had to be there was Ethelberta Parson. Why this was so she could not say, but as she and Dorian approached their goal, she sensed it with growing urgency. They had endured cold and discomfort; their feet were blistered; their food was gone but for a few raw potatoes they kept aside for the pig; they were out of lamp-oil; and still

Ethelberta was undaunted, following the squat snuffling form of Fat Lizzy through the labyrinth of World Below.

Dorian Scattergood had long since given up hope of finding anyone in that endless maze. Even the idea of finding his way home seemed impossible now, though that was not the reason he continued to move on. Ahead of him Ethel was a dim shape against the phosphorescent walls. Patient; tireless; as unafraid of the rats and goblins they had encountered on the upper levels of World Below as she was now of the passing dead.

'We do not need to fear them,' she had told Dorian as the first whispering wave of spirits brushed by them – he had been flattened against the wall, shaking with terror, but she had simply parted the flow and moved on, ignoring the mournful voices all around them – ignoring even the familiar voices of Jed Smith and Audun Briggs as they followed them to the Land of the Dead.

The road into Hel had been bad enough for Maddy. But for Odin it was much worse: *he* could not close his blind eyes to the presence of the dead, nor his ears to their pleas and curses. They sensed it; and for what seemed like miles he was carried along, feet hardly touching the floor of the passage, on wave after wave of the marching dead.

It was not the first time he had risked that journey. Each time had been unpleasant; but this time he felt that something had changed. There was a sense almost of expectancy among the crowd, a knowing quality that made him uneasy. And for the first time they spoke to him – they called him by name.

Blind man on the road to Hel –
(i prayed to you you let me die)
Odin No-Eyes, still alive? Not.
For.
Long.

When at last he heard a living voice, sensed the colours of a living being, he almost missed them both among the clamour and commotion. The voice rose and fell plaintively, seeming to argue with itself at length before falling silent for a moment, then resuming its one-sided argument.

i tell you i can't

i can't an' i won't d'ye kennet it's unnatural you can't make me all right p'raps you can but

mortal peril he sez

mortal peril

The signature was goblin-gold, tinged now with the colours of uncertainty and fear. There was something else too in its vicinity – a token, perhaps, imbued with glam – that bore a very familiar sign.

Now, Odin was not in the least bit interested in Sugar-and-Sack, but he knew Loki's sigil well enough, and it was easy enough, using *Yr* and *Naudr*, to approach the goblin unseen and to grab him before he could make his escape.

A few seconds later Sugar was dangling forlornly from Odin's fist.

'Why, General, Your Honour,' he began. 'What a surpr—'

'Save your blather,' said Odin. He sat down on the rocky floor, keeping a firm hand on Sugar's collar. 'In a moment I'm going to say a name, and you are going to tell me everything you know. You are going to tell me clearly, quickly, truthfully and without a single superfluous word. Otherwise I'll have to break your neck. I may break it anyway. I'm not at my best right now. Understand?'

Sugar nodded so vigorously that his whole body shook.

'Are you ready?'

Once more Sugar nodded.

'Right,' said Odin. '*Loki.*'

Sugar swallowed. Recalling Odin's threat, he delivered his information in a single gabbling breath:

'*Netherworldrescue-missionmaddysfathermortalperiltimerun-ningout—*'

'Wait.' Odin's fingers tightened fractionally around Sugar's neck. 'Again. Slowly.'

Sugar nodded. 'Netherworld,' he said in a strangled voice. 'Rescue mission. Maddy's father. Mortal peril. Time running out.'

'I don't understand a word you're saying,' snapped Odin.

'That's because you're throttlin' me, sir,' said Sugar.

Odin loosened his grip.

'Thank you, sir,' said Sugar apologetically, sitting down on the floor. 'Only it's bin a while since I wet my whistle, sir, and it's a tricky tale. I'd do better telling it in me own words, beggin' your pardon, and with me neck in one piece. Kennet?'

Odin sighed. *Goblins*, he told himself. Might as well interrogate the dead as expect a sensible answer from a goblin. He curbed his impatience and began again.

'Now tell me,' he said. 'Where's my brother?'

14

As it happened, Loki was waiting in a cell in Netherworld as Maddy prepared to meet the Thunderer.

This cell was entirely different to the one Loki had occupied. For a start it looked neat and comfortable: there was a bed with sheets and a thick quilt; there was a standard lamp with a fringed lampshade; a small flowered rug; a window looking out onto green fields. On the window-ledge there was a jar of flowers. A small occasional table stood by the bed, on which Maddy could see something that looked very like a tray of tea and biscuits. And beside the table was a rocking chair, in which a very small, very old lady was working on a piece of knitting.

Behind her Loki began to laugh. 'So *this* is Thor the Thunderer's cell,' he said. 'Gods, Thor, I knew you were twisted, but this is ridiculous.'

Maddy turned to him, bewildered. 'I thought you said my father was here.'

'And so he is,' said Loki, grinning.

'I don't understand.'

Loki indicated the old lady, still rocking and knitting in her chair. 'Meet Ellie,' he said. 'Otherwise known as Old Age.' Once more he began to laugh, his eyes gleaming with mischief and amusement.

Ellie looked up from her knitting and fixed Maddy with a pair of eyes as black and bright as a bird's. 'Be quiet,' she said. 'My husband's asleep.'

Maddy stepped quietly up to the bed. Sure enough, there was someone lying under the quilt; she could just make out the curve of a shoulder, the baby growth of white hair across a skull that was as fine and delicate as a robin's egg.

'You stop that,' said Ellie, standing up with the aid of a walking stick. 'Have some respect for your elders and betters.'

'I'm sorry,' said Maddy. 'I'm looking for my father . . .'

'Your father, eh?'

'Thor, son of Odin. The one they call the Thunderer.'

Now the old lady's apple-doll face split into a thousand wrinkles. 'You must have made a mistake, my dear,' she said. 'There's only me and my man here – and he's sick, poor fellow, almost to the grave . . .'

Maddy turned to Loki. 'You lied,' she said. 'My father's not here.'

Loki shook his head. 'Remember what I told you, Maddy,' he said. 'In the Black Fortress each man makes his own cell; each prisoner appoints his own gaoler from the ranks of his deepest, most inescapable fears.'

'His fears?'

'With me, as you know, it was snakes. With him it's Old Age and a comfortable bed. Each to his own.'

As he spoke, Loki had moved across to the other side of the bed and now Maddy could see him fingering small runes into his left hand like darts, ready to cast. He was still smiling, but now his eyes were narrowed with concentration.

'Now you stop that,' snapped Ellie, grabbing her stick and hobbling quickly to the far side of the bed. 'I'll not have you waking my husband.'

Loki stepped out of her way. She was old, but she was fast; and the stick that she carried crackled with runelight.

'Stand clear,' he told Maddy, and at wildfire speed cast the first of his runes – she recognized *Ós* – at the sleeping figure. Loki's colours dimmed a little more; the old man flinched and muttered; a thin hand clutched at the sheets.

Ellie was looking distinctly menacing now. Her button-black eyes gleamed with rage; her crone's face was a distorted mask. 'Young man, I'm warning you,' she said.

Now Loki flung a second rune – it was *Naudr*, reversed – once more his colours dimmed, and the old man gave a cry, as if in the throes of a fearsome dream.

Ellie gave a squawk of outrage and hit out at Loki with her runestick.

He stepped back in haste, and the blow missed him by a hair's breadth, pulverizing the table that lay between them. She struck again – missed – and the last flickering handful of runes shot out from between Loki's fingers and struck the old man squarely in the chest.

'What are you *doing*?' shouted Maddy above the shrill cries of the angry crone.

Loki said nothing, but stood there and smiled. His signature was fading fast; the violet glow was ghostly pale. But the room was changing. Gone was the window with its pleasant view; now a slit in the wall looked out onto the void of Netherworld. The rest too – chair, curtains, flower vase – had vanished, leaving only the bed – now a simple stone ledge decked with rotting straw – and its single occupant.

And on the ledge before their eyes the old man shifted and flexed; grew muscle; grew bulk and more bulk; grew hair as red as Loki's own; grew a red beard that bristled furiously; opened eyes as hot and dark as embers.

The Thunderer awoke in full Aspect, and the ground shook beneath his tread.

'Now's the time to keep your promise,' Loki told Maddy, backing as far away from the menacing figure as the dimensions of the tiny room would permit.

Thor followed him in a single step, sweeping Ellie aside as he came, and stopped twelve inches away, standing fully two feet higher than Loki, his hands crackling with crimson rune-light.

'What promise?' said Maddy.

'Your promise to intercede on my behalf if any family members happened to – shall we say – take umbrage at my continued survival.'

'Oh,' said Maddy. '*That* promise.'

Thor clamped a fist the size of a Midwinter goose around Loki's neck. '*You*,' he said in a thunderous voice. 'I'm going to break every bone in your body, starting with your miserable neck. And then I'm going to break them all over again, just to make sure I haven't missed any. And then I'm going to grind all the broken bits together. And after *that*' – he gave a large, red, friendly grin – 'I'm going to have to hurt you a bit.'

'I may have omitted to tell you,' said Loki, 'that our friend here and I have certain . . . *issues*—'

Thor's fingers tightened over his throat, cutting off his remaining air supply.

'*Help*—' said Loki.

And as Maddy put her hand on the thunder god's arm and said, '*Father*—' there came a sudden unimaginable sound at the door of the cell and the World Serpent came crashing through it, its massive coils filling the room.

Thor looked at Maddy. 'What d'you mean, *Father*?'

He had loosened his grip on Loki, who was now flattened against the cell wall as far from Jormungand as he could manage while Ellie, incensed at this latest invasion, lashed out at the serpent with her walking stick.

'Terrific,' said Loki under his breath. 'Come to Netherworld. Meet the kids.'

Thor, no quick thinker, was having difficulty coming to terms. 'You're my daughter?' he said slowly. 'Surely I'd have remembered that.'

Behind them the crone was holding out gamely against the World Serpent. Old Age conquers everything in the end, of course, and although the blows that fell against

Jormungand were comparatively feeble, Ellie seemed impervious to the serpent's venom.

'I hate to butt in,' said Loki, 'but if we could keep this to the point . . . ? Thor, this is Maddy. She's come to break you out of here. As have I. Not that you'll appreciate *that*, of course – you're far too busy planning to smash every bone in my body to feel an ounce of gratitude – but we now have *nineteen* minutes left, and personally I'd rather go into this some other—'

'Nineteen minutes for what?' said Thor. In the face of danger he seemed happier and more alert; his beard bristled; in fact his whole Aspect was that of a thunder god preparing for war, and enjoying every minute of it.

'Listen,' said Loki impatiently. 'This is the heart of Netherworld. Just being here creates a disruption you can't imagine. I mean, we've hardly gone out of our way to be discreet. We've already punched holes in a hundred dreams, let a hundred demons escape, including Old Age *and* the World Serpent, so if we're going to get out of here, we'll have to rely on brains, not muscle. Which, let's face it, old friend—'

Thor's face darkened. He shot out his fist—

'You need me,' said Loki.

'Need you why?'

'Because I know how to free the gods.'

Maddy's eyes were very bright as the Trickster explained his latest plan. She was beginning to think she'd misjudged Loki; and she was suddenly ashamed at her past belief that he was the traitor at the gate.

She wanted to tell him so, but there wasn't time. The deathwatch stood at sixteen minutes; and between them, Ellie and Jormungand seemed determined to tear the room apart. Runelight crackled around them both, and the air was so thick with venom that Maddy's eyes burned and stung.

'Now listen,' said Loki urgently. 'You'll have to protect me

– both of you. My glam's almost out, and I don't stand a chance if it comes to a fight. Plus we'll have to be very fast.'

The Thunderer rumbled his assent.

'Well, as we know,' Loki went on, 'our friend Jormungand moves through dreams. Beneath that uncouth exterior he's really just another worm, sliding his way down towards his lair. Or in this case, as it happens, the river Dream. Are you with me so far?'

'Get on with it,' growled Thor.

'Until now,' Loki explained, 'we've done what we could to slow him down. A creature his size attracts attention; makes holes in the fabric of Netherworld like the holes in Ridings cheese. But what if we *wanted* to make those holes? Let Jorgi run amok in the right place and we could engineer a breakout the like of which has never been seen in all of Chaos. All we need is to lay the bait—'

'*Bait?*' said Thor. 'What is this, a fishing trip?'

'Fifteen minutes,' said Loki, looking at Maddy. 'Just follow the snake. And don't stop for *anything*.'

Thor's beard bristled dangerously. 'Tell me, runt. What bait do you use?'

But Maddy had already understood. A chill went down her spine as Loki, corpse-pale in his diminishing colours, *sidestepped* through the cell wall into nothingness.

'Bait?' she said. 'Himself, of course.'

409

15

In a second Jormungand was after him, Old Age still clinging to its sweltering coils. Stone fell away from the damaged wall; a second assault punched right through, giving Thor and Maddy a sudden, dizzying perspective into the next cell. The serpent made for the hole at once, and for what seemed an age they watched its oil-black length squeeze and press itself through the crumbling gap.

'Hang on,' said Maddy to Thor, and flinging her arms around the serpent's tail, she prepared to follow it into the unknown. Beside her, Thor was doing the same; his fingers dug into Jormungand's coils, his knees pressed into the creature's flanks. It was something like riding a bareback horse, Maddy told herself – albeit a legless horse three hundred feet long that oozed a venomous pus. It stank; and yet she held on tight, eyes shut against the poison mist that came from the serpent's mouth.

For an instant she opened them – and found herself flying for the second time above the sickening vista of Netherworld. Cries of torment rose from below; rags of dream fell away beneath her like clouds. And then they were falling into the pit; above them the air was aswarm with ephemera. Maddy closed her eyes—

And opened them again as the World Serpent shrieked through a tunnel of lights at the end of which a single figure – a man, she thought – seemed to hang, turning, on a wheel of stars. Beneath them some creature that seemed all eyes snapped at Jormungand – and then they were through again into open space, where pits of fire released a sulphurous stench and a blonde-haired woman wrestled with a giant spindly armoured cockroach above a crater lined with human bones.

Beside her she was conscious of Thor flinging missiles at the ephemera below. His strength was colossal, and when he struck, the aftershock was great enough to rip holes in the barren land beneath them and to send great chunks of Netherworld spinning wildly into space.

They passed in this way over a dozen vistas, through a dozen cells and a dozen tunnels. In their wake dreams were shattered; cell walls broken; dreamers roused. Maddy could only guess at most of this – her eyes were burning from the serpent's venom and she needed all her strength simply to hold on.

The Thunderer, at least, was enjoying himself. He'd picked up the general idea by now, although the subtleties had more or less passed him by. Thor was not a great thinker; but he knew a demon when he saw one, and this place was filled with them. Back in Aspect, hurling mindbolts, he felt almost happy again; and the memories of five hundred years slipped gently away like a distant dream.

There was no sign at all of Loki. His fading signature was lost among the multitude of ephemera and trails of light; and his figure – desperately small next to the huge bulk of the serpent that pursued him – had long since been lost to Maddy's sight. She could only hope he was still alive; beneath her Jormungand's coils lashed ferociously as the serpent gained strength, cutting and slashing as it went, like a machine chopping into the dream fortress like hay.

Pieces of Netherworld sheared away in its wake; dreamers broke free – though whether they were Æsir or not Maddy had no way of telling; ephemera were scattered to the winds like chaff. Once Maddy even thought she glimpsed what lay *behind* the walls of Netherworld: a spiralling, sucking darkness knitted with dead stars. A chill went through her.

My gods, is that Chaos?

She closed her eyes and held on.

16

Hel's Guardian was watching through the shutter of her dead eye.

'He's really done it this time,' she said, not without a kind of admiration. 'That snake is definitely getting bigger. Of course, if his fears are giving it strength . . .'

In her hands the Whisperer glowed fiercely. 'Just kill him,' it said. 'The girl too.'

'I can't,' said Hel. 'I swore an oath.'

The deathwatch in her hand – the identical twin of the one Loki still wore around his neck – showed the time at fifty-one minutes. He might well make it – he was close: through her all-seeing dead eye she could see him coming, blazing through the air like a comet with the snake on his tail and a trail of dreamers in his wake. Nine minutes – less now – and if he failed to cross the river, then his body and Maddy's would cease to exist, leaving them trapped in a Netherworld that was already coming apart at the seams, showing the dead light of World Beyond.

'What difference does nine minutes make?' said the Whisperer. 'Go on, kill him, before he does any more damage.' Its voice was urgent, and it pulsed now with a greenish light, throwing restless shadows onto Hel's face.

'You're asking me to break my word.'

'Your *word*?' snapped the Whisperer. 'What's your word to such as him? Go on, he's helpless – kill him now, for gods' sakes, kill him before it's too *late* . . .'

'I can't.' Hel looked at the deathwatch. 'My word binds me for another . . . eight minutes.'

The Whisperer glowered, and its colours flared like dragonfire. It had known, of course, that Hel would be difficult to bargain with, even with Loki's full co-operation. But Loki – freed from its influence, restored to his Aspect in Netherworld – Loki had taken Maddy's side – had actually dared to try to *free the gods* . . .

Did you think you could earn their forgiveness, Trickster? Win back your place among the Æsir? Did you think even Thor could protect you from me?

With an effort the Whisperer curbed its rage. The gods might escape, but where would they go? To enter the Underworld would mean only death for all of them – for bodiless they were Hel's property, to do with what she pleased.

Of course, they could always escape into Dream, though this too was not without its perils. For to enter Dream so close to its source was a risk that even the damned might think twice about taking.

Seven minutes remained; and with a wrench the Whisperer turned its gaze from the scene across the river. 'I can help you, lady,' it said in a voice that was suddenly all honey. 'I know what you want, and only I can give it to you . . .'

Hel opened both eyes. 'I don't know what you mean,' she said.

'Don't you?' said the Whisperer.

The seconds passed. Six minutes.

'*Don't* you?' said the Whisperer.

'I can't,' said Hel, but her voice was faint.

'Oh, but you can,' wheedled the Whisperer. 'One little cut – a snip, no more – and everything you've ever wanted can be yours. A life for a life, Goddess. Loki's life – all five minutes of it – and in exchange you could have Balder back again. Imagine that. Balder, alive. Warm. Breathing. And *yours*, Goddess. All yours.'

For long seconds more Hel was silent. 'I can't break my word,' she said at last. 'The balance between Order and Chaos depends on my neutrality.'

'With or without you,' said the Whisperer, 'the balance between Order and Chaos may soon be challenged.'

Hel's living eye was all hunger in her pallid face. 'How so?' she said.

The Whisperer allowed itself the luxury of a smile. 'Do we have a deal, Goddess?'

'Tell me *how*, damn your eyes!'

Glowing, it told her.

Across the river Loki shot like a flaming missile towards the gates of Netherworld. Hel could see that he was almost burned out now, his signature like that of a guttering flame, his face twisted with effort and concentration.

Behind him came Thor, Maddy, the serpent with Old Age still clinging to its tail and, behind that, the dreamers. Dreamers in their hundreds – in their *thousands* – trailing them in shoals as the fortress disintegrated, all of them making for the river.

And now a tremor went through the Underworld; a deep tremor that rocked all of Hel to its foundations, moving rocks that had lain still since the beginning of the world and sending shock waves through the ranks of the dead, making bones dance, dust fly, mist scatter and a howl of outrage rise from Hel's parched throat.

'What is going *on* here?' shrieked the goddess of the Dead. The deathwatch in her hand showed barely eighty-five seconds remaining.

'That's Chaos itself, knocking at your door. Chaos, in search of its prisoners. If Loki escapes, it will break through—'

'*Loki* did this?'

'Kill him now. Save your kingdom and yourself.'

'What if you're wrong, Oracle?'

'You'll still have Balder – will you refuse?'

'Balder.' For the second time in five hundred years Hel gave an involuntary sigh.

'Seventy seconds.'

'But I—'

'Sixty seconds and you'll see Balder alive. Fifty-nine. Fifty-eight. Fifty-seven—'

'All right! All *right*!' Hel stretched out her dead hand – the fingers were bones, brittle and yellow in the eerie light. In its spidery shadow Loki slept, one arm flung out across Hel's sandy floor, a tiny smile on his scarred lips. The silver thread that linked him to Netherworld gleamed like a skein of spiderweb.

'Do it, lady. Take his life.'

Hel reached out her dead hand and snapped the thread.

And at that very moment there came a terrible ripping, splitting, splintering sound – as of Worlds being torn apart at the seams – and all of these things happened at once:

Sugar's runestone turned black as pitch.

Odin felt a wave of energy rush past him as ten thousand of the newly dead poured over him into the Underworld.

In Netherworld Jormungand cleared the gates and plunged headlong towards the river Dream.

Loki followed, with seconds to spare – and ran full-tilt into an invisible barrier that sent him into a deadly spiral, plummeting out of control back into the pit.

And in World's End Magister Emeritus Number 262, a man who in another life had answered to the name of Fortune Goodchild, had time only to ask himself, *How can we possibly march to Netherworld?* before the Nameless spoke a single Word and he fell, stone dead, onto the floor of the Council of Twelve.

'It's beginning,' said the Whisperer.

'What's beginning?' said Hel.

'The end,' said the Whisperer, glowing softly. 'The last meeting between Order and Chaos. The final End of Everything.'

And now Hel saw it starting to change: the stone Head sprouted like a ghastly flower; the air was taking a definite shape; and now she could see its true Aspect, spectral at first but brightening visibly. A shining figure, slightly bent; hooded eyes in a lean face; a staff of runes that gleamed and spun.

'Who are you?' said Hel.

The Whisperer smiled. 'My dear, I've been so many things. I was Mimir the Wise. I was Odin's friend and confidant. I was the Oracle who predicted Ragnarók. My name is Untold, for I have many. But as we're friends, you may call me the Ancient of Days.'

BOOK EIGHT
The Nameless

What is it that the slave dreams?
The slave dreams of being the master.

Book of Mimir, 5:15

1

Everyone felt the psychic blast that slammed throughout the Nine Worlds, so that a hundred miles from the epicentre, purple clouds gathered, doors slammed, dogs howled, ears bled and birds fell screaming from the sky.

The Vanir felt it, and quickened their pace. Frey took the form of a wild boar, and Heimdall that of a grey wolf, and Bragi that of a brown fox, and all three of them set off at a gallop down the tunnels, while Njörd protested and Freyja wailed and Idun sensibly picked up their clothes in case they needed them later.

Fat Lizzy felt it, and knew they were close.

And at the mouth of the Underworld, as the parson and the Huntress gazed in wonderment at the scene unfolding on the plain below, Examiner Number 4421974 heard it and gave a long, harsh sigh of deliverance before slipping gently out of his host and down the passageway into Hel.

It had begun, as the Good Book had foretold.

The dead were on the march. Ten thousand of them.

Silently Hel considered the multitude standing before her on the plain. So many souls; but where was their homage? Why were they ranked like an army? What was this Order, where men could be dead, but where Death herself had no authority?

She turned her terrible half-face upon the ten thousand. 'Be dead,' she ordered.

The men did not move.

'I command you to disperse,' said Hel.

Still no one moved; ten thousand men stood like sheaves, their eyes turned towards Netherworld.

She turned on the Whisperer. 'Is this your doing?'

'Of course it is,' said the Whisperer. 'Now make haste and give me the girl.'

'The girl?' In the commotion she'd almost forgotten.

Hel looked at the deathwatch. Thirty seconds remained. She'd broken her word to Loki, and the balance between Worlds had been shaken to its roots. Break it again, and she dared not think what might happen. Already she could feel the river rising; and beyond it Chaos, like a sick heart beating.

'Quickly,' snapped the Whisperer. 'Every moment she spends in Netherworld is an unnecessary risk.'

'Why?' said Hel.

She looked down at the sleeping girl, tethered to life by a skein of silk. Until now she had spared her hardly a thought; between Loki and the Whisperer there had been no time to notice a fourteen-year-old girl.

Now she watched her most carefully; noted her rust-red signature; once more searched her memory for the resemblance – a family likeness, perhaps, from the days when the Æsir ruled the Worlds . . .

'Who is she?' said Hel.

'No one,' said the Whisperer.

'Funny; that's what Loki said.'

The Whisperer brightened fretfully. 'She's no one,' it said. 'Just give her to me. Cut the thread – do it now, while you can . . .'

Hel's profile was unreadable as she gently reached out with her dead hand. She touched Maddy's face lingeringly.

'Do it now,' urged the Whisperer. 'Do it, and I'll make Balder yours . . .'

Hel smiled and touched the thread that still linked Maddy

to her life. It shimmered faintly at her touch; it glowed like the runemark on her hand . . .

'That runemark . . .' said Hel.

Eighteen seconds.

'Please! There's no time!'

She took the girl's hand in her living one. *Aesk* shone there, a violent red – and in that moment Hel understood. The World Ash. The Lightning Tree. The first rune of the New Script. And now she remembered who Maddy reminded her of – not her Aspect, but her *signature* – and she levelled on the Whisperer the smile that had withered gods.

'So *that's* why you wanted her,' she said. 'That's why you brought her into Hel. And Loki – I see why you wanted him too.'

The Whisperer grimaced desperately. 'I'll build a hall for you, Hel,' it said in its most honeyed voice. 'When Balder rises from the dead, you'll lie together in the Sky Citadel.'

Hel put her fingers to her lips. It was a peculiar sensation; bringing a flush to her living side. She'd thought herself beyond this. Aeons old, dry as dust, she had not expected this rush of feeling; this almost girlish surge of hope . . .

She reached out her hand to break the thread.

2

The World Serpent cleared the gates at twice the speed of dream. Maddy and Thor had just enough time to jump clear before Jormungand hurled itself headlong into the river, Old Age still clinging to its tail. A wall of water rose up; clouds of ephemera exploded in all directions; some of the dreamers were already through and Maddy, now seeing the silvery thread that joined her Aspect to her physical self, made to follow them through the narrowing gap . . .

Behind her the countless dreamers approached. Some were human; some visibly demonic; some bore the runes and colours of gods; others marched like engines, lurched like nightmares, oozed, verminous, towards their freedom.

Thor kept the monstrosities at bay. The inhabitants of Netherworld – dreams and dreamers, creatures of Chaos, engines of destruction, serpents and changelings and any other vermin that might want to breach the gap into the Eighth World – mostly gave him a wide berth, and although it was not possible for him to keep every one away from the gate, it was only the quickest and the most capable that managed to follow Jormungand from Netherworld into Dream.

Before him the Æsir, in their Aspects, had gathered. They were pitifully few – just three of them – shocked into silence by what they saw. Frigg, the Mother, wife of Odin, tall, grey-eyed and with the rune *Sól* on her left arm; Thor's wife Sif, the Harvest Queen, golden-haired and bearing the runesign *Ár*; and Tyr, the Left-Handed, god of battle, burning like a brand in his fiery colours, his spear in his left hand, his right hand like a ghost of itself sketched in fire against the night.

The Thunderer had hoped for more; but the rest had either failed to escape, or fallen into Chaos or plunged into Dream, because he could see no trace of them. Counting himself, a total of four.

Five, if he counted Maddy.

He gestured to Maddy to pass through the gate. Only she could cross into Hel; the others would have to escape through Dream as, all around them, the Ninth World started to tear itself apart. Every few moments some creature – god or demon, she could not tell – lost its grasp on Netherworld and was sucked, screaming, into the emptiness. The noise was apocalyptic; and from the throat of the abyss came a sinister sucking, snickering sound that grew louder and louder with every second that passed.

'Maddy! Go now!' insisted Thor.

But Maddy had seen something moving below. It – *he* – was a long way down; obscured by the mists and the parasites of Netherworld, now swarming like deadly motes through the air. But the signature, though faint, was unmistakable. It was Loki, and he was falling. Beneath him and all around, rifts into Chaos were opening fast, revealing glimpses of the dead starry gulf of World Beyond.

'Go, Maddy!' yelled Thor at her side. 'Through the gap! There isn't much time!'

'But that's Loki,' she cried, pointing at the falling figure.

Thor shook his shaggy head. 'There's nothing you can do . . .' he began.

But Maddy was already in pursuit.

Before Thor could protest, she had dived, not through the gap to the Underworld, but into the cauldron of sizzling air, heedless of ephemera, heedless of the fact that the world she occupied was busily eating itself into oblivion like a serpent swallowing its own tail.

Thor moved to follow her – he wasn't sure why she needed Loki, but there was no time for argument – then he caught sight of what lay behind him and stopped and gazed with widening eyes at the scenes unfolding beyond Dream.

It was as if Hel, for the first time in a thousand years, had blossomed into a kind of life. Clouds gathered in its false sky; a hot, dark wind blew. But that was not why the Thunderer faltered, even though with its gathering clouds and dead sun the plain seemed almost the twin of that other battlefield beyond World's End.

It was the dead at which he stared. Not the dead of Underworld – those lost and pitiable souls, numerous as grains of sand – but a column of dead, just like an army, that reached interminably out of the desert to stand, motionless, ten thousand strong, against the might of Netherworld.

Ten thousand to a man; a magical figure, often mentioned in accounts of the last battle. It was also, as it happened, precisely the number of the Order's membership, a calculated sacrifice of its men – Examiners, Magisters, Professors all – gathered together in a Communion stronger than Death . . .

And now Thor believed he knew that sound – that inhuman sucking, as if Chaos were taking a deep breath – and his face paled beneath his fiery beard. He'd heard it before, at Ragnarók. They'd been outnumbered then, but not as badly; he'd still had his glam – and his hammer too – but even so that sound had struck ice into his heart.

Why, that's— he thought. At which point there came a terrible *crash* across the Worlds – Thor just had time to think, *Uh-oh, here it comes* – and in the final seconds of Maddy's life the legions of the Order began their march, inexorably, across the plains of Hel.

3

She caught up with Loki some thousand levels into Netherworld. He was falling rapidly now, eyes shut, still clasping the deathwatch in his hands. He opened his eyes as Maddy approached, then closed them again with a shake of his head.

'Maddy, I'm dead. Leave me alone.'

'What?' For a moment, with the cacophony of Netherworld in her ears, she'd been sure he had said, *I'm dead*. Then she saw the time on the watch, and her mouth opened in a silent cry.

Forty-five seconds.

'Leave me alone.'

Forty-two seconds.

Forty-one.

'You have to get out,' Loki said.

'We can both get out. Just take my hand . . .'

Loki swore as the rune *Naudr* fastened itself around his wrist. 'Maddy, believe me. You're wasting your time.'

Thirty-nine seconds.

Maddy began to drag him upwards. 'I'm not going to leave you here,' she said. 'I was wrong about you. I thought you were the traitor at the gate—'

And now they were hurtling upwards again, Maddy hauling him with all her glam, Loki trying to reason with her over the deafening sound of the Ninth World's unmaking.

'But I *was* the traitor at the gate!' Loki protested.

'Now you're being noble,' Maddy said. 'You want me to leave you and save myself, so you're trying to make me believe—'

'Please!' yelled Loki. 'I am *not* being noble!'

Thirty seconds left to go. And now their speed rivalled that of the World Serpent at his fastest, crossing what seemed like miles in a fraction of a second; half deafened by the sucking roar of Chaos.

'Listen,' said Loki. 'D'you hear that noise?'

Maddy nodded.

'That's Surt coming through,' said Loki.

Twenty-four seconds.

'*Lord* Surt? The Destroyer?'

'No, another Surt – what the Hel do you think?'

Twenty-two seconds: they could see the gate. The opening looked no greater than a lancet now, and Thor was holding it with both hands, his face dark with the effort, his shoulders bunched like an ox's as they raced towards the narrow slit.

Twenty seconds.

'Don't worry, we'll make it—'

'Maddy – no . . .'

Now Maddy's heart was close to bursting as she plunged towards the closing gate, dragging Loki – still struggling – behind her.

'Listen to me! The Whisperer lied. I know what it wants; I've seen into its mind. I've known it since our journey began. I didn't tell you – I lied – I thought I could use you to save myself—'

Fifteen seconds . . .

Maddy wrenched at Loki's arm—

Naudr, the Binder, gave way with a snap—

And then three things all happened at once:

Hel's deathwatch cracked right across the face, freezing the time at thirteen seconds.

Netherworld crashed shut with a clang.

And Maddy awoke in her own skin and found herself looking into Hel's dead eye.

4

At the entrance to the Underworld the parson and the Huntress stopped. They had tracked their quarry to the mouth of Hel, and now they stood and watched the plain, where a slight dust rose in the wake of the two figures – one tall, one short – that inched their way across the desert.

It was all too much for Adam Scattergood. The bleak sky where no sky had a right to be; the nameless peaks; the dead like thunderheads marching into the blue . . . Even if this was a dream, he thought (and he clung to the idea with all his might), then he'd long since given up any hope of awakening. Death would be infinitely better than this; and he followed, incurious, where the Huntress led, hearing the sound of the dead in his ears, and wondering when it would come for him.

Nat Parson spared him not a thought. Instead he smiled his wolfish smile and opened the Book of Words at the relevant page. His enemy was within range; even across that vastness, he knew, the canticle would strike him down; and he allowed himself a little sigh of satisfaction as he began to invoke the power of the Word.

I name you, Odin, son of Bór . . .

But something was wrong, the parson thought. When first he had used that canticle, it had been with a sense of gathering doom; a power that increased at every word until it became a moving wall, crushing everything in its path. Now, however he spoke the words, the Word declined to reveal itself.

'What's wrong?' demanded Skadi, impatient, as Nat faltered mid sentence and stopped.

'It isn't working,' he complained.

'You must have read it wrong, you fool.'

'I did not read it wrong,' the parson said, angered at being called *fool* in front of his prentice – and by an illiterate, barbarian female at that. He began the canticle again – in his finest pulpit voice – but once more the Word seemed oddly flat, as if something had drained it of its potency.

What's going on? he thought in dismay, reaching for the comforting presence of Examiner Number 4421974 in his mind.

But Elias Rede was strangely silent. Like the Word, the Examiner had somehow lost depth, like a picture faded by the sun. And the lights, he saw – the signature colours and lights that had illuminated everything – they too were gone. One moment they'd been there, and the next – nothing. As if someone had blown out a candle . . .

Who's there?

No inner voice replied.

Elias? Examiner?

Once more silence. A great, dull silence, like coming back one day to an empty house and suddenly knowing that there's nobody home.

Nat Parson gave a cry, and as Skadi turned to look at him, she noticed that something about him had changed. Gone was the silvery skein that had illuminated his colours, transforming a plain brown signature into a mantle of power. Now the parson was plain again; just one of the Folk; undistinguished and unremarked.

The Huntress snarled. 'You tricked me,' she said and, shifting into her animal form, set off across the drifting sand in snarling pursuit of the General.

Nat thought to follow, but she soon outdistanced him,

racing across the endless plain, howling her rage at her enemy.

'You can't leave me here!' the parson said – and that was when the Vanir, drawn by the sound of the white wolf's cry, moved out of the shadows at his back and watched him grimly from the tunnel mouth.

5

In animal guise they had tracked the Huntress, with Frey, Bragi and Heimdall leading the chase. As the passageway broadened, Njörd's sea eagle had joined them, flying low beneath the eaves, and now the four of them resumed their own Aspects, watching intently from their vantage point as the white wolf pursued its distant quarry.

Some distance behind them came Freyja and Idun, turning wondering eyes to the sky of Hel and to the little drama being enacted miles below across the plain.

'I told you Skadi was on our side,' said Njörd. 'She followed him here, she led us right to him—'

'Did she?' Heimdall glanced at the parson, standing not a dozen feet away. 'Then will someone explain to us why *he's* here? And what about the Whisperer? If it was close, I'd have seen it by now.'

'It's obvious,' said Njörd. 'Loki has it.'

'Doesn't make sense,' Heimdall said. 'If Odin and Loki are working together . . .'

'So they quarrelled. He ran. That's what he does. What does it matter?'

'I need to be sure.'

Heimdall turned on the parson, who had backed away. At his feet Adam Scattergood hid his eyes.

'You, fellow,' said Heimdall. 'Where is the Whisperer?'

'Please don't kill me,' pleaded Nat. 'I don't know anything about any Whisperer. I'm just a country parson, I don't even have the Word any more—'

And then the parson stopped and stared, and the Book of Words fell from his hand. He looked like a man having a stroke. His face paled; his eyes bulged; his mouth fell open, but no words came.

His wife was standing at the tunnel mouth. Her hair unpinned; her eyes bright; her plain face very calm.

'Ethel,' said Nat. 'But I saw you die.'

Ethel smiled at her husband's expression. She had expected to feel something when they finally met. Relief perhaps, or anger, fear, resentment. Instead she felt – what *was* that feeling?

'This *is* the Land of the Dead, Nat,' said Ethel with a mischievous smile. And now behind her Nat could see . . . surely that was Dorian Scattergood, and could that possibly be – a pig?

'I asked you a question, fellow,' said Heimdall. 'Where is the Whisperer?'

But it was Ethelberta who replied, looking strangely dignified in spite of her ragged clothes and the dust on her face, and the fact that she was standing next to a man holding a small black pig under one arm.

'The Whisperer is at the gate,' she said. 'I speak as I must, and cannot be silent.'

Heimdall gave her a sharp look. 'What did you say?'

'This is the time that was foretold,' went on Ethel quietly. 'The War of Nine Worlds, when Yggdrasil shall tremble to its roots and the Black Fortress shall be opened with a single Word. The dead shall rise to live again, and the living have no place of refuge as Order and Chaos are finally made one, and the Nameless shall be named, and the formless have form, and a traitor be true and a blind man lead you against ten thousand.'

By this time all eyes were on Ethelberta. Dorian thought how beautiful she was; how luminous and how calm.

'Excuse me,' said Heimdall. 'And you are . . . ?'

'We've met,' she said.

Heimdall looked at her more closely. For a second he frowned at her colours, brighter by far than those of the Folk.

Then he turned accusingly to Idun. 'What did you do to her?' he said.

'She was dying,' said Idun. 'I brought her back.'

There was a rather ominous silence.

'Let me get this straight,' said Heimdall. 'You brought her back.'

Idun nodded happily.

'You gave . . . one of the Folk . . . the food of the gods.'

Idun smiled.

'And you thought that was a good idea?'

'Why not?' said the Healer.

'Why not?' said Heimdall. 'Listen, Idun. She came back from the dead. You've given her the gift of prophecy.' He gave the rock at his side a kick. 'Gods,' he said. 'That's all we need. Another bloody oracle.'

6

'Sir, it's too late,' protested Sugar-and-Sack as they stumbled across the featureless plain. 'The Captain's stone's gone black, d'ye kennet, and that can only mean one thing . . .'

'You're staying with me,' said the General. 'For a start, I'll need your eyes.'

'Me *eyes*?'

'Just take my arm – and keep going.'

In the darkness of World Below Odin had almost welcomed blindness. But here, beneath the false grey sun of the Underworld, he knew that his advantage – such as it was – was at an end. Against the pallor of the desert he and Sugar stood out like two cockroaches on a cake – easy targets for an enemy. Blind, he could still sense that the Vanir were close; and their combined strength was such that even if he'd had the use of his eyes, he would have had little chance against the seven of them at once.

But the Vanir seemed disinclined to attack. Only the white wolf was in pursuit – and so close now that he could hear her panting. But with Sugar as his guide, and a wall of broken rock only yards away, he was almost sure he could make it to some place of shelter; some place from which he might, with luck, strike first at the Huntress just as she shifted back into Aspect.

It was a long shot; but Odin took his chance and, feeling rock at the tip of his staff, he turned abruptly, wedged his back against the wall and fired *Hagall* as hard as he could into the white wolf's open jaws.

If Maddy had fired that bolt, it might have finished there and then. But it was not Maddy; and the mindbolt that would have taken out the Huntress's throat just glanced harmlessly off her shoulder, and lit a string of signature-sparks like crackers off the rock face.

Odin did not have to see the result to know that his blow had gone wide. Sugar squeaked in alarm and dived headfirst into a nest of rocks too small for anything much bigger than a rat to follow, and now he could sense her circling back, her colours flaring like ancient ice.

He reached for the runes, but found them unco-operative. So much of his glam had already gone over the three days of his descent into Underworld that there was less than a spark left now for the fight.

Skadi knew it, and growled with amusement as she closed in for the kill. She had spent so much time in her wolf skin over the past few days that her true Aspect had begun to feel cumbersome and slow; and though she needed it at times (when she wanted to speak or cast runes), she'd always felt better in animal form. She growled again and crouched on her haunches for the leap that would guide her to her enemy's throat.

It never came. Instead she felt a hand on her collar, smelled a not-quite-human scent and was hauled backwards, snarling, by six pairs of hands as Frey and Heimdall cast runes of constraint and Bragi played a farandole that bound her into helplessness. The struggle was short; snarling at her captors, the Huntress regained her natural form and faced them, white and red and spitting with rage, in her own Aspect.

'How *dare* you!' She might have matched them one on one, but against the six she could not triumph. 'I had the right to this kill—'

'The right?' said Freyja. 'To risk our lives for some pointless revenge? Listen, Skadi.' She handed her a cloak, which

Skadi took sullenly. 'We know what you did.'

'Then kill me,' said Skadi, 'because I'm going to do it again the minute I get the chance.'

For a moment they stood face to face: six Vanir and the Huntress, fists clenched and blue eyes glaring, and lastly Odin, leaning on his staff.

Some distance behind them came the others: Ethel, Dorian, Adam and Nat, with the Good Book clasped once more at his chest. It was a tense moment, the stillness broken only by a distant sluicing sound; and with it a vibration that pulled at their eardrums and sucked their teeth and seemed to come from everywhere, nowhere and some other, impossible place in between.

'Listen,' said Odin. 'Do you know that sound?'

Everyone turned to look at him.

Heimdall the Watchman knew it well. He'd heard it on the battlefield at Ragnarók, when the sky had been rent and sun and moon swallowed by a darkness that had nothing to do with the absence of light.

Frey knew it; he'd heard it as he'd fallen, his sword broken and his glam reversed, into the ice.

Freyja knew it too; and remembered a shadow like that of a black bird ringed with fire – a crow, perhaps, or a carrion bird – and that where it fell, nothing remained.

Skadi knew it; and shivered.

Njörd, who had fought from the shores of his own kingdom, had heard it as the river Dream broke its banks and the battle fleet of the dead sailed forth out of the Underworld.

Idun had heard it, and wept.

Bragi too had heard it, though no songs or poems had been written that day. Fire and ice and a black bird shadow; opposing forces so strong that between them the World Tree groaned and swayed. Asgard, the Sky Citadel, the First World, had fallen, crushing continents. And out of Chaos demons had come, slithering between the Worlds in the wake of the blackbird shadow, and all that had been in the Middle World, where the powers of Chaos are at their weakest. And they'd had armies then: warriors, heroes, Tunnel Folk and men . . .

'I see an army poised for battle. I see a General standing alone. I see a traitor at the gate. I see a sacrifice.'

The voice was quiet but distinct, and the Vanir stared at Ethel Parson. Only Odin did not stare; but he stiffened at the sound of her voice.

'Who's that?'

'I'm Ethel Parson, if it please you, sir, and they tell me I'm an oracle.'

For a moment Odin froze. Then a smile touched his harsh features.

'Ethel,' he said. 'I should have known.'

There was a long pause. Then he spoke again, in a gentle voice, and took her hand between his own. 'You felt different. You didn't know why. You could see things you couldn't before. And there was a feeling inside you, wasn't there? A feeling that you had to be somewhere, but you didn't know where . . .'

Ethel nodded silently. Odin didn't see it; but he saw its reflection in her colours and smiled. 'It itched,' he went on. 'And then it took shape. Show me, Ethel. You know what I mean.'

Ethel looked surprised, and she coloured a little. She hesitated – then with a firm gesture she pushed up her sleeve to show them the new runemark on her arm, glowing with a bright-green light.

Nat's mouth fell open in surprise. Dorian gasped; Adam stared; and even the Vanir were stunned into silence.

Only Odin seemed unsurprised, and he smiled as he traced the gleaming sign.

'*Ethel*, the Homeland,' he said. 'Second rune of the New Script. I never thought to find it here – the food of the gods combined with the Word . . .' Slowly he shook his grey head. 'If only there was more time,' he said. 'But I need to talk with you alone.'

Their talk lasted less than five minutes or so; though her eyes were wet at the end of it. 'You're sure of this?' she said at last.

'Quite sure,' said the General. He turned to the Vanir. 'You all heard it, didn't you? That sound. The sound of Chaos coming through. The lines are drawn; the enemy named. And our only hope is beyond that plain. I have to reach it, or everything will fall – not just the gods, not even the Worlds, but *everything*.'

Heimdall frowned. 'The parson's wife told you all this?'

Odin nodded.

'And you believe her?'

'With good cause.'

Skadi gave him a scornful look. 'Even assuming she's telling the truth, there's a whole army between us and the river. You've seen what the Word can do . . .'

'I've seen it, yes.'

'And you think you can win?'

'No,' he said. 'But I think we can fight.'

There was a long and thoughtful silence.

'There are eight of us,' said Heimdall at last.

'Seven,' said Skadi, 'and a blind General.'

Odin grinned. 'Eight of us against ten thousand. My favourite kind of odds.'

Heimdall showed his golden teeth. 'My money's on the General,' he said.

Njörd shrugged. 'Well, if you put it that way—'

'Gods,' said Freyja. 'You're worse than *he* is.'

Frey said: 'I'd like another poke at that bloody black bird . . .'

Bragi began a victory song.

Idun opened her casket of apples, and their scent was enough to wake the dead . . .

And Skadi ground her teeth and said: 'All right – *General* – you win. But that doesn't mean the slate's clean. If we survive, then you and your brother owe me some blood. And this time don't think you can fob me off with promises . . .'

Odin smiled. 'I'll promise you this. There'll be more blood by the end of today than even you could ever want. But if perhaps you want to fight,' he said, pointing, 'then I have reason to believe the battle's *that* way.'

They didn't look like heroes, thought Ethel, and yet with her altered vision she could definitely see something in the air around them; not a signature (she'd been seeing those for days now, and knew the difference) but a kind of *glow*, like the sky before dawn; a promise, if you like, of transformation. She didn't need to be an oracle to know that it might lead to the death of them all; still she went cheerfully in the wake of the gods, humming a little tune under her breath and watching Dorian's broad back as he led the way with Lizzy running at his heels.

All Hel was about to break loose, she thought; and finally, and for the first time, Owen Goodchild's daughter Ethel knew precisely where she wanted to be.

7

In Netherworld – what was left of it – Loki definitely *wasn't* where he wanted to be. He'd felt the severing of his Aspect from his physical self, and his quick mind had come to the following conclusions:

First, and most importantly, he was dead.

That hadn't come entirely as a surprise. In fact as far as Loki was concerned the real surprise was how far he had managed to come before it finally happened. But the face of Hel's deathwatch told its own tale – thirteen seconds remained on the clock, which meant that for the first time in the history of Worlds, Half-Born Hel had broken her word.

All right, he thought. *Let's look on the bright side of this. The bright side is that, though my body may be dead, my Aspect remains here, in Netherworld.*

Not much of a bright side. Still, he thought, the *really* stupid thing at this stage would have been to seek refuge in the Underworld. He'd tried to explain this to Maddy as she dragged him, protesting, towards Hel's borders, but either she hadn't heard him or she simply hadn't understood, because if she'd managed to drag him through, then he would have been Hel's plaything by now, helpless and for ever in her power, like the countless other souls that sighed and keened on the dusty plains of the Land of the Dead.

However (*and now we come to the second point*), to be trapped against an immovable barrier on one side and with Surt on the rampage in his full Aspect on the other (for so he interpreted the sounds coming through from World Beyond) was hardly an enviable position either.

And thirdly, there were the Æsir. He'd managed to evade their attention till now, but as he looked up from the foot of the gate, Loki was uncomfortably conscious of the four familiar Aspects that now flanked him.

Let's face it, he thought. *There is no bright side.*

And bolted.

Predictably he didn't get far. He shifted to his fiery Aspect only to find himself pinned in on all four sides.

'Not so fast,' said Thor. 'You owe us an explanation.'

'He owes us more than that,' said Tyr.

Of course, Loki knew that the one-handed god had more than one reason to distrust him, given that it had been his fault that Tyr lost the hand in the first place. Now he loomed over the Trickster, his signature blazing a fierce orange, his right hand (renewed in Aspect) a miracle of mindweaponry, a gauntlet of glamours that doubled his strength.

'Hit him,' said Sif – whose long hair Loki had once cut off as a joke, and who had never allowed anyone to forget it. 'Go on, Thor, give him one from me.'

'Oh, give me a break,' said Loki. 'I just gave my *life* for you people—'

'How?' said Tyr.

Loki told him.

'So, what you're saying is,' said Tyr, 'that it's actually *your* fault that all this has happened. If you hadn't been so damn careless—'

'*Careless!*'

'Well, unless anyone thinks that destroying half of Netherworld doesn't count as careless, to say nothing of awakening the Destroyer, opening a rift into Chaos, releasing Jormungand back into the Worlds and basically bringing about the second Ragnarók—'

'Leave him alone.'

That was Frigg, the Mother of the gods, and even the

Thunderer hesitated to defy her. A tall, quiet woman with soft brown hair, she might have been unremarkable but for the intelligence in her grey eyes; as it was, her patience and dignity had often overcome trials that even the most powerful weapons had failed to defeat. As one of the few who had visited the Land of the Dead and returned, she had the occasional gift of second sight, and now all eyes were on her as she said, 'There may yet be an escape for all of us.'

Thor made a scornful noise. 'In this shambles? I say fight . . .'

Frigg looked out across the swollen river. The armies of the Order could be seen quite clearly now, eerily still on the dead plain.

'This is not a shambles,' she said. 'All this was planned very carefully. Our escape from the fortress – the closing of the gate – the destruction of Netherworld – even Hel's treachery – none of this was random. It suggests that we were brought here for a specific purpose, and that the enemy – whoever he is – has a plan in which the destruction of the Æsir is only one part.'

Thor grunted again, but Tyr was looking interested. 'Why?' he said.

'No,' said Frigg. 'The question is *who*?'

Everyone thought about that for a moment.

'Well, Surt, I suppose,' said Tyr at last.

Thor nodded. 'Who else is there?'

'Surt was in his kennel, sleeping off Ragnarók. The battle was won. His enemies were dead, or imprisoned in Netherworld. What business would he have in the Middle Worlds? And more to the point' – Frigg turned to Loki, indicating with one hand the silent ranks on the far side of the river – 'what business would he have with such as these?'

'You're right,' said Loki. 'It isn't Surt. Chaos is his business, not Order. He wouldn't know how to raise an army like this. He may be powerful, but behind it all he's just another guard dog, trained to bite on command. Surt doesn't do subtleties.'

Sif flicked her hair. 'You seem to know a lot about it,' she said. 'And *you* do subtleties.'

'Yeah. Like I've always wanted to destroy the Nine Worlds while committing suicide.'

'Well, there's no need to be *rude*,' protested Sif.

'But Loki is right,' said Frigg quietly. 'Surt, for all his power, is just a tool of Chaos. A machine. Someone set him into motion. Someone who knew that we'd be here, that our escape would galvanize his rage.'

The gods were looking puzzled now. 'But there's no one else,' protested Tyr. 'There's no one left after Ragnarók. A few giants, maybe – a demon or two – the Folk . . .'

But Loki's hand had gone to his mouth. His eyes widened.

'He knows,' said Frigg gently.

'*Does* he?' said Thor.

'The girl wanted to rescue her father. She knew he was in Netherworld. But who told her that? Who encouraged her? Who led her here at just the right time, and who made sure Loki was with her – Loki, whose presence ensured maximum havoc in Netherworld, and who could also be used, among other things, as bait?'

'So it *was* his fault . . .'

Frigg shook her head. 'I said, *who*?'

There was a silence.

All around them the screaming, the rushing, the sounds of rocks tearing away from the sides of the fortress and crashing into each other like worlds – everything came to a stop.

And in the silence Loki began to laugh.

And a black bird shadow with a corona of fire reared up its head from between the Worlds, and began to move across the vastness of Chaos towards them.

8

If Hel's living eye was merciless, the dead one was like a burial pit. Maddy bore its gaze for seconds before she managed to look away.

'Am I dead?' she said.

'Damn, she's awake.'

The dry voice was that of the Whisperer, but the figure was one she had never seen: a bent old man, garbed in light, carrying a runestaff that crackled with glam.

'Apparently you're alive, my dear. Against all expectation you made it in time. Of course, it would have been most inconvenient from my point of view to see you discorporated at this stage. But I'd hoped to do things differently. Still, you're here, and that's what counts—'

'What things?' said Maddy.

'Why, my revenge.'

'Revenge against whom?'

'The Æsir, of course.'

Maddy shook her aching head. Still dazed after her wild flight through Netherworld, she stared at the gleaming figure that had blossomed from the Head and tried to understand its ludicrous words.

'The Æsir?' she said. 'But – you're on their side.'

'Their side? Their side?' The ancient voice was harsh with contempt. 'And what side's that, you silly girl? Order? Chaos? A bit of both?'

Maddy tried to sit up, but her head was spinning.

'What have the Æsir done for me? They plundered my talents, they got me killed, then, as if that wasn't enough, they condemned me to this – to be picked up and put away at my master's whim . . .' The Whisperer gave a dry little crack of laughter. 'And for that,' it said, 'I was supposed to feel *grateful*? To let them start all over again?'

'But I don't understand. You helped me . . .'

'Well, you're special,' said the Whisperer.

'And Loki?'

It smirked. 'Well – he was a bit special too.'

Maddy looked round abruptly, half expecting to find Loki gone. She'd dragged him as far as the gate, she knew; but after that everything was blurred. Had she saved him after all?

He was lying beside her, eyes closed. Pale and still though he was, he looked far better than his battered counterpart in Netherworld, and Maddy was immediately reassured. Of course, if he'd died, she told herself, then his body wouldn't be there at all; and his shade would already be walking Hel's halls, along with the ghosts of his family.

Maddy took a deep breath. 'I thought he was the traitor,' she said.

The Whisperer smiled. 'And so did he. In fact he was merely a pawn in my service, as he has been for the best part of five hundred years. He thought I was his prisoner – never suspecting that he was mine. He tried to trick me, as I knew he would, but even a traitor can serve my plan. He'd served it before, at Ragnarók – which in many ways, incidentally, *I* engineered.'

'Engineered it? How?'

'I manipulated the gods to do as I'd planned: I tempted the weak; I flattered the strong; I guided their enemies, made cryptic pronouncements and secret alliances, entered their minds with treacherous thoughts. Odin never saw how he'd been deceived. Even when his brother turned against him, he never suspected the whisperer in the shadows. And now, once more, they have played into my hands. As of course, my dear, have you.'

Maddy listened in growing horror. In front of her she could see the ranks of the Order, silent now, awaiting the Word. Behind her, a single glance told her that the river Dream was rising to flood level: filaments of raw glam hovered over its teeming waters; *things* moved in its unspeakable deeps. Soon, she knew, it would break its banks and spill its nightmare across the plains of Hel. But beyond the river was even worse. Netherworld was coming apart; the illusion of a fortress – or even an island – was long gone now in the churning mess. Rocks circled each other in air that was clotted with ephemera; souls flitted by like moths around a lamp.

'So Loki was right,' she said softly. 'You made a deal with the Order, and you're keeping control of these men somehow.'

The Whisperer smiled. 'A deal?' it said. 'Maddy, I *made* the Order. From Chaos I brought it, after the war. I was free then; the gods were imprisoned; and I sought my disciples among the Folk. The Folk have remarkable minds, you know – rivalling the gods in ambition and pride. I gave them the Good Book – a collection of commandments and prophecies and names of power – and they gave me their minds. By the time your friends escaped from Netherworld, my Order had grown to five hundred men. Scholars; historians; politicians; priests. Five hundred pairs of eyes abroad, linked to me through Communion; the beginnings of an army that would change the Worlds. Little by little; but always through me; the still, small voice of the Nameless.'

'The Nameless?' repeated Maddy blankly.

It gave its dry and humourless laugh. 'Everything has a name, you know. Names are the building blocks of

Creation. And now, at last, my prophecy is fulfilled; and I shall arise as the leader of an invading army. Ten thousand men, all armed with the Word, all loyal to me and incapable of betrayal. With them I can do anything: raise the dead; re-order the Worlds. This time we'll win, no doubt about it, and this time we'll take no prisoners.'

Once more Maddy looked at the Whisperer. It looked insubstantial in this new Aspect, and yet there was no mistaking the power at its fingers; trails of glamour snapped around it, and Maddy knew that just one touch from that staff would be enough to reduce her to a smear of ash.

Where is it getting the power? she thought.

The answer formed itself almost before the question was posed. It was standing before her, set out in orderly columns across the plain.

Slowly she rose to her feet, keeping a distance between herself and the Nameless. From time to time her eyes went back to the figure of Loki at her feet, eyes closed, hands folded neatly over a chest that neither rose nor fell.

'Forget him, he's dead,' said the Whisperer.

'No,' said Maddy. 'He can't be.'

'Of course he can,' said the Whisperer. 'Dead, done and good riddance.'

She put out a hand to touch Loki's face. It was still warm. 'But he's here.' Her voice shook. 'His body is here.'

'Ah yes,' said the Whisperer. 'But I'm afraid it doesn't belong to him any more. You see, Hel and I had a certain arrangement. A life for a life. A bargain, I think.'

Maddy stared at Hel, who stared back impassively, her living hand folded over her dead one, both resting on the deathwatch around her neck. Thirteen seconds remained on the clock.

'You broke your promise,' said Maddy in astonishment.

'By a few seconds—' said Hel.

448

'*That's* why he's still here. You cheated him. You stole his time—'

'Don't be childish,' said Hel crossly. 'A few seconds. He would have died anyway.'

'He trusted you – he spoke of a balance . . .'

Maddy was almost sure she saw a flush against the dead pallor of Hel's living profile.

'No matter,' said Hel. 'What's done is done. Thanks to your friend and his pet snake, Chaos has already breached Netherworld, and it cannot be re-opened without placing *this* world – maybe *all* the Worlds – in jeopardy. Right or wrong, it cannot be changed. And now, Mimir' – she addressed the Whisperer in an altered tone – 'your part of the deal.'

The Whisperer nodded. 'Balder,' it said.

'Balder?' said Maddy.

So that was what he'd promised Hel. Balder's return – in a living body . . .

'And it *had* to be Loki,' she said aloud. 'It couldn't have been me, for instance, or any other casual visitor, because Balder the Fair, of all the Æsir, would never be party to the death of an innocent . . .'

'Well reasoned, Maddy,' said the Whisperer in its dry voice. 'But as we know, Loki's no innocent. And so everyone's happy – well, *almost* everyone. Surt gets Netherworld and everything in it – including our deserters, for whom I imagine he has interesting times in store. Hel gets her heart's desire. And I?' Once more, it smiled. 'My freedom at last. My freedom – from *him*.'

At that the old face twisted in rage, and the eyes, which had always been as cold as glass, blazed with a light from which all sanity had been scoured away.

'Here, in the flesh,' the Whisperer said. 'Here on the plain I'll meet him – and this time I'll kill him, and I will be free.'

'But why?' said Maddy. 'Odin was your *friend*—'

The Whisperer gave a dry hiss. 'Friend?' it said. 'He was no friend to me. He used me when it suited him, that's all. I was his instrument; his slave; and tell me, little girl – what is it a slave dreams of? Do you know? Can you guess?'

'Freedom?' said Maddy.

'No,' said the Whisperer.

'Then what?'

'*The slave dreams of being the master.*'

'First, Balder,' said Hel, who had been watching the river with her dead eye.

'Ah, yes, of course. How could I delay?' And now the Whisperer raised his staff; red lightning crackled from the tip, and Maddy felt the hairs on her arms and head crackle with static in response.

But the power it raised was not against Maddy. It distressed the air like a storm in a bottle, cast shards of lightning onto the plain; it troubled the sky so that crow-coloured clouds gathered overhead, and then the Whisperer raised its staff and opened its mouth to speak the Word.

'Balder,' it said, and the Word it spoke echoed from the mouths of every one of the ten thousand dead. '*Balder,*' it said. '*Come forth.*'

Maddy did not hear the Word, but she felt it. Suddenly her nose bled, her teeth ached; a haze seemed to come between herself and the world and she felt a sensation of *drawing*, of *stretching*. And now a light surrounded Loki's body (she still could not bear to think of it as his corpse) and slowly that Aspect of him began to fade, to alter; so that as she watched, his hair changed colour, his lips lost their scars, the angles of his face softened and changed shape and his eyes opened – not fire-green as before, but a sunny, gold-flecked, summery blue.

If she tried, she could still see Loki behind the new Aspect; but it was like looking at a picture against which a lantern-show had been projected. Nothing was clear; impossible to say where Loki ended and Balder began.

Maddy gave a cry of grief.

Hel's lips parted in a soundless gasp.

The Whisperer bared its teeth in satisfaction.

And Balder the Beautiful, prisoner of Death these five hundred years, stirred, sleepily at first, and then into wide, blue-eyed, astonished life.

'Welcome back, Lord Balder,' said Hel.

But Balder was scarcely paying attention. 'Wait a minute,' he said.

His hand went quickly to his face. Through the gleam of his Aspect Maddy could still see Loki's features, like something glimpsed through thick ice, and as Balder's fingers moved tentatively against his forehead, his cheek, his chin, his air of puzzlement deepened.

'There's something funny about this,' he said. He pressed his fingers once more to his lips. At the pressure, Loki's scars reappeared briefly, then faded again – reappeared – faded – reappeared . . .

His hand went to the glam on his arm. *Kaen*, reversed, now glowing white-hot.

'Hang on,' said Balder. 'I never used to be Loki, did I?'

9

The parson had listened from afar in a state of dull indifference. His Huntress had been defeated, his enemy reinstated; his wife had turned out to be some kind of Seeress – and what did it matter anyway? What did anything matter, now that he had lost the Word?

He looked across at Ethel, standing among the Seer-folk with Dorian to one side of her and that absurd pig on the other. Even the goblin was with them, he thought, and he felt a sudden wrench of self-pity as he realized that no one was watching him; that he could just stand up and walk away into the desert and no one would miss him, or even notice that he had gone. He might be dead, for all they cared – even that damned pig got more respect—

Stop whining, man, for gods' sakes!

Nat jumped as if he'd been stuck with a pin.

Who's that? Who spoke? Examiner?

But Nat knew that it was not the voice of an Examiner. It was no more than a whisper in his mind – and yet he knew it, heard it as if through dreams . . .

Then it struck him with the force of a slap.

Why, that's my *voice*, thought Nat, lifting his head. And with the realization came another thought, one that lit up his eyes with sudden eagerness and set his heart a-fluttering.

Perhaps he didn't need Elias Rede.

Rede was just one man in an army of thousands. And an army of thousands would have its own general – a general whose powers would be unimaginably greater than that of any foot soldier – a general who might be grateful for an insider's help . . .

Nat looked at the Good Book in his hands. Stripped of the powers the Examiner had brought him, he saw that it was just so much worthless ballast now, and he dropped it without a second thought. More important to him now was the knife in his pocket; just a simple clasp-knife, such as any countryman might carry, but sharpened to a lethal sliver.

He knew where to strike; had used it many a time when he was a boy, hunting deer with his father in Little Bear Wood. No one would suspect him now. No one thought him capable. But when the time came, he would know what to do . . .

And so Nat stood up and joined the group; and followed, and watched, and awaited his chance, as the light of Chaos lit the plain, and gods and demons marched to war.

'Gods,' said Heimdall. 'There are so *many* of them . . .'

They had reached the edge of the battle line. It was vaster than any of them had ever imagined; vast with the false perspective of Hel's domain, and lined from one horizon to the other with the dead.

Whatever they had been in life, Odin thought, in death the Order had merged as one: a last Communion; a deadly swarm armed with one Word that, when uttered, would increase its power by ten thousand.

He could already feel it building: it raised his hackles; shivered the ground; made the clouds shift and circle. If there had been birds in those clouds, they would have dropped from the sky; as it was, even the dead felt it, and followed, like dust on a wind of static.

They were waiting, he sensed, for some command, some new word that would galvanize them into movement. All of them silent now, eyes closed; all of them focused with the unbreakable concentration of the dead. The column seemed to stretch out for miles; and yet beyond it the far-sighted Watchman seemed to see something – something impossible, he told himself, and yet if he'd not known, he could almost have *sworn* . . .

But then came a rumbling across the plain; a silent resonance that nevertheless penetrated the listeners to the marrow and beyond.

Bragi heard it as a lost chord.

Idun heard it as the silent sob of a dying man.

Freyja heard it as a cracked mirror.

Heimdall heard it as a blackbird shadow.

Frey heard it as a death wind.

Skadi heard it as creeping ice.

And Odin heard it as a whisper of the Elder Days, a low sound of ancient spite, and suddenly he understood – not everything, but *some* at least – and as once more the ten thousand dead opened their eyes and spoke as one, everyone heard the Word that was spoken, a teasing, seductive whisper of a Word that hung over the desert like a distant smoke signal under the putrid clouds.

Odin, it whispered.

'I hear you,' he said.

Then come, it said. *Come to Me.*

And as the Vanir watched, the ten thousand with their ranks and columns parted silently and in a single fluid movement, leaving a narrow passageway across the sand.

Odin smiled and stepped forward, staff in hand.

Heimdall made as if to guide him.

The dead column seemed to tremble. Ten thousand eyes opened once more and ten thousand heads turned in his direction. The combined weight of their concentration made the Watchman's teeth ache.

Alone, said the Whisperer, and every Examiner mouthed the words in perfect synchronicity. *The General must stand alone.*

There was a long pause. Then Odin spoke. 'At least let me take the goblin,' he said. 'I'll need his eyes to lead me through.'

Agreed, said the Whisperer, and its voice moved through the mouths of the dead, like the wind through a field of corn.

Odin smiled.

'If you think I'm letting you go alone—' said Heimdall.

'I must,' said Odin. 'The prophecy—'

'Damn the prophecy!'

With an effort Odin drew himself up to the full height of his Warrior Aspect. Light and fury blazed from him; the air about him was bright with runes.

'I'm ordering you to stay here,' he said. 'You and the other Vanir too.'

'But why?'

'Because it's the only way. And because if I lose this battle, it may be that the Vanir will be all that stands between Chaos and the Middle Worlds.'

'But you *can't* fight. You can't even *see*—'

'I don't need to see. Now let me go.'

'At least let Idun give you some apple—'

'Listen, Heimdall.' Odin turned towards him, and his one eye, though blind, was shining. 'If my suspicions are right, then even in my youth, armed, in full Aspect, and with my glam intact, I would have been no match for the powers here. You really think fruit is going to help?'

'Then why are you going?' Freyja said.

Ethel could have told her, with her new clear sight; but Odin had bound her to silence. The image of the death ship was strong in her mind – the fallen General with his dog at his feet – and she wished there was something she could say to make him turn back . . .

But by then Odin was already gone, with Sugar leading him carefully across the dusty ground, and the ranks of the Order closed as he passed, erasing him like writing in the sand.

10

Nat Parson had watched with apparent indifference as Odin vanished into the ranks. Inside, however, his heart was racing.

That voice!

He'd heard it as they all had, whispered across the battlefield; and he'd clapped both hands to his face as blood began to drip from his nose. It was the Word – he could sense it as a rabid dog scents water, and for a moment he thought he might go mad from terror and desire.

And now he could almost *touch* the Word; it trembled all around him like the coming of spring; it called him in a voice like gold—

Laws, that power!

Ten thousand times stronger than anything he'd felt before, the pull of the Word was not to be denied, and who could know, when at last it was unleashed, what gifts it might bestow on a faithful servant?

Worlds, Nathaniel. What else is there?

He stared out at the obedient dead, pegged out across the colourless horizon. Ten thousand dead, yet strangely alive – his strained senses could feel their vigilance; their stillness a blind over that horrible alertness. He could feel their unity; the ripples that ran through them like wind through grass; a single flicker of an eye echoed in ten thousand pairs of eyes as they stood in terrible Communion.

That could have been me, he told himself.

Somewhere in those ranks stood his Examiner, the one he had known as Elias Rede. Somewhere, he was certain, Rede was *aware* of him. Surely that made him a part of this

Communion, gave him the right to some of that power . . .

He took a step towards the line.

Ten thousand pairs of eyes looked his way.

He whispered: 'It's me. Nat Parson.'

Nothing happened. No one moved.

Nat took another step.

Behind him the Vanir were lost in debate; their raised voices reached him as if from a distance, but the sounds of the dead were deafening, an artillery of furtive creaking and rustling, as of insects crawling on shifting sand.

He moved closer.

'Prentice?' he said quietly.

Adam, who had been pretending sleep behind a nearby piece of rock, lifted his head.

Nat smiled – to Adam he looked as mad as ale, and Adam began to feel that it might be safer to be as far from his old master as possible.

He backed away—

'Oh no, you don't.' Nat reached out to grab the boy's arm. 'I may need you yet, Adam Scattergood.' He did not mention *why* he might need him; though Adam cringed at the look in his eyes. Nothing was left, Adam thought, of his master. Instead Nat looked like one of the dead; his dull but horribly knowing eyes were fixed on a point Adam could not see, and his grin was like that of a rabid wolf.

'I don't want to go,' said Adam faintly.

'Good lad,' said the parson, and crossed the line to join the army of the dead.

None of the Vanir saw him go. Nat had made no friends among the Faërie, and now that he was no longer a threat, their contempt for him was plain to see. But Ethel had not forgotten him. Her husband still had a part to play, and even she did not know how the game would end.

So she watched as Nat approached the line, dragging Adam in his wake, and she followed quietly, a few paces back. Dorian knew better than to protest. In the short time they had travelled together his respect for Ethel had grown beyond measure, and although he was terribly afraid of the dead men standing on the plain, he would rather have died than let her go alone. And so he followed, his pig at his heels (for Lizzy too knew loyalty), and though the dead pressed in on either side, distressing the air with their stench and their chanting, Ethel Parson stayed calm, her grey eyes kind and compassionate and unafraid.

Someone, she knew, was about to die. And the fate of the Worlds depended on *whom*.

11

Balder the Fair, behind whose shining Aspect fragments of Loki were still apparent, looked down at himself with a puzzled expression. He examined his hands, his chest, his arms and legs. He pulled a hank of hair over his eyes and squinted at it. Even through his colours it still showed faintly red.

'What *is* this?' said Balder, looking at Hel.

But it was the Whisperer who replied. 'A life for a life, o Fairest One. You're free to go. Your new Aspect will take you anywhere – back to the Middle Worlds, if that's what you want—'

'To Asgard?' said Balder.

'Sorry, no deal. Asgard fell – well, of course, you wouldn't be expected to know that, would you? – but you can take your pick of the other Worlds, and feel smug at the thought that you're the first dead person to leave the Underworld by legitimate means since before the Elder Age began . . .'

But Balder was no longer listening. 'Asgard fell?' he repeated numbly.

'Yes, lord,' said Hel. 'At Ragnarók.'

'And Odin?'

'Him too.'

'The others?'

'Everyone, lord. Everyone fell,' said Hel with a trace of impatience. She'd been waiting for a sign of gratitude for some time now, and this footling concentration on petty details seemed to her pointless and quite annoyingly masculine.

She gave him a glimpse of her living profile, keeping her dead face turned away, and was irritated to find that he did not notice. It was trying, she thought, after everything she had sacrificed.

'Well, Loki didn't fall,' went on Balder, oblivious. 'Otherwise his body wouldn't be here. And what exactly am I doing in Loki's body, and how did you manage to get him out of it in the first place?'

Maddy told him of Loki's promise, Hel's betrayal, the release of the Æsir—

'What?' said Balder. 'The Æsir escaped?'

'Well, they *would* have done if Hel hadn't stopped them—'

'You don't understand,' said Hel. 'The Ninth World's unstable – if I open it now, anything might get through—'

'Including the Æsir,' said Maddy at once.

'The Æsir,' said Hel. 'Where would they go? Into Dream, or the ranks of the dead . . .'

'Whereas I—' said Balder.

'*You* have a body, lord. A glam . . .' She hesitated, and her living eye shifted modestly downward. 'I thought perhaps that you and I—'

He stared at her with an astonishment that Hel found quite unflattering. She flushed a little and turned to the Whisperer. 'You promised . . .' she began.

But the Whisperer was not paying attention. Instead it stood in its hazy Aspect, glamour twisting around it like smoke, watching the distant, dark figure crossing the grey strand towards it. A silence fell, in which Maddy could hear individual grains of sand dropping onto the dead plain.

'One-Eye,' she said.

The Whisperer smiled.

The ranks of the Order parted like cornstalks as Odin passed through, and closed like spears again at his back.

'Odin,' it said.

'Mimir, old friend.'

Odin, in Aspect, mindsword to hand, his hat pulled down to conceal his face, with Sugar trotting at his heels. The Nameless, in Aspect, hooded and cloaked, its runestaff spitting glamours. Maddy on one side, Hel on the other; Balder in the middle.

'Not Mimir,' it said. 'Not any more.'

'You'll always be Mimir to me,' he said.

And now the General could see them all – their colours, at least. His truesight perceived them as figures of light: he saw Maddy, weakened and depleted by her flight through Netherworld, her colours touched with the grey-violet of grief; he saw Balder revealed in Loki's glam; saw Hel in her colours; saw what had once been the Whisperer standing in a column of light, the stone Head that it had inhabited for so long lying discarded at its feet.

'Old friend,' it said. 'It's been too long.'

'Five hundred years,' said Odin, moving closer.

'Longer by far,' said the Nameless softly, and though its voice was calm, Odin could see the killing rage in its heightened colours. He supposed it had just cause to hate him; all the same his heart was heavy. So many friends lost or dead. Such a price to pay for a few years' peace.

Does it have to be like this?

The answer came as quick as thought. *To the death*, it said. *To the victor, the Worlds.*

In silence the enemies faced each other. Behind them the river Dream boiled and seethed. Beyond that lay the darkness.

BOOK NINE
Dream

Anything that can be dreamed is true.

Fabrications, 12

BOOK NINE

Dream

1

The shadow that reared over the Ninth World – the blackbird shadow with feathers of fire – was beyond anything seen since Ragnarók.

It was Surt, the Destroyer, in full Aspect; and whatever fell beneath the shadow of its wing vanished as if it had never been, leaving only Chaos in its place, a Chaos full of stars that grew and swelled as the world receded.

Little was left of the Black Fortress as, piece by piece it reverted to its raw material of glamours, ephemera and dream. Fragments still floated in the void – here a piece of city wall, there a rock, a ditch, a bend in a river, blown like snowflakes on the dark wind.

It was on one of these fragments that the Æsir had settled to make their final stand; an outcrop of some rocky something overlooking the Underworld; with Thor, in Aspect, mindbolts in hand, and Tyr with his gauntlet raised to strike; Frigg watching the scene unfolding in Hel; Loki crouching in the shelter of the rock, and Sif, who was no warrior, holding a running commentary on when, exactly how and how soon they were all about to die.

'It's all *your* fault,' she said, pointing at Loki who, ignoring her, was picking off passing demons with a series of small, quick cantrips that sliced through the air like shrapnel.

'Your fault,' repeated Sif, 'and now you're dead, and everything's going to Pan-daemonium – and what in the Worlds are you grinning at *now* . . . ?'

But Loki wasn't listening. Instead he allowed his mind to run – he found that shooting demons sharpened his concentration – turning over the events of past days until he understood – albeit too late – how cleverly he had been manipulated.

Frigg's words had brought it home to him: how it had used him from the start; how he had been sent to his death on a fool's errand while the Whisperer made its bargain with Hel – how it had tricked her into serving its purpose, how Hel's betrayal had opened the rift in Chaos, and how the Whisperer stood now, at the head of an army, poised, not to do battle, as Odin supposed, but to unleash that Chaos into the Worlds, and watch as they fell, one by one . . .

He realized he'd underestimated the Whisperer's ambition. He'd thought that it was simply out for revenge; that once its debt was settled with Odin, then perhaps it would be satisfied. Now he knew better. It wanted its turn; it wanted the power of Order and Chaos, to be the One and Only God . . .

He pegged *Kaen* at a cloud of ephemera and saw it disperse like a swarm of bees. Desperation had restored his sense of humour, and in the minutes he had left, Whisperer or not, he was determined to go out in flames. Fire-runes shot from his fingertips; his eyes gleamed and his face, though bearing the marks of exhaustion, was alight with pleasure. He supposed it was the Chaos in his blood; but to his own surprise Loki found he was having more fun than he had in five hundred years.

Behind him Thor and Tyr stood back to back, each one covering the other as they struck mindbolts at the blackbird shadow. It kept coming. Behind it came silence; the spinning space between the stars; the unimaginable emptiness of World Beyond.

Inch by inch, it glided closer. Clouds of ephemera fizzled

and died in its wake. Demons – some as huge as oliphants – were sucked like seeds into its maw, and still it came, unstoppable; oblivious. It was almost upon them now; Netherworld had fallen, and only the shores of the river remained. On came Surt; the shadow clipped the edge of the rock upon which the Æsir had made their stand . . .

Then, suddenly, even as the rock began to disintegrate beneath them—

Everything stopped. A silence fell. Netherworld froze at the moment of its unmaking, and Odin and the Nameless began to move closer, barely at first, circling each other almost imperceptibly, like dancers in some long, slow ceremony.

Maddy, whose heart had leaped at the sight of her old friend, took a step forward, but Balder put a hand on her arm.

'Leave him,' he said in a quiet voice. 'Interfere, and you risk both your lives.'

She knew he was right – this was Odin's battle, not hers – but she could not help but feel a little hurt that her old friend had not even acknowledged her. Was he angry? Didn't he care? Or had she simply served her purpose, to be put aside like so many before?

The two warriors were closing now; Odin looking tired and drab next to the dazzling form of the Nameless. The staff in its hands crackled with runes; Odin's mindsword gleamed kingfisher-blue.

Behind them, ten thousand voices of the Order began to recite from the Book of Invocations.

I name you Odin, son of Bór . . .

'You've lost,' said the Nameless. 'Your time is done. Out with the old gods. In with the new.'

Odin smiled. 'The new?' he said. 'There's nothing new about this, old friend. This is the way the Worlds turn. Even betrayal serves one side or another. And even Chaos has its rules.'

'Not this time,' said the Nameless. 'This time *I* will set the rules.'

'The rules are already set. You serve them, whether you like it or not.'

The Whisperer hissed. 'I'll serve no one. Not Order. Not Chaos. And if everything else has to fall – then so be it. I'll rule alone. Nothing but Me throughout the worlds: all-seeing, all-knowing, all-powerful Me.'

'I can see Wise Mimir has lost none of his wisdom,' mocked Odin.

In fact he had rarely felt less like laughing. The strength of the Nameless was even greater than he had anticipated; its glam was like the heart of a star, and although its Aspect was still only half formed, he knew that it was already lethal.

Behind him the army of the Order intoned:

'I name you Grim and Gan-glari,

Herian, Hialmberi,

Thekk, and Third, and Thunn, and Unn.'

Every name weakened him further; he lashed out at the figure dimly glimpsed through his truesight, but his mindsword struck nothing but air. Behind him, in the ranks, a single man fell. Another stepped forward to take his place.

In its turn, the Nameless struck. The runestaff only brushed Odin's wrist – but it burned like hot iron and the force of it sent him sprawling, half stunned, across the sand.

'I name you Bolverk,

I name you Grimnir,

I name you Blindi,

I name you Svidri . . .'

Odin stood up, rubbing his wrist. 'You've grown stronger,' he remarked calmly, transferring his mindsword to his uninjured hand.

'I wish I could say the same of you,' said the Nameless.

Odin feinted; parried; struck. The sword in his hand sped

like a dart, but a flick from the runestaff was enough to divert it, and the weapon flipped harmlessly away, cleaving the ground where it fell and leaving a crater six feet deep.

'I name you Omi, Just-as-High,
I name you Harbard, Hropta-Tyr.'

Once more the runestaff flashed; Odin dodged, but the Nameless was faster. The tip of the staff just grazed his knee, and One-Eye fell, rolled, casting Yr one-handed as he did; so when the runestaff struck again – at the head this time – it glanced away as Odin cast Tyr at his attacker.

In the ranks of Examiners another man fell, vanishing like a puff of smoke into the desert air. But still the Nameless stood unscathed, stronger than ever and with a smile of triumph across its harsh features.

Odin struck out again with the strength of despair. In the crowd another Examiner fell, but the Nameless struck back with snakelike speed, this time catching him squarely on the shoulder.

'I name you Sann and Sanngetal,
Fiolsvinn, Skilfing—'

It was a weak spot, barely healed from the crossbow bolt, and he went down heavily under the blow. He rolled out of range, casting Tyr left-handed as he pushed himself back onto his feet.

Tyr hit the Nameless squarely between the eyes.

Odin staggered back to see the result.

In the ranks, a knot of Examiners vanished like smoke, and the rest closed in to take their place. Odin did not see it; instead he saw the bolt pass right through the airy form of the Nameless, dispersing its glam harmlessly on the dead air.

The Nameless gave its dry laugh.

The river Dream swelled and rose.

Grimly he drew his mindsword again.

2

On the far side of the battlefield the Vanir heard the Nameless speak. Every syllable was relayed to them as ten thousand voices spoke the words:

'*I name you Odin, son of Bór . . .*'

It was beginning, Heimdall thought. Eight against the multitude . . .

He took a step closer to the line of men. This time no eye followed him. Every man's gaze was fixed on the same point; their backs were turned; he sensed the depth of their concentration. A dry wind blew, charged with dust, but no man so much as shielded his eyes; and from the widening gyre in the crow-coloured clouds came a heightened glare the colour of fresh blood.

He'd sworn to Odin that he would not follow. It rankled; but an oath was an oath. Still, he thought, no oath had been sworn concerning the dead men standing so passively, apparently lost in thought, watching the fight by the riverside.

He could sense the power of that canticle, and knew that for Odin each word was a blow. If he could break their Communion, he thought – stop that damned chanting, at least for a moment.

He drew a mindbolt from the rune *Hagall* and shot it into the nearest column.

Nothing happened; no man fell.

Frey joined him, mindsword in hand, but the Reaper's blade was no more effective than his own weapon; it passed through the line as if through smoke.

He called Skadi; then Njörd; but neither mindwhip nor trident had any effect; nor had fire-runes, ice-runes, or runes of victory. The ears of the dead were impervious even to Bragi's most potent music; the eyes of the dead were blind to Freyja's most seductive glamours; and still they continued to chant the secret names of Allfather:

'Ialk and Ygg and Veratyr,
Vakr and Thror and Varmatyr –
Herteit, Bileyg, Oski and Gaut . . .'

And in the general consternation and the assault of the Word it was as many as twelve verses later that the Vanir realized that the parson and his prentice – not to mention the farmer, the woman and the pot-bellied pig – were missing.

3

The battle, he knew, was nearly done. Time after time Odin had struck; he was bleeding from a dozen wounds, but no damage had come to the Whisperer. Instead his blows had cleared a narrow swathe among the silent troops of the Order – but for every man that fell, another stepped in to take his place, and the ghastly Communion went unbroken. One-Eye fought on like a cornered rat – but in his heart he was coming to believe that the creature was invincible.

Now, at last, the General was reaching the end. Every name, every canticle cut deeper than the last. His glam was burned out; his right arm useless; his mindsword worn right down to a nub. He'd struck the Nameless a hundred times; but not once had he dealt it so much as a scratch.

If anything, it had gained strength as they fought, its Aspect taking shape around it so that, even blind, Odin could almost see the face now beneath the hermit's cowl, the shape of the mouth, the intelligence behind its eyes. And its colours – surely he knew that rust-red trail, flaring at the edges towards bright orange . . .

But it was not yet the Word made *flesh*. That Aspect, he knew, might wield power here, in the Land of the Dead, but to conquer the Worlds it needed bone and muscle and living flesh . . .

A life for a life.

His flesh. His bone.

'*I name you Wotan, Vili, and Ve . . .*'

'Is this what you wanted, Mimir, old friend? I wish you joy of it,' he said. 'For myself, I'm beginning to tire of this body.'

The Nameless gave a dry laugh. 'Oh no,' it said. 'Your body wouldn't do for me. Oh no. Not at all. It might have been all right a hundred years ago, but it's far too damaged to be of any use to me now. No, this, my friend, is for fun – and because I hate to see an old score go unsettled.'

It raised its staff to strike again and Odin rolled sharply out of the way, ignoring the pain in his wounded shoulder.

'So whom did you have in mind?' he said. 'This is the Land of the Dead, in case you hadn't noticed—'

And then it suddenly came to him.

A life for a life.

Without a body (or even a head), the thing could never leave the Underworld, and if it wished to conquer Worlds . . .

A life for a life.

Maddy's life.

And now he saw the Nameless's plan, and he struck out in rage and desperation at the thing that danced just out of reach. He fell to one knee—

The Nameless parried his blow with ease.

'So that's what you wanted all along,' gasped Odin as he struck out again. 'To be reborn into living flesh – to rebuild Asgard and to rule it yourself. To become Modi – to steal her glam and make it your own – to fulfil the prophecy you had to make . . .'

'At last,' said the Nameless. 'You always were slow. Well, old friend, you know what they say. Never trust an oracle.'

And now they had come to the final verse. Thirty-three verses were written under the name of Odin Allfather in the Book of Invocations; ten thousand voices recited the final couplet.

'I name you Warrior, One-Eye and Wanderer.

Thus are you named, and thus are you . . .'

And now, at last, the General fell, defeated, onto the sand.

4

Now Maddy had heard the prophecy. *I speak as I must*, the Oracle had said – and although it had misdirected them, told fragmentary truths to deceive and delay, she knew that an Oracle cannot lie.

I see a death ship on the shores of Hel
And Bór's son with his dog at his feet . . .

And yet as she'd watched the two terribly mismatched opponents, she had never lost the conviction that something, somehow, would happen to turn the battle to One-Eye's advantage. Some unexpected turn of events, like in her favourite stories.

But now it was over. Her friend was lying face-down on the bone-grey sand, his colours so faint that he might have been dead.

No, not you too, she mourned, and shaking off Balder's restraining hand, she ran across the blood-spattered sand to where he lay. The Nameless stood over them, its runestaff raised, its face illuminated with triumph, but Maddy hardly noticed it.

She knelt down. Touched his hair. He was still alive.

'Maddy.'

'I'm here.'

Painfully he raised his head. Out of Aspect he looked very old – very *human* – as if a hundred years had passed since their last meeting on Red Horse Hill. He had lost his eye-patch during the fight and his ruined face was a mask of blood and dirt. His one eye stared sightlessly, and she realized that he was totally blind. Her heart gave a wrench of pity and grief – but behind it the feelings of anger and hurt that had come to her when she learned the truth were still alive, still crying for release.

'Why did you have to come here?' she said. 'I knew that if you came here, you'd die.'

Odin sighed. 'Same – impatient – Maddy.' He spoke in a broken, breathless whisper, but she could still hear a trace of the old irritable One-Eye in his voice, and that made her want most terribly to cry.

'I wanted to stop the war,' she said. 'I wanted to stop all this from happening. I wanted to save *you*—'

'Can't,' said Odin. 'Prophecy.'

Maddy began to protest, but Odin shook his head. 'Let me – see you – again,' he said as, blindly, and with great gentleness, he raised his hand to Maddy's face.

For a moment Maddy held her breath as his fingers moved from her cheek to her chin, lingered at her forehead; traced the lines of sorrow and stubbornness around her mouth, the slight wetness around her eyes.

A good face, Odin thought. Strong, but gentle – though perhaps not so wise . . .

He smiled and lowered his head to the sand.

As behind them the Nameless stepped in to deliver the final blow.

Meanwhile, at last, Nat and the Folk had reached the clearing. Passing unseen through the ghostly ranks, they found themselves mesmerized by the scene unfolding before them.

Ethel recognized it, and sighed.

Adam gaped at it, open-mouthed.

Dorian clutched Fat Lizzy.

Sugar looked down at the Captain's runestone resting in the palm of his hand, and his stomach lurched as he saw it pulse with a violet light – just once, and faintly, like a heart that has not quite stopped beating.

Oh, no, Sugar thought. *Surely not. Not* now . . .

The runestone flared, a little brighter this time, and a strange little shiver went up Sugar's spine, almost as if a familiar voice—

You're beyond reprieve. You said it yourself. There's nothing I can do.

He made as if to drop the stone. But as he emerged from the Order's ranks, he found himself still gripping it tightly and pushed it deep into his pocket. Perhaps there *was* something, after all. You never did know with runes.

Nat Parson stared in wonderment, his eyes filled with the glory of the Nameless. He had travelled so far – suffered so much for the sake of this moment that he hardly dared hope that he had reached it at last.

This Being shot through with wonderful lights; this terrible, glorious, all-powerful Being, born in Aspect from the stone Head – could *this* be the Word his heart had longed for? Slowly he began to push his way through air that was curdled with glamours and barbs. No one reached a hand to stop him; no one saw the joy in his eyes as he moved towards the two opponents.

'Don't cry, my dear,' the Nameless said. 'I *told* you you were special.'

Maddy turned to look at it as it stood over her, lifting its staff. Glamours clung to it like wool to a spindle, spitting sheaves of static into the dead air. It was impressive; Maddy sensed she should have been impressed. But the ground was wet with One-Eye's blood and the colour of it was all she could see; that red, like Harvestmonth poppies on the desert sand . . .

'I'm not afraid of you,' she said, as once she had told a one-eyed journeyman long ago, on Red Horse Hill.

The Nameless smiled. 'I'm glad,' it said. 'Because you and I are going to be very close.'

Now, Maddy had not heard the conversation between Odin and the Nameless as they fought it out across the plain. But she was no fool, and the thought had already crossed her mind that if Loki's body could be used to make Balder live again, then perhaps the same was true of hers. An unmarked body was best, of course; One-Eye's was damaged – perhaps beyond repair – but her own was healthy and, more importantly, her unbroken glam would give its bearer the power of gods . . .

She narrowed her eyes at the Nameless. 'Special?' she said.

'Very special, Maddy,' it said. 'You're going to take us to the stars. Together we're going to rewrite Creation from the top. Rebuild the Sky Citadel. Remake what the Æsir destroyed through their greed and carelessness. Instead of Nine Worlds in opposition, there will be only One World. Our World. A World where things make proper sense. A World with Good and Evil in their proper places, and One God ruling everything, for ever and always—'

Maddy gave it a scornful look. 'That sounds a lot like something One-Eye used to call *gobshite*.'

The Nameless brightened angrily. 'You think you have a choice?' it snapped. 'You heard the prophecy.'

Maddy smiled. '*I see an army poised for battle. I see a General standing alone. I see a traitor at the gate. I see a sacrifice.*' She levelled her dark-grey eyes at the Whisperer. 'I asked you once if you thought *I* was supposed to be the sacrifice.'

'*No*—' said Odin.

No one heard.

Maddy looked around – at Hel, this time, standing in silence with her dead profile averted; at Balder, clothed in

Loki's flesh; at the ten thousand troops – minus a few – standing in eerie silence before them.

'Don't think of it as a sacrifice,' it said in its most soothing voice. 'Think of it as a new beginning. You won't be dead – you'll just be Me, as everything else will just be Me. I'll leave My mark on every blade of grass, every drop of water, every human heart – and everything will worship Me, and love Me, and fear Me, and be judged . . .'

It paused for effect, and pulled back its hood. Its Aspect was almost completed now, the stone Head it had occupied for so many years now standing forgotten to one side. Now Maddy could see her own colours swimming faintly behind those of the Whisperer, and feel a kind of static in her hair and teeth as the Word gathered all around her.

Ten thousand dead were ready with it; ten thousand corpses drew breath. And in the anticipation of the Word, no one saw the small, cautious figure of Sugar-and-Sack as he left the shelter of his group and moved softly across the dead sand, unremarked and unregarded, in the direction of the two adversaries.

Now, Sugar was far from heroic material. As far as he was concerned, he should never have been a part of this business in the first place. The General was dead – or as good as – the Captain was dead – or worse than – and Maddy was about to be consumed by the Nameless, which made her at least as dead as both of them.

He really didn't know why he didn't just run. No rune or cantrip forced him to act. No profit was likely to come to him. Not even the runestone bound him now, though he could still feel the force of its pulse, as if some part of the Captain were still trapped there, urging him on in a soft voice.

It wasn't even as if he quite understood what he was expected to do – or why – and yet he kept moving, low to the ground, towards the nasty old glam – the Whisperer – that had started all this off in the first place, and that now lay forgotten to one side, as the thing that had blossomed out of the stone moved closer to Maddy and spoke.

'Dear girl,' said the Nameless. 'Listen to Me.'

And such was its glamour that she almost obeyed, almost succumbed to the mellifluous voice. 'You're so tired, Maddy,' the Nameless went on. 'You deserve to rest. Don't fight me now that we've come so close . . .'

And now the dead began to speak, their voices toneless as the drifting sand.

'*I name you Modi, child of Thor,*
Child of Jarnsaxa, child of wrath.
I name you Aesk,
I name you Ash—'

Maddy had fewer names than One-Eye, and she knew that her canticle was likely to be short. Already she could feel it working on her: her head was heavy; her legs half rooted to the ground . . .

With an effort she shook herself. 'Fight you?' she said. 'I suppose I could try.' And she pulled out of her pocket – not a rune, not a glamour, not a mindsword, but a simple country clasp-knife, such as might be carried by any smith or farmer's boy in Malbry and beyond.

And now Maddy could see something truly surprising – Maddy, who had thought never to be surprised by anything ever again. It might be a mirage, she told herself, but wasn't that Ethelberta Parson, with Dorian Scattergood at her side, and Adam Scattergood, and Nat Parson – and could that be . . . *a pot-bellied pig*?

She was going mad, she thought. It was the only possible explanation. It galled her slightly that in her last desperate moments of life she should have to endure visions of Nat

Parson and Adam Scattergood, but if things went according to plan, she thought, then at least she wouldn't have to see them for very much longer.

'With that?' said the Nameless, and began to laugh. Ten thousand dead laughed with it, and their voices were like a flock of carrion birds rising into the gunmetal sky.

But Maddy's gaze stayed straight and true.

'You need my body unharmed,' she said. 'If I die here, my spirit stays in Hel, and the rest of me just goes to dust. I can't kill *you*, but I can do *this* . . .'

And she raised the knife to her own throat.

480

5

Once again there was silence in Hel. Everyone watched Maddy, standing in the circle of gods and Folk with the clasp-knife held to her own throat.

Loki watched from Netherworld, and in spite of his peril, he grinned.

Thor watched, and thought, *That's my girl.*

Odin did not watch, but he knew, all the same.

Balder watched and saw the solution clearly for the first time; not a battle, nor even a war, but a *sacrifice*—

'Maddy! No!' the Nameless howled, and ten thousand voices echoed its cry. 'Think what I'm offering – Worlds, Maddy—'

Maddy took a deep breath. It would have to be a clean blow – there might not be time for another, she thought. She pictured her blood – a necklace of it – spraying out onto the sand . . .

Her hand was shaking a little, she saw. She tried to steady it—

And found that neither hand would move.

It was too late. She was paralysed; at last the Book of Invocations had done its work. And now all she could do was watch in despair as the Nameless closed in, exultant, its poisonous voice whispering in her ears, promising:

Worlds, Maddy. What else is there?

Nat Parson gave a strangled cry. He had no idea what he was doing; no thought of danger crossed his mind. All he could think of was the wretched girl; the girl who had foiled him at every turn; the girl who had laughed at him, thwarted him, ridiculed him and was now about to take what he himself had longed for: the Word that was rightfully his . . .

'*No!*' He hurtled towards her, knife in hand, head lowered like a charging boar. 'She never wanted it! Give it to me!' And, grabbing Maddy by the hair, remembering those hunting parties with his father, so many years ago, he pulled back her head to cut her throat.

Sugar reached the discarded Head and, grasping it in both arms, began to run furiously across the open sand. It burned his skin like a sulphur-stone, but Sugar held on, dodging and running for all he was worth, eyes squinting almost shut in concentration.

Find it, the Captain had said. *And throw it into the deepest part* . . .

Well, all of it looked deep enough. The question was, could he reach it in time?

He scuttled through Nat Parson's legs, going *Ouch-ouch-ouch* from his blistered hands and, looking for all the Worlds like a squirrel carrying a baked apple, he ran as fast as his short legs would go (which was faster than you might expect, and very quick for his size) towards the river Dream.

Nat was taken by surprise. All his attention had been on the girl, and when the goblin shot between his legs, he tripped and half fell forward onto the sand. He dropped the knife, bent to retrieve it, and found himself face-to-face with something that hissed and crackled and gleamed, and seethed with fury and thwarted ambition. Nat did not pause for a second to think; instead he opened his arms and clasped it, howling, to his chest.

The Nameless had not seen the parson approach, had not given the little party of Folk more than a second's thought. But first had come this mad creature scuttling in between it and the girl, and now here was the fool parson flailing out of the desert, eyes staring, mouth twisted and shouting, '*No! Take me!*' – reaching out hands already stiffened and blackening from its touch as—

Ten thousand troops cried out in alarm and still the parson begged, *Take me!* – arching, reaching, yearning, *burning* for Communion, his mouth agape in an O of horror and amazement as the Nameless struggled to free itself and the Word blossomed like an early rose . . .

To Nat it felt like tumbling into a pit of snakes. The Nameless's mind was nothing like that of Elias Rede – Rede at least had once been human, with human thoughts and aspirations. But there was nothing human – nor even godlike – about the Nameless. No pity, no love, nothing but a sump of hate and fury.

No human consciousness could survive such a blast, and in a second Nat fell to the ground, bleeding from his nose and ears. For if the Word had been violent at a distance, here, at the source, it was cataclysmic. The force made the ventings from the Whisperer's firepit seem like nothing more than a milk-pan boiling over on the fire; the aftershock knocked the living from their feet and dispersed the dead like motes of dust.

The Nameless gave a howl of rage. Robbed of its victim, suddenly finding itself in the body of the wrong man – a man with neither glam nor training – it acted without thought or restraint. Its first instinct was to annihilate the interloper; its second to regain the safety of its original vessel—

But the stone Head that had contained it since the beginning of the Elder Age was no longer lying on the ground. The Nameless gave another howl – of desperation, this time.

Without a suitable vessel, it knew, it would be no more than another soul in Hel – Hel's property and Hel's slave. Robbed of a leader, its army would disperse like the dust it was; its great plan would remain unfulfilled. Ten thousand troops echoed its cry as the Nameless focused every particle of its glam on a single, frantic, all-important objective:

To possess the girl. Once and for all.

It was then that the river burst its banks. The Word, unleashed and uncontrolled, multiplied by ten thousand and flung out towards the rift in the Worlds, had finally proven too much to contain.

The thing that had been the Ancient of Days wailed aloud – *Not yet – not yet!* – as the river Dream – a tidal wave – came rushing across the desert towards them.

Ethel Parson knew what it meant. She didn't know *how* she knew – but she did – just as she knew that the only hope of the Nine Worlds was beyond that river, and that they were almost out of time.

Sugar heard it and dropped the Head before setting off, no less urgently, in the opposite direction.

Odin heard it and thought, *At last.*

Across the plain the Vanir heard it, and braced themselves for the End of All Things.

In Netherworld the Æsir heard it, as the blackbird shadow began once more to descend. Still clinging to the spur of rock – now the only piece of solid matter as far as their eyes could see – they felt the approach of Chaos like a shrieking black wind and fell back once again, still flinging mindbolts into the thing's lightless maw, until they were actually *pressing against* the gate dividing World from World, feeling its texture hard at their backs.

Loki had time to think, *Damn gate should be charging me rent by now*, when suddenly it gave way and he tumbled backwards into the flow.

Hel's living eye shot open in sudden comprehension to rest upon the hands of the deathwatch, as they now began to move together once more. She had just enough time to think, *Gods, what have I done?* when the tidal wave hit and all at once the desert was submerged in Dream.

6

The world of Dream is barely a world at all, but more an accumulation of possible worlds; a world in which land-masses come and go as easily as sandbanks in a fast-flowing river and nothing is ever as it seems to be.

The river itself is really nothing like a river. Although the eye gives it a river's length and breadth, what flows along it is strangely volatile; shining; mercurial; almost alive, ready to take shape whenever it touches a stray thought.

There is little sense of distance in Dream; little sense of scale or time. Dream's territory is strictly neutral, like Death's; it exists equally in Order and Chaos; no rules apply, or all of them. Like Netherworld, it is beyond these things, and, like Netherworld, it is different for every creature that falls under its influence.

Here, at the source, it can be deadly.

Loki fell into a dream of snakes, and went under struggling and gasping.

Thor fell into a dream of being stark naked at an important function, at which a beautiful woman with flowers for eyes and two mouths, both of them ringed with carnivorous teeth, made a speech in a language he did not understand, but to which he was expected to reply.

Frigg dreamed of a woman neither beautiful nor young, but gentle, and with a quiet strength. She wore a simple homespun gown; one cheek was scratched and marked with dirt. She pulled up her sleeve, and the Mother of the gods saw a glam on her arm, still faint as yet, but growing steadily more clear. She held out her hand . . .

Maddy dreamed of a floating rock, and climbed aboard into another dream. She was back in Malbry, on Red Horse Hill, and the gorse was in bloom on the hillside. One-Eye sat next to her; not Odin, but the old One-Eye as she had first known him, watching her with his rare smile.

'One-Eye!' she cried out in relief – and suddenly she knew that everything that had happened over the past few days had simply been another dream; a nightmare from which she had now awoken. She reached out her arms to her old friend, but he warned her away with an outstretched hand.

Be careful, he said. *You're safe here. But don't touch anyone you meet – that is, if you want to stay yourself. There's a few odd things in the air today . . .*

Maddy said, 'I dreamed you were dead . . .'

One-Eye shrugged. *It wouldn't be the first time. Now I have to go – there's a harvesting at Pog Hill I promised to attend—*

'But you'll be back, won't you?' she said.

Aye, between Beltane and Harvestmonth. Look for me then – in dreams.

Odin dreamed of his son, Thor. He was aware it was only a dream, and yet he saw Thor very clearly, and slipped under the surface into a dream in which he sat under a tree in Asgard as it was and watched the clouds race past – and Odin still had both his eyes, and Loki was not yet in disgrace (well, no more than usual, anyway), and Maddy, though as yet unborn, stood close by, and Frigg was there, and Erda, Thor's mother, and Thor himself, looking just the same as they had five hundred years ago.

That's because you're dead, Dad, said Thor, as if he'd read his mind.

Dead? said Odin. *But this is—*

Look at the facts, said Thor kindly. *Your eyes – this place – us – what other explanation could there be?*

Well, I could be dreaming, Odin said.

You always were a dreamer, said Thor.

And now, as Odin slipped deeper into the dream, he seemed to hear Loki's voice crying for help. And he understood that Loki was in another dream; and that Loki's dream was killing him.

I have to help him, Odin said.

Leave him, said Thor. *He deserves to die.*

He freed you from Netherworld, Odin said.

Freed us only to save his skin!

That sounded typical enough, thought Odin. Since the beginning of the Elder Age, Loki had helped the gods only inasmuch as he'd usually caused the trouble in the first place. And yet hadn't Odin himself known this from the start? And in his arrogance, hadn't he always been shamefully eager to blame Loki for his own mistakes?

In the dream next door, Loki was screaming. He sounded so close, Odin thought. All he had to do was reach out his hand . . .

If you do, said Thor, *then I can't answer for the continued integrity of this place. I mean, wouldn't you rather die here, surrounded by your loved ones, in a place that can only exist now in dreams, or would you rather die in Hel, defeated, as the world comes to an end around you? Your choice, Dad – but is he worth it?*

He's my brother, Odin said.

You never learn, do you? said Thor.

Odin smiled and reached out his hand.

Sugar dreamed of pork roast, and kept an eye open in case Fat Lizzy should happen to drift by.

Dorian dreamed of Ethel Parson. *You always were too good*

for me, he thought, *and now* . . . Now Ethel was two women in one – one the dowdy parson's wife, the other the woman of almost blinding beauty he'd glimpsed at intervals as they drew closer to their goal. They stood, face to face, like the January Man; Ethel looking forwards, the other looking sweetly back.

Don't leave me, said Dorian.

Then take my hand, said the two-in-one.

And as Dorian reached to take her hand, he saw a man standing in her place; a big red-bearded man whose hands, though large, were far from clumsy and whose face he felt he should know. For a second he paused . . .

Fat Lizzy dreamed of Dorian Scattergood, and sighed.

Hel the Half-Born never dreamed. Dreaming was for lesser folk, and anyway, she had lived alongside Dream for too long to be affected by its tides and vagaries. With a word, she conjured her citadel, and repaired with Balder to one of its higher turrets, the better to observe what happened next.

Time acts differently in Dream. Though hours seemed to have passed since then, the gate between the Worlds had been open for a mere six of the thirteen seconds remaining on the face of Loki's deathwatch.

Six short seconds – but the damage was done. The Black Fortress was now no more than a foundering patch of rubble against the rising swell of the river. Demons, prisoners and pieces of ephemera thrashed and tumbled in the hectic flow. And now the space between the Worlds looked just like a waterspout, sucking obscenely and at random, sending pieces of flotsam – some as large as skerries – lurching into the filthy air.

'It has to be stopped,' said Balder to Hel. 'Any more of this, and Chaos will find its way into the other Worlds.'

Hel shot him a glance from her living eye. 'It's safe

enough in here,' she said. 'Even Surt knows better than to mess with Death.'

'And the others?'

She shrugged. 'They knew the risks when they came here. Anything happens to them, I'm not responsible.'

How tiresome he was, thought Hel. For the first time in centuries she had Balder to herself, and all he could think about was the possible disruption to the other Worlds. To be sure, she had made a stupid mistake—

You broke your word. You cheated Loki out of thirteen seconds . . .

And now the time had come for Hel to pay.

Balder the Beautiful looked down from his turret, and though his eyes were blue as summer skies, they were far from dreamy. He saw Odin far below, struggling with some dream of drowning.

He saw Ethel and Dorian holding hands, and Fat Lizzy perched on a spur of rock. He saw Adam Scattergood, lost in a dream of giant spiders, and Loki, surrounded by poisonous snakes.

He saw Nat Parson, and knew he was dying.

He saw the thing that had been the Nameless, its face twisted with rage and chagrin, as it stood hip-deep in the river and *screamed* at the rising tide, like the Fool King in the old tale: *STOP, I SAY! I COMMAND YOU, STOP!*

But words – even *Words* – have no power in the realm of Dream. Dream has no rulers; no servants; no kings. Dream cannot be summoned, commanded or banished. And as the Nameless ranted and raved, Nat Parson – Nathaniel Potter, as was – fell into a dream of his own, a dream in which he was a young boy again in his father's house, watching his father at work in the shop.

Look at the clay, his father said.

I see it, said Nathaniel. The clay was blue and smelled of the riverbed from which it had been gathered. Nat's father cupped it between his hands like a bird that might otherwise fly away. The potter's wheel turned as he pumped the treadle, and the lump of clay began to take shape.

A fat-bottomed pot, with a neck that grew slim as the wheel went round. Nat thought he had never seen anything as delicate as his father's big hands cupping the clay; teasing it round, making it smooth.

You try, said Fred Potter.

Nat cupped his fingers around the pot.

But he was only a boy, not even a prentice, and the beautiful pot with its swan's neck and gracious curves wobbled, leaned and collapsed on the wheel.

Nathaniel began to cry.

Don't cry, said Fred, and put his arm around the sobbing boy's shoulders. *We can always make another one.*

He began to pump the treadle again, and the pot began to rise anew, to become, if anything, more beautiful than before.

Fred Potter turned and smiled at his son. *See, son?* he said. *Our lives are like these things I make. Turn 'em, build 'em, bake 'em in fire. That's what you've been, son. Baked and fired. But a pot don't have the right to choose whether he be for water, wine, or just left empty. You have, son. You have.*

This was where Nat realized – to his sorrow – that this was all a dream. Fred Potter could never have voiced such thoughts. And yet Nat, who hadn't thought about his father more than twice since the old man's death, now found himself wanting to believe.

It's too late, Dad. It's all gone wrong.

It's never too late. Come on, take my hand . . .

And as Nat Potter took his father's hand, he found himself at peace for the first time in many years, and slipped quietly away to a place where even the Nameless could not find him.

The Nameless gave a roar of frustration as it plunged, bodiless, into Dream. At the same time there came a kind of rushing sigh – like the sound of the sea coming in on the sand. Ten thousand souls gave a single gasp as Dream struck them with a giant wave and they were lost in a moment, like grains of sand, rolling, roiling, sifting, seething, drifting, drowning, marvelling – for so few of them had ever dreamed, and here they were, at Dream's very source . . .

Some wept.

Some ran splashing into it, like children at the seaside.

Some went insane.

The dead of Hel, who had gathered like dust and ash and smoke and sand on the deserts of Hel for centuries, were drawn to the movement and flocked like birds to the edge of Dream . . .

And Elias Rede, the Examiner once known as 4421974, had time to think, *No more numbers for me*, as he plunged with joy into the wave.

'That rift,' said Balder, 'in Netherworld. You know what caused it, don't you, Hel?'

Hel's face was impassive, but he thought her living profile flushed a little.

'You have to mend it now,' he said. 'Your dead are escaping. Your realm is at risk.'

'There are always plenty of dead,' said Hel. 'I can bear a few losses.'

'But the rift is widening. If Chaos gets through—'

'It won't,' she said. 'Dream will contain it.'

'It may not, Hel. You broke your word.'

Hel's word is unbreakable. Balder knew this, as everyone did; it was one of the axioms of the Middle World.

But it seemed the unbreakable *had* been broken – and now there was turmoil in her realm. He knew what *that* meant – that the forces of Chaos were very close, and that if nothing was done to halt it now, then the rift between Worlds would widen and tear, opening up similar rifts into the Eighth World, and the Seventh, unravelling through the fabric of Worlds like a ladder in some fine lady's silk stocking until, at last, the Chaos was everywhere, and Ragnarók would come again.

Hel the Half-Born knew it too. The promise of Balder had blinded her to danger as well as to consequences, but the face of the deathwatch was beyond argument. Slowly but nonetheless relentlessly as Dream flooded the land, the hands of the deathwatch were moving together, and when they met . . .

She spoke aloud, in a voice still rusty from under-use. 'I can buttress this tower if Chaos breaks through. Seal it off from the rest of the Worlds. We can be beyond Order, beyond Chaos. You and I – my love – alone.'

Balder's expression, though habitually sunny, was bleak. 'I can't,' he said. 'To stand by and watch the Worlds swallowed up, one by one, for my sake—'

'You don't have a choice,' said Hel grimly. The six seconds of dreamtime had dwindled to three. 'There's nothing either of us can do . . .'

So many times she'd dreamed of this moment – Hel, who never dreamed – and now the dream was within her grasp . . .

'There is,' said Balder. 'Pay Loki his debt.'

For a moment she stared at him. 'Do you know what you're saying? No one can stop what's happening now. Even if I were to take your life . . . Besides, this is Loki we're talking about – Loki, whose mischief caused your death—'

'It doesn't matter,' Balder said. 'You broke your word to bring me to life. What kind of a basis is that for a meaningful relationship?'

'But here you can be *safe*,' protested Hel. 'You can have

anything, do anything you ever wanted. My face offends you? There are glamours I could use to make myself beautiful. I could look like anyone – Sif, Freyja even—'

Balder's eyes went cold as midwinter. 'Tricks,' he said.

Now Hel's living eye twitched in growing annoyance. *Tricks?* she thought. *What does he think the others use? Does he really think Freya's hair was ever naturally that shade? Or that Sif's waist doesn't benefit from a little tight lacing?*

For the first time she began to wonder whether she hadn't made a big mistake, bringing Balder to this place. She should have drugged him first, she thought; a single draught of the river Dream would have ensured his co-operation, at least until the danger was done.

Still, it was too late for that now. Balder was looking out of the window again, searching, his eyes narrowed in concentration. For a second he thought he saw Loki suspended over a pit of snakes, and Odin desperately holding onto his hand—

With a flick of her dead fingers, Hel made the window disappear. A fine silk tapestry, cleverly and lasciviously embroidered with scenes of lovers, now hung in its place.

Balder saw it and turned away. 'Send me back,' he said in a flat voice.

Hel ignored him, and with another gesture made a banqueting hall appear around them, with tables set with fine crystal and pomegranates (a traditional favourite in Hel) and honey cakes and oysters and sweetmeats and wines of every colour from spring-green and deepest amber to rose-gold and tulip-black.

But Balder looked at them in disgust. 'Do you really want to please me?' he said. 'Then let me go!' And once more he turned away, and Hel, gnashing her teeth, made one last gesture in the air—

'My love,' she said, and stood before him as Nanna, his

wife, who had died upon Balder's funeral pyre rather than live for a day without him; and nothing could have been sweeter and more joyful than her smile, and nothing as soft as her gleaming hair, but Balder closed his eyes in loathing, and tightened his lips and said nothing at all.

Hel gave a cry of rage and disappointment. She looked at the deathwatch, its hands now separated by nothing but the smallest whisker of time.

'*Then go!*' she screamed, and in an instant her citadel was gone, and Balder was standing once more in the desert with the river gleaming and churning all around him and Dream, in all its gorgeous disarray, laid out at his feet.

Loki, he thought. And plunged headlong into the rapids.

Meanwhile Odin's strength was fading. The pull of Loki's dream had intensified, as if to combat his attempt to escape. Below him Odin could see the rift between the Worlds, now a vortex through which the gulf of Chaos could be glimpsed like the pupil of a monstrous eye.

Hang on! he said, but his arm was numb, his hand slick with Loki's sweat, and it was hopeless, he knew; they would both be sucked into the gap between the Worlds where the blackbird shadow would blot them from existence as if they'd never been at all . . .

Well, said Loki between gritted teeth. *At least you tried, brother – which is more than I was expecting from you, to be totally honest* . . .

Now Loki was clinging on by his fingertips. He could feel them slipping, one by one: index, median, annular . . . *This little piggy went to Chaos*, thought Loki with a sudden desperate crack of laughter. *This little piggy stayed at home—*

Hold on! said Odin one last time. And then the fingers slipped from his grasp and he was left clutching shadows while –

– Another hand reached out from behind him and grabbed hold of Loki by the hair.

Got you – said a voice Odin thought he recognized, and he had just enough time to marvel at how very like Balder's that voice was when there came an almighty crashing sound, as if every door in the Nine Worlds had suddenly been blown shut, and all these things happened at once:

The hands on the deathwatch snapped together.

The rift between Worlds closed as if it had never been there at all.

The river Dream pulled back, leaving an untold acreage of mudflats of evaporating dreamtime across the deserted plains of Hel.

And the dreamers suspended there awoke with a start, and some awoke to their former selves, and some paused as dancers in the middle of some complicated fugue, who find themselves unexpectedly partnered with a total stranger as the music comes to a sudden stop.

Maddy awoke sobbing on the far shore of Dream, but could no longer recall exactly why she had wept.

Frigg awoke in the body of a woman who had seemed to her at first both plain and middle-aged, but who, with the rune *Ethel* shining brightly from her arm, made middle age and plainness into virtues far greater than the most transcendent beauty.

Dorian Scattergood awoke to find the sign of *Thuris* emblazoned across his scarred right arm and Ethel watching him with a quizzical expression on her face – a face that was no longer quite hers, but which nevertheless radiated beauty and love.

'Thor,' she said, and held out her hand.

Adam Scattergood awoke feeling perfectly normal – except for the tiny voice that whispered and whined at the back of his head . . .

Brave Tyr awoke to find himself three feet shorter than he used to be.

Sugar awoke to find himself clutching Fat Lizzy desperately in both arms. For a moment they stared at each other, nonplussed, then the pot-bellied sow gave a squeal of outrage, as around her an Aspect began to form – that of a shapely, well-rounded woman with hair the colour of ripe corn and a face now twisted with fury and disbelief.

Sif the Harvest Queen awoke in a state of rage that, if expressed in the Middle Worlds, would have levelled trees, blighted crops and killed every flower from here to World's End. As it was, there were no trees or flowers, and she was only able to scream in a voice that would have shattered glass, had there been any: 'A *pig*? You brought me back as a stinking *pig*?'

Loki awoke in his own skin, and laughed until his guts were aching and—

Hel hissed – *Men!* – and closed her eyes, while around her the dead settled back like dust, to lie silent and undisturbed for another long age.

7

Silently Maddy let her eyes wander over the mudflats of Hel.

Dreamstuff still littered them, looking like the usual flotsam and jetsam of any river or sea, but the little group that stood assembled on the shore of Dream knew better than to investigate too closely the shining fragments, the not-quite-rocks, the seductive vapours that had been left behind.

The Vanir had joined them from their vantage point in the heart of the desert, and there had been some discussion over what had happened – discussion that had proved for the most part inconclusive. Skadi was particularly resentful, given that Odin was now beyond revenge, and Loki . . .

'Basically, what you're saying is that I'm not allowed to kill him,' she said for the fourth time. She had already tried this argument on Njörd, Frey and Bragi, and now it was Heimdall's turn to try to placate her (none of the others had managed yet).

Heimdall showed his golden teeth.

'Why?' said the Huntress. 'Because he saved the world? Well, if that's your excuse—'

'It's not.' That was Idun, breaking in, sounding unusually down-to-earth and taking Skadi by surprise. 'You can't kill Loki,' she said simply, 'because Balder wanted him to live.'

There was a long silence.

'Balder?' said Skadi.

Idun nodded.

There was another silence, during which Idun thought, with some surprise, that Skadi's ice-blue eyes looked a little misty. It was no secret that Balder had broken hearts while he was alive, but—

'Balder wanted him to live?' repeated Skadi in a doubtful voice.

'He sacrificed his life for him – for all of us,' said Idun.

There was another long and chilly pause.

'That's the most ridiculous thing I've ever heard,' said Skadi. 'You'll be saying he's in charge next.'

'Well,' said Idun. 'Officially, as the General's second-in-command—'

'Oh, bite me,' growled the Huntress, and put away her mindwhip before slouching off across the sand.

Adam was watching all this from afar. He felt surprisingly unafraid – he thought that perhaps the events of the past few days had cured him of fear for ever – but his eyes were narrowed in hate as he watched, his skinny body curled up beneath a rock some distance from where the gods were standing.

No one had paid him the least attention; no one had searched for him, called or even noticed that he was missing.

That was good, said Adam to himself; if he took the wide road across the plain, he would be long gone before anyone remembered he'd been there at all.

He moved quickly, and with a peculiar confidence quite unlike the Adam Scattergood who had left Malbry half a life-time ago. He remembered that Adam with some contempt now – that boy who was afraid of dreams. Now he stood reborn – a man – perhaps even the *Last* Man – and he was aware of a great responsibility. In one hand he held a golden key, and he kept his fist clenched tight around it as he began to run, low and fast, across the colourless expanse of Hel, while in his mind that little voice still whispered and coaxed, promising:

Worlds?

The dead gave him a wide berth, which didn't surprise Adam one bit.

Meanwhile Maddy was trying to come to terms with recent events. It was hard enough to believe that they had survived at all – and yet more so to accept the four new-comers from across the river, the Æsir, who stood in Aspect among them.

Thor the Thunderer, who also happened to be Dorian Scattergood; Frigg the Mother, who had once been Ethel Parson; Bright-Haired Sif, the Harvest Queen, whose sigil *Ár* was echoed on the belly of a pot-bellied sow; and finally Tyr, One-Handed no more, but who seemed to be having problems with his host.

'I *can't* be Tyr,' protested Sugar-and-Sack. 'That's Brave-Hearted Tyr. Tyr the Warrior. I mean, do I even *look* like a warrior? There's been a bloody mistake. You've mistaken me for someone *brave*.'

'You were brave,' Maddy told him. 'You stole Mimir's Head.'

'I didn't mean to!' said Sugar in alarm. 'It was the Captain made me do it! He's who you want, not me!' Around and above him the Warrior's Aspect stood tall; and his colours – which were a vibrant red, with a hint of goblin-gold at the edges – glowed fiercely. On his left palm a runemark burned – *Tyr*, reversed, bright as blood. 'Take it off!' said Sugar, hold-ing out his hand.

The Mother smiled. 'It isn't that easy.'

'*But I'm not me any more!*' wailed the reluctant Warrior.

'Of course you are,' said Maddy gently. 'You'll carry his Aspect, but you'll always be you. Just as I'll always be Maddy Smith, though I'll also be Modi, child of Thor. Think about it, Sugar. You've done a wonderful thing. All of you have.' She looked at Ethel, Dorian and Fat Lizzy – looking very strange in the Aspect of Bright-Haired Sif – and then at Loki, who was standing alone with his back turned.

Maddy went over to him, but he did not look at her. Instead he watched the river Dream, with its islands, eddies, skerries and rocks, and for once there was no trace of laughter in his eyes, but only a bleakness that Maddy could not identify.

'Cheer up, you escaped,' she said at last.

Loki kept right on not looking at her. Across the river the Black Fortress of Netherworld was already rebuilding itself, piece by piece, turret by impossible turret.

'Just wondering what else escaped,' Loki remarked, without taking his eyes from the Black Fortress.

'More of the Æsir, perhaps.'

'Perhaps.'

Maddy thought he didn't sound particularly convinced.

'Or Balder, do you think?'

'Balder's dead.' He looked at her then, and there was anger as well as bleakness in his eyes. 'Balder died to save *me*. Or rather, he died to ensure Hel's word was not broken; the word that keeps the balance between Order and Chaos in this place.' He paused for a moment. 'The smug bastard.'

In spite of herself, Maddy smiled.

'Well, I hope he doesn't expect gratitude. I never was much good at that. And as for the General . . .' He paused again, his eyes moving to the place where Odin had fallen. 'If he thinks this puts me under any kind of obligation . . .'

There was a silence, in which Loki glared fiercely into the middle distance.

'It's all right,' said Maddy. 'I'll miss him too.' And, hand-in-hand, they walked to the shore of Dream, where the funeral was already preparing itself.

8

There should have been a ship, Maddy thought – a long grey ship to set on fire as they pushed it away from the shore – instead they made do with a flat piece of floating debris, some shard of the fortress that had fallen away. They laid Odin's body on this makeshift barque, along with his weapons and his hat, and then all of them, the lost children of Order and of Chaos, stood watching as finally Loki stood at the foot of the boat and torched it with wildfire.

No one spoke as the river took the last of Odin One-Eye into fire and darkness. No one dared voice the hope that he might somehow have escaped into Dream – though if he had died in Hel, Maddy thought, then surely Hel would have claimed him as she had the rest, and there would have been no body to burn.

But Hel was in her citadel, and no amount of calling or petitioning could persuade her to show her face again.

And so all remained lost in thought, the ragged survivors, Æsir and Vanir; pale, bruised, and grieving.

Is this really how it was supposed to end? thought Maddy. *The General dead, the balance regained, the Order wiped out and us – the gods of yesteryear – standing like beggars on the shore of Dream, waiting – waiting for what?*

She looked up, angry at the tears that threatened. And saw––

The gods, in full Aspect, all twelve of them, standing like columns of colour and light, heroes and heroines of the Elder Age. And as Maddy watched, the tears began to stream down her face – Maddy Smith, who never cried – and in that moment of grief and uncertainty she felt a sudden and unexpected lurch of joy.

She had always been a lonely child, playing alone, keeping apart, hated and feared even by her own Folk, even by her father and sister. During all her years in Malbry there had only been One-Eye to take her side, and that only for a few days in the year. She had never expected things to be different; had always believed she would die alone, unknown and uncherished, friendless, childless, fatherless.

But these people standing by the riverside . . .

She watched as one by one the Vanir stepped forward to pay their respects. The Watchman, the Reaper, the Man of the Sea, the Healer, the Poet, the Huntress, the goddess of desire; slowly they passed, one by one, to salute the little barque as the river took it and to cast their runes of luck and protection into the river Dream.

And now came the Æsir. All filed past: the Thunderer, the Mother, the Harvest Queen, the Warrior, the Trickster . . .

These were her family, Maddy thought. Her father was there, and her grandmother; her allies and her friends. They shared her grief; they were bound to her, as she was to them, and she knew – suddenly and without any doubt – that whatever came, fair weather or foul, they would face it together.

It isn't over, Maddy thought. *This battle has been fought many times already, and will be fought many times again. Who knows what new face the enemy will take? Who knows how it will end next time?*

All she knew was that she wanted to be a part of it – *was* a part of it, whether she wished it or not – just as the leaves and roots of the World Tree play their part in the balance of Order and Chaos. Everything was linked: sorrow and joy; healing and loss; beginning and ending and all the seasons in between.

The Order might be gone – at least for now. But there would be other enemies, other pretenders to threaten the balance. There was a citadel to be built – Asgard, as was –

friends to be made, a brother to be found and a world of tales to be discovered and told.

One-Eye would have understood – One-Eye, who had collected tales like they were penknives, or butterflies, or stones. For a teller of tales will never die, but will live on in stories – for as long as there are folk to listen.

The Order knew it – which was why they had outlawed stories and books – and the first thing Maddy intended to do was to change that Law, and to free all the people in Malbry and beyond, to free them from sleep and into dream . . .

For Maddy knew that where Folk dream, the gods will never be far away. And she smiled as she remembered something One-Eye had said, back in the days when such things had seemed as remote and unattainable as Asgard itself.

Anything that can be dreamed is true.

The river Dream, like the World Tree, has many branches, many routes. In World Below it joins the Strond and filters into World Above. It gushes under Red Horse Hill and bubbles out into Little Bear Wood, and trickle by trickle, it runs under the mountains, down the valleys, across the fens and finally to World's End and into the One Sea, the place from which all things came and all things may one day return.

Look for me in dreams, he'd said.

And Maddy smiled as she watched the burning boat drift down the river and out of sight.

RUNES OF THE NEW SCRIPT

Aesk: the Ash Tree, Yggdrasil

Ethel: the Homeland, Motherhood

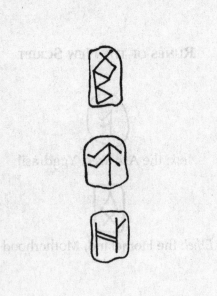